George Barnett Smith

Life of Her Majesty Queen Victoria

George Barnett Smith

Life of Her Majesty Queen Victoria

ISBN/EAN: 9783337059064

Printed in Europe, USA, Canada, Australia, Japan

Cover: Foto ©Raphael Reischuk / pixelio.de

More available books at **www.hansebooks.com**

LIFE OF HER MAJESTY

QUEEN VICTORIA

Compiled from all Available Sources

BY

G. BARNETT SMITH

AUTHOR OF

"THE PRIME MINISTERS OF QUEEN VICTORIA," ETC.

JUBILEE EDITION

LONDON

GEORGE ROUTLEDGE AND SONS

BROADWAY, LUDGATE HILL

NEW YORK: 9 LAFAYETTE PLACE

1887

PREFACE.

THE approaching Jubilee of the Queen's reign offers a
favourable opportunity for relating the story of her
Majesty's life. This I have endeavoured to trace in
the following pages. All sources of information have
been consulted, and I have dealt as fully as possible
with the inner life of the Sovereign from the time of
childhood to that of mature age. Although deprived
of a father's care in her infancy, it will be seen how,
in her early years, she was tended by the loving
ministrations of a wise mother. The chapter " Victoria
Regina " gives a full account of her accession to the
throne, while the one immediately ensuing deals with
her happy marriage, when she found a devoted partner
in the Prince Consort, and one able to guide her in
important matters as well as to sustain her by his
affection. Succeeding chapters show the home life of
the royal couple and their children, together with

their movements and public appearances. One section furnishes details of the severe affliction which befell the Queen and the nation by the death of the Prince Consort; and the remaining chapters describe the Queen's life and public labours since that melancholy event. While Englishmen may differ upon theories of government, all may unite, after a study of her Majesty's character and career, in recognizing in her the dutiful child, the loving wife, the watchful and affectionate mother, and the judicious Sovereign.

G. B. S.

CONTENTS.

ILLUSTRATIONS.

—◆—

THE LIFE

OF

QUEEN VICTORIA.

———•+•———

¡2

CHAPTER I.

EARLY YEARS.

IN the long and chequered annals of the British Empire two reigns have been especially illustrious, and in both those reigns a woman wielded the sceptre of England. Probably there is no age more brilliant in history than that of 'The Maiden Queen.' Rome vaunted its martial renown; Constantinople its opulence and magnificence; Greece its superb triumphs of art; but the age of Elizabeth had a glory which is destined to outlive them all. It was an epoch of lofty genius and of many-sided power. Invincible in arms, it was also transcendent in intellect. The age of Raleigh, of Frobisher, and of Drake, was likewise the age of Burleigh and of Bacon, of Spenser and of Shakespeare. These great Englishmen have bequeathed to us an undying inheritance; and down to the latest syllable of recorded time their descendants will continue to catch some echoes from 'the spacious times of great Elizabeth.'

B

The other noble epoch in British history is that associated with our own beloved Sovereign. If in the Elizabethan age our literature touched its culminating point of splendour, and the fame of our prowess travelled beyond the seas; in the Victorian age we have, on the other hand, witnessed an expansion of England that would have seemed incredible to our ancestors, while the triumphs of science and the arts, and the progress of the people, are without a parallel in the history of the world. In these various developments, as in all that concerns the welfare and happiness of her people, the Queen has taken a deep and continuous interest; and it has been vouchsafed to her, as it has been vouchsafed to few sovereigns, to look back upon a long period of beneficent governance, whose record will be writ large in the history of Britain. And now, as she reaches the jubilee of her reign, the hearts of all her subjects will turn towards her Majesty with gratefulness as they remember the past, and with affectionate solicitude as they contemplate the future.

I propose in the following pages to relate the life of the Queen, and not the history of her reign, which may be read in various forms elsewhere. Nevertheless, the personal narrative will necessarily be interwoven with public events, for a monarch, beyond all other persons, cannot escape the pressure and burden of the times. An ideal sovereign, besides his or her private joys and sorrows, bears in remembrance those of the people; and such a sovereign has Queen Victoria been, from the time when, still youthful in years, she assumed her high destiny as ruler of these realms, to the present year of grace, which is not the least memorable in a memorable reign.

Only six sovereigns of England since the Norman Conquest attained an age equal to or beyond that which the Queen will attain on the 24th of May 1887. These were: Queen Elizabeth, who reached 69 years; James II., 68 years; George II., 77 years; George III., 82 years; George IV., 68 years; and William IV., 72 years. Her Majesty's reign has only been twice exceeded in length; namely, by Henry III., who reigned for 56 years; and by George III., who reigned for 60 years; but the reign of one other sovereign, Edward III., equalled it, by extending to 50 years. Queen Victoria is only eighth in descent from James I., a long stretch of history being covered by the seven intervening lives. She is fourteenth in descent from Edward VI.; twenty-eighth in descent from Henry I.; thirty-fifth in descent from Alfred the Great; and thirty-seventh in descent from Egbert, the first sole monarch of England. The ramifications of her pedigree connect her with many other illustrious personages, in addition to those already named.

Her Majesty was born at Kensington Palace on the 24th of May 1819. She was the only child of Edward, Duke of Kent, and her Serene Highness Victoria Mary Louisa, daughter of the Duke of Saxe-Coburg Saalfeld, widow of Emich Charles, Prince of Leiningen, and sister of Prince Leopold. After their marriage, in 1818, the Duke and Duchess of Kent retired to Amorbach, the residence of the Leiningen family; but when there was good hope of an heir being born to the Duke, the Duchess yielded to her husband's patriotic wish that their child should be born on English soil. Upon their return, so anxious was the Duke for the safety of his wife and his expected offspring, that he himself drove the carriage throughout the whole of the land journey from the Castle of Amorbach to Kensington Palace, where they arrived early in April 1819. As the time of her accouchement approached, the Duchess of Kent, following the custom of her native land, confided herself to the care of 'Dr.' Charlotte Siebold, though the regular medical attendants were available in case of need. The birth took place at about 4 A.M., and it was immediately notified to the Ministers and Privy Councillors, who had assembled in an adjoining room, and amongst whom were the Duke of Sussex, the Duke of Wellington, the Archbishop of Canterbury, Lord Lansdowne, the Bishop of London, and George Canning.

The little Princess was baptized on the 24th of June in the grand saloon of Kensington Palace. The Archbishop of Canterbury (Dr. Manners Sutton) performed the ceremony, being assisted by the Bishop of London (Dr. Howley); and the child received the names of Alexandrina Victoria. The Prince Regent was godfather, and the sponsors were the Emperor Alexander of Russia (represented by the Duke of York), the Queen Dowager of Würtemberg (represented by the Princess Augusta), and the Duchess Dowager of Coburg (represented by the Duchess Dowager of Gloucester). It is stated by the Hon. Amelia Murray, in her *Recollections*, that the Duke of Kent wished to name his child Elizabeth, that being a popular name with the English people; but at the baptism the Prince Regent gave only the name of Alexandrina. The Duke requested that another name might be added, whereupon the Prince said: 'Give her her mother's also, then; but it cannot precede that of the Emperor.' So the Princess came to be called Alexandrina Victoria. Greville says that George IV. wished her to be christened Georgiana. It is interesting to note that the Princess Victoria was successfully vaccinated in the following August, and that she was the first member of the royal family of Britain who received the benefit of Jenner's remarkable discovery.

There seemed little probability that the child thus ushered into the world would ever become Queen of England. The Duke of Kent was the fourth son of George III. ; but a series of unexpected changes soon brought his daughter near the throne. Upon the death of the deeply lamented Princess Charlotte, the only child of George IV., the Duke of York had become heir-presumptive to the crown. His Royal Highness had no children, however, and the Duke of Clarence, the third son of George III., came next in succession. The Duke of Clarence had married, and his wife, the Princess Adelaide, bore him a daughter, who, if she had lived, would in the natural order of things, have become Queen. But this child died in infancy, leaving the Princess Victoria the only scion of the royal stock.

The Duke and Duchess of Kent, with their infant daughter, went to Sidmouth, on the east coast of Devon, at the close of 1819. Early in the following year the Princess had a narrow escape from death. A youth, who had obtained possession of a gun, fired at some small birds so near to the residence of their Royal Highnesses that the charge broke the nursery windows, and some of the shot passed quite close to the head of the infant Princess, then in the arms of her nurse. The offender was brought before the Duke, but, owing to the kindliness of disposition of his Royal Highness, he escaped with a reprimand on promising not to pursue his pleasures so recklessly.

The stay at Sidmouth, however, was destined to have a sad and fatal termination. The Duke of Kent was seized with a severe indisposition, occasioned by delaying to change his wet boots after a walk through the snow. Affection for his child had drawn him to the nursery immediately on reaching home. To a severe chill succeeded inflammation of the chest, with high fever, which resulted fatally. The Duke was perhaps more highly esteemed than any other son of George III. His public conduct was judicious and self-sacrificing. In the army he initiated many healthful reforms; after he ceased from active service in it, he interested himself in humanitarian movements of all kinds, especially devoting himself to the cause of the widow and the orphan. The result was, that he became known as the ‘ Popular Duke,’ and no royal personage ever better deserved the title. He was of regular and temperate habits, kind to all, and the firm friend of those who put their trust in him. His generosity was such that it frequently outran discretion, causing embarrassment to himself; but the poor had the benefit of it. I find that the Duke was officially connected with sixty-two societies, every one of which was devoted to some noble religious or charitable object. The personal virtues of the Duke, the love he bore his country, and the untiring exertions he displayed in the cause of philanthropy and religion, justly gave him a high place in the affections of his fellow-countrymen. It was auspicious that the Queen should have had such a father, for many of his traits, with the gentleness and uprightness which distinguished the mother, descended in large measure upon the child.

Two days after the death of the Duke, the Duchess of Kent, accompanied by her babe and her brother, Prince Leopold, set out for London. Where all was sad and mournful there was one gleam of sunshine; for the infant, ' being held up at the carriage window to bid the assembled population of Sidmouth farewell, sported and laughed joyously, and patted the glasses with her pretty dimpled hands, in happy unconsciousness of her melancholy bereavement.' The Duchess arrived at Kensington Palace on the 29th of January, and on that very day the Prince Regent succeeded to the throne by the death of his father. The likeness of the Duke of York to her lost father deceived the little Princess Victoria, and when the former came on his visit of condolence, and also subsequently, she stretched out her hands to him in the belief that he was her father. The Duke was deeply touched by the appeal, and clasping the child to his bosom, he promised to be indeed a father to her. Many addresses of condolence were received by the Duchess, and as she generally received them with her infant in her arms, there was frequently a painful contrast witnessed between the tear-stained face of the mother and the happy countenance, wreathed with smiles, of the daughter.

Interesting stories are told of the times when Princess Victoria appeared, at fifteen months old, in a child's phaeton, tied safely to the vehicle with a broad ribbon round her waist. Her half-sister,

Princess Feodore, some years her senior, would draw
the child in this carriage. The baby liked to be
noticed, and answered all who spoke to her : she
would say 'lady' and 'good morning,' and, when
told, would hold out her soft dimpled hand to be
kissed, with an arch expression on her face. 'Her
large blue eyes, beautiful bloom, and fair complexion,
made her a model of infantine beauty.' On one
occasion she was nearly killed by the upsetting of
the pony carriage. A private soldier, named Maloney,
claimed the honour of having saved England's future
sovereign on this occasion. He was walking through
Kensington Gardens, when he saw a very small pony
carriage, in which was seated a child. The pony was
led by a page, a lady walked on one side, and a
young woman beside the chaise. A large water dog
having got between the pony's legs, the startled pony
made a sudden plunge on one side, and brought the
wheels of the carriage on to the pathway. The child
was thrown out head downwards, and would in a
moment have been crushed beneath the weight of the
carriage, then toppling over, had not Maloney grasped
her dress before she came to the ground, and swung
her into his arms. He restored her to the lady, and
was praised by a number of persons, who speedily
collected, for rescuing 'the little Drina,' as the child
was called. He was told to follow the carriage to
the Palace, where he received a guinea, and the
thanks of the Duchess of Kent, for 'saving the life
of her dear child, the Princess Alexandrina.' Such
was the statement of Maloney, made late in life, and
published in the daily journals.

William Wilberforce had a very early introduction

HER ROYAL HIGHNESS THE DUCHESS OF KENT, THE QUEEN'S MOTHER.

After an Engraving by R. J. Lane, A.E.

to the Princess Victoria, and the way in which he
records it testifies to the childlike simplicity of his
own nature. Writing to Hannah More on the 21st of
July 1820, he says : 'In consequence of a very civil
message from the Duchess of Kent I waited on her
this morning. She received me, with her fine
animated child on the floor by her side, with its
playthings, *of which I soon became one.*' The widowed
Duchess resolved that her child should be brought up
under her own eye, and to this work she religiously
devoted herself. 'A few months after the birth of
my child,' said the Duchess, describing her situation
at this time, ' my infant and myself were awfully
deprived of father and husband. We stood alone,
almost friendless and unknown, in this country. I
could not even speak the language of it. I did not
hesitate how to act. I gave up my home, my kindred,
and other duties, to devote myself to a duty which
was to be the sole object of my future life.' And an
admirable home training, after the best of English
traditions, was the result of this devotion. Simplicity
of diet, regularity of hours, and no excitement, were
the main principles upon which the Duchess proceeded in rearing her offspring. The life at Kensington
was as simple as that of any English household.
'The family party met at breakfast at eight o'clock
in summer-time, the Princess Victoria having her
bread and milk and fruit put on a little table by her
mother's side. After breakfast, the Princess Feodore
studied with her governess, Baroness Lehzen, and the ·
Princess Victoria went out for an hour's walk or drive.
From ten to twelve her mother instructed her ; after
which she would amuse herself by running through the

suite of rooms, which extended round two sides of the palace, and in which were many of her toys. Her nurse was a Mrs. Brock, whom the Princess used to call her "dear, dear Boppy." At two came a plain dinner, while the Duchess took her luncheon. After this, lessons again till four ; then would come a visit or drive ; and after that the Princess would ride or walk in the gardens ; or occasionally, on very fine evenings, the whole party would sit out on the lawn under the trees. At the time of her mother's dinner, the Princess had her supper laid at her side; then, after playing with her nurse, she would join the party at dessert ; and at nine she would retire to her bed, which was placed by the side of her mother's.'

King George the Fourth presented the Princess on her fourth birthday with a superb token of remembrance, being a miniature portrait of himself richly set in diamonds. He also gave a State dinner party to the Duchess and her daughter. In the following year, in response to a message from his Majesty, Parliament voted an annual grant of £6000 to the Duchess of Kent for the education of the young Princess. A suitable preceptor was now sought for, and the choice of the Duchess fell upon the Rev. George Davys, afterwards Bishop of Peterborough. She made it a rule that the Bible should be daily read to the young Princess. The Duchess confided fully in Dr. Davys; and when it was suggested to her, after her daughter became direct heir to the throne, that some distinguished prelate should be appointed instructor, she expressed her perfect approval of Dr. Davys, and declined any change ; but hinted that if a clergyman of superior dignity were indispensable to fill the important office of tutor, there would be no objection to Dr. Davys receiving the preferment he had always merited. Earl Grey acted upon the hint, and made Dr. Davys Dean of Chester not long after-wards. The Baroness Lehzen was also retained through the whole term of the Princess's education, and proved an excellent instructress. After six years spent under the care of her tutors, the Princess could lay claim to considerable accomplishments. Owing to the exercise of unusual natural abilities, she could speak French and German with fluency, and was acquainted with Italian; she had made some progress in Latin, being able to read Virgil and Horace with ease; she had commenced Greek, and studied mathe-matics, in which difficult science she evinced much proficiency; and she had likewise made considerable progress in music and drawing.

Occasionally the child longed for companions of her own age, and a delightful anecdote is related in illustration of this. As the youthful Princess took great delight in music, her mother sent for a noted child performer of the day, called Lyra, to amuse her with her remarkable performances on the harp. On one occasion, while the young musician was playing one of her favourite airs, the Duchess of Kent, perceiving how deeply her daughter's attention was engrossed with the music, left the room for a few minutes. When she returned she found the harp deserted. The heiress of England had beguiled the juvenile minstrel from her instrument by the display of some of her costly toys, and the children were discovered, 'seated side by side on the hearthrug in a state of high enjoyment, surrounded by the Princess's play-

things, from which she was making the most liberal
selections for the acceptance of poor little Lyra.'
The chronicler of this incident states that among the
flowery bowers of Claremont the Queen's education
was informally yet delightfully promoted by the
conversation of her accomplished uncle, Prince
Leopold, who, taking advantage of the passionate
love his young niece and adopted daughter manifested
for flowers, gave her familiar lessons in botany, a
science in which he greatly excelled. A daily journal
of the studies of the Princess Victoria, of her progress
and mode of conduct, was kept by the Baroness
Lehzen, and submitted once a month to the inspection
of Prince Leopold, whose affectionate solicitude for
his niece's welfare was not without its beneficial
results.

Lord Albemarle, Leigh Hunt, and others, have
testified in almost identical terms to the many charms
of the Queen as a young girl, and the natural artless-
ness and attractiveness of her disposition. From an
account written by one of those who saw her in childhood I must quote the following paragraph : ' Passing
accidentally through Kensington Gardens a few days
since, I observed at some distance a party, consisting
of several ladies, a young child, and two men-ser-
vants, having in charge a donkey gaily caparisoned
with blue ribbons, and accoutred for the use of the
infant. The appearance of the party, and the
general attention they attracted, led me to suspect
they might be the royal inhabitants of the Palace.
I soon learned that my conjectures were well founded,
and that her Royal Highness the Duchess of Kent was
in maternal attendance, as is her daily custom, upon

her august and interesting daughter in the enjoyment
of her healthful exercise. On approaching the royal
party, the infant Princess, observing my respectful
recognition, nodded, and wished me a " good morning "
with much liveliness, as she skipped along between
her mother and her sister, the Princess Feodore,
holding a hand of each. Having passed on some
paces, I stood a moment to observe the actions of the
child, and was pleased to see that the notice with
which she honoured me was extended in a greater or
less degree to almost every person she met. Her
Royal Highness is remarkably beautiful, and her gay
and animated countenance bespeaks perfect health
and good temper. Her complexion is excessively
fair, her eyes large and expressive, and her cheeks
blooming. She bears a very striking resemblance to
her late royal father, and indeed to every member of
our reigning family.'

Charles Knight, in his *Passages of a Working Life*,
furnishes a glimpse of the Princess as he saw her in
1827. 'I delighted to walk in Kensington Gardens,'
he observes. ' As I passed along the broad central
walk I saw a group on the lawn before the Palace,
which to my mind was a vision of exquisite loveliness.
The Duchess of Kent and her daughter, whose years
then numbered nine, are breakfasting in the open
air—a single page attending upon them at a respectful
distance; the matron looking on with eyes of love,
whilst the fair, soft English face is bright with smiles.
What a beautiful characteristic it seemed to me of
the training of this royal girl, that she should not
have been taught to shrink from the public eye ; that
she should not have been burdened with a premature

conception of her probable high destiny; that she should enjoy the freedom and simplicity of a child's nature; that she should not be restrained when she starts up from the breakfast-table and runs to gather a flower in the adjoining parterre; that her merry laugh should be as fearless as the notes of the thrush in the groves around her. I passed on, and blessed her; and I thank God that I have lived to see the golden fruits of such training.'

A tender consideration for others was inculcated systematically upon the young Princess, and the effects of this were demonstrated in a variety of ways. Perhaps none is more pleasing than an incident that occurred at a London jeweller's, in which the Princess was one of the chief actors. She was in the habit of amusing herself by going *incognita* in a carriage to different shops, and not only making purchases herself, but observing with interest the movements of others. Being one day at the jeweller's referred to, she perceived a young and intelligent lady, who was engaged in looking over different gold chains for the neck. She at length fixed upon one, but finding the price more than she expected, she regarded the chain very wistfully. 'Could it not be offered cheaper?' she inquired. 'Impossible,' was the reply. The would-be purchaser was obliged to give up all idea of the chain, which she did most reluctantly, and to be content with a cheaper article. After she had left, the Princess Victoria, who had observed everything, inquired of the jeweller who she was, and on receiving satisfactory information, she ordered the much-admired chain to be packed up and sent to the young lady. A card was forwarded with it, intimating that the

Princess Victoria was so well pleased in observing
that the young lady who had been so much taken
with the beauty and workmanship of the chain had
yet so much command of her passions as not to suffer
those to overcome her prudence, that she desired her
to accept the chain which she so much admired, in
the hope that she would always persevere in that
laudable line of conduct upon which female happiness
so much depended.

Another illustration of the Princess's kindness of
heart, and of her filial solicitude in carrying out the
wishes of her parents, occurred in connection with the
family of a soldier named Hillman. It appears that
Hillman was with the Duke of Kent when he was at
Gibraltar. The Duke's regiment were inclined to
mutiny, but Hillman remained faithful. Upon his
return to England, the Duke provided a cottage for
Hillman near his palace at Kensington. Just before
his death his Royal Highness begged his wife to look
after the soldier and his family. This wish the
Duchess faithfully observed, taking her daughter with
her on her visits. Hillman at length died, leaving
one son and a daughter. The boy was very ill, and the
Princess Victoria visited him at frequent intervals
until his death. The daughter also suffered from
a complication of diseases. Two days after the
Princess's accession to the throne, the child's regular
pastor visited her, and found her unusually bright and
cheerful. Being questioned as to the cause of this,
she drew forth from under her pillow a book of
Psalms. 'Look there,' she exclaimed, 'look what the
new Queen has sent me to-day by one of her ladies,
with the message that, "though now Queen of Eng-

land, as she had to leave Kensington, she did not forget me." ' The messenger from the Queen told the sick girl that the lines and figures in the margin of the book were the dates of the days on which the Queen herself used to read the Psalms, and that the marker with the little peacock on it was worked by the Princess's own hand. 'Was it not beautiful, sir?' added the girl, bursting into tears. The words above quoted, 'She did not forget me,' emphasize a very admirable trait in the Queen's character.. From her very earliest years she remembered and studied to the last the welfare of those in whom she had once taken an interest.

Considering the principles in which she was reared, there was no wonder that the Princess developed from a dutiful daughter into a loving wife, a vigilant mother, a kind mistress, a generous benefactor, and an exemplary Christian. She had been schooled in habits of sobriety and religion, and the sentiments of obedience and self-control, which were from the first impressed upon her, bore their legitimate fruit in after-life.

The Princess was an excellent singer, and had for her master the famous Lablache. She was also a good dancer, and excelled in archery. But of all out-door exercises she was most passionately fond of that of riding. She was much devoted to the animals that bore her, from a favourite donkey presented to her by her uncle, the Duke of York, to the pony which carried her in her latest Highland excursions.

A Yorkshire lady has related an anecdote of the youthful days of the Princess. She went with the Duchess on a visit to Earl Fitzwilliam, at

Wentworth House, and while there found great delight in running about alone in the gardens and shrubberies. She was thus disporting herself one wet morning, when the old gardener—unaware of the little visitor's name and rank—saw her about to descend a treacherous piece of ground from the terrace, and called out, 'Be careful, miss; it's slape!'—this being a Yorkshire word for slippery. The Princess turned and asked, 'What's slape?' and immediately received a practical answer, for her feet flew from under her, and she fell down. As the old gardener carefully lifted her up he remarked, ' *That's* slape, miss.' Another account states that it was Earl Fitzwilliam himself who called out, ' Now your Royal Highness has an explanation of the term " slape " both theoretically and practically.' ' Yes, my Lord,' the Princess replied, ' I think I have. I shall never forget the word " slape." '

The Princess had a ready wit. On one occasion her teacher had been reading in her classical history the story of Cornelia, the mother of the Gracchi—how she had proudly presented her sons to the first of Roman ladies with the words, ' These are my jewels. ' ' She should have said my *Cornelians*,' immediately remarked the Princess. Of course, ' the divinity that doth hedge a king' extends in popular eyes in some degree to a Princess, and people are apt only to look on the roseate side. But none knows better than the Queen herself that human nature is a complex thing, and that, however a child may desire perfection, there is a good deal of the old leaven of imperfection in every one. So the Princess Victoria, noble in character as she was, exhibited some of those imperfections which no child is without, unless it be

C

those precocious creatures in whom supernatural goodness is developed from the first at the expense of
a healthy organization.   The Princess was impulsive,
sometimes not a little wilful and imperious; but
the affections being strong and the head well trained,
these matters always righted themselves, and the
young offender was herself quick to acknowledge the
wrong.   She had an ingrained sense of justice which
could always redress the balance.

The first grief which the Princess was able to
appreciate to the full arose from the death of the
Duke of York.   The Princess was at this time in
her eighth year, and as she had ever experienced great
kindness and affection at the hands of her uncle, his
loss affected her keenly.   The Duke of York and the
Duchess of Clarence were the two members of the
royal family towards whom her youthful heart was
most strongly drawn out.   At the time of the Duke's
death she was unconscious that his demise brought her
one step nearer the throne.   The marriage of her
sister, the Princess Feodore, to Prince Hohenlohe-
Langenbourg, was another wrench to the child, and one
which seriously narrowed her restricted home circle.

The gaieties of Court life were first brought within
the actual apprehension of the future Queen in 1828,
when she was in her tenth year.   At a Drawing Room
held during the season the Princess had an opportunity of observing how a queen but little older than
herself was received with royal honours at the Court
of George IV.   This young Sovereign was Donna
Maria da Gloria,. Queen of Portugal. The two children
had previously exchanged some formal State visits, but
official etiquette did not admit of a close intimacy.

The first occasion on which the Princess Victoria
danced in public was at a juvenile ball given by the
King to Donna Maria. The young queen presented
an appearance of great splendour, for her dress blazed
with all the jewels of the Portuguese crown; she was
surrounded by her Court, and was led to the ballroom
by the hand of the King himself. Little Victoria was
dazzled by so much magnificence; but, as a chronicler
of the scene remarks, 'the elegant simplicity of the
attire and manners of the British heiress formed
a strong contrast to the glare and glitter around the
precocious queen. These royal young ladies danced in
the same quadrille, and though the performance of
Donna Maria was greatly admired, all persons of
refined taste gave the preference to the modest graces
of the English-bred Princess.' The Princess Victoria
had for partners at her first ball Lord Fitzalan, heir
to the Dukedom of Norfolk, Prince William of Saxe-
Weimar, the young Prince Esterhazy, and the sons of
Lords De-la-Warr and Jersey.

Getting away from the lights of the ballroom into
the open air, we have another sketch of the Princess
as she appeared, untrammelled by State surroundings,
to a well-known literary man. 'We remember well,'
writes Leigh Hunt in *The Old Court Suburb*, 'the
peculiar pleasure which it gave us to see the future
Queen, the first time we ever did see her, coming up a
cross path from the Bayswater gate, with a girl of her
own age by her side, whose hand she was holding as
if she loved her. A magnificent footman in scarlet
came behind her, with the splendidest pair of calves in
white stockings which we ever beheld. He looked
somehow like a gigantic fairy, personating for his

C 2

little lady's sake the grandest kind of footman he
could think of; and his calves he seemed to have
made out of a couple of the biggest chain lamps in
the possession of the godmother of Cinderella.'

In a cottage in the demesnes of Claremont there
dwelt in the first quarter of the present century the
aged mother of a distinguished novelist, with her two
daughters. One of those daughters was Miss Jane
Porter, the author of *The Scottish Chiefs, Thaddeus of
Warsaw,* &c. She had abundant opportunities of
observing the Princess Victoria in her childhood, and
in a private letter which she wrote shortly after the
Queen's accession she detailed her reminiscences at
length. From this letter I extract the following
entertaining passages :—' My mother had warmly loved
the noble virtues of Princess Charlotte. She did not
less admire their corresponding continuance in Prince
Leopold; and she delighted in thinking the young
Princess Victoria resembled Princess Charlotte in her
infancy. My mother, attended by a favourite little
white poodle dog, with a crook-headed stick in her
hand, assisting, but not yet supporting, her still unen-
feebled steps, generally chose her places for walking
where she would be most likely to meet the young
hope of England taking her morning exercise; and
great was the pleasure with which she marked every
animated movement of the youthful Victoria, whether
walking by the side of her governess, or running
forward in the eagerness of childhood's happy im-
pulses, with a bounding elasticity of active enjoyment
which full health only, or the spring of earliest youth,
can know.

'My own opportunities were not less than my

gratified mother's of seeing the Princess, being,
indeed, with my dear sister, a sharer in these walks;
and we had yet more frequent occasions given to us
of knowing her most interestingly developing character from persons whose duty or other circumstances brought them almost domestically under the
royal roof.

'In describing the infancy of the Princess I would
say she was a beautiful child, with a cherubic form of
features, clustered round by glossy fair ringlets. Her
complexion was remarkably transparent, with a soft
but often heightening tinge of the sweet blush-rose
upon her ·cheeks, that imparted a peculiar brilliancy
to her clear blue eyes. Whenever she met any
strangers in her usual paths she always seemed, by
the quickness of her glance, to inquire who and
what they were? The intelligence of her countenance was extraordinary at her very early age; but
might easily be accounted for on perceiving the extraordinary intelligence of her mind.

'I remember a little incident that may illustrate
this. One Sunday, at Esher Church, when the
Princess Victoria might be about six years old, my
attention was particularly attracted to the Claremont
pew, in which she and the Duchess of Kent and her
royal uncle (then the widowed Prince Leopold) sat.
It occupies a colonnaded recess, elevated a little, in
the interior south wall of the church. Parallel to it
runs a small gallery of pews, from one of which (my
mother's), being directly opposite to the royal seat, I
could see all that passed. I should not voluntarily
have so employed myself at church, but I had seen a
wasp skimming backwards and forwards over the

head and before the unveiled summer bonnet of the
little Princess ; and I could not forbear watching the
dangerous insect, fearing it might sting her face.
She, totally unobserving it, had meanwhile fixed her
eyes on the clergyman, who had taken his seat in
the pulpit to preach the sermon, and she never withdrew them thence for a moment during his whole
discourse.

' Next day, a lady, personally intimate at Claremont,
called at our humble little abode, and I remarked to
her the scene I had witnessed the preceding morning
at church ; wondering what could possibly have engaged the young Princess's attention so unrecedingly
to the face of the Rev. Dr. ——, a person totally
unknown to her, and whose countenance, though
expressive of good sense, was wiry and rough-hewn,
and could present nothing pleasing enough to fix the
eyes of a child. "It was not himself that attracted
her fixed eyes,". replied our visitor; "it was the
sermon he was preaching. For it is a custom with
her illustrious instructress to inquire of Princess
Victoria, not only the text of the discourse, but also
the heads of its leading subjects. Hence she neither
saw the wasp when in front of her, nor heard the
whisking of the protective handkerchief behind her.
Her whole mind was bound up in her task—a rare
faculty of concentration in any individual, therefore
more wonderful in one hardly beyond infancy. And
with a most surprising understanding of the subjects,
she never fails performing her task in a manner that
might grace much older years." '

After citing numerous incidents illustrative of the
Princess Victoria's goodness of heart, of a character

similar to those I have already given, Miss Porter goes
on to say : ' There were several mistaken reports about
this period, representing the Princess in a feeble state,
unable to walk, &c.; and as they made their way
into the newspapers, the public anxiety became painfully excited.   But not a word of truth was in the
statement.   At the very time they were deploring
her weakened steps she was running like an antelope
over Claremont lawn, or moving with an elastic
grace in the rudiments of dancing which only perfect
symmetry of foot and ankle could possess ; and where
perfect symmetry of form exists there needs no
words to prove that perfect health must be in all its
parts.

' This sweet spring of the Princess's life was thus
dedicated to the sowing of all precious seeds of knowledge, and the cultivation of all elegant acquirements ;
in the midst of the indigenous flowers which everywhere sought her eager eye, imparting the sportive
gladness of the ever gay butterfly to her youthful
spirit, just awakened into this beautiful world—a
reflection of Paradise!   The heavenward lark was
also in that infant bosom, for, young as she was, she
sang with sweetness and taste ; and my brother, Sir
Robert (who when in England frequently had the
honour of dining at Claremont), often had the pleasure of listening to the infant chorister, mingling its
cherub-like melody with the mature and delightful
harmonies of the Duchess of Kent and Prince
Leopold.

' But time wore on, with its succession of months
(we hardly may count a march by years to youth
only yet advancing to its teens), and the young

Princess gradually found a closer attention to her graver pursuits grow upon her. She read general history, under the guidance of one of England's best scholars in that essential branch of education—and more especially she "fixed the eyes of her mind" on the ancient annals of her own future dominions. Not being satisfied with our celebrated historians, Hume, Rapin, and others of modern date, she sought after the original authorities; and those venerable pen-men in *black-letter* were constrained to give up their lore (generally hidden lore from woman's eye) to the youthful heiress of their almost worshipped themes— our Saxon Alfred, our Norman Henries and Edwards. Succeeding chroniclers also yielded to her the same genuine tribute, till they told of the happily united royal streams in the bosoms of the Stuart and the Brunswick race—herself a nobly conscious daughter of both. And now that she has become the bride of a Prince of the most revered Saxon line—of the glorious posterity of John Frederick, Elector of Saxony, the friend of Luther and Melancthon, and the defender till death of the restored purity of the Christian Church—let us hail the auspicious sign as a pledge from Heaven that the present constitution of this realm, bequeathed by Alfred, and the Christian Church, established in simplicity and truth amongst us, most especially by the Brunswick race, are to remain in our land firm as the rock in which its soil is bedded.'

The Duchess of Kent early familiarized her illustrious daughter with the features of her own country, interesting her in it by personal visits to its chief cities and towns. Mother and child visited

together Birmingham, Worcester, Kenilworth, and
Carnarvon, with their strange commingling of historic interest and modern enterprise. They were
also seen alternately at Malvern, Broadstairs, Ramsgate, Brighton, Leamington, and Tunbridge Wells;
and they further honoured by their presence various
members of the English aristocracy at their country
seats.

The portraits of the Princess Victoria, executed
during her infancy and childhood, are somewhat
numerous. Sir William Beechey painted a picture in
oil, representing the Duchess seated on a sofa, upon
which her young daughter stood beside her, and this
painting is in the possession of the King of the
Belgians. Turnerelli, the sculptor, executed an excellent bust of the Princess when she was in her
third year; and in 1827 Mr. Behnes produced a
marble bust, which is now in one of the corridors of
Windsor Castle. It was justly regarded as one of
the most beautiful specimens of sculpture ever exhibited in the British schools of art, the likeness being
perfect, the features delicately portrayed, and the
expression admirable. Mr. Fowler, an artist of
Ramsgate, executed two portraits of the Princess, one
in her ninth year. This latter portrait Sir Thomas
Lawrence declined to admit into the Royal Academy
Exhibition, and an argumentative correspondence
ensued between the Duchess of Kent and the President. The Duchess regarded the portrait as the best
that had been taken of her daughter, with the exception of the bust by Behnes; and the attitude of
Sir T. Lawrence led to a good deal of prejudicial
feeling against him. Mr. Westall, R.A., painted a

trustworthy full-length portrait of the Princess as she appeared when in her twelfth year.

It was not until the spring of 1830 that the Princess Victoria became aware of her nearness to the British throne. One account states that she was reading English history with her governess, the Baroness Lehzen, and in the presence of her mother, when some question arose in connection with the succession to the crown. The point had probably been purposely suggested. Her Royal Highness studied her genealogical table for some time; and the account thus proceeds, the discussion being opened by a question from the Princess:

'In the event of the death of the King, my uncle, who would be the presumptive successor to the throne?'

The Baroness parried the question by the reply: 'The Duke of Clarence will succeed on the death of the present King.'

'Yes,' said the Princess, 'that I know; but who will succeed him?'

The governess, who saw the bearing of the inquiry, hesitated a moment, and then answered, 'Princess you have several uncles!'

Her Royal Highness now became agitated; the colour rose rapidly to her cheek, and she observed with much seriousness, 'True, I have; but I perceive here,' pointing to her table, 'that my papa was next in age to my uncle Clarence; and it *does* appear to me, from what I have just been reading, that when he and the present King are both dead, I shall become Queen of England!'

The Baroness looked silently towards the mother

of the Princess, who, after a short pause, replied to the following effect :

' We are continually looking forward, my beloved child, in the hope that your dear aunt, the Duchess of Clarence, may yet give birth to living children. Should it please God, however, that this be not the case, and that you are spared to the period, very distant I trust, which terminates the valuable lives of our revered Sovereign and the Duke of Clarence, you will indeed, by the established laws of our country, become their undoubted successor. Should this event—at present too remote and uncertain to engage our attention, further than to stimulate our endeavours so to form your mind as to render you not unworthy so high a destiny—should this event indeed occur, may you prove a blessing to your country and an ornament to the throne you are called to fill ! '

But we have another account of this interesting and, to the youthful participator in it, momentous conversation, and one which contains more tender and childlike touches. It is furnished in a letter written by the Baroness Lehzen, and as the Queen has herself placed the letter before her subjects, its authenticity may be accepted beyond question. This narrative, which fixes a year later than that given in the preceding account as the date of the conversation, is as follows :—

" I ask your Majesty's leave to cite some remarkable words of your Majesty when only twelve years old, while the Regency Bill was in progress. I then said to the Duchess of Kent, that now for the first time your Majesty ought to know your place in the succession. Her Royal Highness agreed with me, and

I put the genealogical table into the historical book. When Mr. Davys (the Queen's instructor, afterwards Bishop of Peterborough) was gone, the Princess Victoria opened the book again as usual, and seeing the additional paper said, 'I never saw that before.' 'It was not thought necessary you should, Princess,' I answered. 'I see I am nearer the throne than I thought.' 'So it is, madam,' I said. After some moments the Princess answered, 'Now, many a child would boast, but they don't know the difficulty. There is much splendour, but there is more responsi-bility.' The Princess having lifted up the fore-finger of her right hand while she spoke, gave me that little hand, saying, 'I will be good. I understand now why you urged me so much to learn even Latin. My aunts Augusta and Mary never did ; but you told me Latin is the foundation of English grammar and of all the elegant expressions, and I learned it as you wished it ; but I understand all better now.' And the Princess gave me her hand, repeating, 'I will be good.' I then said, 'But your aunt Adelaide is still young and may have children, and of course they would ascend the throne after their father William IV., and not you, Princess.' The Princess answered, 'And if it was so, I should never feel disappointed, for I know by the love aunt Adelaide bears me how fond she is of children.' " This is much more simple and natural, and the incident throws an agreeable light upon the early life of the Queen.

When William IV. ascended the throne in 1830, it became necessary to provide for the contingency of the Princess Victoria's accession before attaining the age of eighteen, that being the period of her majority.

A Regency Bill was introduced by Lord Lyndhurst, but a change of Government occurring before it was carried, it devolved upon Lord Brougham, the Lord Chancellor in Lord Grey's Administration, to take up and adopt the measure. The position was a singular one, because Parliament had to contemplate the possibility that William IV. might die leaving a posthumous child. Lord Brougham could not find a parallel case in English history since the death of Geoffrey, son of Henry II., who left a son, Prince Arthur, whose claims were thrust aside by the usurpation of King John. The possibility of posthumous issue in William's case having been provided for, the Bill passed both Houses and became law. The Duchess of Kent was named guardian of the infant Princess and regent of the kingdom, but she was to be assisted by a Council of Regency drawn from the royal family and the Ministers of State. Some months afterwards further provision was made for the education and maintenance of the Princess, and for the support of her honour and dignity as heiress presumptive. A sum of £10,000 a year was voted, in addition to the original annual grant of £6,000.

The Princess Victoria's first appearance at Court during the new reign was made at the celebration of Queen Adelaide's birthday, on the 24th of February 1831. The drawing-room held by her Majesty was stated to have been the most magnificent witnessed since that which signalized the presentation of the Princess Charlotte of Wales on the occasion of her marriage. The Princess Victoria stood on Queen Adelaide's left hand. Her dress was made entirely of articles manufactured in the United Kingdom.

She wore a frock of English blonde over white satin, a pearl necklace, and a rich diamond agrafe fastened the Madonna braids of her fair hair at the back of her head. She was the object of interest and admiration on the part of all assembled. The scene was one of the most splendid ever remembered, and the future Queen of England contemplated all that passed with much dignity, but with evident enjoyment.

When King William prorogued his first Parliament an interesting circumstance occurred, which caused much enthusiasm amongst those who witnessed it. Queen Adelaide and the princesses witnessed the spectacle of the royal State procession. The people cheered the Queen lustily, but, forgetting herself, that gracious lady took the young Princess Victoria by the hand, led her to the front of the balcony, and introduced her to the happy and loyal multitude. In January 1831 the Princess made her first appearance at the theatre, visiting Covent Garden, and thoroughly entering into the pleasures of the children's entertainment provided.

A strange omission, and one which gave rise to much comment, was observed in connection with the coronation of King William IV. and Queen Adelaide, in Westminster Abbey, on the 8th of September 1831. The absence of the heiress presumptive, Princess Victoria, from the ceremony was particularly remarked upon; and it appears that no place had been assigned to her, nor any preparation made in expectation of her gracing or witnessing the coronation. Here was a splendid opportunity for the quidnuncs, and amongst the items of gossip served up it was roundly asserted that Earl Grey, the Prime

Minister, obstinately opposed all idea of inviting the Princess to be present. Others affirmed that the Duchess of Northumberland, the governess of the Princess, in the exercise of a superior and enlightened judgment, and in consideration of the then alleged delicate health of her young charge, advised that her pupil should not be present at the coronation of King William and Queen Adelaide. No other explanation being at the moment forthcoming, this was accepted by those who did not throw the blame of that 'conspicuous absence' on Queen Adelaide herself and her royal consort; but, as an anonymous writer observed, 'Who that knew the good King William and his incomparable Queen, would believe that any slight was put by them on their well-beloved niece and the heiress presumptive to the throne?' Another report stated that 'the Duchess of Northumberland was seeking to give a political bias to the education of the Princess; and some uneasiness was therefore created at the palace.' A morning journal asserted that the Duchess of Kent had 'refused to attend—yes, refused to attend,' and it reproved her in somewhat harsh terms, alluding to the impertinence of the widow of a mediatized German prince in withholding her daughter from a ceremony at which she could never at one time have expected to see a daughter of hers as heiress presumptive to the crown of England! Other papers made the alleged refusal to attend rest on the course taken by Lord A. Fitzclarence, who, in marshalling the coronation procession on paper, had assigned a place to the Princess Victoria after the other members of the royal family, instead of next to the King and Queen. This singular controversy was finally set at rest by an `authoritative statement to the effect that, the Duchess having pleaded the delicate state of her daughter's health, had obtained the King's sanction to her absence ; a natural explanation which might have occurred to any one who was not interested in finding a more ambiguous one.

Meanwhile, away from the Court, the Princess continued her studies. In addition to the tuition she received from Dr. Davys and the Baroness Lehzen, she was taught music by W. J. B. Sale, first engaged at the special request of George IV. ; and dancing by Madame Bourdin. In writing and arithmetic she was instructed by Mr. Steward, the writing-master at Westminster School, and under his guidance she acquired that free and bold hand manifested by her autograph signature. She learnt with facility all that was taught her, and exhibited a special talent in the acquisition of living languages. In the Isle of Wight and at Claremont she also received daily instruction from the Duchess; and the future Queen gave good promise in every way both as to talent and disposition. In the summer and autumn of 1832 the Duchess of Kent took her daughter upon a tour through many of the English counties, and also through the Welsh principality. The main objects of this royal progress were of an intellectual character. Coventry, Shrewsbury, Powis Castle, Wynnstay, and Beaumaris were visited in turn, and all matters of historical, statistical, or industrial interest were closely examined. The royal pair took up their residence for some time in the Isle of Anglesey, and the Princess visited the Eisteddfod at Beaumaris, investing the musical victors with the prizes awarded for their performances. Returning in October through the Midland counties, the travellers were warmly welcomed at Worcester, Chester, Chatsworth, Matlock, and other places. During this autumnal tour the Princess Victoria laid the foundation-stone of a school, named a bridge, planted an oak, and stood godmother to the infant daughter of Lord and Lady Robert Grosvenor. The Duchess zealously strove to interest her in all ranks and classes of the people over whom she was destined to govern. The Princess was cosmopolitan in her tastes. At Lichfield Cathedral she was struck with admiration by Chantrey's exquisite group of the 'Sleeping Children'; while at Bromsgrove she exhibited a keen interest in the works of the nailers and other iron manufactures in the vicinity. She was especially delighted with a present from the nailers of Bromsgrove, consisting of a thousand little nails of all patterns enclosed in a quill and presented in a small gold box. Oxford University stirred in her other sentiments and emotions; and at the University the visitors were welcomed by an address from the Vice-Chancellor. The Princess also received at the famous University Press a present of a magnificent Bible, and the history of her visit printed on white satin.

In the following year (1833) the Duchess and her daughter took up their residence at their beautiful seat of Norris Castle, Isle of Wight. Unembarrassed by the trammels of society, they were able to enjoy the delightful scenery of the island, sometimes taking long walks and excursions alone. A tourist on one occasion strolled into the old churchyard at Arreton,

D

to search out the grave of Elizabeth Wallbridge, the heroine of Legh Richmond's popular religious story, *The Dairyman's Daughter*.   Beside a grassy mound he discovered a lady and a young girl seated, 'the latter reading aloud, in a full melodious voice, the touching tale of the Christian maiden.   The tourist turned away, and soon after was told by the sexton that the pilgrims to that humble grave were the Duchess of Kent and Princess Victoria.'

From Norris Castle the royal ladies made many marine excursions in the *Emerald* yacht.   Southampton, Carisbrooke, and Winchester were visited; while at Plymouth and Torquay minute attention was paid by the future Sovereign to the details of marine affairs. In acknowledging an address from the inhabitants of Torquay on the anniversary of one of England's great naval victories, the Duchess of Kent said : ' It has ever been my pride to lead the Princess to regard with warm feelings all the recollections that belong to this day in relation to the naval service of the country.' And in replying to an address from Plymouth she referred with satisfaction to her residence in the Isle of Wight, which permitted her, as a part of the education of her daughter, to visit the coast, and the great arsenal so associated with the naval renown of Britain.   Another providential escape from destruction marked the Princess Victoria's homeward voyage from the Eddystone to Norris Castle in the *Emerald* yacht. It seems that the vessel ran foul of the *Active* hulk, and the mainmast of the *Emerald* being sprung, her sail and a piece of heavy wood were detached.   The pilot, Mr. Saunders, quick as thought, sprang to where the Princess was standing, lifted her in his arms to a

more safe position further aft, and the next moment
crash came the topmast down where the Princess had
originally stationed herself. But for the prompt action
of Mr. Saunders she must have been crushed to death.
Her Royal Highness bore herself with calmness while
the event was passing, but after fully perceiving her
imminent danger she burst into tears, and thanked her
preserver with artless grace for his great presence of
mind. The pilot was promoted to be a master, and
when the Princess became Queen of England he was
invited to Court. On the death of Mr. Saunders,
moreover, the Queen made provision for his wife and
family.

After the return to Kensington Palace the Princess
suffered from a severe attack of illness. For some
time preceding her fifteenth birthday she looked pale
and languid, and the violent changes of temperature
subjected her to the only serious indisposition she had
hitherto experienced. She soon recovered her health,
however, and was able to accompany King William
and Queen Adelaide to the Grand Musical Festival in
Westminster Abbey, when she was greeted with
enthusiasm and affection by the loyal crowds which
had assembled on the occasion.

The Ascot races of June 1835 were witnessed
by a brilliant gathering. On the principal day the
Princess Victoria made her first appearance on a race-
course with the Royal Family. The Life Guards
preceded the royal *cortége*, and the *coup d'œil* when the
latter appeared on the ground was splendid in the
extreme. The uniforms of the soldiery, and the
magnificent attire of the ladies of rank and fashion,
who attended in their thousands, combined with the

glorious summer day, gave *éclat* to a scene never to
be forgotten. The Princess was then just sixteen, not
very tall in stature as yet, but glowing with youth,
health, and happiness. Her hair, which appeared of
an almost flaxen hue, was braided in what were known
as Clotilde bands, the ancient style worn by the Plantagenet queens, and it became the Princess's contour
of face exceedingly well. For costume she wore
a large pink bonnet and a rose-coloured satin dress,
broché, with a pelerine cape trimmed with black lace.
Though the cynosure of all eyes, it is stated that the
Princess seemed much more delighted at any expression of loyalty bestowed on her royal uncle, the
King, than by all the intoxicating applause lavishly
accorded to herself. N. P. Willis, the American
author, then on his travels, viewed this scene at Ascot,
and thus described the illustrious personages present :
' In one of the intervals I walked under the King's
stand, and   saw her Majesty the Queen and the
young Princess Victoria very distinctly. They were
leaning over the railing, listening to a ballad singer,
and seeming as much interested and amused as any
simple country folk could be. The Queen is undoubtedly the plainest woman in her dominions, but the
Princess is much better-looking than any picture of
her in the shops, and for the heir to such a crown as
that of England, unnecessarily pretty and interesting.
She will be sold, poor thing ! bartered away by those
great dealers in royal hearts, whose grand calculations
will not be much consolation to her if she happens to
have a taste of her own.' The plain-spoken American
was wrong in his prophetic vision. There was no such
bartering as he anticipated, for not long after this the

girl of whom he wrote plighted her troth in a genuine love-match, if ever there was one in the annals of royal houses.

On the 30th of August 1835 the Princess Victoria was confirmed by the Archbishop of Canterbury, assisted by the Bishop of London, in the Chapel Royal, St. James's. In addition to the Princess and the Duchess of Kent, only the King, Queen Adelaide, and the Duchess of Saxe-Weimar, with some other members of the Royal Family, were present. The scene was very touching. We read that the young Princess exhibited great marks of sensibility during the beautiful and pathetic exhortation in which the Archbishop represented to her the great responsibility attaching to her high station; and when he spoke of the struggle she must prepare for between the world and Heaven, and, above all, of the absolute necessity of her looking up to the King of kings for counsel and support in all the trials that awaited her, her composure gradually gave way, till at length she was bathed in tears, and, unable to subdue the violence of her emotion, she laid her head upon her mother's shoulder and sobbed aloud. The Duchess of Kent was scarcely less affected, while the King and Queen were also much moved.

In strange contrast to this scene, Greville relates one which is alleged to have occurred at Windsor on the 21st of August 1836. It was the King's birthday. Being Sunday, the celebration was what was called private, but there were a hundred persons at dinner, either belonging to the Court or from the neighbourhood. The Duchess of Kent sat on one side of the King, and one of his sisters on the other;

the Princess Victoria opposite. All that passed was heard by Adolphus Fitzclarence, who would seem to have reported it. By the Queen's desire the King's health was drunk, and by way of reply his Majesty delivered an extraordinary and outrageous speech. 'I trust in God,' he is reported to have said, 'that my life may be spared for nine months longer, after which period, in the event of my death, no regency would take place. I should then have the satisfaction of leaving the royal authority to the personal exercise of that young lady (pointing to the Princess), the heiress presumptive of the crown, and not in the hands of a person now near me, who is surrounded by evil advisers, and who is herself incompetent to act with propriety in the station in which she would be placed. I have no hesitation in saying that I have been insulted—grossly and continually insulted—by that person; but I am determined to endure no longer a course of behaviour so disrespectful to me. Amongst many other things, I have particularly to complain of the manner in which that young lady has been kept away from my Court; she has been repeatedly kept from my drawing-rooms, at which she ought always to have been present; but I am fully resolved that this shall not happen again. I would have her know that I am King, and I am determined to make my authority respected; and for the future I shall insist and command that the Princess do upon all occasions appear at my Court, as it is her duty to do.'

Though the King concluded with an affectionate allusion to the Princess and her future reign, it may readily be conceived that such a speech as this, if delivered in the precise terms reported, would create a most painful sensation. Greville adds that the awful philippic was uttered with a loud voice and excited manner; that the Queen was in deep distress, while the Princess burst into tears, and the whole company were aghast. As for the aggrieved and insulted Duchess of Kent, she said not a word, but announced her immediate departure, and ordered her carriage. However, a sort of reconciliation was patched up, and she was prevailed upon to stay till next day. We will hope that the whole scene, though no doubt unseemly enough, was greatly exaggerated; but it is unfortunately true that the King's temper too frequently got the better of him, and that he more than once, in unkingly and ungentlemanly terms, and terms the reverse of fraternal, vented it upon the Duchess of Kent.

In May 1836 the Duke of Coburg, together with his two sons, Prince Ernest and Prince Albert, paid a visit to England, and spent nearly four weeks at Kensington Palace with the Duchess of Kent. It was now that the Princess Victoria saw for the first time her future husband. The distinguished visitors were *fêted* at Windsor and at St. James's by the King and Queen, and by every member of the Royal Family in England. In the company of the Duchess of Kent and her daughter they also visited the chief attractions of the metropolis. Before Prince Albert bade farewell to his fair cousin they went together to behold the touching spectacle of the anniversary of the London Charity Schools at St. Paul's. Both were much moved by the scene, especially when the children joined in singing that sublime composition, the Hundredth

Psalm. After the proceedings were over, the royal party were entertained at luncheon at the Mansion House by the Lord Mayor and Lady Mayoress. The large party of citizens who had the honour of being invited, says a contemporary account, were charmed with the fresh, healthful beauty of the Princess, and with the frank, unaffected manner of the Princes her cousins, all three of whom entered freely into conversation with their host and hostess, and the other guests, and expressed themselves as highly delighted with the scene they had just witnessed.

The Princess Victoria attained her legal majority on the 24th of May 1837, being then eighteen years of age. She was serenaded at Kensington Palace, at seven in the morning, by a band of thirty-seven vocal and instrumental performers in full dress. Her Royal Highness sat at one of the windows during the performance of the concert (she was always an early riser), and she graciously requested the repetition of one of the songs, which contained an allusion to her illustrious parent. The performance concluded with 'God save the King,' in which the assembled spectators joined in full chorus. During the day many congratulatory visits were paid to the Duchess of Kent and the Princess; and amongst the birthday gifts to her Royal Highness was a magnificent grand pianoforte, of the value of 200 guineas, from the King. It was asserted that his Majesty offered to give the Princess £10,000 a year from his privy purse, provided she would allow him to name the officers of her establishment; but that she declined to accept the money on that condition.

The royal birthday was observed as a holiday in

London, and neither House of Parliament sat. A grand State ball was given at St. James's Palace, at which a brilliant party assembled to do honour to her Royal Highness; but the King and Queen were absent on account of the severe indisposition of the former. At this ball the Princess Victoria for the first time took precedence of her mother, occupying the central chair of State, supported by the Duchess of Kent and the Princess Augusta. The metropolis was brilliantly illuminated in the evening, and the happy event was likewise celebrated in various parts of the country by demonstrations of public rejoicing.

The celebration was rendered further memorable by addresses of congratulation being voted by the City of London in Council to the Princess and her illustrious mother the Duchess of Kent. As the circumstance was without precedent, touching an heir presumptive to the throne, some members of the Corporation opposed the resolution; but the addresses were carried, and the Lord Mayor and aldermen, &c., duly attended at Kensington Palace to present them. The Duchess, in her reply, first referred to the loss of her husband and the education of her daughter, to which she had devoted herself after the Duke's death; and then came these interesting passages: ' I have in times of great difficulty avoided all connection with any party in the State; but if I have done so, I have never ceased to impress on my daughter her duties, so as to gain by her conduct the respect and affection of the people. This I have taught her should be her first earthly duty as a constitutional sovereign. The Princess has arrived at that age which now justifies my expressing my confident ex-

pectation that she will be found competent to execute
the sacred trust which may be reposed in her; for,
communicating, as she does, with all classes of society,
she cannot but perceive that the greater the diffusion
of religion, knowledge, and the love of freedom in a
country, the more orderly, industrious, and wealthy is
its population, and that with the desire to preserve
the constitutional prerogatives of the Crown ought
to be co-ordinate the protection of the liberties of the
people.'   The address to the Princess Victoria was
then read ; and her Royal Highness, very simply and
naturally, but with blushing timidity, replied : 'I am
very thankful for your kindness, and my mother has
expressed all my feelings.'

Addresses continued to be presented to the
Duchess and Princess for many days, and on one day
alone no fewer than twenty-four addresses were
received and acknowledged.   Mr. Attwood, in presenting an address from the Birmingham Political
Union, said a few words, with peculiar solemnity and
earnestness, expressive of the gratitude and respect
due to the Duchess for her wise maternal conduct,
which caused her Royal Highness to be deeply moved.
Another address which the Princess received with
special pleasure was one presented by the inhabitants
of Kensington, through their reverend vicar, Arch-
deacon Pott.   When this venerable clergyman was
introduced the young Princess advanced to meet him
with a smiling welcome, and assured him of the high
gratification with which she received the warm sentiments of affectionate attachment he was commissioned
by his parishioners to lay before her ; and at the same
time promised him that 'the welfare and interest of

her native town should never fail to be zealously forwarded by any means which it might please God to
place in her power.'

The Queen's last appearance at Court as Princess
Victoria was at the drawing-room in honour of the
King's birthday, May 29, 1837; and shortly afterwards she made her final appearance in public as heiress
presumptive at the memorable charity ball given at
the Opera House for the benefit of the Spitalfields
weavers. Her life as Princess thus closed with a
charitable act, and she had the satisfaction of knowing that the terrible sufferings which afflicted the
poor in the East End were soon afterwards alleviated.

We have now come to the parting of the ways.
The life of the Princess has been traced from her birth,
and through her childhood and girlhood, up to the
verge of womanhood. She had grown up a fair and
graceful type of the English maiden, and notwithstanding her high destiny she had been reared in
the paths of duty and of self-sacrifice. Who knows
not how to serve, knows not how to govern. The
people owed a debt of gratitude to the Duchess of
Kent for the admirable all-round training she gave
her child. None knew of the nearness of that blow
which was soon to fall upon the Royal House, removing the King from the midst of his subjects; but
that his successor was prepared for her lofty position
whenever he should be called away, was due to that
constant teaching and supervision which had nourished
her soul in rectitude and in affectionate solicitude for
the welfare of the people.

CHAPTER II.

VICTORIA REGINA.

THE illness which prevented King William IV. from taking part in the birthday festivities of the Princess Victoria developed rapidly towards the close of the month of May. His Majesty exhibited signs of great debility and exhaustion, with oppression of breathing; and he had lost the power of walking. Preparations had been made to convey him to Brighton for change of air early in June, but these had to be abandoned. On the 9th he experienced some relief from the most distressing symptoms, and transacted business with Sir Herbert Taylor. All who came in contact with the King observed how his illness had refined him and made him gentle and resigned. Indeed, his unwearied patience and cheerfulness excited the admiration and astonishment of all who had opportunity of witnessing them. All his sailor-like bluntness of speech had disappeared. On the morning of the 16th he observed to the Queen: 'I have had some quiet sleep; come and pray with me, and thank the Almighty for it.' When the King's devotions were over, the Queen said: 'And shall I not pray to the Almighty that you may have a good day?' To which his Majesty replied: 'Oh, do! I wish I could live ten years for the sake of my country. I feel it my duty to keep

well as long as I can.' On the morning of Sunday
the 11th, seeing Lady Mary Fox occupied with a
book, the King inquired what she was reading, and
being told that it was a Prayer-book, his countenance
beamed with pleasure. The Queen asked whether it
would be agreeable if she read the prayers to him.
His Majesty answered : ' Oh, yes ! I should like it
very much ; but it will fatigue you.' Ascertaining
that the Rev. Mr. Wood was the preacher that morning in the chapel of the Castle, the King desired him
to be sent for. When he entered, the royal sufferer
said : ' I will thank you, my dear sir, to read all the
prayers till you come to the prayer for the Church
militant.' By this injunction the King intended to
include the Communion Service and all the other
parts of the Liturgy used in the celebration of public
worship. It is stated to have been both an affecting
and an instructive lesson to observe the devout
humility of the King, who fervently dwelt, as could be
perceived from his manner and the intonation of his
voice, on every passage which bore even the most
remote application to his own circumstances. ' It has
been a great comfort to me,' he exclaimed afterwards
to the Queen. Nor was it a transitory feeling, for on
each day of the ensuing week Lord Augustus Fitzclarence received his Majesty's command to read to
him the prayers either of the morning or evening
service.

By Sunday the 18th the King's illness had become
so alarming that only a fatal result could be apprehended. Nevertheless, he transacted official business,
and his last act of sovereignty was to sign a free
pardon to a condemned criminal. Shortly afterwards

the Archbishop of Canterbury attended, and administered the sacrament to the King and Queen, the
former appearing calm and collected, and his attitude
being one of humility and gratitude to God. Early
on the morning of this day the King had remembered
that it was the anniversary of the battle of Waterloo,
and he had said to Dr. Chambers: 'Let me but live
over this memorable day—I shall never live to see
another sunset.' Dr. Chambers answered : 'I hope
your Majesty may live to see many.' To which the
King replied in a phrase which he commonly employed: 'Oh! that is quite another thing.' When he
awoke on the morning of the 19th the King
remarked to the Queen, 'I shall get up once more to
do the business of the country;' and as he was
wheeled in his chair from the bedroom to the dressing-room, he looked with a gracious smile on the
Queen's attendants, who were standing in tears near
the door, and said, 'God bless you!' and waved his
hand. When the Archbishop came and read the
Service for the Sick, and the Articles of Faith, the King,
though much exhausted, enunciated with distinct
and solemn emphasis the words, 'All this I steadfastly believe.' For the first time the Queen was
now overpowered by the weight of her affliction. The
King perceived her emotion, and said in a tone of
encouragement, 'Bear up, bear up.' Once or twice
during the day he raised his eyes and exclaimed,
'Thy will be done!' When the Archbishop left him
for the last time he said to the King, 'My best
prayers are offered up for your Majesty;' whereupon
the dying monarch replied, with feeble yet distinct
utterance, 'Believe me, I am a religious man.' At

twelve minutes past two on the morning of the 20th, the King passed away, leaving behind him the memory of a sovereign who was just and upright, while as a man he was a sincere friend, a forgiving enemy, and a gracious and indulgent master. His defects were mainly surface defects, and these were forgotten in the wide and genuine tribute called forth by his sterling virtues.

The King is dead! God save the Queen! To the veteran of threescore and ten has succeeded the maiden of eighteen. The manner in which the young Sovereign received the news of her accession has been told by Miss Wynn in her *Diary of a Lady of Quality*, and the account is extremely interesting. The Archbishop of Canterbury (Dr. Howley) and the Lord Chamberlain (the Marquis Conyngham) left Windsor immediately after the King's death, posting to Kensington Palace, to inform the Princess Victoria of the melancholy event. Leaving Windsor shortly before half-past two, they did not reach Kensington until five o'clock in the morning. 'They knocked, they rang, they thumped for a considerable time before they could rouse the porter at the gate. They were again kept waiting in the courtyard, then turned into one of the lower rooms, where they seemed forgotten by everybody. They rang the bell, and desired that the attendant of the Princess Victoria might be sent to inform her Royal Highness that they desired an audience on business of importance. After another delay and another ringing to inquire the cause, the attendant was summoned, who stated that the Princess was in such a sweet sleep that she could not venture to disturb her. Then they said : " We are come on business of State to the Queen, and even her sleep must give way to that." It did ; and to prove that she did not keep them waiting, in a few minutes she came into the room in a loose white nightgown and shawl, her nightcap thrown off, and her hair falling upon her shoulders, her feet in slippers, tears in her eyes, but perfectly collected and dignified.'

Bishop Fulford states that on being informed of her new dignity, the first words which the young Queen uttered were these, addressed to the Archbishop : 'I ask your prayers on my behalf.' They knelt down together, and Victoria inaugurated her reign, like the young King of Israel in the olden time, by asking from the Most High, who ruleth over the kingdoms of men, an understanding heart to judge so great a people.

Another incident which redounds to the honour of the youthful Sovereign is recorded. The first act of her life as Queen was to write a letter, breathing the purest and tenderest feelings of affection and condolence, to Queen Adelaide. Her manner of doing it evinced a spirit of generosity and consideration which obtained for her golden opinions everywhere. Her Majesty wrote the letter spontaneously, and having finished it, folded and addressed it to ' Her Majesty the Queen.' Some one in her presence, who had a right to make a remark, noticing this, mentioned that the superscription was not correct, and that the letter ought to be addressed to ' Her Majesty the Queen Dowager.' 'I am quite aware,' said Queen Victoria, ' of her Majesty's altered character ; but I will not be the first person to remind her of it.'

The Queen's first Privy Council was held at Ken-

sington Palace on the morning of the 21st. The
incidents of this memorable Council have been preserved in the pages of Greville, and that acid diarist
himself seems to have been struck with admiration at
the bearing of the young Queen : 'Never was anything like the first impression she produced, or the
chorus of praise which is raised about her manner and
behaviour, and certainly not without justice. It was
very extraordinary, and something far beyond what
was looked for. Her extreme youth and inexperience,
and the ignorance of the world concerning her,
naturally excited intense curiosity to see how she
would act on this trying occasion, and there was
a considerable assemblage at the Palace, notwithstanding the short notice which was given. The first
thing to be done was to teach her her lesson, which
for this purpose Melbourne had himself to learn. I
gave him the Council papers, and explained all that
was to be done, and he went and explained all this to
her.'

Melbourne asked the Queen if she would enter the
room accompanied by the great officers of State, but
she said she would go in alone. When the Lords
were assembled the Lord President informed them of
the King's death, and suggested, as they were so
numerous, that a few of them should repair to the
presence of the Queen and inform her of the event,
and that their lordships were assembled in consequence ; and accordingly the two Royal Dukes of
Cumberland and Sussex, the two Archbishops, the
Lord Chancellor, and Melbourne, went with him. The
Queen received them in the adjoining room alone. As
soon as they had returned, the proclamation was read,

E

and the usual order passed. When the doors were thrown open and the Queen entered, accompanied by her two uncles, who advanced to meet her, she was quite plainly dressed, and in mourning. The Queen bowed to the lords, took her seat, and then, in a clear, distinct, and audible voice, and without any appearance of fear or embarrassment, she read the following declaration to the Council :—

'The severe and afflicting loss which the nation has sustained by the death of his Majesty, my beloved uncle, has devolved upon me the duty of administering the government of this empire. This awful responsibility is imposed upon me so suddenly, and at so early a period of my life, that I should feel myself utterly oppressed by the burden, were I not sustained by the hope that Divine Providence, which has called me to this work, will give me strength for the performance of it, and that I shall find in the purity of my intentions, and in my zeal for the public welfare, that support and those resources which usually belong to a more mature age and to long experience.

'I place my firm reliance upon the wisdom of Parliament, and upon the loyalty and affection of my people. I esteem it also a peculiar advantage that I succeed to a Sovereign whose constant regard for the rights and liberties of his subjects, and whose desire to promote the amelioration of the laws and institutions of the country, have rendered his name the object of general attachment and veneration.

'Educated in England, under the tender and enlightened care of a most affectionate mother, I have learned from my infancy to respect and love the Constitution of my native country.

'It will be my unceasing study to maintain the Reformed religion as by law established, securing at the same time to all the full enjoyment of religious liberty; and I shall steadily protect the rights and promote to the utmost of my power the happiness and welfare of all classes of my subjects.'

Greville goes on to say with regard to the subsequent proceedings : 'After she had read her speech and taken and signed the oath for the security of the Church of Scotland, the Privy Councillors were sworn, the two Royal Dukes first, by themselves; and as these two old men, her uncles, knelt before her, swearing allegiance, and kissing her hand, I saw her blush up to the eyes, as if she felt the contrast between their civil and their natural relations, and this was the only sign of emotion which she evinced. Her manner to them was very graceful and engaging: she kissed them both, and rose from her chair, and moved towards the Duke of Sussex, who was farthest from her, and too infirm to reach her.

'She seemed rather bewildered at the multitude of men who were sworn, and who came one after another to kiss her hand, but she did not speak to anybody, nor did she make the slightest difference in her manner, or show any in her countenance, to any individual of rank, station, or party. I particularly watched her when Melbourne and the Ministers and the Duke of Wellington and Peel approached her. She went through the whole ceremony—occasionally looking at Melbourne for instruction when she had any doubt what to do, which hardly ever occurred— with perfect calmness and self-possession, but at the

E 2

same time with a graceful modesty and propriety
particularly interesting and ingratiating.'

But the Queen's speech had not passed over without a curious colloquy between two eminent men.
Although generally admired, Brougham found fault
with it, and worked himself into a state of considerable excitement. He said to Sir Robert Peel, by
whom he was standing, but with whom he was not in
the habit of communicating :

'*A*melioration—that is not English ; you might
perhaps say *m*elioration ; but improvement is the
proper word.'

'Oh,' rejoined Peel, 'I see no harm in the word ;
it is generally used.'

'You object,' said Brougham, 'to the sentiment ;
I object to the grammar.'

'No,' said Peel, 'I don't object to the sentiment.'

'Well, then, she pledges herself to the policy of *our*
Government,' said Brougham.

Greville adds : 'Peel told me this, which passed in
the room, and near the Queen. He likewise said how
amazed he was at her manner and behaviour, at the
apparent deep sense of her situation, her modesty, and
at the same time her firmness. She appeared in fact
to be awed, but not damped ; and afterwards the
Duke of Wellington told me the same thing, and
added that if she had been his own daughter he
could not have desired to see her perform her part
better.'

In signing the State documents the Queen simply
wrote her name 'Victoria,' without the 'Alexandrina,' and this necessitated many alterations in the
records. The written rolls of the House of Lords,

and the printed forms of the oath at the House of
Commons, described the Queen as her Majesty
' Alexandrina Victoria ;' but after the proceedings at
the Council, when her Majesty signed ' Victoria,' the
forms required to be altered. In some instances new
forms were provided ; but in others there was not
time, and the pen was consequently run through
the first name, ' Alexandrina.' The Lord Chancellor
attached a foot-note to the rolls, recording that such
erasures were made after the morning sitting, and
after the peers' signatures then affixed had been
written. There also became necessary an important
and curious interlineation in the oath—namely, the
addition, within parenthesis, of the words, ' saving
the right of any issue of his late Majesty King
William the Fourth, which may be born of his late
Majesty's consort.'

The Princess Victoria was formally proclaimed
Queen of Great Britain and Ireland on the 21st of
June, from St. James's Palace. Long before the
hour fixed for the ceremony all the avenues to the
palace were crowded, every balcony, window, and
elevated position being filled with spectators. The
space in the quadrangle, in front of the window at
which her Majesty was to appear, was crowded with
ladies and gentlemen, and even the parapets above
were filled with people. The great Irish agitator,
O'Connell, in the front line opposite the windows,
attracted considerable attention by waving his hat and
cheering most vehemently.

The guns in the park fired a salute at ten o'clock,
and immediately afterwards the Queen made her
appearance at the window of the Presence Chamber.

She stood between Lords Melbourne and Lansdowne, and was received with deafening cheers. Her mother also, who was close behind her, received most cordial plaudits. The Queen looked very fatigued and pale, but returned the repeated cheers with which she was greeted with remarkable ease and dignity. She was dressed in deep mourning, with a white tippet, white cuffs, and a border of white lace under a small black bonnet, which was placed far back on her head, exhibiting her light hair in front simply parted over her forehead. The Queen and the Duchess of Kent regarded the proceedings with much interest. As her Majesty appeared at the window the band of the Royal Guards struck up the National Anthem. On its conclusion, Sir William Woods, acting for the Garter King-at-Arms, and accompanied by the Duke of Norfolk as Earl Marshal of England, read aloud the proclamation containing the official announcement of the death of King William IV., and of the consequent accession of Queen Victoria to the throne of these realms. The proclamation was as follows :—

' Whereas it has pleased Almighty God to call to His mercy our late sovereign lord, King William the Fourth, of blessed and glorious memory, by whose decease the imperial crown of the United Kingdom of Great Britain and Ireland is solely and rightfully come to the high and mighty Princess Alexandrina Victoria (saving the rights of any issue of his late Majesty King William the Fourth which may be born of his late Majesty's consort) : We, therefore, the lords spiritual and temporal of this realm, being here assisted with those of his late Majesty's Privy Council, with numbers of others, principally gentlemen of quality, with the Lord Mayor, aldermen, and citizens of London, do now hereby, with one voice and consent of tongue and heart, publish and proclaim that the high and mighty Princess Alexandrina Victoria is now, by the death of our late Sovereign of happy memory, become our only lawful and rightful liege lady, Victoria, by the grace of God Queen of the United Kingdom of Great Britain and Ireland, Defender of the Faith, saving as aforesaid: To whom, saving as aforesaid, we do acknowledge all faith and constant obedience, with all hearty and humble affection, beseeching God, by whom kings and queens do reign, to bless the royal Princess Victoria with long and happy years to reign over us. God save the Queen!'

While the proclamation was being read there was considerable movement among the crowd, who continued to cheer and cry 'God save the Queen!' until the stentorian voice of Daniel O'Connell commanded 'Silence!' Her Majesty stood during the whole rehearsal of the proclamation. She was deeply affected at the acclamations which rent the air, and was observed to shed tears. This touching incident was commemorated by Mrs. Browning (then Miss Elizabeth Barrett) in a poem, of which the following were the last two stanzas:—

'God save thee, weeping Queen!
Thou shalt be well beloved:
The tyrant's sceptre cannot move
As those poor tears have moved.
The nature in thine eyes we see
Which tyrants cannot own—
The love that guardeth liberties.
Strange blessing on the nation lies,
Whose Sovereign wept—
Yea, wept to wear its crown.

'God bless thee, weeping Queen!
   With blessing more divine,
   And fill with better love than earth's
      That tender heart of thine;
   That when the throne of earth shall be
      As low as graves brought down,
   A piercèd hand may give to thee
      The crown which angels shout to sce:
         Thou wilt not weep
      To wear that heavenly crown.'

Auspicious as her accession was, the gravity of the occasion and the weight of her new responsibilities caused the Queen to be overcome more than once by her emotion on that trying day. As soon as she found herself disengaged from all the duties of the solemn ceremonial, she traversed the palace with hasty steps till she arrived at her mother's apartment, and flinging herself on her bosom, she gave vent to her contending feelings in a flood of tears. The Duchess gently soothed her, and then the Queen said :

'I can scarcely believe, mamma, that I am Queen of England; but I suppose I really am so—am I not ?'

'You know, my love, you are. You have just left a scene which must have assured you of it.'

'And in time,' replied her Majesty, 'I shall become accustomed to my change of character; meanwhile, since it really is so, and you see in your little daughter the Sovereign of this great country, will you grant her the first request she has had occasion in her regal capacity to put to you ?   I wish, my dear mamma, to be left for two hours alone.'

The Duchess understood the reason for this request,

and for the first day in her daughter's life she left
her alone. The young Queen desired in human
solitude, but in the presence of her Maker, to com-
mune with herself upon the duties which would now
lie before her, day after day, and year after year, as
the monarch of a great and powerful empire.

One result of the Queen's accession escaped without
comment in almost all the journals. The descent of
the English crown to a female necessitated the
separation from it of the kingdom of Hanover, which,
according to Salic law, passed to the Queen's uncle,
Ernest, Duke of Cumberland.

Her Majesty's first assumption of royalty in the
Council Chamber at Kensington Palace formed the
subject of a historical picture by Sir David Wilkie.
In that picture the 'Maiden Queen' is seen at the
head of the table, while at the foot, facing her, is the
Duke of Sussex in his black velvet skull-cap. Other
noticeable figures in the group are those of the great
Chancellor Lyndhurst; Brougham, the clever and
indiscreet, with his restless features ceaselessly in
action; the Duke of Wellington, with his striking
countenance; Lord John Russell, a statesman whose
capacity was not to be measured by his inches, and
who was humorously described, when he married the
stately young widow,' Lady Ribblesdale, as 'the
widow's mite'; John Campbell, the writer of the
'Lives of the Chancellors'; and Lord Melbourne,
gentleman and statesman, and one who was soon high
in the confidence of his Sovereign.

When the news of Queen Victoria's accession
became known to Prince Albert, who was then a
student at Bonn, he wrote to her Majesty as follows

on the 26th of June :—'Now you are queen of the
mightiest land of Europe, in your hand lies the
happiness of millions. May Heaven assist you and
strengthen you with its strength in that high but
difficult task. I hope that your reign may be long,
happy, and glorious, and that your efforts may be
rewarded, by the thankfulness and love of your subjects.' The Prince's demeanour at this time was
diffident and retiring ; he was strongly averse to
putting himself forward in any way ; and it was
determined by the friends both of the Queen and the
Prince that, to prevent the premature report of a
formal engagement between the cousins, as well as to
allow the young Queen time for the consideration of
her own feelings, Prince Albert should travel for some
months. This he accordingly did, in company with
his brother, through Switzerland and Northern
Italy.

The first honour conferred by the Queen upon any
one was the bestowal of the Grand Cross of the Order
of the Bath upon the Earl of Durham. His lordship
was a well-known Whig, and all the associations of
the young Sovereign were with that party. Her
father had been a decided Liberal, and the Duchess
held similar views, which were shared also by Leopold,
King of the Belgians. Lord Melbourne, was the
Queen's adviser, and although in many other relations
of life he was careless and *insouciant*, in this capacity
he was ever earnest, sincere, and judicious. He was
not greedy of power, nor did he use any unfair means
of getting or keeping it. 'The character of the
young Sovereign seems to have impressed him deeply.
His real or affected levity gave way to a genuine and

lasting desire to make her life as happy and her reign as successful as he could. The Queen always felt the warmest affection and gratitude for him, and showed it long after the public had given up the suspicion that she could be a puppet in the hands of a Minister.' But the boastful tone of some of the Whigs, who spoke of the accession too much in the tone of a party triumph, ruffled the Tories so greatly that there was not always on the part of the latter that cordial loyalty which might have been expected.

The Queen took up her residence at Buckingham Palace on the 13th of July, and four days later she went in State to dissolve Parliament. An immense concourse of persons witnessed the procession, and the cheering all along the route was most deafening. As she entered the House all the peers and peeresses present rose at the flourish of trumpets, and remained standing. Her Majesty was attired in a splendid white satin robe, with the ribbon of the Garter crossing her shoulder, and a magnificent tiara of diamonds on her head, and a necklace and stomacher of large and costly brilliants. When she had ascended the throne and taken her seat, Lord Melbourne, who stood close to her right hand, whispered to her that it was customary to desire the peers and peeresses to be seated; whereupon her Majesty, in rather a low voice, and bowing condescendingly, said, 'My lords, be seated.' The usual formalities having been gone through, the Queen read her first speech from the throne. The closing passages of this document, which breathed of the constitutional spirit that has marked the whole course of her Majesty's reign, ran as follows :

' I ascend the throne with a deep sense of the responsibility which is imposed upon me; but I am supported by the consciousness of my own right intentions, and by my dependence upon the protection of Almighty God. It will be my care to strengthen our institutions, civil and ecclesiastical, by discreet improvement wherever improvement is required, and to do all in my power to compose and allay animosity and discord. Acting upon these principles, I shall upon all occasions look with confidence to the wisdom of Parliament and the affections of my people, which form the true support of the dignity of the Crown, and ensure the stability of the Constitution.'

Her Majesty read the speech deliberately, and with a sweet voice which was heard all over the House, while a natural grace and modest self-possession characterized her demeanour. Fanny Kemble, who was present on this historic occasion, thus wrote concerning its central figure: 'The Queen was not handsome, but very pretty, and the singularity of her great position lent a sentimental and poetical charm to her youthful face and figure. The serene, serious sweetness of her candid brow and clear soft eyes gave dignity to the girlish countenance; while the want of height only added to the effect of extreme youth of the round but slender person, and gracefully moulded hands and arms. The Queen's voice was exquisite, nor have I ever heard any spoken words more musical in their gentle distinctness than "My Lords and Gentlemen," which broke the breathless silence of the illustrious assembly, whose gaze was riveted on that fair flower of royalty. The enunciation was as perfect as the intonation was melodious, and I think it is im-

possible to hear a more excellent utterance than that
of the Queen's English by the English Queen.'

Soon after her Majesty's accession she was called
upon to sign her first death-warrant. It was presented to her by the Duke of Wellington, and concerned a deserter who had been condemned to death
by court-martial. The Queen, with tears in her eyes,
asked, ' Have you nothing to say in behalf of this
man ? '

' Nothing ; he has deserted three times,' replied the
Duke.

' Oh, your Grace, think again ! '

' Well, your Majesty,' said the brave veteran, ' though
he is certainly a very bad *soldier*, some witnesses spoke
for his character, and, for aught I know to the contrary, he may be a good *man.*'

' Oh, thank you for that a thousand times ! ' exclaimed the Queen ; and writing ' pardoned ' on the
paper, she pushed it across the table to the Duke, her
hand trembling with emotion.

Another anecdote also deserves to be recorded. It
was told by Lord Melbourne. Immediately she was
in a position to do so, she said to the Prime Minister :
' I want to pay all that remain of my father's debts.
I *must* do it. I consider it a sacred duty.' Lord
Melbourne said that the earnestness and directness of
that good daughter's manner, when speaking of her
father, brought the tears into his eyes. The Duke of
Kent had not had a very large allowance, considering
his position and his natural generosity, which caused
him to contribute beyond his means to excellent institutions of all kinds. However, the Queen never rested
until all his liabilities had been conscientiously dis-

charged.   Amongst the Duke's creditors were the late
Lords Fitzwilliam and Dundas.   Representatives of
these peers received the amounts of their debts, accompanied by a valuable piece of plate from the Queen,
with a letter expressive of the obligations she felt
towards those who had been her father's friends, and
the pleasure she and the Duchess of Kent felt in being
enabled thus to express their feelings.

The Queen was exceedingly popular with all classes.
At one time, when some foolish person talked of
deposing 'the all but infant Queen' and putting the
Duke of Cumberland in her place, O'Connell said : ' If
necessary, I can get 500,000 brave Irishmen to defend
the life, the honour, and the person of the beloved
young lady by whom England's throne is now filled.'
Charles Dickens also was but the representative of
many others who were filled with enthusiasm over the
grace and beauty of the young Sovereign.   Occasionally the devotion of her admirers was somewhat
embarrassing.   This was especially so in the case of a
gentleman who, for some time before the Queen left
Kensington Palace, laboured under the delusion that
he was one day destined to marry her Majesty.   His
attentions became very annoying, and on one occasion
he actually succeeded in writing his name in the
visiting-book, only to be erased, however, as soon as
the autograph was discovered.   Although a gentleman
in means, he would actively assist the workmen in
weeding the piece of water in Kensington Gardens, in
the hope of obtaining a sight of her Majesty ; and
every evening he would wait in his phaeton in the
Uxbridge Road until the Queen's carriage appeared in
sight, when he would follow it in whatever direction it

might proceed. Once the Duchess directed a page to request the pertinacious one to drive off, but he refused. When the Queen left Kensington for Buckingham Palace he was noticed as being most vociferous in his demonstrations of loyalty. As soon as her Majesty entered her carriage, he rushed out of the courtyard, and, running at full speed down the avenue, and jumping into his phaeton, preceded the royal *cortége* to the palace at Pimlico. It was some time before he discovered that he had misread his destiny.

From the general consensus of praise induced by the Queen's conduct and demeanour immediately after her accession, Greville in his later volumes is somewhat of a dissentient. As history or biography cannot claim to be candid which does not set forth all possible aspects of a question, I shall give some extracts from Greville's pages. At the same time, two things should be borne in mind : first, that Greville himself always found a keener pleasure in animadverting and criticizing than he did in admiring and approving ; and secondly, his informants frequently permitted their confidences to be tinged with personal feeling or prejudice.

Writing on July 30th, 1837, Greville says : Madame de Lieven told me yesterday that she had an audience of the Queen, who was very civil and gracious, but timid and embarrassed, and talked of nothing but commonplaces. Her Majesty had probably been told that the Princess was an *intrigante,* and was afraid of committing herself. She had afterwards an interview with the Duchess of Kent, who (she told me), it was plain to see, is overwhelmed with vexation and disappointment. Her daughter

behaves to her with kindness and attention, but
has rendered herself quite independent of the Duchess,
who painfully feels her own insignificance. The almost
contemptuous way in which Sir John Conroy has been
dismissed must be a bitter mortification to her.   The
Duchess said to Madame de Lieven, " *Qu'il n'y avait
plus d'avenir pour elle, qu'elle n'était plus rien ;* " that for
eighteen years this child had been the sole object
of her life, of all her thoughts and hopes, and now
she was taken from her, and there was an end of all
for which she had lived heretofore. Madame de Lieven
said that she ought to be the happiest of human
beings, to see the elevation of this child, her pro-
digious success, and the praise and admiration of
which she was universally the object ; that it was
a triumph and a glory which ought to be sufficient for
her ; at which she only shook her head with a melancholy smile, and gave her to understand that all this
would not do, and that the accomplishment of her
wishes had only made her to the last degree unhappy.
King William is revenged, he little anticipated how or
by what instrumentality ; and if his ghost is an ill-
natured and vindictive shade, it may rejoice in the
sight of this bitter disappointment of his enemy.   In
the midst of all her propriety of manner and conduct,
the young Queen begins to exhibit slight signs of a
peremptory disposition, and it is impossible not to
suspect that, as she gains confidence, and as her
character begins to develop, she will evince a strong
will of her own.   In all trifling matters connected
with her Court and her palace she already enacts the
part of Queen and mistress, as if it had long been
familiar to her.'

The Queen having, in a letter to her uncle King
Leopold, spoken of her sad childhood, Greville assumes
that the expression referred to the Duchess's treatment
of her, but all other accounts of the Queen's childhood take a different view.   Nevertheless, the Court
gossip gives this passage : 'The person in the world
she (the Queen) loves best is the Baroness Lehzen, and
Lehzen and Conroy were enemies. There was formerly
a Baroness Spaeth at Kensington, lady-in-waiting
to the Duchess, and Lehzen and Spaeth were intimate
friends. Conroy quarrelled with the latter and got her
dismissed, and this Lehzen never forgave. She may
have instilled into the Princess a dislike and bad
opinion of· Conroy, and the evidence of these sentiments, which probably escaped neither the Duchess
nor him, may have influenced their conduct towards
her ; for, strange as it is, there is good reason to believe
that she thinks she has been ill-used by both of them
for some years past. Her manner to the Duchess is,
however, irreproachable, and they appear to be on
cordial and affectionate terms. Madame de Lehzen is
the only person who is constantly with her. When any
of the Ministers come to see her, the Baroness retires
at one door as they enter at the other, and the
audience over, she returns to the Queen.'

The statement as to the Baroness Lehzen's domi-
nant influence over the Queen is scarcely consistent with her well-known dependence on Melbourne.
So complete was this dependence that, as Greville
himself says, 'her reliance upon Melbourne's advice
extends at present to subjects quite beside his constitutional functions, for the other day somebody asked
her permission to dedicate some novel to her, when she

F

said she did not like to grant the permission without knowing the contents of the work, and she desired Melbourne to read the book and let her know if it was fit that she should accept the dedication. Melbourne read the first volume, but found it so dull that he would not read any more, and sent her word that she had better refuse, which she accordingly did.'

In the light of knowledge gathered from other sources we must also regard the ensuing passage as containing exaggerated statements, which cannot be implicitly accepted. The Queen 'now evinces in all she does an attachment to the memory of her uncle, and it is not to be doubted that, in the disputes which took place between him and her mother, her secret sympathies were with the King; and in that celebrated scene at Windsor, when the King made so fierce an attack upon the Duchess's advisers, and expressed his earnest hope that he might live to see the majority of his niece, Victoria must have inwardly rejoiced at the expression of sentiments so accordant with her own. Her attentions and cordiality to Queen Adelaide, her bounty and civility to the King's children, and the disgrace of Conroy, amply prove what her sentiments have all along been.' Whatever may have been the Queen's feelings with regard to Sir John Conroy, it is impossible for a moment to conceive that her Majesty could have borne with the least complacency William IV.'s unwarrantable and passionate attack upon her mother; and although she was civil and considerate towards the King's children, her thoughts invariably turned first towards the Duchess of Kent.

Greville has a weakness for accentuating too much any roughness of speech or character in the persons

whom he describes. Now, another chronicler has
a very interesting anecdote relating to the Queen ; but
while he illustrates the discipline which the Sovereign
inculcated in her household, he does not omit to add an
incident which also testifies to the kindness of her
heart. A certain high and noble lady, who had been
appointed to a place of great distinction about the
royal person, did not observe with strict punctuality
her hours of official duty. On the second or third
morning that this circumstance occurred her Majesty
received her noble attendant with her watch in her
hand.

'I am afraid I have unfortunately been the occasion of detaining your Majesty,' observed her ladyship in an apologetic tone.

'Yes, full ten minutes,' rejoined the Queen,
gravely; 'and I beg this want of punctuality may
not happen again.'

Then, perceiving that her ladyship, in the agitation
caused by this reproof, experienced some embarrassment in the arrangement of her shawl, her Majesty,
as if to prove that no unkind feeling had prompted
her remark, condescended to assist her with her own
hand, observing with great sweetness as she did so,
'We shall all become more perfect in our duties in
time, I hope.'

On the 22nd of August the Queen removed with
her Court to Windsor Castle, where a week later she
received her uncle the King of the Belgians and his
consort, Queen Louise. Later in the autumn her
Majesty visited Brighton, returning to London on the
4th of November.

There was a magnificent pageant on the occasion

of her first visit to the City as Queen, on Lord
Mayor's Day, the 9th of November. A general
holiday was observed that day in London, and crowds
of persons assembled along the whole route from
Buckingham Palace to the Guildhall. The Queen
sat in the royal state carriage, attended by the
Duchess of Sutherland as Mistress of the Robes, and
the Earl of Albemarle as Master of the Horse. Her
Majesty wore a splendid pink satin robe shot with
silver, her hair encompassed with a splendid tiara;
and she looked the picture of health. As the procession filed along the Strand the church bells rang
forth merrily, and mingling with their peals enthusiastic cheers came from thousands of human voices.
Rows of national flags and heraldic banners were
stretched across the thoroughfare at several points,
and busts and portraits of the Queen were placed in
conspicuous positions. Her Majesty, who was in
high spirits, acknowledged the continuous greetings
of her subjects in the most gracious manner. After
the Queen, the only distinguished person generally
cheered was the Duke of Wellington, though the
King's College boys gave a warm greeting to the
Archbishop of Canterbury.

Temple Bar was a point of great interest, for here
the City bounds began. The Lord Mayor and sheriffs,
with the aldermen, who had been accommodated in
Messrs. Childs' banking-house, proceeded to mount
their chargers a little before two o'clock. In the case
of one worthy alderman the equestrian exercise
proved too much for him. Desiring to perform with
unusual grace and gallantry an obeisance to a
fair lady at a window, he was sent sprawling upon

HER MAJESTY IN MILITARY COSTUME AT A REVIEW AT WINDSOR, SEPT. 28, 1837.

From the Picture by Prentice.

(By Permission of Mr. Thomas McLean, Haymarket.)

the gravel, while his horse walked over him. Never since the days of John Gilpin did feat of a London citizen excite so much masculine laughter and feminine sympathy. He sustained little injury, however, and was successfully hoisted into the saddle again. The incident was quickly forgotten in the near approach of the royal procession. When the arrival of the Queen was announced, the Lord Mayor dismounted, and taking the City sword in his hand, stood on the south side of Temple Bar. Her Majesty's carriage then drew up within the gateway, and the Lord Mayor presented the keys of the City to the Queen, which her Majesty, after keeping them for a few moments, restored in a gracious manner. At this moment the multitude of spectators rent the air with their acclamations. The Lord Mayor remounted, and, holding the City sword aloft, took his place immediately before the royal carriage; after which the aldermen, the members of the Common Council, and other civic authorities formed in procession.

One of the most interesting episodes of the day occurred in front of St. Paul's Cathedral, where a booth had been erected for the accommodation of the boys of Christ's Hospital. The royal carriage stopped in the middle of the road opposite the cathedral gate, and a platform was wheeled out on which were Mr. F. G. Nash, senior scholar of Christ's Hospital, and the head-master and treasurer. The scholar, in conformity with an old usage, delivered an address of congratulation to her Majesty, concluding with an earnest prayer for her welfare. 'God save the Queen' was then sung by the scholars and a great part of the other spectators. The Queen was much pleased with

the proceedings, and in 'subsequently returning his
oration to Master Nash with her signature added, she
wrote a note expressive of her approbation.'

On arriving at the Guildhall, whose rooms had been
sumptuously fitted up and decorated, the Queen
received the chief guests in the drawing-room.
Another address was presented, and the dinner was
announced. The Queen descended the hall preceded
by the Lord Mayor, and was conducted by the Lord
Chamberlain to the throne, the band playing ' O ! the
roast beef of Old England.' The dinner was much
like other dinners for the viands, but one dish deserves
special mention. This, was a salmon, and the only
one at the banquet. It had been caught in the River
Tivy, near Kenarth, in the county of Carmarthen, by
William Griffiths, a poor lame fisherman, who with
unbounded loyalty sent it by the mail to the Lord
Mayor, requesting that it might form part of the
civic entertainment to the Queen. ' The health of
our Most Gracious Sovereign Queen Victoria' was
drank amidst loud applause, and in response the
Queen rose and bowed several times very affably to
the company. Her dress attracted much attention.
It was richly embroidered with silver; and over
her left shoulder the Queen wore the riband of the
Order of the Garter, with the George appended;
on her head she had a splendid diadem and circlet;
she also wore diamond earrings, and had a stomacher
of brilliants. At the royal table were the Dukes of
Sussex and Cambridge; the Duchesses of Kent,
Gloucester, Cambridge, and Sutherland; Prince George
and Princess Augusta of Cambridge; and the Countess
of Mulgrave. Her Majesty was rather flurried at one

point of the proceedings, when the common crier
shouted in stentorian tones, ' Her Majesty gives the
Lord Mayor, and prosperity to the City of London.'
The Queen proceeded to drink the toast. Unfortunately, after doing so her lace ruffles accidentally
became entangled with her bouquet and fan, which
with her smelling-bottle she had laid on the table
beside her plate, and this was the occasion of her
breaking the glass in which she had drunk the
popular toast. This little accident appeared to cause
her some concern.

, Only one more toast was given, that of ' The
Royal Family,' and then the Queen retired from the
hall to the drawing-room, where she was served with
tea in a splendid gold service. The value of the
plate at the whole entertainment was estimated at
£400,000. Sir George Smart conducted the orchestra
on this occasion, which included all the chief vocal and
instrumental performers of the metropolis. At the final
rehearsal, on the preceding day, Sir George had said
to the performers, ' We must be very particular ; for
if we are at all at fault, her Majesty's ear will detect
our blunder.'

At half-past eight o'clock a flourish of trumpets
announced the arrival of the Queen's carriage.
Her Majesty then left, and when she arrived
at the carriage door she turned round to the
Lord Mayor, who stood at the step, and said with a
smile, ' I assure you, my Lord Mayor, that I have
been most highly gratified.' She then warmly shook
hands with the chief magistrate, and drove off amid
ringing cheers. On the homeward route the royal
carriage pulled up for a few minutes at the end of

Cheapside, where, under the direction of the Sacred Harmonic Society, several hundred voices sang 'God save the Queen.'

Her Majesty afterwards conferred a baronetcy on the Lord Mayor, Sir John Cowan, and knighted the two sheriffs, Sir John Carroll and Sir Moses Montefiore. The latter gentleman was the first Jew to receive the honour of knighthood from a British Sovereign, and the country warmly approved this act of distinction.

About this time a German named Stuber was arrested for threatening to shoot the Queen and the Duchess of Kent. He was proved to be insane, and was sent to the Hoxton Lunatic Asylum. On the 4th of November also, as the Queen was passing through the Birdcage Walk, St. James's, in an open carriage, a person in the garb of a gentleman sprang suddenly to the side of the vehicle, and holding up his fist in a threatening manner, made use of very offensive language towards the Queen, adding, 'I'll have you off the throne, and your mother too.' He then ran off, but was subsequently taken into custody, and discovered to be one John Goode, formerly a captain in the 10th Hussars. He likewise was found to be insane.

Her Majesty opened her first Parliament on the 20th of November, her progress to the House being marked by the most loyal demonstrations. When she had ascended the throne in the House of Lords, the Queen directed the Lord Chancellor to read the following declaration, which we are told she repeated after his lordship, sentence by sentence, very articulately, and with much feeling and solemnity :—

'I, Victoria, &c., do solemnly and sincerely, in the presence of God, testify and declare that I do believe that in the Sacrament of the Lord's Supper there is not any transubstantiation of the elements of bread and wine into the body and blood of Christ, at or after the consecration thereof, by any person whatsoever; and that the invocation or adoration of the Virgin Mary, or any other saint, and the sacrifice of the Mass, as they are now used in the Church of Rome, are superstitious and idolatrous. And I do solemnly, in the presence of God, profess, testify, and declare, that I do make this declaration, and every part thereof, in the plain and ordinary sense of the words read unto me, as they are commonly understood by English Protestants, without any evasion, equivocation, or mental reservation whatsoever, and without any dispensation already granted me for this purpose by the Pope, or any other authority or person whatsoever, and without thinking that I am or can be acquitted before God and man, or absolved of this declaration, or any part thereof, although the Pope, or any other person or persons or power whatsoever, shall dispense with or annul the same, or declare that it was null and void from the beginning.'

The question of the Civil List was settled by Parliament this session. The Queen placed unreservedly in the hands of Parliament the hereditary revenues transferred to the public by her immediate predecessor. In the House of Commons the Chancellor of the Exchequer pointed out that, whilst former Sovereigns had inherited considerable personal property, Queen Victoria had not done so, and would further be deprived of the revenues of Hanover, which had now

become a separate kingdom. The sum of £385,000 was
therefore voted as the annual income of the Sovereign.
The amount was thus distributed : Her Majesty's privy
purse, £60,000 ; salaries of her Majesty's household
and retired allowances, £131,260; expenses of her
Majesty's household, £172,500 ; royal bounty, alms,
and special services, £13,200 ; and unappropriated
balances, £8,040.   Mr. Joseph Hume made an in-
effectual attempt to reduce the whole grant by
£50,000.   At the suggestion of the Queen, Parliament also voted an additional grant of £8,000 a
year to the income of the Duchess of Kent, thus
raising it to £30,000 per annum.

. The Queen entered fully into all business matters
brought before her by the Prime Minister.   She
would know the why and the wherefore of everything.
Indeed, one authority says that Melbourne was heard
to declare that he would rather have ten kings to
manage than one queen.   He could not place a
single document in her Majesty's hand for signature
but she first asked an infinite variety of questions
respecting it, and she not infrequently ended her
interrogatories by declining to put her name to the
paper in question until she had taken further time to
consider its merits.   The Premier on a certain occasion had submitted an Act of Government for her
Majesty's approval, and was proceeding to urge its
expediency, when he was thus stopped short by the
Queen :

. 'I have been taught, my lord, to judge between
what is right and what is wrong ; but expediency is
a word which I neither wish to hear nor to understand.'

Again, when Melbourne was anxious to obtain the Queen's signature to an important State document, he argued for it with all the force and eloquence at his command. But the Sovereign had resolved upon having further information before affixing her signature. It was in vain that he explained and argued, and in the end, when he pleaded the paramount importance of the matter he was met by the reply:

'It is with me a matter of paramount importance whether or not I attach my signature to a document with which I am not thoroughly satisfied.'

But the other side of the picture reveals the admirable relations existing between the Queen and her Minister. George Villiers told Greville that he had been exceedingly struck with Melbourne's manner to the Queen, and hers to him—his, so parental and anxious, but always so respectful and deferential; hers, indicative of such entire confidence, such pleasure in his society. 'She is continually talking to him,' continues Greville, 'let who will be there; he always sits next her at dinner, and evidently by arrangement, because he always takes in the lady-in-waiting, which necessarily places him next her, the etiquette being that the lady-in-waiting sits next but one to the Queen. It is not unnatural, and to him it is peculiarly interesting. I have no doubt he is passionately fond of her, as he might be of his daughter, if he had one—and the more because he is a man with a capacity for loving, without having anything in the world to love. It is become his province to educate, instruct, and form the most interesting mind and character in the world. No occupation was ever more engrossing or involved greater responsibility. I have no doubt that Melbourne is both equal to and worthy of the task, and that it is fortunate she has fallen into his hands, and that he discharges this great duty wisely, honourably, and conscientiously. It is a great proof of the discretion and purity of his conduct and behaviour that he is admired, respected, and liked by all the Court.'

As soon as her Majesty's State duties were despatched, she occupied the time (when not engaged in riding or walking) with music, reading, or drawing. She took great delight in Italian music, and also in the compositions·of Handel, Haydn, Beethoven, and Mozart. To these was subsequently added Mendelssohn, who was also a favourite with the Prince Consort. Her voice was a *mezzo-soprano* of good tone, and her singing was excellent. Her talents for drawing were such that one of her masters said : 'The Princess Victoria would have made the best female artist of the age if she had not been born to wear a crown.' After she became queen, she would frequently entertain her distinguished guests by singing in the drawing-room, after dinner, choice popular airs, in which she was accompanied by the Duchess of Kent on the piano. Some other personal details may be mentioned. As her Majesty has herself declared that ' she is rather small for a queen,' we are emboldened to give her stature, which is just five feet two inches. But her carriage and imposing appearance always seem to indicate a considerably greater height. Her head is finely and fully developed, and those professedly skilled in such matters affirm that benevolence, justice, and firmness are very prominent organs ; that self-esteem also is fully developed; while veneration is scarcely enough so. The whole expression of face is intellectual. About the time of her marriage the Queen's complexion was delicately transparent; her cheeks were beautifully tinted if exertion or animation flushed their natural fairness; her nose was a well-formed and very delicate aquiline; her eyes blue, but with well-marked eyebrows. Altogether she had a comeliness which pertained to none of the Brunswick line since the time of Augusta of Saxe-Gotha, Princess of Wales, and the Queen's great-grandmother.

But we must now pass on to the coronation, the great event of 1838, and the greatest spectacle of her Majesty's reign. Long before the day fixed for the ceremony the deepest interest was manifested in it. Amongst the proclamations issued was one declaring it to be the Queen's royal will and pleasure to dispense with, at her approaching coronation, all the ceremonies usually performed in Westminster Hall on such an occasion. These ceremonies included the entry of the Champion of England on horseback, whose right it was to throw down his gauntlet in defence of the Sovereign, challenging any one to take it up. Another proclamation stated that the peers were to be relieved from doing homage in the usual fashion by kissing the left cheek of the Sovereign. One can imagine the girl-Queen's dismay if this ancient custom had been maintained in her case. For her royal uncles to kiss her cheek was only a natural proceeding, but that some six hundred spiritual and temporal peers should follow each other in kissing the Sovereign's left cheek would have been an appalling prospect. The old custom was for each peer, according to his rank and profession, singly to ascend the throne, to touch with his hand the crown on the Sovereign's head, and then to kiss her on her cheek. Though all the peers would no doubt have taken care to be present on such an interesting occasion, it cannot be matter of surprise that they were relieved from this and other onerous duties.

The first issue of sovereigns bearing the impress of Queen Victoria took place on June 14, but the bankers were only supplied with limited numbers, and could not gratify the whole of their clamorous cus-. tomers at once.

The crown in which the Queen was to appear at the coronation was made, and exhibited for public inspection, by Messrs. Rundell & Bridge. It was more tasteful than that worn by George IV. and William IV., which had been broken up. The old crown weighed more than seven pounds, and the new, which was smaller, only about three pounds. It was composed of hoops of silver, enclosing a cap of deep blue velvet; the hoops were completely covered with precious stones, surmounted by a ball covered with small diamonds, and having a Maltese cross of brilliants on the top of it. The cross had in its centre a splendid sapphire; the rim of the crown was clustered with brilliants, and ornamented with *fleur-de-lis* and Maltese crosses, equally rich. In the front of the large Maltese cross was the enormous heart-shaped ruby which had been worn by Edward, the Black Prince, and which afterwards figured in the helmet of Henry. V. at the battle of Agincourt. Beneath this, in the circular rim, was a large oblong sapphire There were many other precious gems, emeralds rubies, and sapphires, and several small clusters of drop pearls. The lower part of the crown was surrounded with ermine. The value of the jewels on the crown was estimated at £112,760. The following is a summary of the precious stones comprised in the crown :— 1 large ruby, irregularly polished ; 1 large broad-spread sapphire ; 16 sapphires ; 11 emeralds ; 4 rubies ; 1,363 brilliant diamonds ; 1,273 rose diamonds ; 147 table diamonds ; 4 drop-shaped pearls ; 273 other pearls.

Amid great pomp and ceremony the coronation of her Majesty took place in Westminster Abbey, on Thursday, the 28th of June. London was awake very early on that day, and by six o'clock strings of vehicles poured into the West End. Crowds of foot-passengers also were on the move, all converging towards one point. From Hyde Park Corner to the Abbey there was scarcely a house without a scaffolding, soon to be filled with sightseers. Seats were sold at a very high rate, while tickets for the interior of the Abbey were bought on the eve of the ceremony at more than twenty guineas each ; and the Earl Marshal had to apprise the public that forged tickets were in circulation, the holders of which would not only be stopped but given into custody. Notwithstanding the immense number of persons in the Green Park and St. James's Park, and in the vicinity of Buckingham Palace, the police and military preserved admirable order.

At ten o'clock a salute of twenty-one guns, and the hoisting of the imperial standard in front of the palace, intimated that her Majesty had entered the State carriage. The procession then set forth, pre-

ceded by trumpeters and a detachment of Life Guards.
Then came the foreign ministers and ambassadors,
followed by the carriages of the Royal Family, containing the Duchess of Kent, the Duchess of Gloucester,
the Duke and Duchess of Cambridge, and the Duke of
Sussex; next her Majesty's carriages, containing the
members of the household and others; and then, after
officers and guards of various kinds, came the State
coach, drawn by eight cream-coloured horses, conveying
the Queen and the Mistress of the Robes and Master
of the Horse.　All the royal personages were loudly
cheered, but when the State carriage bearing the
young Sovereign came in view the enthusiasm was
something tremendous.　Her Majesty appeared in
excellent spirits, and highly delighted with the
imposing scene.　The troops saluted in succession as
she passed, and remaiued with presented arms until
the royal carriage had passed the front of each
battalion, the bands continuing to play the National
Anthem.　To the credit of the crowd, a hearty cheer
was raised for Marshal Soult, which the French veteran
acknowledged with great satisfaction, not unmingled
with surprise.　It is said that every window along
the route was a bouquet, every balcony a parterre of
living loveliness and beauty; and as the Queen passed,
scarfs, handkerchiefs, and flowers were waved with
the most boisterous enthusiasm.　Her Majesty was
more than once visibly affected by these exhilarating
demonstrations, and occasionally turned to the
Duchess of Sutherland to conceal or express her
emotion.

　　Westminster Abbey was reached at half-past eleven.
On each side the nave, galleries were erected for the

spectators, with accommodation for a thousand persons. Under the central tower of the Abbey, in the interior of the choir, a platform was raised, covered with a carpet of cloth of gold, and upon it the chair of homage, superbly gilt, was placed, facing the altar. Further on, within the chancel, and near the altar, was Edward the Confessor's chair. The altar was covered with massive gold plate. Galleries were provided for members of the House of Commons, foreign ambassadors, and other persons of distinction, the Judges, Masters in Chancery, Knights of the Bath, the Lord Mayor, and the members of the Corporation, &c.

Shortly before noon the grand procession began to enter the choir. It was headed by the prebendaries and Dean of Westminster, followed by the great officers of her Majesty's household. Then came the Lord Privy Seal, the Lord President of the Council, the Lord Chancellor of Ireland, the Archbishop of Armagh, the Archbishop of York, the Lord Chancellor of England, and the Archbishop of Canterbury. The Princesses of the blood royal succeeded: the Duchess of Cambridge, in a robe of estate of purple velvet and wearing a circlet of gold, her train borne by Lady Caroline Campbell, and her coronet by Viscount Villiers; the Duchess of Kent, in a robe of estate of purple velvet and wearing a circlet of gold, her train borne by the hapless Lady Flora Hastings, and her coronet by Viscount Emlyn. Next came one of the most interesting parts of the procession—the Regalia. St. Edward's staff was borne by the Duke of Roxburghe; the golden spurs by Lord Byron; the sceptre with the cross by the Duke of

G

Cleveland; the curtana, or sword of mercy, by the
Duke of Devonshire; the second sword by the Duke
of Sutherland, and the third sword by the Marquis
of Westminster. Black Rod and Deputy Garter
were succeeded by Lord Willoughby d'Eresby, Lord
Great Chamberlain of England. The Princes of the
blood royal now appeared: the Duke of Cambridge,
in his robes and carrying his bâton as Field Marshal;
and the Duke of Sussex, also in his robes of estate.
Then in order were the High Constable of Ireland,
the Duke of Leinster; the High Constable of Scotland, the Earl of Erroll; the Earl Marshal of
England, the Duke of Norfolk; Viscount Melbourne,
bearing the sword of State; the Lord High Constable of England, the Duke of Wellington; the
Bishop of Bangor, bearing the patina; the Bishop of
Winchester, bearing the Bible; and the Bishop of
London, bearing the chalice. After these came
the Queen, in her royal robe of crimson velvet,
furred with ermine and bordered with gold lace,
wearing the collars of her Orders, with a circlet of
gold upon her head. On one side of her was the
Bishop of Bath and Wells, with ten gentlemen-at-
arms; and on the other the Bishop of Durham, also
with ten gentlemen-at-arms. Her Majesty's train
was borne by the following eight young ladies, the
daughters of well-known noblemen of high rank in
the peerage: Lady Adelaide Paget, Lady Frances
Elizabeth Cowper, Lady Ann Wentworth Fitzwilliam,
Lady Mary Augusta Frederica Grimston, Lady Caroline Amelia Gordon Lennox, Lady Mary Alethea
Beatrix Talbot, Lady Catherine Lucy Wilhelmina
Stanhope, and Lady Louisa Harriet Jenkinson.

The last distinguished personages in the procession were the Lord Chamberlain of the Household; the Duchess of Sutherland, Mistress of the Robes; the Marchioness of Lansdowne, First Lady of the Bedchamber; six other ladies of the bedchamber; eight maids of honour; eight women of the bedchamber; Gold Stick of the Life Guards; the Master of the Horse; the Captain of the Guard, and other high officials.

The scene which followed her Majesty's entry into the Abbey was one of the most impressive which could possibly be conceived. From a variety of sources we have gathered our description of its most interesting features. The Queen looked extremely well, and had a very animated expression of countenance. Some of the foreign ambassadors had numerous and splendid suites, and were magnificently attired; but by far the most gorgeous was Prince Esterhazy, whose dress, down to his very bootheels, sparkled with diamonds. The scene within the choir which presented itself to the Queen on her entrance was very gorgeous, and indeed almost overwhelming. The Turkish ambassador, it is reported, was absolutely bewildered; he stopped in astonishment, and for some time would not move up to his allotted place.

The Queen was received with hearty plaudits as she advanced slowly towards the centre of the choir; the anthem, ' I was glad when they said unto me, Let us go into the house of the Lord,' being meanwhile sung by the musicians. Then, with thrilling effect and full trumpet accompaniment, ' God save the Queen' was rendered. The booming of the guns outside was

G 2

deadened by the tumultuous acclamations of those
within the Abbey, which did not close till the
beloved object of this enthusiastic homage reached
the recognition-chair, on the south-east of the altar.
Here the Queen knelt at the faldstool, engaging in
silent prayer. Her mind must have been agitated
with deep and conflicting emotions at this awful
moment, when the vast weight of her responsibilities
pressed in upon her. There were many who shed
tears as the simple maiden, the centre of so much
splendour and the cynosure of a whole empire, im-
plored the Divine strength in the fulfilment of her
sovereign duties.

When she rose from her devotions the pealing
notes of the anthem rang through the arches of the
Abbey. Scarcely had the music ceased when, in
pursuance of their prescriptive right, the Westminster scholars rose up with one accord and
acclaimed their Sovereign. They shouted in almost
deafening chorus, ' *Victoria, Victoria ! Vivat Victoria
Regina !* ' This was the first actual incident in the
proceedings of the coronation.

The Archbishop of Canterbury now advanced from
his station at the great south-east pillar to the east
side of the theatre or platform, accompanied by the
Lord Chancellor, Lord Great Chamberlain, the High
Constable, and the Earl Marshal, preceded by Garter
King-at-Arms; and presenting the youthful monarch
to her people, made the recognition in these words :

' Sirs, I here present unto you Queen Victoria, the
undoubted queen of this realm; wherefore, all you
who are come this day to do your homage, are you
willing to do the same ? '

In response there was a rapturous and general shout
of 'God save Queen Victoria!' The Archbishop and
the great officers of State made the same recognition
to the people on the other three sides of the Abbey,
south, west, and north ; the Queen remaining standing,
and turning herself about to face her loyal lieges on
each side as the recognition was made, which was
answered with long and repeated acclamations. The
last recognition over, the drums beat, the trumpets
sounded, and the band struck up the National Anthem.
This part of the ceremonial has been described as one
of the most striking and picturesque.

The bishops who bore the patina, Bible, and
chalice in the procession, now placed the same on
the altar. The Queen, attended by the Bishops of
Durham and Bath and Wells and the Dean of Westminster, with the great officers of State and noblemen
bearing the regalia, advanced to the altar, and kneeling upon the crimson-velvet cushion, made her first
offering, being a pall or altar-cloth of gold, which she
delivered to the Archbishop of Canterbury, by whom
it was placed on the altar. Her Majesty next placed
an ingot of gold, of one pound weight, in the hands
of the Archbishop, by whom it was put into the oblation basin. The bearers of the regalia, except those
who carried the swords, then proceeded in order to the
altar, where they delivered St. Edward's crown, the
sceptre, dove, orb, spurs, and all the other insignia of
royalty, to the Archbishop, who delivered them to the
Dean of Westminster, by whom they were placed on
the altar. The religious ceremony now began with
the reading of the Litany by the Bishops of Worcester
and St. David's. Then followed the Communion

Service, read by the Archbishop of Canterbury and the Bishops of Rochester and Carlisle. The Bishop of London preached the sermon from the following text, in the Second Book of Chronicles, chap. xxxiv. verse 31st:—

'And the king stood in his place, and made a covenant before the Lord, to walk after the Lord, and to keep his commandments and his testimonies and statutes, and with all his heart and all his soul to perform the words of the covenant which are written in this book.'

Her Majesty paid profound attention to the words of the sermon, in the course of which the Bishop praised the late King for his unfeigned religion, and exhorted his youthful successor to follow in his footsteps. The earnest manner in which she listened, and the motion with which, at the mention of her dead uncle, she bowed her head on her hand to conceal a falling tear, were highly touching.

On the conclusion of the service the Archbishop advanced towards the Queen, addressing her thus:

'Madam, is your Majesty willing to take the oath?'

The Queen replied, 'I am willing.'

'Will you solemnly promise and swear,' continued the Archbishop, 'to govern the people of this United Kingdom of Great Britain and Ireland, and the dominions thereto belonging, according to the statutes in Parliament agreed on, and the respective laws and customs of the same?'

In an audible voice the Queen answered, 'I solemnly promise so to do.'

'Will you, to your power, cause law and justice, in mercy, to be executed in all your judgments?'

'I will.'

Then said the Archbishop; 'Will you, to the utmost of your power, maintain the laws of God, the true profession of the Gospel, and the Protestant reformed religion established by law? And will you maintain and preserve inviolably the settlement of the united Church of England and Ireland, and the doctrine, worship, discipline, and government thereof, as by law established within England and Ireland, and the territories thereunto belonging? And will you preserve unto the bishops and clergy of England and Ireland, and to the churches there committed to their charge, all such rights and privileges as by law do or shall appertain to them or any of them?'

Clearly and firmly the Queen replied, 'All this I promise to do.'

Her Majesty, with the Lord Chamberlain and other officers, the sword of State being carried before her, then went to the altar and took the coronation oath. Laying her right hand upon the Gospels in the Bible carried in the procession, and now brought to her by the Archbishop, she said, kneeling:

'The things which I have here before promised I will perform and keep. So help me, God!'

Then the Queen kissed the book, and to a transcript of the oath set her royal sign manual. The Duchess of Kent was observed to be deeply affected during the whole of this office. After signing, her Majesty knelt upon her faldstool while the choir sang *Veni, Creator, Spiritus.*

The next part of the ceremony, the anointing, was extremely interesting. The Queen sat in King Edward's chair; four Knights of the Garter—the

Dukes of Buccleuch and Rutland, and the Marquises of Anglesey and Exeter—held a rich cloth of gold over her head; the Dean of Westminster took the ampulla from the altar, and poured some of the oil it contained into the gold anointing-spoon; then the Archbishop anointed the head and hands of the Queen, marking them in the form of a cross, and pronouncing these words:

'Be thou anointed with holy oil, as kings, priests, and prophets were anointed. And as Solomon was anointed king by Zadok the priest and Nathan the prophet, so be you anointed, blessed, and consecrated queen over this people, whom the Lord your God hath given you to rule and govern. In the name of the Father, and of the Son, and of the Holy Ghost. Amen.'

The Archbishop then pronounced a prayer or blessing over the Sovereign.

The spurs were presented by the Lord Chamberlain to the Queen, who returned them to the altar. The sword of State was presented by Lord Melbourne to the Archbishop, who in delivering it into the Queen's right hand said: 'Receive this kingly sword, brought now from the altar of God, and delivered to you by the hands of us, the servants and bishops of God, though unworthy. With this sword do justice, stop the growth of iniquity, protect the holy Church of God, help and defend widows and orphans, restore the things that are gone to decay, maintain the things that are restored, punish and reform what is amiss, and confirm what is in good order; that doing these things, you may be glorious in all virtue, and so faithfully serve our Lord Jesus Christ in this

life that you may reign for ever with Him in the life
which is to come.   Amen.'

Lord Melbourne, according to custom, redeemed the
sword 'with a hundred shillings,' and carried it un-
sheathed before her Majesty during the remainder
of the ceremony.   Then followed the investing with
the royal robe and the delivery of the orb.   At this
point there was some little confusion, and when the orb
was put into the Queen's hand she turned to Lord
John Thynne and said : ' What am I to do with it ? '
' Your Majesty is to hold it, if you please, in your
hand.' ' Am I ? ' she said : ' it is very heavy.' As each
article of the regalia was given to the Queen the
Archbishop accompanied it with a suitable exordium.
When the investiture *per annulum et baculum*—the
ring and sceptre—was performed, it was found that the
ruby ring had been made for her Majesty's little finger
instead of the fourth, on which the rubric prescribes
that it should be put.   When the Archbishop was to
put it on, she extended the former, but he said it
must be on the latter.   She replied that it was too
small, and that she could not get it on.   The Archbishop said it was right to put it there, and as he insisted, she yielded, but had first to take off her other
rings, and then this was forced on, but it hurt her
very much, and as soon as the ceremony was over, she
was obliged to bathe her finger in iced water in order
to get it off.

One curious custom was observed by the Duke
of Norfolk, who, as lord of the manor of Worksop,
holds an estate by the service of presenting to the
Sovereign a right-hand glove during the ceremonial of
the coronation.   The Duke left his seat, and approach-

ing the Queen, kneeling, presented to her a glove for
her right hand, embroidered with the arms of Howard,
which her Majesty put on. His Grace afterwards
occasionally performed his high feudal office of supporting the Sovereign's right arm, or holding the
sceptre by her side.

The Archbishop, in delivering the sceptre with the
cross into the Queen's right hand, said : ' Receive the
royal sceptre, the ensign of kingly power and justice.'
Next he delivered the rod with the dove into the
Queen's left hand, this being ' the rod of equity
and mercy.' The Archbishop then took the crown into
his hands, and laying it upon the altar, offered up
a prayer. Turning from the altar with the other
bishops, he now received the crown from the Dean of
Westminster, and placed it on her Majesty's head;
whereupon the people, with loud and repeated shouts,
cried ' God save the Queen!' At the moment the
crown was placed on the head of the Sovereign
the act was made known by signal to the semaphore
at the Admiralty, from whence it was transmitted to
the outports and other places. A double royal salute
of forty-one guns was fired, and the Tower, Windsor,
Woolwich, and other guns gave a similar greeting to
the crowned monarch of the British realms.

On the assumption of the crown, the peers and
peeresses put on their coronets, the bishops their caps,
and the kings-of-arms their crowns ; while the trumpets
sounded, the drums beat, and the Tower and park
guns fired their volleys. Then the full burst of the
orchestra broke forth, and the scene was one of such
grandeur as to defy description. The Queen was
visibly agitated during the long-reiterated acclama-

tions. Her bosom heaved with suppressed emotion, and she turned her expressive eyes involuntarily, as if for maternal support, on her sympathizing mother, who, with infinitely less command of her feelings, was drowned in tears, and occasionally sobbed most audibly. By a strong effort her Majesty regained her composure, and the august ceremonial proceeded.

After an anthem had been sung, the Archbishop presented the Bible to the Queen, who gave it to the Dean of Westminster to be placed on the altar. The benediction was then delivered by the Archbishop, all the bishops, with the rest of the peers, responding to every part of the blessing with a loud and hearty 'Amen!' The choir then began to sing the *Te Deum*, and the Queen proceeded to the chair which she first occupied, supported by two bishops. She was then 'enthroned,' or 'lifted,' as the formulary states, into the chair of homage, by the archbishops, bishops, and peers surrounding her. Then began the ceremony of homage. The Archbishop of Canterbury knelt and did homage for himself and other lords spiritual, who all kissed the Queen's hand. The royal dukes, with the temporal peers, followed according to their precedence, class by class. Ascending the steps leading to the throne, and taking off their coronets, they repeated the oath of homage in the following quaint and homely Saxon form :—

'I do become your liegeman of life and limb, and of earthly worship ; and faith and truth I will bear unto you, to live and die, against all manner of folks. So help me God !'

Each peer then in his turn touched the cross on her Majesty's crown, in token of his readiness to support it against all adversaries. He then kissed the Sovereign's hand and retired.

A pretty and touching scene took place when the royal dukes, who alone kissed her Majesty's cheek, come forward to do homage. The Duke of Sussex, who was suffering from indisposition, was feebly and with great difficulty ascending the steps of the throne, when the Queen, yielding to the impulse of natural affection, flung her fair arms about his neck and tenderly embraced him. The Duke was so overcome by this genuine display of feeling that he was supported from the theatre by some of the peers, being unable to repress his emotion.

The Duke of Wellington, Earl Grey, and Lord Melbourne were loudly cheered as they severally ascended the steps of the throne. Another incident which went to the heart of the people—for it showed that the Queen's kindness of heart had not forsaken her even in the midst of so great a ceremony—occurred when old Lord Rolle, who was between eighty and ninety years of age, went up to do homage. Harriet Martineau, who was in the Abbey and witnessed the scene, thus describes it: 'The homage was as pretty a sight as any: trains of peers touching her crown and then kissing her hand. It was in the midst of that process that poor Lord Rolle's disaster sent a shock through the whole assemblage. It turned me very sick. The large infirm old man was held up by two peers, and had nearly reached the royal footstool, when he slipped through the hands of his supporters, and rolled over and over down the steps, lying at the bottom coiled up in his robes. He was instantly lifted up, and

he tried again and again, amidst shouts of admiration
of his valour. The Queen at length spoke to Lord
Melbourne, who stood at her shoulder, and he bowed
approval ; on which she rose, leaned forward, and held
out her hand to the old man, dispensing with his
touching the crown. He was not hurt, and his self-
quizzing on his misadventure was as brave as his
behaviour at the time. A foreigner in London
gravely reported to his own countrymen, what he
entirely believed on the word of a wag, that the
Lords Rolle held their title on the condition of
performing the feat at every coronation ! '

Another account observes that the Queen's ' first
impulse was to rise, and when afterwards Lord Rolle
came again to do homage she said, " May I not get
up and meet him ? " and then rose from the throne
and advanced down one or two of the steps to prevent
his coming up—an act of graciousness and kindness
which made a great sensation. It is in fact the
remarkable union of *naïveté*, kindness, and native
good nature, with propriety and dignity, which makes
her so admirable and so endearing to those about her,
as she certainly is. I have been repeatedly told that
they are all warmly attached to her, but that all feel
the impossibility of for a moment losing sight of the
respect which they owe her. She never ceases to be
a queen, but is always the most charming, cheerful,
obliging, unaffected queen in the world.'

While the lords were doing homage, the Earl of
Surrey, Treasurer of the Household, threw coronation
medals in silver about the choir and lower galleries,
which were scrambled for with great eagerness. A
London alderman was thrown on the ground and

rolled over in the struggle for one of these medals. It was feared that a battle-royal would ensue between some of the competitors. One of the sons of the Duke of Richmond secured thirteen of the medals, which he placed in his page's sash, in Oriental fashion. High-born ladies entered into the struggle as well as the sterner sex.

At the conclusion of the homage the choir sang the anthem, ' This is the day which the Lord hath made.' The Queen received the two sceptres from the Dukes of Norfolk and Richmond ; the drums beat, the trumpets sounded, and the Abbey rang with exultant shouts of 'God save Queen Victoria! Long live Queen Victoria! May the Queen live for ever!' The members of the House of Commons raised the first acclamation with nine cheers. Of the House of Commons as then constituted there survive only three members who are members of the Lower House at the present time—Mr. Gladstone, Mr. Villiers, and Mr. Christopher M. Talbot.

The solemn ceremony of the coronation being now ended, the Archbishop of Canterbury went to the altar. The Queen followed him, and having divested herself of the symbols of sovereignty, she knelt down before the altar. The Gospel and Epistle of the Communion Service having been read by two bishops, her Majesty made her offering of bread and wine for the communion, in the paten and chalice. A second oblation was a purse of gold, which was placed on the altar. The Queen received the sacrament kneeling on the faldstool by the chair. Afterwards she put on her crown, and with her sceptres in her hands, took her seat again upon the throne. The Archbishop then proceeded with the Communion Service, and pronounced the final blessing. The choir sang the noble anthem, 'Hallelujah! for the Lord God omnipotent reigneth.'

The Queen then left the throne, and attended by two bishops and noblemen bearing the regalia and swords of State, passed into King Edward's Chapel, the organ playing. The Queen delivered the sceptre with the dove to the Archbishop of Canterbury, who laid it on the altar. She was then disrobed of her imperial robe of State, and arrayed in her royal robe of purple velvet by the Lord Chamberlain. The Archbishop placed the orb in her left hand. The gold spurs and St. Edward's staff were delivered by the noblemen who bore them to the Dean of Westminster, who placed them on the altar. The Queen then went to the west door of the Abbey wearing her crown, the sceptre with the cross being in her right, and the orb in her left hand. The swords and regalia were delivered to gentlemen who attended to receive them from the Jewel Office. It was nearly four o'clock when the royal procession passed through the nave at the conclusion of the ceremony. As the Queen emerged from the western entrance of the Abbey, there came from the thousands and tens of thousands of her subjects assembled in the vicinity thunders of acclamation and applause. Similar greetings awaited her on the whole of the homeward route; and the scene was even more impressive than in the morning, as her Majesty now wore her crown, and the peers and peeresses their robes and their jewelled coronets.

To the coronation succeeded the festivities. The

Queen gave a grand banquet to one hundred guests, and the Duke of Wellington a ball at Apsley House which was attended by 2000 persons. On the next day, and for three succeeding days (omitting Sunday), a fair was held in Hyde Park, this popular festive entertainment being visited by her Majesty on the Friday. All the theatres in the metropolis, and nearly all other places of public amusement, were by the Queen's command opened gratuitously on the evening of the coronation. The peaceable and orderly behaviour of hundreds of thousands of persons belonging to the middle and lower classes during the festivities extorted the admiration of foreign residents in London, and was much commented upon. The accidents and offences reported were extraordinarily few. Enthusiastic demonstrations took place throughout the country, and public dinners, feasts to the poor, processions, and illuminations were the order of the day. Every town in England had its rejoicings; while in the chief continental cities British subjects assembled to celebrate the auspicious event.

A parliamentary return showed that the entire expenses of the coronation amounted to £69,421 1s. 10d. of which sum nearly half was incurred by the fitting up of Westminster Abbey. The coronation expenses of George IV., which the Chancellor of the Exchequer estimated would not exceed £100,000, amounted to £238,000.

There was quite a shower of honours and dignities in connection with the Queen's coronation; but the peers need not detain us, and out of the twenty-nine baronets created, only two will enjoy a permanent fame—namely, Edward Bulwer Lytton, as representing

literature, and John Frederick William Herschel, as
representing science.

A Sovereign is exposed to annoyances from which
private individuals are free. Mary Queen of Scots,
Marie Antoinette, and other female monarchs, attracted
by their loveliness and other qualities an admiration
which frequently proved embarrassing. We have
already seen that this was the case with the Princess
Victoria, and after she became queen she had both
her admirers and assailants. She was subjected to
many annoyances during the year succeeding her
coronation. A Scotch youth travelled from the far
North to Windsor that he might become personally
acquainted with her Majesty, whom he announced
he was destined to espouse. His mental malady
having become only too apparent, he was placed under
restraint. Another individual succeeded in obtaining
admission to the Chapel Royal, and planted himself
opposite to the royal closet. After greatly disturbing
the Queen by his rude and eager gaze, he began to
bow and kiss his hand to her, till he was removed by
the proper authorities. Incoherent letters, the result
of similar aberrations of reason, were addressed to the
Queen in great numbers, and some of them found
their way into the public journals.

In the spring of 1839 her Majesty was passing in
her carriage through the triumphal arch facing the
Duke of Wellington's mansion in Piccadilly, when a
man rushed from the crowd and threw a letter into the
coach with such violence that it struck the Queen
upon the face. She remained quite calm, and
indicated the offender, who was seized and conveyed
to the police station, when it was found that he was

H

the victim of a hallucination. Amongst other cases
were those of Thomas Flowers, who was found in the
Queen's apartments at Buckingham Palace; and
Charles Willets, traveller to a commercial house in
Basinghall Street. The conduct of the latter was
especially offensive. As the Queen was taking an
airing in Hyde Park in July 1839, he followed
her on horseback, and endeavoured to get by the side
of her Majesty. Foiled in this, he kept crossing and
recrossing in front of the Queen, and endeavoured to
attract her attention by placing his hand on his left
breast, waving his hand, and otherwise acting in a
most ridiculous manner. As nothing could be done
with him, Colonel Cavendish gave him into custody.
Being brought up at Bow Street, he was fined £5 for
assaulting the Queen's outrider, and ordered to find
bail, himself in £200, and two respectable house-
holders in £100 each, to keep the peace for six
months.

But more important events still must have kept
the young Sovereign's mind under high tension at
this time. The Ministry was falling into disrepute;
there' was war in Canada, and much discontent at
home; while a great Court scandal arose in consequence of the painful case of Lady Flora Hastings.
The Queen did all she could to smooth matters, and
was much distressed by the turn of events. But there
were some persons so animated by party spirit that
they strove to make the innocent young ruler account-
able for the mistakes committed by her ladies. It
seems incredible that Melbourne, who was generally most
judicious in Court matters, should have permitted the
case of the unfortunate Lady Flora to go as far as it

did, with the necessary consequence of the strongest
public sympathy being manifested in her favour.
The death of Lady Flora Hastings was prematurely
hastened by the cruel, and, as the event proved,
unnecessary, indignity to which she was subjected.
There can be no doubt that her Majesty was very
badly advised in this matter.

But turning from this melancholy incident to a
more agreeable subject, the following account of the
Queen's daily life at Windsor will be read with great
interest:—'She gets up soon after eight o'clock,
breakfasts in her own room, and is employed the
whole morning in transacting business : she reads all
the despatches, and has every matter of interest and
importance in every department laid before her. At
eleven or twelve, Melbourne comes to her, and stays
an hour, more or less, according to the business he
may have to transact. At two she rides with a large
suite (and she likes to have it numerous); Melbourne
always rides on her left hand, and the equerry-in-
waiting generally on her right; she rides for two
hours along the road, and the greater part of the
time at a full gallop. After riding she amuses herself
for the rest of the afternoon with music and singing,
playing, romping with children, if there are any in
the Castle (and she is so fond of them that she
generally contrives to have some there), or in any
other way she fancies. The hour of dinner is nomi-
nally half-past seven o'clock, soon after which time
the guests assemble, but she seldom appears till near
eight. The lord-in-waiting comes into the drawing-
room and instructs each gentleman which lady he is
to take into dinner.

'When the guests are all assembled the Queen comes in, preceded by the gentlemen of her household, and followed by the Duchess of Kent and all her ladies; she speaks to each lady, bows to the men, and goes immediately into the dining-room. She generally takes the arm of the man of the highest rank, but on this occasion she went with Mr. Stephenson, the American Minister (though he has no rank), which was very wisely done. Melbourne invariably sits on her left, no matter who may be there; she remains at table the usual time, but does not suffer the men to sit long after her, and we were summoned to coffee in less than a quarter of an hour. In the drawing-room she never sits down till the men make their appearance. Coffee is served to them in the adjoining room, and then they go into the drawing-room, when she goes round and says a few words to each, of the most trivial nature—all, however, very civil and cordial in manner and expression. When this little ceremony is over, the Duchess of Kent's whist table is arranged, and then the round table is marshalled; Melbourne invariably sitting on the left hand of the Queen, and remaining there without moving till the evening is at an end. At about half-past eleven she goes to bed, or whenever the Duchess has played her usual number of rubbers, and the band have performed all the pieces in their list for the night. This is the whole history of her day. She orders and regulates every detail herself; she knows where everybody is lodged in the Castle; settles about the riding and driving; and enters into every particular with minute attention.'

While it was quite natural that her Majesty should

cling to Melbourne, seeing that she had had no other
instructor and adviser in matters of State, there were
those who regarded the Premier's monopoly of the
Queen as injudicious. They argued that whenever a
change of Government came about, she must feel the
separation from her Minister and friend very keenly.
Such a trial came sooner than was expected, though
it could not in any case have been much longer
delayed. The Melbourne Ministry resigned office on
the 7th of May 1839, in consequence of having been
placed in a minority of five on the question of the
government of Jamaica. The Queen sent for the
Duke of Wellington, and subsequently for Sir Robert
Peel. The latter undertook to form a Cabinet, and
on the 9th submitted a list of his proposed colleagues.
At the same time, as a public evidence of the Queen's
confidence, he asked for the dismissal of certain ladies
related to members of the ex-Ministry, and holding
high appointments in her Majesty's household. This
was construed as undue action on Peel's part, and
was afterwards spoken of as 'The Bedchamber Plot.'
Various and conflicting accounts have been published
of this semi-political imbroglio, but as the latest, given
by Greville, contains many details which are not to
be found elsewhere, I shall follow his account of the
transaction. Peel being unable to bring the Queen
round to his views, sent Lord Ashley, in the hope
that he might be able to influence her, but Lord
Ashley fared no better. Then the Duke of Wellington
and Peel saw her together, but only to find her firm
and immovable. She was prepared with answers
and arguments to all that they could advance. They
told her that she must consider her ladies in the same

light as her lords, to which she replied, 'No; I have lords besides, and these I give up to you.' When they still pressed her, she said: 'Now, suppose the case had been reversed—that you had been in office when I had come to the throne; Lord Melbourne would not have required this sacrifice of me.'

Peel was obliged to consult his friends, and in the meantime a meeting of the old Cabinet was convened at Melbourne's house. The ex-Premier laid before the ex-Ministers a letter from the Queen, written in a strain such as Elizabeth might have used. She said: 'Do not fear that I was not calm and composed. They wanted to deprive me of my ladies, and I suppose they would deprive me next of my dressers and my housemaids; they wished to treat me like a girl; but I will show them that I am Queen of England!' A letter was composed for her Majesty, and in accordance with its terms she wrote to Sir Robert Peel that, 'having considered the proposal made to her yesterday by Sir Robert Peel, to remove the ladies of her bedchamber, she cannot consent to a course which she conceives to be contrary to usage, and is repugnant to her feelings.' Peel then resigned his commission. As soon as the affair became known it caused the greatest excitement in London. The Queen was warmly applauded for the part she had taken, but the Tories were bitterly incensed against the Whigs. An opinion strongly adverse to Peel speedily gained ground, though a different complexion has since been given to his conduct by a statement made by Lord Wharncliffe. His lordship said that, so far from there being a lack of deference and consideration on the part of Peel, he manifested a desire to consult her

wishes and feelings in every respect ; and that, instead
of a sweeping demand for the dismissal of all her
ladies, he merely suggested the expediency of some
partial changes. There was no disposition on the
part of Peel to regard her with distrust, or to fetter
her social habits ; and when she said, 'You must not
expect me to give up the society of Lord Melbourne,'
he replied that 'nothing could be further from his
thoughts than to interfere with her Majesty's society
in any way, or to object to her receiving Lord Melbourne as she pleased, and that he should always feel
perfectly secure in the honour of Lord Melbourne that
he would not avail himself improperly of his intercourse with her.' But when he began to talk of 'some
modification of the ladies of her household' she stopped
him at once, and declared that she would not part
with any of them. As no point of agreement could
be formed, Lord Melbourne was recalled by her
Majesty, and he and his late colleagues agreed to
resume their places. There was a good deal of
recrimination in consequence between Whigs and
Tories, and a debate in Parliament, and it was long
before the public excitement subsided.

But the time had come when the Queen felt that
she desired a nearer and yet a dearer one than any of
the companions or counsellors of either sex by whom
she was surrounded. The cares of State weighed
heavily upon that young heart, and she required some
one upon whom she could lean in times of anxiety and
trouble, and whose love and counsel would cheer and
sustain her in periods of perplexity. Speculation had
long been rife as to when, and with whom, she would
enter upon the wedded state. Fortunately, however,

for her happiness, no reasons of State were allowed to dictate her course in this the most momentous change in a woman's life.   We shall presently see that when her marriage came to be celebrated, it was one of affection, and that it was the woman as well as the Queen who stood before the hymeneal altar.

CHAPTER III.

BETROTHAL AND MARRIAGE.

ON the 26th of August 1819—the same year which
witnessed the birth of the Queen—there was born to
the reigning Duke of Saxe-Coburg-Saalfeld a son,
who was afterwards named Albert. The birth took
place at the Rosenau, the summer residence of the
Duke, about four miles from Coburg. This child,
who was destined to be closely allied with England,
was lineally descended from those great Saxon
princes ' whose names are immortalized in European
history by the stand they made in defence of their
country's liberties against the encroaching power of the
German emperors, as well as by the leading part they
took in the Reformation.'

Albert was brought up with his elder brother
Ernest, and the two boys would seem to have vied
with each other in their winning ways and affectionate disposition. When the younger was but
five years old the Duke and Duchess separated in
consequence of an unhappy estrangement, and a
divorce followed, and the little brothers never saw
their mother again. But their two grandmothers
were passionately attached to them, and have left many
interesting descriptions of the boys. Albert was a
delicate, nervous child, with a beautiful countenance—

almost too much of a seraph, it was thought, for this
mundane sphere; but by the time he was six years
old he showed that he was pretty much like other
boys, and in a *naïve* little diary which he kept there
occur these two somewhat startling items :—' 9th
April. I got up well and happy; afterwards I had a
fight with my brother.' ' 10th April. I had another
fight with my brother: that was not right.' The
young Princes were active and courageous, but they
were also very studious. Albert's grandmamma
Coburg led him to take an interest in his cousin the
Princess Victoria, and to correspond with her at an
early date. The Duchess was the mother of Prince
Leopold and the Duchess of Kent. She died when
Prince Albert was twelve years old. The young
Prince's training was very thorough, embracing
tuition in various branches of science, languages,
music, literature, ethics, and politics. He had also a
fine moral and physical training, so that as he
advanced towards manhood he was upright both in
mind and body. A programme of studies which he
drew up for himself when in his fourteenth year is of
a most comprehensive and useful character. His
mind was further enlarged by travel, and after tours
in Germany, Austria, and Holland, he visited England, spending some time, as we have seen, with the
Duchess of Kent and his cousin at Kensington
Palace. At the close of his university career at
Bonn, Prince Albert travelled with Baron Stockmar
in Switzerland and Italy. The King of the Belgians
had always favoured a marriage between the cousins
Victoria and Albert, but King William IV. had
strongly discouraged it.

However, the Princess Victoria repeatedly declared that she would marry nobody else (though five suitors were found for her), and when she became Queen she of course had her right of choice without let or hindrance.

In his home at Erenburg, in the spring of 1839, Prince Albert was agreeably surprised, on entering his apartments after a long journey, to receive a smiling welcome from the features of his fair cousin, the young Queen of England. It appears that she had sent her portrait, executed by Chalon, for his acceptance, and it was privately placed, by her desire, so that it should be the first object to meet his view on his return.

The two brothers, Ernest and Albert, again visited England in the ensuing October, this being the third occasion on which they had done so. They reached Buckingham Palace on the 10th, and were conveyed thence in the royal carriages to Windsor Castle. The Queen appears to have been still more impressed than before with her younger cousin, and in writing to her uncle Leopold she remarked : ' Albert's beauty is most striking, and he is most amiable and unaffected ; in short, very fascinating.' Then, with maidenly reserve, as though she had been too communicative, she hastened to add : ' The young men are *both* amiable, and delightful companions, and I am glad to have them here.'

The manner of life at Windsor during the stay of the Princes is thus described : ' The Queen breakfasted at this time in her own room ; they afterwards paid her a visit there ; and at two o'clock had luncheon with her and the Duchess of Kent. In the afternoon

they all rode—the Queen and the Duchess and the
two Princes, with Lord Melbourne and most of the
ladies and gentlemen in attendance, forming a large
cavalcade.   There was a great dinner every evening,
with a dance after it three times a week.'   The
Queen now put off the monarch, and was the woman
alone. She danced with Prince Albert, and showed him
many attentions which she could never show to others.
' At one of the Castle balls, just before the Queen
declared her engagement with her royal cousin to her
Council, she presented his Serene Highness with her
bouquet.   This flattering indication of her favour
might have involved a less quick-witted lover in an
awkward dilemma, for his uniform jacket was fastened
up to the chin, after the Prussian fashion, and offered
no button-hole wherein to place the precious gift.
But the Prince, in the very spirit of Sir Walter
Raleigh, seized a penknife, and immediately slit an
aperture in his dress next his heart, and there trium-
phantly deposited the royal flowers.'

Royal courtships naturally excite curiosity, for
those undistinguished in position are eager to learn
whether love is after all the ' leveller' he is represented.   Her Majesty's experience proved that he
was.   One report says that the Queen endeavoured
to encourage her lover by asking him how he liked
England, to which he responded ' Very much.'   Next
day the query was repeated, and the same answer
was returned.   But on the third occasion, when the
maiden-monarch, with downcast eyes and tell-tale
blushes, asked ' If he would like to live in England ? '
he rose to the occasion.   Emboldened by the Queen's
demeanour, it is stated that ' on this hint he spoke '

of feelings that he had treasured up in strictest
secrecy since his first visit to England ; having, with
that sensitive delicacy which is the inseparable companion of true love, waited for some encouraging
token before he ventured to offer his homage to the
'bright particular star' of his devotions.

Another account says that her Majesty inquired of
his Serene Highness whether his visit to this country
had been agreeable to him ?—whether he liked England ?   And on the answer being given, 'Exceedingly,'
'Then,' added the Queen, 'it depends on you to make
it your home.'

All this is very pretty and very pleasant, but as a
matter of fact the Queen actually proposed to the
Prince, and was necessitated to do so from the circumstances of her position.   We have it on her own
admission that she directly made the proposal.   Some
days after she had done so she saw the Duchess of
Gloucester in London, and told her that she was to
make her declaration the next day.   The Duchess
asked her if it was not a nervous thing to do.   She
said, ' Yes; but I did a much more nervous thing a
little while ago.'   ' What was that ? '   ' I proposed to
Prince Albert.'

The engagement was made on the 15th of October.
Prince Albert had been out hunting with his brother,
and returned to the Castle about noon.   Half an hour
afterwards he received a summons from the Queen,
and went to her room, finding her alone.   After a few
minutes' conversation on other subjects, the Queen
told him why she had sent for him, and the whole
story of mutual love was once more quickly told.
' Though as Queen,' observes one writer, ' she offered

the Prince her coveted hand—that hand which had
held the sceptre of sceptres, and which princes and
peers and the representatives of the highest powers
on earth had kissed in homage—it was only as a poor
little woman's weak hand, which needed to be upheld
and guided in good works by a stronger, firmer hand;
and her head, when she laid it on her chosen husband's
shoulder, had not the feel of the crown on it. Indeed,
she seems to have felt that his love was her real coronation, his faith her consecration.'

She was not long in communicating the joyful news
to her dear friend, Baron Stockmar. It came with
some little surprise upon him, for, shortly before, the
Queen had assured him that she did not intend to
change her unmarried state for a long period. And
now she wrote : 'I do feel so guilty I know not how to
begin my letter; but I think the news it will contain
will be sufficient to ensure your forgiveness. Albert
has completely won my heart, and all was settled
between us this morning. I feel certain he will make
me happy. I wish I could feel as certain of my
making him happy.'

The Prince himself, writing to his affectionate
grandmother of Gotha, said : 'The Queen sent for me
alone to her room the other day, and declared to me,
in a genuine outburst of affection, that I had gained
her whole heart, and would make her intensely happy
if I would make her the sacrifice of sharing her life
with her, for she said she looked on it as a sacrifice;
the only thing which troubled her was that she did
not think she was worthy of me. The joyous openness
with which she told me this enchanted me, and I was
quite carried away by it.'

Her Majesty appears to have repeatedly dwelt on the Prince's sacrifices. In one of the typical entries in her Journal we read : ' How I will strive to make Albert feel as little as possible the great sacrifice he has made ! I told him it *was* a great sacrifice on his part, but he would not allow it.' Although many would have regarded the Prince as only to be envied, in one sense the Queen was quite right. She was not called upon to surrender anything, while she received the love and devoted care of a good husband. He, on the other hand, left his native home to dwell amongst strangers, with whom he had yet to make his way. He expatriated himself from Germany and from his much-loved brother, and took upon himself a portion of the burdens of the English Sovereign, without taking equal rank with her in the rights and privi- leges of sovereignty.   .

But the young couple were very happy. They had many tastes and sympathies in common. The Prince had considerable facility as an artist, and still more as a composer. The music he composed to the songs written by his brother was beyond the average in sweetness of melody, and some of his sacred com- positions, notably the tune ' Gotha,' were of a high order, and found their way into the psalmodies. He also sang well and played with skill. During his stay at Windsor Castle her Majesty frequently accom- panied him on the pianoforte, and at a later period they often sang together the admired productions of Rossini, Auber, Balfe, and Moore. Before he left the Castle, his engagement being then known, the Prince drew a pencil portrait of himself, which he presented to the Duchess of Kent. Both he and his brother were exceedingly fond of outdoor and field sports of all kinds.

Of course Greville has something to say about the royal engagement, and, as is frequently the case, his remarks are not of the pleasantest character. According to his account, her Majesty treated the Prime Minister rather slightingly. 'The Queen,' he says, 'settled everything about her marriage herself, and without consulting Melbourne at all on the subject—not even communicating to him her intentions. The reports were already rife, while he was in ignorance ; and at last he spoke to her : told her that he could not be ignorant of the reports, nor could she ; that he did not presume to inquire what her intentions were ; but that it was his duty to tell her that if she had any, it was necessary her Ministers should be apprised of them. She said she had nothing to tell him ; and about a fortnight afterwards she informed him that the whole thing was settled : a curious exhibition of her independence, and explains the apprehensions which Lady Cowper has recently expressed to me of the serious consequences which her determined character is likely to produce. If she has already shaken off her dependence on Melbourne, and begins to fly with her own wings, what will she not do when she is older, and has to deal with Ministers whom she does not care for, or whom she dislikes ?'

Now, this does not quite accurately represent what really occurred. There was no soreness felt by Melbourne, who was as kind as ever when the Queen, feeling that the time had come when she could confide in him, told him of her intentions. This she did on the 14th of October, the day before the engagement

was made. She said she had made her choice, whereupon Melbourne expressed his great satisfaction, and
added (as it is stated in the Queen's Journal) : ' I
think it will be very well received, for I hear that
there is an anxiety now that it should be, and I
am very glad of it.' Then he said, in a paternal
tone : ' You will be much more comfortable, for a
woman cannot stand alone for any time in whatever
position she may be.'

The King of the Belgians took a special interest in
the engagement. Before he was aware of its conclusion he had written to the Queen as follows concerning his nephews : ' I am sure you will like them
the more the longer you see them. They are young
men of merit, and without that puppy-like affectation
which is so often found with young gentlemen of
rank ; and though remarkably well-informed, they are
very free from pedantry. Albert is a very agreeable
companion. His manners are so quiet and harmonious
that one likes to have him near one's self. I always
found him so when I had him with me, and I think
his travels have still further improved him. He is full
of talent and fun, and draws cleverly.' Then comes a
very direct hint in the King's letter : ' I trust they will
enliven your *séjour* in the old castle, and may Albert
be able to strew roses without thorns in the pathway
of life of our good Victoria. He is well qualified
to do so.'

A letter from the Queen to the King crossed this
one. ' My dearest uncle,' she wrote, ' this letter will I
am sure give you pleasure, for you have always shown
and taken so warm an interest in all that concerns me.
My mind is quite made up, and I told Albert this

1

morning of it. The warm affection he showed me at
learning this gave me great pleasure. He seems perfection, and I think I have the prospect of very great
happiness before me. I love him more than I can say,
and shall do everything in my power to render this
sacrifice (for such in my opinion it is) as small as
I can. It is absolutely necessary that this determina-
tion of mine should be known to no one but yourself
and uncle Ernest, until after the meeting of Parliament, as it would be considered otherwise neglectful
on my part not to have assembled Parliament at once
to inform them of it.' The writer added : 'Lord
Melbourne has acted in this business as he has always
done towards me, with the greatest kindness and
affection. We also think it better—and Albert quite
approves of it—that we should be married very soon
after Parliament meets, about the beginning of
February.'

King Leopold sent a very affectionate reply from
Wiesbaden : 'My dearest Victoria, nothing could
have given me greater pleasure than your dear letter.
I had, when I learnt your decision, almost the feeling
of old Simeon—"Now lettest thou thy servant depart
in peace." Your choice has been for these last years
my conviction of what might and would be best for
your happiness ; and just because I was convinced of
it, and knew how strangely fate often changes what
one tries to bring about as being the best plan one
could fix upon—the maximum of a good arrangement
—I feared that it would not happen.'

We have glimpses of the royal lovers in their correspondence with each other and with their friends
and relatives. Thus, Prince Albert, writing to Baron

Stockmar, remarks: 'An individuality, a character which shall win the respect, the love, and the confidence of the Queen and of the nation, must be the groundwork of my position. If, therefore, I prove a "noble" Prince in the true sense of the word, as you call upon me to be, wise and prudent conduct will become easier to me, and its results more rich in blessings.' But his new position brought anxieties with it. 'With the exception of my relation to her (the Queen),' he wrote to his stepmother, 'my future position will have its dark sides, and the sky will not always be blue and unclouded. But life has its thorns in every position, and the consciousness of having used one's powers and endeavours for an object so great as that of promoting the good of so many, will surely be sufficient to support me.'

The Princes Ernest and Albert remained for a month at Windsor, and we hear of a beautiful emerald serpent ring which the latter presented to his lady-love. In the bracing November weather the engaged couple were present at a review, in the Home Park, of the battalion of the Rifle Brigade quartered at Windsor. Her Majesty has thus described this interesting scene: 'At ten minutes to twelve I set off in my Windsor uniform and cap, on my old charger "Leopold," with my beloved Albert, looking so handsome in his uniform, on my right, and Sir John Macdonald, the Adjutant-General, on my left, Colonel Grey and Colonel Wemyss preceding me, a guard of honour, my other gentlemen, my cousin's gentlemen, Lady Caroline Barrington, &c., for the ground. A horrid day: cold, dreadfully blowy, and, in addition, raining hard when we had been out

I 2

a few minutes. It, however, ceased when we came to the ground. I rode alone down the ranks, and then took my place as usual, with dearest Albert on my right, and Sir John Macdonald on my left, and saw the troops march past. They afterwards manœuvred. The Rifles looked beautiful. It was piercingly cold, and I had my cape on, which dearest Albert settled comfortably for me. He was so cold, being *en grande tenue*, with high boots. We cantered home again, and went in to show ourselves to poor Ernest, who had seen all from a window.'

The Princes returned to the Continent on the 14th of November. After so many happy weeks the Queen felt her loneliness very much, and she spent a good deal of her time in playing over the musical compositions which she and her lover had enjoyed together. She had also another reminder of him in the shape of a beautiful miniature, which she wore in a bracelet on her arm when she subsequently announced her intended marriage to the Privy Council. Writing to his aunt, the Duchess of Kent, the Prince observed : ' What you say about my poor little bride sitting all alone in her room, silent and sad, has touched me to the heart. Oh, that I might fly to her side to cheer her !' The Queen herself afterwards wrote : ' For the " poor little bride " there was no lack of those sweet words, touched with the grateful humility of a manly love, to receive which was a precious foretaste to her of the happiness of the years to come.' The Prince wrote to his bride : ' That I am the object of so much love and devotion often comes over me as something I can hardly realize. My prevailing feeling is, what am I that such happiness should be mine ? For

excess of happiness it is for me to know that I am so
dear to you.' And again, alluding to his grandmother's
regret at the impending separation from her: 'Still
she hopes, what I am convinced will be the case, that
I may find in you, my dear Victoria, all the happiness
I could possibly desire. And so I *shall*, I can truly
tell her for her comfort.' Yet once more, writing
from 'dear old Coburg,' he says: 'How often are my
thoughts with you! The hours I was privileged to
pass with you in your dear little room are the radiant
points of my life, and I cannot even yet clearly
picture to myself that I am indeed to be so happy as
to be always near you, always your protector.' Telling the Queen that in an hour he was to take the
sacrament in the church at Coburg, he added, with
mingled affection and solemnity: 'God will not take it
amiss if in that serious act, even at the altar, I think
of you, for I will pray to Him for you and for
your soul's health, and He will not refuse us His
blessing.'

The Queen had more than one trying ordeal before
her. She left Windsor with the Duchess of Kent on
the 20th of November for Buckingham Palace, and
immediately summoned a Council for the 23rd. It
was held in the bow-room of the palace, on the ground
floor. Amongst those assembled was the venerable
Duke of Wellington, respecting whom and the
Sovereign an amusing anecdote had just been current.
It was gravely reported that in an interview with
her Majesty Lord Melbourne had represented to the
Sovereign the advisability of her marriage, and had
begged her to say whether there was any person for
whom she entertained a preference. Her Majesty

deigned to acknowledge that there was one man for whom she could conceive a regard, and that was Arthur, Duke of Wellington! If this anecdote were as true as it is good, it bore testimony to the sly humour of the Queen.

Her task before the Council was an embarrassing one, but her courage, as she tells us, was inspired by the sight of the Prince's picture in her bracelet. 'Precisely at two I went in,' writes the Queen in her *Journal*. 'The room was full, but I hardly knew who was there. Lord Melbourne I saw looking kindly at me with tears in his eyes, but he was not near me. I then read my short declaration. I felt my hands shook, but I did not make one mistake. I felt most happy and thankful when it was over. Lord Lansdowne then rose, and in the name of the Privy Council asked that this most gracious and most welcome communication might be printed. I then left the room, the whole thing not lasting above two or three minutes. The Duke of Cambridge came into the small library where I was standing, and wished me joy.'

The Queen's declaration to her Council was as follows: 'I have caused you to be summoned at the present time in order that I may acquaint you with my resolution in a matter which deeply concerns the welfare of my people and the happiness of my future life. It is my intention to ally myself in marriage with the Prince Albert of Saxe-Coburg and Gotha. Deeply impressed with the solemnity of the engagement which I am about to contract, I have not come to this decision without mature consideration, nor without feeling a strong assurance that, with the blessing of Almighty God, it will at once secure my domestic felicity and serve the interests of my country. I have thought fit to make known this resolution to you at the earliest period, in order that you may be apprised of a matter so highly important to me and to my kingdom, and which, I persuade myself, will be most acceptable to all my loving subjects.'

In her new-found bliss as an affianced bride, and while receiving and exchanging daily warm assurances of mutual affection, the Queen did not forget her subjects, and especially those who were the most unfortunate of her own sex. Only on the day before she opened Parliament she sent a donation ot £50 to the Manor Hall Refuge for Destitute Females released from prison, signifying at the same time, in a gracious communication to Mrs. Fry—that noble friend of the outcast and the degraded—her intention of always supporting the above-mentioned benevolent and truly serviceable institution.

Parliament was opened by the Queen in person on the 16th of January 1840. It had been rumoured that the recent death of her Majesty's aunt, the Landgravine of Hesse Homburg, would prevent the Queen from attending the House of Lords, but this proved not to be the case. The Queen had consulted her royal aunts, the Princess Augusta and the Duchess of Gloucester, on the subject, and they both advised her to pursue the course of performing her duty to the Senate. 'You are, my dear, the highest public functionary,' said the Princess Augusta, 'and must not permit your private respect to your family to interfere with the proper discharge of your duties to your empire.' In her course to the Houses of Parliament the Queen was received with fervent demonstrations of loyalty, and the knowledge of the happy errand she was upon lent additional interest to her progress on this occasion. The marriage that was soon to be solemnized touched the people deeply, for they knew it was one of affection, and not one ' arranged ' merely for purposes of State.

The first part of her Majesty's speech, which was delivered with some amount of trepidation, was as follows : ' Since you were last assembled I have declared my intention of allying myself in marriage with the Prince Albert of Saxe-Coburg and Gotha. I humbly implore that the Divine blessing may prosper this union, and render it conducive to the interests of my people, as well as to my own domestic happiness ; and it will be to me a source of the most lively satisfaction to find the resolution I have taken approved by my Parliament. The constant proofs which I have received of your attachment to my person and family, persuade me that you will enable me to provide for such an establishment as may appear suitable to the rank of the Prince and the dignity of the Crown.'

A Bill for the naturalization of Prince Albert was at once passed through both Houses, and the Queen subsequently conferred upon her future husband the title of ' His Royal Highness,' as well as the rank of a Field Marshal in the British army. The question of the Prince's annuity created a good deal of discussion in the House of Commons on the 27th of January. Lord John Russell proposed an annual sum of £50,000, but this was opposed by Mr. Joseph Hume on the ground of economy. He sought to reduce the amount to £21,000, and caused much laughter by a remark to the effect that 'the noble lord must know the danger of setting a young man down in London with so much money in his pockets.' The amendment was negatived by 305 to 38; but another amendment, proposed by Colonel Sibthorp, reducing the sum to £30,000, was carried by 262 to 158. A curious rumour had got afloat that her Majesty had incurred debts beyond the amount of her allowance; and Government was asked if such were the fact, and also whether Parliament was to be called upon to contribute towards the expenses of the approaching royal nuptials. Lord John Russell stated that both reports were entirely unfounded. With regard to the pecuniary position of Prince Albert, it may be stated, on a Coburg authority, that when he attained his majority he was put in possession of the property bequeathed to him by his mother, which produced a revenue of 28,000 florins (about £2,400) per annum. When it was decided that he should leave the country to marry Queen Victoria, the Prince granted certain pensions to persons attached to his household, and then transferred the estate to his elder brother.

The royal marriage was fixed for the 10th of February, and on the afternoon of the 8th Prince Albert arrived at Buckingham Palace, accompanied by his father and elder brother. The Prince brought as a wedding gift to his bride a beautiful sapphire and diamond brooch; and her Majesty in return presented the Prince with the Star and Badge of the Garter, and the Garter itself, set in diamonds. The Queen had been exceedingly gratified by the high

tribntes paid to the personal character of Prince
Albert by men of all parties.   Sir Robert Peel, the
leader of the Opposition in the House of Commons,
had especially spoken in generous terms, and felici-
tated the Sovereign and the country upon the forthcoming auspicious union.

The question of the precedence of Prince Albert,
however, caused a great deal of difficulty, and much
annoyance to the Queen.   Greville has told the inner
and secret history of the struggle.   Writing in his
diary under the date of February 4th, he says: ' On
Friday the Cabinet agreed to give up the precedence
over the Prince of Wales; but to a question of
Brougham's, the Lord Chancellor said he had no
other concession to offer.   It was then agreed that
the discussion should be taken on Monday.   On
Saturday, Clarendon spoke to Melbourne himself, and
urged him to consider seriously the inconvenience of
a battle on this point, and prevailed upon him to go
to the Duke of Wellington and talk it over with him.
He wrote to the Duke, who immediately agreed to
receive him.   Then he went to Apsley House, and
they had an hour's conversation.   Melbourne found him
with one of his very stiffest crotchets in his head,
determined only to give the Prince precedence after
the Royal Family, and all he could get from him was
that it would be *unjust* to do more.   All argument
was unavailing, and he left him on Saturday evening
without having been able to make any impression on
him, or to move him by a representation of the
Queen's feelings to make concessions to meet those
the Government were prepared to make; for the
Queen would have been content to accept precedence

for her life, and saving the rights of the Prince of
Wales. This, however, they would not consent to;
and so determined were they to carry their point, that
they made a grand whip up, and brought Lord
Clarendon all the way from Grimsthorpe to vote upon
it. Under these circumstances the Government resolved to withdraw the clause, and they did so, thus
leaving the Prince without any specific place assigned
by Parliament, and it remains with the Queen to do
what she can for him, or for courtesy, tacit consent, and deference for her Consort, to give him the
precedence virtually which the House of Lords refuses
to bestow formally.

'I think the Duke of Wellington has acted
strangely in this matter, and the Conservatives
generally very unwisely. *Volentibus non fit injuria,*
and the Dukes of Sussex and Cambridge, who alone
were concerned, had consented to the Prince's precedence. The King of Hanover, it seems, was never
applied to, because they knew he would have refused;
and they did not deem his consent necessary. There
is no great sympathy for the lucky Coburgs in this
country, but there is still less for King Ernest, and
it will have all the effect of being a slight to the
Queen out of a desire to gratify him. There certainly was not room for much more dislike in her
mind of the Tories; but it was useless to give the
Prince so ungracious and uncordial a reception, and
to render him as inimical to them as she already is.
As an abstract question, I think his precedence unnecessary; but under all the circumstances it would
have been expedient and not unjust to grant it.'

The precedence controversy became so warm that

Greville looked up the authorities and the ancient practice on the subject. He came to the conclusion that the Queen had power to grant the Prince precedence everywhere but in Parliament and in Council, and on the whole he considered that *her husband* ought to have precedence. He accordingly wrote a pamphlet on the subject, which was very favourably regarded by the Queen. In the end the Queen settled the precedence problem, so far as England was concerned, by declaring it to be her royal will and pleasure, under her sign-manual, that her husband should enjoy place, pre-eminence, and precedence next to her Majesty.

Sunday, the 9th of February, Prince Albert spent in paying visits to the various members of the Royal Family, remaining for some time with the Queen Dowager and the Princess Augusta. His frank and manly bearing impressed all the Queen's relatives in his favour. So deeply did his religion enter into everything, tinging all with seriousness, though not with gloom, that only a very short time before the wedding ceremony he wrote to the venerable Dowager Duchess of Saxe-Coburg, who had enacted the part of a second mother to him, as follows : ' In less than three hours I shall stand at the altar with my dear bride. In these solemn moments I must once more ask your blessing, which I am well assured I shall receive, and which will be my safeguard and future joy. I must end. God help me, or rather God be my stay !' He could not, even in the prospect of so much happiness with his wife, lose sight of the fact that as a stranger in the land he would have much to live down, and would have as it were to make a position for himself in the affections of the English people.

An anecdote of a different but interesting kind is told of the Queen and her approaching wedding. It is said that the Archbishop of Canterbury waited upon her Majesty, and inquired if it were her wish that any alteration should be made in that portion of the Service appointed in the Liturgy for the solemnization of matrimony which included the promise of ' obedience '—a curious promise for the Sovereign of Great Britain to make to her newly naturalized subject Prince Albert, who had just taken the oath to her as his liege lady. The Queen, according to the report, replied that ' it was her wish to be married in all respects like any other woman, according to the revered usages of the Church of England, and that, though not as a *queen*, as a *woman* she was ready to promise all things contained in that portion of the Liturgy.'

Many were the ejaculations of ' God bless her ! ' which went up from the citizens of London on the morning of the 10th of February as they thought of the royal bride. The wedding ceremony was one of unusual interest, for more than a century had elapsed since the nuptials of a reigning Queen of England had been celebrated, besides which the youth and grace of Victoria had touched all loyal hearts. At an early hour a dense throng of persons assembled in front of Buckingham Palace, from whence the procession was to set out for St. James's, where the marriage was to be solemnized. At a quarter before twelve the bridegroom's procession issued forth, consisting of Prince Albert, his father, the Duke of

Saxe-Coburg-Gotha, his brother Prince Ernest, and their suites. At ten minutes past twelve the signal was given for the departure of the Queen. Accompanied by the Duchess of Kent, and attended by the Duchess of Sutherland, her Majesty seated herself in her full-dress carriage. For the benefit of lady readers I may state that the Queen wore on her head a wreath of orange blossoms and a veil of Honiton lace, with a necklace and earrings of diamonds. Her dress was of white satin, with a very deep trimming of Honiton lace, in design similar to that of the veil. The body and sleeves were richly trimmed with the same material, to correspond. The train, which was of white satin, was trimmed with orange blossoms. The cost of the lace alone on the Queen's dress was £1,000. The satin was manufactured in Spitalfields, and the lace at a village near Honiton. More than two hundred persons were employed upon the latter for a period of eight months, and as the lace trade of Honiton had seriously declined, all these persons would have been destitute during the winter had it not been for the Queen's express order that the lace should be manufactured by them.

As her Majesty entered her carriage she was extremely pale and agitated, but the cheers of the people quickened her spirits, and brought the blush to her cheeks and the smiles to her eyes. She bowed repeatedly in response to the joyous acclamations which greeted her on every side as the carriage moved off. All the way to St. James's Palace nothing was to be heard but enthusiastic cheering, and nothing to be seen but the waving of brides' favours and snow-white handkerchiefs.

At St. James's, the colonnade through which the procession passed to the chapel was excellently arranged and fitted up, rows of spectators being accommodated on each side. A host of celebrities, and of young and fashionable women, assembled here as early as ten o'clock. Smiles were exchanged as the band marched into the court, playing the appropriate air, 'Haste to the wedding.' Many of the grand functionaries of State, and favoured persons invited to view the nuptial ceremony, passed through the colonnade to the Chapel Royal. The first arrival of interest was the Duke of Sutherland, escorting his two beautiful daughters, the Ladies Elizabeth and Evelyn Leveson Gower, to their seats in the chapel. They were said to be the prettiest girls there, and were elegantly dressed in trains of the palest pink, trimmed all round with blush roses. The Bishop of London and the Archbishop of Canterbury next gravely passed by, followed by the Duke of Somerset and his handsome Duchess. Then came the Duke of Devonshire, the Earl of Carlisle and one of his many beautiful daughters; the Duke of Wellington in his uniform as a Field Marshal, and with his truncheon; and the Marquis of Anglesey in his splendid uniform as colonel of the 7th Hussars, covered with Orders, and wearing conspicuous bridal favours. The hero of Waterloo, who looked infirm, and did not move with his usual alacrity, was the only individual the spectators stood up to honour and to cheer. He bowed with great dignity in return, but appeared to be sinking under the weight of his years and his honours. The Baroness Lehzen, the Queen's governess and friend, attracted considerable attention. She was a lady with dark eyes and hair, and a complexion white as marble, which appeared all the whiter by contrast with her black velvet Spanish hat, which was surmounted by a white plume. Her countenance exhibited great energy and talent.

At twenty minutes past twelve a flourish of trumpets and drums gave notice of the approach of the royal bridegroom, and shortly afterwards the band played the triumphant strains of 'See the conquering hero comes!' The Prince wore a Field Marshal's uniform, with the star and ribbon of the Garter, and the bridal favours on his shoulders heightened his picturesque appearance. One who stood near him thus made notes of his person: 'Prince Albert is most prepossessing. His features are regular; his hair pale auburn, of silken glossy quality; eyebrows well defined and thickly set; eyes blue and lively; nose well proportioned, handsome mouth, teeth perfectly beautiful, small mustachios, and downy complexion. He greatly resembles the Queen, save that he is of a lighter complexion; still, he looks as though neither care nor sorrow had ever ruffled or cast a cloud over his placid and reflective brow. There is an unmistakable air of refinement and rectitude about him, and every year will add intellectual and manly beauty to his very interesting face and form.'

Contemporary accounts state that as the Prince moved along he was greeted with loud clapping of hands from the men, and enthusiastic waving of handkerchiefs from the assembled ladies. In his hand he carried a Bible bound in green velvet. Over his shoulders was hung the collar of the Garter surmounted by two white rosettes. On his left knee was

HIS ROYAL HIGHNESS PRINCE ALBERT.

After a Drawing by J. Louise De Meÿern Hurenberg.

the garter itself, which was of the most costly workmanship, and literally covered with diamonds. He had
suffered much from sea-sickness in coming over from
Germany, but the effects of this had passed away;
and his graceful and engaging manners, and pensive
looks, won golden opinions from the fair spectators.
The Prince's father and brother also received a cordial
welcome, with which they were apparently much
pleased. When the bridegroom's procession reached
the chapel, the drums and trumpets filed off without
the door, and the procession advancing, his Royal
Highness was conducted to the seat provided for him
on the left hand of the altar. Here he was engaged
for some time in conversation with the Queen
Dowager.

At half-past twelve the drums and trumpets sounded
the National Anthem as a prelude to the arrival of the
bride. Every person rose as the doors were again
opened, and the royal procession came in with solemn
steps and slow. The *coup d'œil* was now magnificent,
as floods of sunshine streamed through the windows
upon the many gorgeous costumes in which the royal
and distinguished persons who appeared in the procession were attired. The Princesses attracted much
attention. First came the Princess Sophia Matilda of
Gloucester, still very beautiful, and dressed in lily-
white satin; then the Princess Augusta of Cambridge,
in pale blue, with blush roses round her train; next
the Duchess of Cambridge, in white velvet, leading by
the hand the lovely little Princess Mary, who was
dressed in white satin and swansdown, the mother all
animation and smiles at the applause which greeted
her child; and lastly the Duchess of Kent, regal in

K

stature and dignity, and dressed in white and silver, with blue velvet train. The Duke of Cambridge and the Duke of Sussex succeeded, the latter 'looking blithe and full of merry conceits.' One account says that the Duchess of Kent appeared somewhat disconsolate and distressed, and that there were traces of tears upon her countenance.

Immediately after Lord Melbourne, who carried the sword of State, came the Queen herself, the central figure, and one of universal interest. She wore a chaplet of orange-blossoms on her head, and her bridal veil was fastened to the back of her head with a small brilliant pin. She had round her neck the collar of the Garter, but wore no other ornaments or jewels. She looked anxious and excited, and with difficulty restrained her agitated feelings. Her Majesty's train was borne by twelve unmarried ladies, the daughters of well-known peers. These noble demoiselles were the Ladies Adelaide Paget, Sarah Frederica Caroline Villiers, Frances Elizabeth Cowper, Elizabeth West, Mary Augusta Frederica Grimston, Eleanora Caroline Paget, Caroline Amelia Gordon Lennox, Elizabeth Anne Georgiana Dorothea Howard, Ida Hay, Catherine Lucy Wilhelmina Stanhope, Jane Harriet Bouverie, and Mary Charlotte Howard. The bridesmaids, like their royal mistress, were attired in white. Their dresses were composed of delicate net, trimmed with festoons of white roses over slips of rich gros de Naples, with garlands of white roses over the head. The Duchess of Sutherland walked next to the Queen, and the ladies of the bedchamber and the maids of honour closed the bride's procession.

The Chapel Royal was specially prepared and

decorated for the ceremony. The altar and *haut pas* had a splendid appearance, the whole being lined with crimson velvet. The wall above the communion-table was hung with rich festoons of crimson velvet edged with gold lace. The Gothic pillars supporting the galleries were gilt, as were the mouldings of the oaken panels, and the Gothic railing round the communion-table. The communion-table itself was covered with a rich profusion of gold plate. On one side was a stool for the Archbishop of Canterbury, and on the other one for the Bishop of London. On the left-hand side of the altar, and on the *haut pas*, were four stools, with footstools to match, for the Dukes of Sussex and Cambridge, the Princess Augusta and the Duchess of Gloucester; while on the opposite side were six stools of a like description for the Duchess of Cambridge, the two Princesses of Cambridge, Prince George of Cambridge, Prince Ernest and the reigning Duke of Saxe-Coburg-Gotha, the brother and father of the bridegroom. To the left side of the altar, and in front of the four stools, first described, were two State chairs—that next the railing of the altar for her Majesty, and that nearer to the aisle for the Duchess of Kent. On the opposite side were also two State chairs—that next the railing for Prince Albert, and that nearer the aisle for the Dowager Queen Adelaide. Close to the railing of the altar were two fald-stools for her Majesty and Prince Albert, to be used during the ceremony. The entire floor was covered with a blue-and-gold pattern carpet, with the Norman rose. The whole of the remaining part of the interior was decorated; and the ceiling, which is adorned with the arms of Great Britain in various coloured devices and compartments, presented a very tasteful appearance, having been completely renewed.

The royal and illustrious personages having all taken their places in the chapel, after the lapse of a few minutes her Majesty rose, and with the Prince advanced to the steps of the altar. The Archbishop of Canterbury then began the service with impressive solemnity, the Bishop of London making the responses. All eyes were now fixed upon the Queen. Preparatory to the commencement of the holy rite, her Majesty bowed her head upon her hand, and remained for some moments in silent prayer. When she had concluded her devotions, the Archbishop began the exhortation in the usual words. The entire service was precisely that of the Church liturgy, the simple names of 'Albert' and 'Victoria' being used. To the usual questions Prince Albert answered firmly 'I will.'

The corresponding inquiries were then addressed to her Majesty, 'Victoria, wilt thou have Albert to thy wedded husband, to live together after God's ordinance in the holy estate of matrimony? Wilt thou obey him and serve him, love, honour, and keep him, in sickness and in health, and, forsaking all other, keep thee only unto him, so long as ye both shall live?'

The Queen—in accents which, though full of softness and music, were audible at the most extreme corner of the chapel—replied, 'I will;' and in so responding, she 'accompanied the expression with a glance at his Royal Highness, which convinced all who beheld it that the heart was with her words.'

When the Archbishop inquired, 'Who giveth this woman to be married to this man?' the Duke of Sussex advanced, and holding the Queen's hand, said, 'I do.' The Archbishop then took her Majesty's hand, and placed it in that of Prince Albert, whereupon the usual forms of trothing faith were gone through. Both bride and bridegroom spoke in a tone of voice and with a clearness of enunciation which are seldom witnessed on similar occasions in the humbler walks of life. One who was present at the ceremony has observed that her Majesty's expression of the words 'love, cherish, and obey,' and the confiding look with which they were accompanied, were inimitably chaste and beautiful. .

Prince Albert then took the wedding-ring, which was quite plain, off his own finger, and gave it to the Archbishop. His Grace handed it back to the Prince, who then placed it, as directed, on his wife's finger. At this moment the Earl of Uxbridge gave the signal, and the cannon fired the royal salute, which was answered by the Tower artillery firing alternately with the Park guns, while all the bells in London and Westminster rang out a joyous peal of congratulation. Every citizen in the metropolis knew at the same moment that his beloved Sovereign had become a wedded wife.

Returning to the scene in the chapel; the remaining portions of the ceremony were impressively read by the Archbishop of Canterbury. Upon the conclusion of the service, the Queen shook hands cordially with the various members of the Royal Family, who now took up their positions in the procession as arranged for the return. The Duke of Sussex, after

shaking the royal bride by the hand with great
warmth, affectionately kissed her cheek.   Her Majesty
then crossed over to the other side of the altar, where
the Queen Dowager was standing, and the two illustrious ladies embraced with evident and unaffected
cordiality.   Prince Albert next kissed the hand of
Queen Adelaide, and acknowledged her congratulations.

The procession, being formed, left the chapel much
in the same order as it had entered.   But her Majesty
and her newly wedded consort now walked together
hand-in-hand, ungloved—Prince Albert with spark-
ling eyes and a heightened colour smiling down upon
the Queen, and she appearing very bright and
animated.

When the Queen and her husband passed through
the corridor, after leaving the chapel, the clapping of
hands and waving of handkerchiefs were renewed
again and again, until they had vanished out of sight.
Whether by accident or design, Prince Albert enclosed her Majesty's hand in his own in such a
way as to display the wedding-ring, which appeared
more solid than is usual in ordinary weddings.   The
various royal ladies in the procession were warmly
cheered, but an ovation more prolonged and enthusiastic than any other given during the whole day,
was reserved for the Duke of Wellington as he left
the chapel.   The Duke was not part of the royal procession, and it had passed to some distance before he
made his appearance.   But no sooner had the veteran
saviour of his country arrived in the centre of the
colonnade, than the whole company rose spontaneously,
and, without signal of any kind, gave him three

hearty cheers. The Duke was visibly touched by this greeting.

The procession passed on to the State apartments, but the Queen and Prince Albert, with their royal relatives and the principal Ministers of State and members of the Privy Council proceeded to the throne-room, where they were joined by the Archbishops of Canterbury and York, and the Bishop of London. The attestation of the marriage now took place upon a splendid table prepared for the purpose. Her Majesty and Prince Albert signed the marriage register, and it may here be mentioned that the name of the Queen is Alexandrina Victoria Guelph, while that of the Prince Consort was Francis Albert Augustus Charles Emanuel Busici. The marriage was attested by the Duke of Sussex and twenty-nine other persons. The attestation book, which is bound in rich purple velvet, is a speaking memento of royal nuptial ceremonies for many generations past. It is in the custody of the Archbishop of Canterbury. Amongst the witnesses who signed at the Queen's marriage was the Duke of Wellington, and it is an interesting fact that his signature also appeared at the attestation of her birth.

When all was concluded within St. James's, the procession to Buckingham Palace was reformed in almost the same order as when it set out in the morning. Prince Albert now took his place in the same carriage with her Majesty, while the Duchess of Sutherland took her place in another carriage with the Earl of Albemarle, who on this occasion alone waived his official right to be in the same carriage with her Majesty. In the royal carriage the Queen occupied the place of honour, and Prince Albert and the Duchess of Kent sat opposite. Her Majesty's faithful subjects were so desirous of seeing her, and were so eager in their demonstrations of loyalty, that she put down the closed windows of the carriage, and bowed, with much sweetness upon her smiling features, on the right hand and on the left.

The wedding-breakfast was given at Buckingham Palace, the guests including the various members of the Royal Family, the officers of the household, the Ministers of State, and the Archbishop of Canterbury and the Bishop of London. The wedding-cake, which was admirably designed, was a great object of attraction. It was more than nine feet in circumference by sixteen inches deep. Its weight was three hundred pounds, and the materials of which it was composed cost one hundred guineas. On the top of the cake was the figure of Britannia in the act of blessing the illustrious bride and bridegroom. The figures were nearly a foot in height, and by the feet of the Prince was the effigy of a dog, intended to represent fidelity, while at the feet of the Queen were two turtle-doves, denoting the felicities of the marriage state. A Cupid, beautifully modelled, was writing in a volume expanded on his knees the date of the day of the marriage, and various other Cupids were disporting themselves after the manner of Cupids. There were numerous bouquets of white flowers, tied with true-lovers' knots of white satin riband, on the top of the cake ; and these were intended for presents to the guests at the nuptial breakfast. There were large medallions upon shields bearing the letters ' V.' and ' A.,' and supported by Cupids on pedestals, while all round and over the cake were wreaths and festoons of orange-blossom and myrtle, entwined with roses.

Another matter of interest to the fair sex is that each of the royal bridesmaids received a magnificent brooch, the gift of her Majesty. This brooch was in the shape of a bird, the body being formed entirely of turquoises; the eyes were rubies and the beak a diamond; the claws were of pure gold, and rested on pearls of great size and value. The whole workmanship was very exquisite, and the design was furnished by the Queen.

Shortly before four o'clock the royal party left Buckingham Palace for Windsor amid the acclamations of a vast multitude. The first carriage contained the Queen and Prince Albert, the second Prince Ernest of Saxe-Coburg, and three others the members of the royal suite. Just as the procession left the palace the sun shone forth brilliantly upon the newly married pair, an emblem, it was universally hoped, of their future happiness. Prince Albert was very simply attired in a plain dark travelling dress, and the Queen appeared in a white satin pelisse, trimmed with swansdown, with a white satin bonnet and feather.

On the road to Windsor the principal houses in the villages were illuminated, and crowds came forth to testify their loyal delight on the happy occasion. Eton College presented one of the finest spectacles on the route. Opposite to the college was a representation of the Parthenon at Athens, which was brilliantly illuminated by several thousand variegated lamps; it was surmounted by flags and banners, and under the royal arms was displayed the following motto: ' *Gratu-*

latus Etona Victoriæ et Alberto.' Beneath the clock-tower of the college there was a blaze of light, and a number of appropriate devices were displayed in various coloured lamps. A triumphal arch, composed of ever-greens and lamps tastefully displayed, extended across the road. The Etonians, wearing white favours, were marshalled in front of the College. They received the Queen with loud acclamations, and escorted her to the Castle gates.

By the time Windsor was reached the shades of evening had gathered. The whole town could be perceived therefore brilliantly illuminated before the royal carriage entered it. A splendid effect was created by the dazzling lights as they played upon the faces of the multitude. The crowd on the Castle-hill was so dense at half-past six that it was with the utmost difficulty a line was kept clear for the royal carriages. The whole street was one living mass, whilst the walls of the houses glowed with crowns, stars, and all the brilliant devices which gas and oil could supply. At this moment a flight of rockets was visible in the air, and it was immediately concluded that the Queen had entered Eton. The bells now rang merrily, and the shouts of the spectators were heard as the royal cortége approached the Castle. At twenty minutes before seven the royal carriage arrived in the High Street, Windsor, preceded by the advanced guard of the travelling escort. The shouts were now most loud and continuous, and from the windows and balconies of the houses handkerchiefs were waved by the ladies, whilst the gentlemen huzzaed and waved their hats. The carriage, owing to the crowd, proceeded slowly, the Queen and her royal consort bowing to the people. Her Majesty looked remarkably well, and Prince Albert seemed in the highest spirits at the cordiality with which he was greeted. When the carriage drew up at the grand entrance the Queen was handed from it by the Prince; she immediately took his arm and entered the Castle. To the royal dinner party which followed only Lady Sandwich, the lady-in-waiting, the maids of honour, the Hon. Misses Cocks and Cavendish, Lord Torrington, Major Keppel, and Mr. Seymour, the groom and equerry in waiting, had the honour of being invited.

A splendid State banquet in celebration of the royal wedding was given at St. James's Palace in the grand banqueting-room. The Duchess of Kent, who was the only royal personage present, did the honours of the occasion, being supported on her right by the Earl of Erroll, and on her left by the Earl of Albemarle. Upwards of a hundred distinguished persons received invitations, and all attended in court dresses, the members of the orders of knighthood wearing their respective insignia. The Queen Dowager gave a banquet at Marlborough House, at which several members of the Royal Family were present; and dinners were given by Viscount Melbourne, Lord John Russell, Lord Palmerston, and other members of the Cabinet. The theatres were thrown open free, and at every house the National Anthem was sung with rapturous enthusiasm. The gaieties in London and several of the provincial towns were kept up for some days.

The Dowager Lady Lyttelton, who was an eye-witness of the marriage, and who was thrown much into the company of the Sovereign as a lady of the bedchamber, and subsequently as governess to the royal children, wrote at a later date respecting the wedding : 'The Queen's look and manner were very pleasing, her eyes much swollen with tears, but great happiness in her countenance, and her look of confidence and comfort at the Prince when they walked away as man and wife was very pleasing to see. I understand she is in extremely high spirits since ; such a new thing to her to *dare* to be unguarded in conversation with anybody, and, with her frank and fearless nature, the restraints she had hitherto been under from one reason or another with everybody must have been most painful.'

For one day only, the 11th of February, were the Queen and Prince alone together at Windsor, and on that day her Majesty wrote to Baron Stockmar, 'There cannot exist a dearer, purer, nobler being in the world than the Prince.' On the 12th the Duchess of Kent, the Duke of Coburg, the hereditary Prince, and the whole Court joined the happy couple, who would doubtless have been glad if the exigencies of State could have been relaxed a little more. After two more brief days the Court returned to London, for royalty was not able to indulge in a honeymoon as ordinary folk. On the 18th the Queen held a Court at Buckingham Palace for the reception of congratulatory addresses from the Houses of Parliament. Subsequently she received addresses from the London clergy, the Corporation of London, the University of Cambridge, the Society of Friends, and the General Assembly of the Church of Scotland. The Duke of Wellington also headed a deputation from Oxford, and read a complimentary address to her Majesty; and several hundred students of the University were present in academic costume. On the 26th of February the Queen and Prince Albert visited Drury Lane Theatre in State, receiving a most enthusiastic welcome, and we read afterwards of visits to the hunting-field, to the Royal Academy, and other sources of outdoor and intellectual enjoyment. Further honours were conferred upon the Prince. He was made a Knight Grand Cross of the Order of the Bath, and appointed Colonel of the 11th Regiment of Light Dragoons, which was now armed, clothed, and equipped as Hussars, and called 'Prince Albert's Own Hussars.'

The Duke of Coburg left England on the 28th of February on his return to Germany. Prince Albert's sorrow at parting with his father was very great, for it now meant permanent separation. The Queen, writing in her *Journal*, remarks concerning Prince Albert's feelings at this time: 'He said to me that I had never known a father, and could not therefore feel what he did. His childhood had been very happy— Ernest, he said, was now the only one remaining here of all his earliest ties and recollections; but if I continued to love him as I did now, I could make up for all. . . . . Oh! how I did feel for my dearest, precious husband at this moment! Father, brother, friends, country, all has he left, and all for me. God grant that I may be the happy person, the *most* happy person to make this dearest, blessed being happy and contented. What is in my power to make him happy I will do.' Another severe trial for the Prince occurred some weeks later, when he said adieu to his brother Ernest. 'They bade farewell, German student fashion, singing together the parting song, *Abschied.*' The brothers embraced each other affectionately, ' poor Albert being pale as a sheet, and his eyes full of tears.'

The Queen was absolutely obliged for her own comfort, as well as to establish the rights of her husband, to issue letters patent conferring on him precedence next to herself. All kinds of objections and disputes would have arisen but for this step, and some indeed did so before the issue of the patent. As to the general conduct of the Prince, it was most wise and unexceptionable. He sank himself in order to smooth the course of the Queen, but was always ready with his counsel and advice. As the Prince himself subsequently expressed it, he resolved ' to sink his own individual existence in that of his wife, to aim at no power, by himself or for himself, to shun all ostentation, to assume no separate responsibility before the public ; continually and anxiously to watch every part of the public business in order to be able to advise and assist her at any moment, in any of the multifarious and difficult questions brought before her— sometimes political or social, or personal—as the natural head of the family, superintendent of her household, manager of her private affairs, her sole confidential adviser in politics and only assistant in her communications with the affairs of the Government.' Again, writing to his father he said, 'I endeavour quietly to be of as much use to Victoria in her position as I can.'

How well and judiciously on the whole the Prince fulfilled his functions as the Queen's adviser, history has already borne testimony. If he sometimes made mistakes, he certainly made fewer than might have been expected from one in his difficult position. But his unquestioned integrity, his sincerity, honesty, and high principle, stood him in good stead; and they were a sheet-anchor upon which the Queen could always rely. Neither her Majesty nor her husband expected to find life easy in their exalted station; but as both were in deep sympathy with each other, and as love, trustful and unfeigned, was the moving spring of both, difficulties were overcome instead of becoming themselves insurmountable. If ever it could be said of any marriage—and I rejoice that it can be so said in thousands of cases—the Queen's was a marriage of profound happiness and mutual trust, for it was a real union of souls.

CHAPTER IV.

WEDDED HAPPINESS.

AUSPICIOUSLY as the Queen's married life began, it necessarily caused some friction in quarters which were ruled by old Court principles. It was difficult for the officials of the palaces to settle down under the new conditions. All was altered, and Prince Albert found that even in his own home it was necessary to be stern sometimes and to exercise his authority. Writing to his old comrade, Prince Löwenstein, he said he was very happy and contented, but that he had difficulty in filling his place with proper dignity, as he was only the husband and not the master of the house. When the Queen was appealed to on the subject she stated that she had pledged herself to obey as well as to love and honour her husband, and that 'this sacred obligation she could consent neither to limit nor define.'

Dickens has covered with everlasting contempt the system of red-tapeism, but the red-tapeism of the public offices never approached in sheer ridiculousness to that which presided over the domestic arrangements of the royal palaces. Some ludicrous examples of the working of the system are furnished in Sir Theodore Martin's 'Life of the Prince Consort,' and in Baron Stockmar's 'Memoirs.' For instance, the three great officers of State, the Lord Steward, the Lord Chamberlain, and the Master of the Horse, who were changed with the removal of the Ministry for the time being, had each a governing voice in the regulation of the household. 'Thus one section of the palace was supposed to be under the Lord Chamberlain's charge, another under that of the Lord Steward, while as to a third it was uncertain whose business it was to look after it. The above high officials were responsible for the interior of the building, but the outside had to be taken care of by the department of the Woods and Forests. The consequence was, that as the inside cleaning of the windows belonged to the Lord Chamberlain's department, the degree of light to be admitted into the palace depended proportionably on the well-timed and good understanding between the Lord Chamberlain's office and that of the Woods and Forests. One portion of the *personnel* of the establishment again was under the authority of the Lord Chamberlain, another under that of the Master of the Horse, and a third under the jurisdiction of the Lord Steward.' Baron Stockmar writes that 'the Lord Steward finds the fuel and lays the fire, and the Lord Chamberlain lights it. In the same manner, the Lord Chamberlain provides all the lamps, and the Lord Steward must clean, trim, and light them. Before a pane of glass or a cupboard door could be mended, the sanction of so many officials had to be obtained, that often months elapsed before the repairs were made.'

The absurd rules prevailing operated curiously and inconveniently in other ways. 'As neither the Lord Chamberlain nor the Master of the Horse has a regular deputy residing in the palace, more than two-thirds of all the male and female servants are left without a master in the house. They can come on and go off duty as they choose; they can remain absent for hours and hours on their days of waiting, or they may commit any excess or irregularity; there is nobody to observe, to correct, or to reprimand them. The various details of internal arrangement whereon depend the well-being and comfort of the whole establishment, no one is cognizant of or responsible for. There is no officer responsible for the cleanliness, order, and security of the rooms and offices throughout the palace.' This anomalous state of things was ultimately altered owing to the exertions of the Prince, but not until several years had elapsed and the needed reforms had been strongly insisted upon.

The Queen and Prince Albert spent their first Easter together at Windsor, and here also they took the Sacrament in common for the first time. Reference has already been made to the Prince's religious convictions, and the Queen has remarked concerning the taking of the Sacrament: 'The Prince had a very strong feeling about the solemnity of the act, and did not like to appear in company either the evening before or on the day on which he took it, and he and the Queen almost always dined alone on these occasions.' Describing one of these evenings in the *Early Years of the Prince Consort*, her Majesty says: 'We two dined together. Albert likes being quite alone before he takes the Sacrament. We played part of Mozart's Requiem, and then he read to me out of *Stunden den Andacht* (Hours of Devotion) the article on *Selbster Kentniss* (Self-Knowledge).' In how many Courts have evenings been spent after this fashion?

Towards the end of April there was a wedding in Paris which had a special interest for the Queen and Prince Albert. The Duc de Nemours led to the altar Princess Victoria of Saxe-Coburg, only daughter of the head of the Catholic branch of the family, sister of the King Consort of Portugal, and first cousin both to the Queen and Prince Albert. The Princess had spent much of her youth at Coburg, and had been the playmate of the Prince. She had also been the friend of the Queen from girlhood. Her Majesty wrote of their friendship : ' We were like sisters : bore the same name—married the same year. There was in short a similarity between us which, since 1839, united us closely and tenderly.'

At this time the Queen parted with her mother, who now felt it right to retire to a separate establishment. The Duchess consequently removed to Ingestre House, Belgrave Square, which henceforth became her home. But even this separation did not interrupt the close sympathy and affection which had always existed between mother and child. There were still frequent occasions when the loving counsel of the parent was sought by the daughter, and their intercourse continued to be of the same intimate character as before.

Her Majesty spent her birthday at Claremont, and in the company of her husband enjoyed her first period of uninterrupted leisure and relaxation from the affairs of State. The attractions of that charming seat afforded great delight to the royal couple, who wandered about at their will, undisturbed by the bustle and cares of a full Court. On one occasion they were caught in a shower, and sought shelter in a cottage inhabited by an old and solitary dame. This good cottager entertained her visitors with many stories touching the Princess Charlotte and Prince Leopold, once the owners of Claremont, little imagining the rank of her listeners. When the royal visitors left she lent them her umbrella, with many strict injunctions to Prince Albert that it should be taken care of and faithfully returned. Report speaks not of her demeanour when she ultimately became aware of the high station of her visitors.

Prince Albert early revealed his predilections towards music and art. Music especially moved him to enthusiasm, and his first appearance in this connection was at the Ancient Music Concerts. In private he played and sang much with the Queen, the organ being his favourite instrument. Lady Lyttelton thus records her impressions of one musical evening: 'Yesterday evening, as I was sitting here comfortably after the drive by candle-light, reading M. Guizot, there suddenly arose from the room beneath—oh, such sounds! It was Prince Albert, dear Prince Albert, playing on the organ, and with such master skill as it appeared to me—modulating so learnedly, winding through every kind of bass and chord, till he wound up with the most perfect cadence; and then off again, louder, and then softer: no tune, as I was too distant to perceive the execution or small touches, so I only heard the harmony; but I never listened with much more pleasure to any music. I ventured at dinner to ask him what I had heard. "Oh! my organ—a new possession of mine. I am so fond of the organ! It is the first of instruments; the only instrument for expressing one's feelings."' In painting, and etching also, the Prince passed a considerable portion of his time; and as an outdoor occupation he developed great taste in landscape gardening.

The first occasion on which the Prince manifested his deep sympathy with humanitarian movements—one of the conspicuous features of his career—was on the 1st of June, when he presided over a meeting called to promote the abolition of the slave trade. He had carefully prepared his speech beforehand, committed it to memory, and repeated it to the Queen. The Prince made a successful *entrée* upon public life. Caroline Fox, the Quaker, makes mention of the Prince's appearance in her Memoirs : ' The acclamations attending his entrance were perfectly deafening, and he bore them all with calm, modest dignity, repeatedly bowing with considerable grace. He certainly is a very beautiful young man—a thorough German, and a fine poetic specimen of the race. He uttered his speech in a rather low tone, and with the prettiest foreign accent.'

London was startled on the evening of the 10th of June by the report of Oxford's attempt to assassinate the Queen. From the various accounts published at the time, and subsequently, it appears that the Queen and Prince Albert left Buckingham Palace by the garden gate opening from Constitution Hill for a drive. The hour was about six o'clock. They were seated in a very low German droschky, drawn by four horses, with postillions, preceded by two outriders and followed by two equerries. As soon as the carriage had proceeded a short distance up Constitution Hill, thus getting clear of spectators, a young man on the park side of the road presented a pistol, and fired it directly at the Queen. The Prince, hearing the report, turned his head in the direction whence it came; her Majesty at the same instant rose, but Prince Albert immediately pulled her down by his side. 'The report of the pistol,' said a witness of the occurrence, 'attracted my attention, and I heard a distinct whizzing or buzzing before my eyes, between my face and the carriage. The moment he fired the pistol he turned himself round, as if to see whether any one was behind him. He then set himself back again, drew a second pistol with his left hand from his right breast, presented it across the one he had already fired, which he had in his right hand, and fired again, taking very deliberate aim.' Several persons rushed upon the miscreant. The fellow was quite calm and collected, admitted having fired the pistols, and went quietly with two of the police to the Queen Square station. He was discovered to be one Edward Oxford, seventeen years of age, and recently employed as barman at a public-house in Oxford Street.

The Queen, as might naturally be supposed, was seriously alarmed at the occurrence, but besides being extremely pale did not betray any outward agitation. Rising to show that she was unhurt, she ordered the postillions to drive to Ingestre House, her first thought being for her mother. The Duchess of Kent received her daughter safely before there had been time for her to be shocked by the news of the attempted assassination. The Queen and the Prince remained with the Duchess for a short time, and then returned by way of Hyde Park. The royal pair were received with every symptom of deep satisfaction by a large gathering of ladies and gentlemen in the park, and escorted to Buckingham Palace. Large numbers of the nobility called in the evening to offer their congratulations.

For many days after the dastardly affair there was an exhibition of almost unbounded loyalty. The journals of the day report that thousands of people continued to assemble before the palace, and hundreds of noblemen, members of the Government, and private ladies and gentlemen, called to congratulate or inquire, and to present their grateful addresses on such a happy and providential deliverance. Whenever her Majesty and the Prince drove out they were escorted by hundreds of ladies and gentlemen on horseback, who accompanied them like a bodyguard; whilst the immense sympathizing crowds cheered most enthusiastically. At first there was a surmise as to a widespread conspiracy being on foot, but this report was discovered to be unfounded, though there had been some slight countenance for it.

At the different theatres, and at places where public dinners were held, as soon as the news transpired on the Wednesday evening, the day of the attempt, 'God save the Queen' was sung with loyal fervour. A grand concert was being held at the Opera House for the benefit of the New Musical Fund: it was to have terminated with Mozart's overture to *Idomeneo*, but Sir George Smart, the conductor, stepped forward, and having informed the audience of the attempt on her Majesty's life, proposed to substitute the National Anthem. His suggestion was received with great enthusiasm.

On the 12th a remarkable scene of loyalty was witnessed at Buckingham Palace. The sheriffs of London, the Cabinet Ministers, and others, attended early to present addresses of congratulation ; but the great event of the day was the presentation of addresses from the two Houses of Parliament.   At two o'clock the State carriage of the Speaker of the House of Commons entered the court, followed by 109 carriages filled entirely with members of Parliament : never before, it is said, was the Speaker followed by so numerous a *cortége* on the occasion of present-ing an address. As soon as the carriages of the Commons had left the court, the procession of the Lords began to enter—the barons first, and then the other peers, rising in rank to the royal Dukes of Sussex and Cambridge ; the Lord Chancellor bringing up the rear.   There were eighty-one carriages in the peers' procession, which was brilliant and imposing to an extraordinary degree.   Many of the lords wore splendid uniforms and decorations of various Orders : the Duke of Wellington especially was attired with much magnificence.   The procession of the Commons passed with little notice from the crowd ; but on the Duke's appearance the cheering was enthusiastic and universal.   The Dukes of Sussex and Cambridge also were cheered.   Whilst the lords were alighting from their carriages the grand terrace in front of the palace was crowded with distinguished persons in splendid costumes.

'The Queen received the address on the throne. The Lord Chancellor and the Speaker of the House of Commons advanced side by side. The Dukes of Sussex and Cambridge walked in a line with the Lord Chancellor, the peers and commoners following. Prince Albert stood on the left of the throne ; the great officers of State and of the household on the right.

The Lord Chancellor read the address, and the Queen was graciously pleased to receive it.'

Similar enthusiasm was manifested all over the country. On the 16th and 18th the Queen and Prince Albert went to Ascot races, receiving a remarkable ovation. Two days later the Queen visited the opera for the first time after the atrocious attempt on her life, and the appearance of the Sovereign here was likewise the signal for a loyal demonstration of a very striking character. The vast audience rose, the National Anthem was sung with great enthusiasm, the assembly loudly cheering at the end of each verse; Her Majesty standing all the time, and graciously acknowledging the congratulations of the audience. As soon as the singing of the anthem was concluded Prince Albert was called, and received three hearty cheers.

Her Majesty and the Prince paid a visit to Greenwich Hospital on the 27th, going down from Whitehall in the Admiralty barges. They had lunch with the Governor, Vice-Admiral Fleming, and then walked through the different halls, and inspected the dinners prepared for the veteran tars. Grace having been said, the Queen partook of the soup, bread, and meat provided for the gallant inmates of the Hospital, and handed a piece of the bread to one of the ladies of her suite. The veterans were highly delighted with the affable manners of the Queen, and the kind manner in which she inquired after their welfare. Round the grand square 1,000 pensioners of all classes were drawn up, while 800 schoolboys and the nurses and girls in the establishment took up various positions assigned to them. The day was a memorable one, and the royal visitors were much struck by the excellence of the arrangements.

Oxford was brought to trial at the Central Criminal Court on the 8th of July. There had been found at his lodgings, after he was searched, a quantity of powder and shot, and the rules of a secret society styled 'Young England,' prescribing, among other things, that every member should, when ordered to meet, be armed with pistols and a sword, and a black crape cap to cover his face. The charge against Oxford was high treason in its most exaggerated form—that is, a direct attempt on the life of the Queen. The Attorney-General prosecuted, and a considerable number of witnesses were examined. There was a curious *nonchalance* on the part of the prisoner all through, which pointed to insanity.

When Lord Uxbridge visited him in his cell, Oxford coolly and impudently asked, 'Is the Queen well?' to which his lordship responded, 'How dare you ask such a question?' The prisoner frankly owned having fired the pistols, which he stated were well loaded. Mr. Fox Maule put in the following deposition, which the misguided youth had voluntarily made and signed at the Home Office :—'A great many witnesses against me. Some say that I shot with my left, others with my right hand. They vary as to the distance. After I fired the first pistol, Prince Albert got up as if he would jump out of the carriage, and sat down again, as if he thought better of it. Then I fired the second pistol. This is all I shall say at present.—EDWARD OXFORD.'

Witnesses were called for the defence to show that a predisposition to insanity existed in the prisoner's mind, and that it was hereditary in his family, his grandfather having died in a lunatic asylum. The prisoner himself, it was shown, had before behaved in an alarming manner. There seemed to be no doubt that Oxford was suffering from insanity, which manifested itself in a morbid desire for notoriety; and the jury found him guilty, at the same time declaring him to be insane. The prisoner, who had remained unmoved during the whole of the proceedings, was ordered to be confined during her Majesty's pleasure.

It seems, perhaps, to have been a great hubbub created over one miserable, crazy youth—addresses, rejoicings, grand processions, and a great State trial; but then even a small pistol and a crazy youth might have been the means of causing a great disaster, and plunging a whole nation into mourning. Little wonder, then, that it should have been plunged into universal rejoicing instead. With regard to the future of Oxford, he was confined first in Bedlam, and then in Dartmoor. He always explained his act as having been prompted by sheer vanity and desire for notoriety. After about thirty-five years' imprisonment he was released on condition that he would go to the Antipodes. Not many years ago he was earning his living as a house-painter in Australia.

Towards the close of the parliamentary session of 1840 a Regency Bill was introduced. The prospect of an heir to the throne rendered it necessary to make provision for her Majesty's possible death or lengthened disqualification for reigning. Both political parties were consulted in the matter, and a Bill was brought forward, providing that Prince Albert should be

Regent in the event of the death of Queen Victoria before her next lineal descendant and successor should have attained the full age of eighteen years. The measure was well received, and, with the exception of a speech made by the Duke of Sussex in the Lords, it passed both Houses unanimously and without objection, and became law.

The daily life of the royal pair has been described in the *Early Years of the Prince Consort*. From the pages of this work we learn that the Queen and Prince breakfasted at nine, and took a walk every morning soon afterwards. When in London these walks were taken in Buckingham Palace gardens, which the Prince had already enlivened with different kinds of animals and aquatic birds. ' In their morning walks in the gardens it was a great amusement to the Prince to watch and feed these birds. He taught them to come when he whistled to them from a bridge connecting a small island with the rest of the gardens.'

After the walk ' came the usual amount of business (far less heavy, however, then than now), besides which they drew and etched a great deal together, which was a source of great amusement, having the plates bit in the house. Luncheon followed at the usual hour of two o'clock. Lord Melbourne, who was generally staying in the house, came to the Queen in the afternoon; and between five and six the Prince usually drove her out in a pony phaeton. If the Prince did not drive the Queen he rode, in which case she drove with the Duchess of Kent or the ladies. The Prince also read aloud most days to the Queen. The dinner was at eight o'clock, and always with the company. In the evening the Prince frequently played at double chess, a game of which he was very fond, and which he played extremely well.' On returning from his rides, which were generally into those London districts where improvements were going on, the Prince ' would always come through the Queen's dressing-room, where she generally was at that time, with that bright loving smile with which he ever greeted her, telling her where he had been, what new buildings he had seen, what studios he had visited.' The practice in English houses for gentlemen to remain alone at the table for a considerable time after dinner was never favourably viewed by the Queen; and in this she had a seconder in her husband, who was a very temperate man, and not addicted to the pleasures of the table. Lord Campbell thus speaks of a royal dinner at which he was present : ' The Queen and the ladies withdrawing, Prince Albert came over to her side of the table, and we remained behind about a quarter of an hour, but we rose within the hour from the time of our sitting down. A snuff-box was twice carried round and offered to all the gentlemen. Prince Albert, to my surprise, took a pinch.'

The Prince made his way with all classes, even with those Tories who at first looked rather askance at him. He was conciliatory and judicious ; and to show the way he had advanced in the public esteem, the remark which Melbourne made to the Queen on the Regency Bill may be quoted : ' Three months ago they would not have done it for him ; it is entirely his own character.' The Duke of Wellington was so completely won over that he remarked : ' Let the Queen put the Prince where she likes, and settle it herself ; that is the best way.' His Grace also made

short work of questions of State etiquette, and when
Lord Albemarle, Master of the Horse, held out about
his right to sit in the Sovereign's coach on State
occasions, he said, on being asked for his opinion :
'The Queen can make Lord Albemarle sit at the top
of the coach, under the coach, behind the coach, or
wherever else her Majesty pleases.'

The Queen prorogued Parliament on the 11th of
August, Prince Albert accompanying her for the first
time. Next day the Court left for Windsor. On
the 26th his Royal Highness attained his majority,
and the event was celebrated by a breakfast at Adelaide
Lodge.   The Prince went to London on the 28th for
the purpose of receiving the freedom of the City. At
this ceremony the names of six aldermen and common
councilmen, who undertook to vouch for the eligibility
of the Prince, were read, together with the declaration
upon oath.   The oath was as follows : 'We declare,
upon the oath we took at the time of our admission to
the freedom of the city, that Prince Albert is of good
name and fame ; that he does not desire the freedom
of this city whereby to defraud the Queen or this city
of any of their rights, customs, or advantages ; but
that he will pay his scot and bear his lot : and so we
all say.'

The Chamberlain then proposed the freeman's oath
to the Prince, and it was remarked that he was
evidently moved at that part where he swore to keep the
peace towards her Majesty.   Husbands do not always
voluntarily swear to keep the peace towards their wives.
The Chamberlain having next addressed his Royal
Highness, the Prince delivered the following answer
very distinctly and audibly : ' It is with the greatest

pleasure that I meet you upon this occasion, and offer you my warmest thanks for the honour which has been conferred upon me by the presentation of the freedom of the City of London. The wealth and intelligence of this vast city have raised it to the highest eminence amongst the cities of the world; and it must therefore ever be esteemed a great distinction to be numbered amongst the members of your ancient Corporation. I shall always remember with pride and satisfaction the day on which I became your fellow-citizen; and it is especially gratifying to me, as marking your loyalty and affection to the Queen.'

Prince Albert was sworn a member of the Privy Council on the 11th of September, and it is stated that so anxious was he to discharge conscientiously every duty which might devolve upon him, that in his retirement at Windsor he set to work to master Hallam's *Constitutional History* with the Queen, and also began the study of English law with a barrister.

Early in November preparations were made at Buckingham Palace for the approaching accouchement of the Queen. The Court removed from Windsor to London on the 13th, and on the 21st the Princess Royal was born at Buckingham Palace at 1.40 P.M. In the Queen's chamber were the Duchess of Kent, Prince Albert, and the medical men, with Mrs. Lilly, the nurse, and some of the ladies of the bedchamber. In an adjoining apartment, the door of which was open, were the Duke of Sussex, the Archbishop of Canterbury, the Bishop of London, the Lord Chancellor, Lord Melbourne, Lord Palmerston, Lord Erroll, Lord Albemarle, Lord John Russell, and other Privy

Councillors, whose constitutional duty it was to be present at the birth of an heir to the throne. At ten minutes before two Mrs. Lilly entered the ante-chamber where the Privy Councillors were assembled, with the 'young stranger'—a beautiful, plump, and healthful princess—wrapped in flannel, in her arms. Sir James Clark followed the nurse. The babe was for a moment laid upon the table, but the loud tones in which she indicated her displeasure at thus being made 'the observed of all observers,' while they proved the soundness of her lungs and the maturity of her frame, rendered it advisable that she should be returned to her chamber to receive her first attire. Prince Albert received the congratulations of all present, and then the officials retired to spread the happy news throughout the metropolis. The Tower guns were fired in honour of the event. According to the gossip of the time, Prince Albert expressed a fear that the people might be disappointed, whereupon the Queen reassured him by saying, 'Never mind; the next shall be a boy,' adding that she hoped she might have as many children as her grandmother, Queen Charlotte. The Queen has recorded the traits of tenderness shown by her husband during her seclu-sion. 'He was content to sit by her in a darkened room, to read to her, and write for her. No one but himself ever lifted her from her bed to her sofa, and he always helped to wheel her on her bed or sofa into the next room. For this purpose he would come instantly when sent for, from any part of the house. His care for her was like that of a mother, nor could there be a kinder, wiser, more judicious nurse.'

On the very day after the birth of the Princess Royal, 'the boy Jones'—who seems to have had a mania for surreptitiously entering Buckingham Palace —was found concealed under a sofa in a room next to the Queen's. It was not the first time he had entered the palace, and when he was questioned as to how he had come there, he impudently replied, ' The same way as before,' adding that he could find his way into the palace at any time he pleased. It was believed that he scaled the garden wall about half way up Constitution Hill, and effected an entrance through one of the windows of the palace. On the last occasion on which he was caught, he was found about 1 A.M. crouched in a recess, with his shoes off, by the police-sergeant on duty in the interior of the palace. The rascally youth boasted that, screened by some article of furniture, he had coolly listened for some time to the conversation of the Queen and her Royal Consort. Jones was taken to the Home Office, but the authorities scarcely knew what to do with him. Being deemed too young for serious punishment, he was committed to the House of Correction, Tothill Fields, as a rogue and vagabond for three months. He behaved remarkably well while in prison. Some time after his release he was induced to become an apprentice for five years on board a vessel bound for Australia, where he learned discipline and became a steady seaman.

The Queen speedily recovered from her accouchement, and opened Parliament in person on the 26th of January 1841. Prince Albert, in the uniform of a field marshal, entered the House of Lords with the royal procession, and took his seat on the chair of

M

State appropriated for him on the left of the throne.
The Queen's speech was not an exciting document.
Happily, affairs were peaceful at home at this time,
though abroad there were wars and rumours of wars.
We were just passing through one of our many difficulties with China ; serious differences had arisen between
Spain and Portugal on the navigation of the Douro ;
and affairs in the Levant were in a serious condition.
England had concluded with Russia, Prussia, Austria,
and Turkey a convention intended to effect a pacifica-
tion of the Levant, to maintain the integrity and
independence of the Ottoman Empire, and thereby to
afford additional security for the peace of Europe.
We had also just concluded treaties with the Argen-
tine Republic and the Republic of Hayti for the sup-
pression of the slave trade.

An accident happened to Prince Albert on the
9th of February, which, but for the Queen's presence
of mind, might have had serious consequences.   His
Royal Highness was skating in Buckingham Palace
Gardens when the ice suddenly gave way, and he was
immersed in deep water.   He had to swim for several
minutes before he was got out.   The Queen was close
by the Prince when the accident occurred, and was
the only person who had sufficient presence of mind
to render him any material assistance.

The christening of the Princess Royal took place
on the 10th, in the throne-room at Buckingham
Palace.   The font, new for the occasion, was very
elegant in form and exquisitely finished.   It was of
silver gilt, elaborately carved with the royal arms, &c.
The water used for the ceremony was brought from
the river Jordan.   The Archbishop of Canterbury

officiated, with the assistance of the Bishops of London and Norwich, and the Dean of Carlisle. The Duke of Wellington appeared as sponsor on behalf of the Duke of Saxe-Coburg and Gotha, and the other sponsors present were the Queen Dowager, the Duchess of Gloucester, the Duchess of Kent, the King of the Belgians, and the Duke of Sussex. Queen Adelaide named the royal infant ' Victoria Adelaide Mary Louisa.' Prince Albert wrote to the Dowager Duchess of Gotha : ' The christening went off very well ; your little great-grand-daughter behaved with great propriety and like a Christian. She was awake, but did not cry at all, and seemed to crow with immense satisfaction at the lights and brilliant uniforms, for she is very intelligent and observing. The ceremony took place at half-past six P.M. ꞏ After it there was a dinner, and then we had some instrumental music. The health of the little one was drank with great enthusiasm.'

The ensuing summer saw the Queen and her husband entering into the pleasures of the people and sharing them with much zest. They listened to the moving declamation of the great French actress, Rachel, and welcomed Adelaide Kemble, who made her first appearance in opera this season. The Queen's influence upon the stage was a healthful and restraining one. As Mrs. Oliphant has observed, she was ' in the foreground of the national life, affecting it always for good, and setting an example of purity and virtue. The theatres to which she went, and which both she and her husband enjoyed, were purified by her presence ; evils which had been the growth of years disappearing before the face of the young Queen.'

The Whig Ministry, having been defeated in the House of Commons by a majority of one, on a vote of want of confidence proposed by Sir Robert Peel, determined to appeal to the country. Parliament was dissolved accordingly, and the elections were held in July. The Conservatives gained a great majority, and when the new Parliament assembled in August, Ministers were placed in a minority of 91 in a House of 629 members. Lord Melbourne and his colleagues consequently resigned office. The Queen's parting with the Premier was a very trying one on both sides. In taking his leave of the Sovereign, Melbourne congratulated her on the great advantage she possessed in the presence and counsel of the Prince, which would have the effect of softening to her the trial of the first change of Ministers in her reign. 'For four years,' added Melbourne, 'I have seen you every day; but it is so different from what it would have been in 1839. The Prince understands everything so well, and has a clever, able head.' This tribute to her husband greatly touched the Queen, who has recorded her regret at parting with 'a faithful and attached friend, as well as Minister.' It was with great pleasure and pride that she listened to Melbourne's praise of her royal husband.

Sir Robert Peel came into power as Prime Minister, and his bearing appears to have been everything that was admirable and judicious. Care had been taken to avoid any such *esclandre* as the 'Bedchamber Plot,' for when it was becoming apparent that a change of Ministry must take place, it was arranged that those of the Queen's ladies whose removal the Tories considered essential, on account of their close relationship to leading Whig Ministers, should voluntarily retire. As the result of this understanding, the Duchess of Bedford, the Duchess of Sutherland, and Lady Normanby resigned their positions as ladies of the bedchamber. A passage in the *Life of the Prince Consort*, referring to the bearing of the new Premier, says: 'Lord Melbourne told Baron Stockmar, who had just returned from Coburg, that Sir Robert Peel had behaved most handsomely, and that the conduct of the Prince throughout had been most moderate and judicious.' All the friction caused by that little matter of Peel's attitude towards the Royal Annuity Bill had entirely passed away from the Prince's mind.

One of the earliest acts of the new Minister was to propose a Fine Arts Commission, with Prince Albert as chairman. Its more immediate object was the superintendence of the artistic work at the new Houses of Parliament. Nothing could have been suggested which would have afforded greater pleasure to the Queen and the Prince than this commission, and the latter spoke of it as his real initiation into public life. It gave him an opportunity to display his taste, and to advance the liberal arts in the country. As to social reforms, it should be stated to the Prince's credit that it was owing to his influence, and that of the Duke of Wellington, that the practice of duelling disappeared from the British army.

There was great rejoicing at Buckingham Palace on the 9th of November 1841, when the Queen gave birth to her first-born son, and consequently the heir to the throne. The Archbishop of Canterbury, the Premier, and all the great officers of State were summoned to the palace as early as seven o'clock in the

morning, and the Duchess of Kent arrived at nine.
The Queen was then very ill, and had been so at
intervals during the two preceding hours.   Prince
Albert manifested the greatest anxiety and interest,
as he remained in attendance with the medical men,
Sir James Clark, Dr. Locock, and Mr. Blagden.
Shortly before eleven o'clock the Prince was born.
He was conveyed by the nurse to the Privy Councillors and others in the adjoining apartment, who there-
upon signed a declaration as to the birth of an heir to
the British Crown.   Intelligence of the happy event
was immediately communicated to all the members of
the Royal Family, including the Queen Dowager, who
was at Sudbury Hall; the Duchess of Cambridge, who
was at Kew; the Princess Sophia, who was at Black-
heath; and the Duchesses of Gloucester and Cambridge,
and the Duke of Cambridge and Prince George, who
were in London.

Official etiquette, usually as strong as the law of
the Medes and Persians, was for once set aside in the
great joy over the birth of a Prince.   It appears that
almost every influential individual in the household of
her Majesty stepped out of his proper sphere, and
gave directions which belonged to the departments of
others.   There was a complete confusion of places for
at least half an hour after the event, and Court officials
rushed hither and thither with the gratifying intelligence of the birth of a Prince; three messengers
arrived at Marlborough House within two minutes, all
desirous of being the first to convey the news to the
Queen Dowager.   An act of royal clemency marked
the happy occasion of the birth of an heir to the
throne.   Her Majesty was pleased to notify to the

Home Secretary that those convicts who had behaved well should have their punishment commuted; and that those deserving this clemency on board the various hulks should have their liberty at once granted to them.   On the 11th of November the Lord Mayor and Lady Mayoress, and the sheriffs, were received at Buckingham Palace.   After having had candle served, the party were conducted by the Lord Chamberlain to the apartments of Prince Albert, to pay a visit of congratulation to his Royal Highness.   The infant Prince was brought into the room in which the company were assembled, and was carried round to all the distinguished visitors present.   The Archbishop of Canterbury issued a special prayer to be offered up in all churches on behalf of the Queen and the infant Prince.

For the post of nurse to the royal child there had been many applications, some being from ladies of wealth and position.   The choice of the Queen fell upon Mrs. Brough, an under-servant at Claremont, who was herself, before her marriage, a housemaid in the establishment.   At the birth of the Princess Royal the previous wet-nurse received £500; but on the birth of the Prince of Wales all the gratuities were doubled.

There was great happiness within the palace.   At Christmas the Queen wrote in her *Journal*: 'To think that we have two children now, and one who enjoys the sight already (the Christmas-tree); it is like a dream.'   Prince Albert, writing to his father, said: 'This is the dear Christmas Eve on which I have so often listened with impatience for your step, which was to convey us into the gift-room.   To-day I have two children of my own to make gifts to, who, they know not why, are full of happy wonder at the German Christmas-tree and its radiant candles.' Her Majesty gives us another sketch of a peaceful 'interior': 'Albert brought in dearest little Pussy (Princess Victoria), in such a smart, white merino dress, trimmed with blue, which mamma had given her, and a pretty cap, and placed her on my bed, seating himself next to her, and she was very dear and good; and as my precious, invaluable Albert sat there, and our little love between us, I felt quite moved with happiness and gratitude to God.' Writing some weeks later to King Leopold, she said: 'I wonder very much whom our little boy will be like. You will understand how fervent are my prayers, and I am sure everybody's must be, to see him resemble his father in every respect, both in mind and body.' And in another letter she remarked: 'We all have our trials and vexations; but if one's home is happy, then the rest is comparatively nothing.'

When the baby Prince was a month old the Queen issued a patent creating 'our most dear son' Prince of Wales and Earl of Chester. He was already Duke of Saxony, Duke of Cornwall and Rothesay, Earl of Carrick, Baron of Renfrew, Lord of the Isles, and Great Steward of Scotland. With regard to his new Welsh dignity the patent ran: 'As has been accustomed, we do ennoble and invest him with the said principality and earldom, by girting him with a sword, by putting a coronet on his head and a gold ring on his finger, and also by delivering a gold rod into his hand, that he may preside there, and may direct and defend those parts.'

The christening of the Prince of Wales, which was
made a very imposing ceremony, took place on the
25th of January 1842 in St. George's Chapel,
Windsor Castle. The King of Prussia had arrived at
the castle three days before, on a visit to the Queen,
and to stand as chief sponsor at the christening. He
was accompanied by the famous *savant*, Baron
Alexander von Humboldt. The Archbishops of
Canterbury and York, and the Bishops of London,
Winchester, Oxford, and Norwich, officiated at the
baptismal ceremony. The sponsors were the King of
Prussia, the Duke of Cambridge, the Duchess of Cambridge (proxy for the Duchess of Saxe-Coburg), and
the Princess Augusta of Cambridge (proxy for the
Princess Sophia). When the infant Prince was
brought in and given into the hands of the Archbishop of Canterbury, the sponsors named him
' Albert Edward,' by which names he was accordingly
christened by his Grace. On the conclusion of the
ceremony the *Hallelujah Chorus* was sung by the
full choir, by request of Prince Albert, and the
overture to Handel's oratorio of *Esther* was performed.
The name of Albert was given to the young Prince,
after his father, and that of Edward, after his maternal
grandfather, the Duke of Kent.

After the christening the Queen held a chapter of
the Order of the Garter, when the King of Prussia,
as ' a lineal descendant of King George I.,' was
elected a Knight Companion, the Queen buckling the
garter round his knee. Then followed luncheon in
the White Breakfast Room, and in the evening there
was a grand banquet in St. George's Hall. The display of plate was amazing, and there was one immense

gold vessel, described as more like a bath than anything else, capable of containing thirty dozens of wine.
To the great surprise of the Prussian visitors, it was
filled with mulled claret.   Four toasts were drank,
which were given by the Lord Steward, the Earl of
Liverpool, in the following order: ' His Royal Highness the Prince of Wales,' 'The King of Prussia,'
' The Queen,' and ' His Royal Highness Prince Albert.'
An immense royal christening cake was placed in the
Waterloo Chamber after the banquet.   The expenses
incurred in connection with the christening ceremony
and the subsequent festivities amounted to about
£200,000.

The Queen paid special honour' and deference to
her august visitor, the King of Prussia.   When she
first met him, on his arrival at Windsor, she kissed
him twice, and made him two low curtseys.   In her
Journal she writes of the King: ' He was in common
morning costume, and complained much of appearing
so before me.   He is entertaining, agreeable, and
witty; tells a thing so pleasantly, and is full of
amusing anecdotes.'   The King was magnificently
entertained during the whole of his stay by the
Queen, and also by many of the leading members of
the aristocracy.   He manifested great interest in the
historic buildings and other sights of London, and
was indefatigable in visiting the chief points of
attraction.

There never was a period in her Majesty's life
when she was more jubilant in spirits, or more
profoundly happy, than this which immediately
succeeded upon the birth of the Prince of Wales.
Supremely blest in the choice she had made of a

husband, she rejoiced to see her royal Consort daily making his way in the affections of the people, and now that there was an heir to the crown, the Sovereign and the people were drawn closely together by a new and auspicious bond. The weight of State cares no longer pressed heavily upon her, and her cup of happiness was full even to overflowing.

CHAPTER V.

THE JOYS AND CARES OF HOME AND STATE.

BUT the year 1842 brought with it many sad episodes. Terrible news came from Afghanistan, where 'the fatal policy of English interference with the fiery tribes of Northern India in support of an unpopular ruler had ended in the murder of Sir Alexander Burnes and Sir William Macnaghten, and the evacuation of Cabul by the English.' Other disasters succeeded, chief amongst which was the destruction of her Majesty's 44th Regiment. The soldiers were cut down almost to a man, and only one individual of the whole British force was able to reach Jellalabad. This was Dr. Brydon, who arrived there, faint and wounded, on the 13th of January. The story of his sufferings, as well as a graphic narrative of the whole campaign, is to be read in the journals of the period. The British army marched through the Khyber Pass, defeated Akbar Khan in the Tezeen Valley, and eventually reached Cabul, when the prisoners, long pent up within that city, were released. Cabul was subsequently evacuated, and Jellalabad was destroyed. The British arms ultimately triumphed, but only after a fearful and bloody campaign, in which many of the finest of our troops were cut off by a harassing guerilla warfare.

As the year opened we were also at war with

China. Fortunately, the uniform success which had attended our previous hostile operations against that Power once more smiled upon our arms, and brought the Celestials to reason. After the taking of Chin-keang-foo by the British, and the appearance of our squadron before Nankin, hostilities were suspended, and negotiations for peace were entered into and concluded between the Chinese Commissioners and Sir Henry Pottinger.

But the condition of things at home was very serious. Not only was there a continuous fall in the revenue, but an ever-growing agitation throughout the country on the subject of the Corn Laws. Loud and general complaints were heard of depression in all the principal branches of trade, accompanied by distress among the poorer classes; and after all allowance had been made for exaggeration there still remained a real and lamentable amount of misery and destitution. Though the people bore their sufferings with exemplary patience and fortitude, there could be no doubt that they were passing through a period of deep trial and privation.

It was not, therefore, without a shadow over her happiness that the Queen opened Parliament in person on the 3rd of February. The ceremony was attended by more than usual pomp and splendour in consequence of the presence of the King of Prussia. Madame Bunsen, who was a spectator of the scene in the House of Lords, wrote: 'The opening of Parliament was the thing from which I expected most, and I was not disappointed. The throngs in the streets, in the windows, in every place people could stand upon, all looking so pleased; the splendid Horse Guards, the

Grenadiers of the Guard, of whom might be said as
the King said on another occasion, "An appearance
so fine, you know not how to believe it true;" the
Yeomen of the Bodyguard; then in the House of
Lords, the peers in their robes, the beautifully dressed
ladies with very many beautiful faces; lastly, the procession of the Queen's entry, and herself, looking
worthy and fit to be the converging point of so many
rays of grandeur. It is self-evident that she is not
tall, but were she ever so tall, she could not have
more grace and dignity, a head better set, a throat
better arching; and one advantage there is in her
looks when she casts a glance, being of necessity cast
up and not down, that the effect of the eyes is not
lost, and they have an effect both bright and pleasing.
The composure with which she filled the throne while
awaiting the Commons I much admired; it was a
test—no fidget, no apathy. Then her voice and
enunciation cannot be more perfect. In short, it
could not be said that she *did well*, but that she was *the
Queen*—she was, and felt herself to be, the descendant
of her ancestors. Stuffed in by her Majesty's mace-
bearers, and peeping over their shoulders, I was
enabled to struggle down the emotions I felt at
thinking what mighty pages in the world's history
were condensed in the words so impressively uttered
by that soft and feminine voice : peace and war, the
fate of millions, relations and exertions of power felt
to the extremities of the globe : alterations of corn
laws, birth of a future Sovereign : with what should it
close but the heartfelt aspiration, God bless her, and
guide her for her sake, and the sake of all.'

From the throne to the home is but a step. The

Queen and Prince Albert were profoundly interested in March by the news of the approaching marriage of Prince Ernest to the Princess Alexandrina of Baden. Writing to King Leopold on the subject, her Majesty said: 'My heart is full, very full, of this marriage; it brings back so many recollections of our dear betrothal—as Ernest was with us all the time, and longed for similar happiness. I have entreated Ernest to pass his honeymoon with us, and I beg you to urge him to do it, for *he* witnessed *our* happiness, and *we must therefore witness his.*' Prince Albert much wished to go over to Carlsruhe for the wedding, which took place on the 3rd of May, but he felt that he could not leave the Queen at this anxious time. The prevalent distress, which led to rioting in the English and Scotch mining districts, the agitation on the subject of the Corn Laws, the fears of a Chartist rising, and the unsettled condition of affairs abroad, all impelled him to remain by the side of her Majesty, and amongst the people whose sufferings he was anxious to alleviate.

On the 12th of May the Queen gave a grand *bal masqué* at Buckingham Palace, which is spoken of as 'the Queen's Plantagenet Ball.' The object of the ball was to endeavour to give a stimulus to trade in London, which had gradually been getting worse. At the Palace on this brilliant occasion a past age was revived with great picturesqueness and splendour. Her Majesty appeared as Queen Philippa, consort of Edward III., and Prince Albert as Edward III. himself; the costumes of those of the Queen's own circle belonging mostly to the same era. Fabulous sums were spent upon dresses, diamonds, and jewels, which

could hardly have a direct effect upon the trade of the
East-end, though they undoubtedly did upon that of
the West.   Her Majesty's dress, however, was entirely
composed of materials manufactured at Spitalfields.
In her crown she had only one diamond, but that was
a treasure in itself, being valued at £10,000.   The
leading feature of the ball, according to the journals
of the day, was the assemblage and meeting of the
Courts of Anne of Brittany (the Duchess of Cambridge)
and Edward III. and Philippa.   All the arrangements
were made in exact accordance with the period.
Amongst those representing distinguished characters
were the Princess Augusta of Cambridge as Princess
Claude, the Duke of Beaufort as Louis XII., the Earl
of Pembroke as the Comte d'Angoulême, Prince
George of Cambridge as Gaston de Foix,the Marchioness
of Ailesbury as the Duchesse de Ferrare, Lord Cardigan as Bayard, Lady Exeter as Jeanne de Conflans,
Lord Claud Hamilton as the Comte de Chateau-
briand, and Lady Lincoln as Anne de Villeroi.   There
were French, German, Italian, Scotch, Greek, and
Russian quadrilles, as well as a Crusaders' quadrille
led by the Marchioness of Londonderry, and a
Waverley quadrille, led by the Countess De-la-Warr.
Subsequently there were dancing reels, Russian
mazurkas, &c.

   Some other characters in this famous historic scene
must be mentioned.   There were the Duchess of
Beaufort as Isabella of Valois, Queen of Spain; Lady
Clementina Villiers as Vittoria Colonna; the Ladies
Frances and Alexandrina Vane as Rowena and Queen
Berengaria; the Countess of Chesterfield as Donna
Florinda; the Countess of Westmorland as Joan

Beaufort, daughter of John of Gaunt; Earl De-la-Warr in the armour of his ancestor as worn at the battle of Crecy; the Earl of Warwick as Thomas Beauchamp, Earl of Warwick, England's Marshal-General at the battle of Poictiers; the Duke of Norfolk as Queen Elizabeth's Earl Marshal; the Duke of Roxburghe as David Bruce, the captive King of Scotland; Mr. Monckton Milnes (Lord Houghton) as the poet Chaucer; and Sir E. Bulwer Lytton in an anonymous dress of dark velvet slashed with white satin.

About a fortnight after this pageant a grand ball was given in her Majesty's Theatre for the benefit of the Spitalfields weavers, at which the Queen was present with a brilliant circle. Fancy balls were also given at Stafford House and Apsley House for the same charitable object.

Two daring attempts to assassinate the Queen were made this year, within a few weeks of each other. The first was by a man named John Francis. Towards seven o'clock on the evening of May 30, her Majesty and party were proceeding down Constitution Hill. When about halfway down, the would-be assassin Francis was seen to take a pistol from his side, and to fire it in the direction of the royal carriage, from which he was distant not more than seven feet. The Queen manifested her usual courageous demeanour under the outrage. Francis was immediately seized by Private Allen, of the Fusilier Guards, and Police Constable Turner, who was attempting to dash the pistol out of his hand when the shot was fired. The culprit was taken to the lodge adjoining the Palace, where he was searched; and a ball, with a little

N

powder, and the still warm pistol, were taken from his person. The man maintained a dogged silence as to his motive, and refused to give any explanation about his antecedents; but it was subsequently ascertained that he was the son of a machinist in Drury Lane Theatre, and had for some months been out of employment. When the news of the outrage reached the Houses of Parliament, both Lords and Commons adjourned in confusion, as it was found impossible to carry on the public business amidst the excitement which the attempt occasioned.

All concurrent accounts speak of the admirable bravery and presence of mind of the Queen. It appears that on the previous Sunday, while the Queen and Prince were driving along the Mall, having been to service at the Chapel Royal, St. James's, Prince Albert saw a man step out of the crowd of cheering spectators and present a pistol at him. Happily, the pistol did not go off, and the Queen, who was bowing to the people on the other side, neither heard nor saw anything. As the Prince's own knowledge of the attempt was corroborated by an independent witness, her Majesty was apprised of the occurrence. The Prince, in afterwards writing to his father, said that both he and the Queen were naturally much agitated, and that his wife had become nervous and unwell. Her Majesty's doctor desired her to continue going out, however. The Queen herself was strongly in favour of this. She 'never could have existed,' she herself said afterwards, ' under the uncertainty of a concealed attack. She would much rather run the immediate risk at any time than have the presentiment of danger constantly hovering over her.' But with that generous consideration which has always distinguished her, she would not permit her female attendants to accompany her, in accordance with the usual practice, on her dangerous drive. Lady Bloomfield, who was then Miss Liddell, one of the maids-of-honour in waiting, has described how her Majesty's attendants waited at home all the afternoon, expecting a summons, which never came, to go the usual drive. The Queen went out with the Prince alone, and when they came back the news of the dastardly attempt spread through the palace. To Miss Liddell her royal mistress said : ' I dare say, Georgy, you were surprised at not driving with me this afternoon, but the fact was, that as we returned from church yesterday a man presented a pistol at the carriage window, which flashed in the pan ; we were so taken by surprise that he had time to escape ; so I knew what was hanging over me, and I was determined to expose no life but my own.' The Queen and her husband had driven out by Hampstead, being warmly cheered along the route, and had nearly accomplished the return journey, when between the Green Park and the garden wall, and just opposite to where Oxford had made his attempt two years before, the miscreant Francis, who was lying in wait, fixed his pistol, being then about five or seven paces off. The Prince at once recognized the man as the same ' little swarthy ill-looking rascal ' who had made the abortive attempt on the preceding day.

' We felt as if a load had been taken off our hearts,' wrote the Prince when all was safely overpast, ' and we thanked the Almighty for having preserved us a second time from so great a danger.' The Duchess of

N 2

Kent was deeply affected when she met the Queen at the palace after the affair. Falling upon her daughter's neck, she burst into tears, and the Queen ' endeavoured to reassure her with cheerful words and affectionate caresses.' As for the Sovereign lady herself, she soon recovered her wonted equanimity, and writing to King Leopold on the following day, she said : ' I was really not at all frightened, and feel very proud at dear uncle Mensdorff calling me "very courageous," which I shall ever remember with peculiar pride, coming from so distinguished an officer as he is.' It may be stated that the ' uncle Mensdorff' here mentioned was a private gentleman, a French *émigré*, who became a distinguished officer in the Austrian service, and who married the Duchess of Kent's eldest sister.

Her Majesty attended the Royal Italian Opera on the evening of the attempt, desirous of showing herself as early as possible to her subjects. There was a scene of extraordinary enthusiasm, and the National Anthem was performed to the accompaniment of repeated bursts of cheering. On the following day congratulatory addresses were voted by both Houses of Parliament to the Queen on her escape from assassination ; and numerous similar addresses were subsequently forwarded by corporate bodies throughout the kingdom. At Windsor, on the 13th of June, the Queen received an address of congratulation from the Eton boys ; and she and the Prince were enthusiastically cheered on leaving the Castle for London by the scholars, who had assembled on the Mount. The journey to London on this occasion was the first which the Queen had made by railway, and the time occupied in travelling from Slough to Paddington was twenty-five minutes.

The trial of John Francis for shooting at the Queen took place on June 17th, when the prisoner was found guilty and sentenced to death. On the conclusion of Chief Justice Tindall's address, Francis fell insensible into the arms of one of the turnkeys, and in that state was carried out of the court. The Queen directed a reprieve of the sentence, although she was 'fully conscious of the encouragement to similar attempts which might follow from such leniency.' The death sentence on Francis was commuted to transportation for life, and he was sent out to Tasmania.

On the very day following this noble exercise of the royal clemency—that is, Sunday the 3rd of July—another daring attempt was made to shoot the Queen. It occurred while she was driving to the Chapel Royal, St. James's, accompanied by her uncle the King of the Belgians. A deformed youth, named John William Bean, levelled a pistol at the Queen and attempted to fire it. The pistol was loaded, but very fortunately did not go off. The hunchback was seized by a youth named Dassett, but the police at first treated the thing as a joke. But when Dassett was in danger of being arrested as the actual culprit, witnesses came forward who proved the real state of the case. The pistol was found to contain only powder, paper, and some bits of a tobacco-pipe, rammed together. It was also discovered that Bean, who was a chemist's assistant, had written a letter to his father stating that he 'would never see him again, as he intended doing something which was not dishonest, but desperate.'

The Queen had no knowledge of Bean's attempt until her return to the palace, and when apprised of it she betrayed no alarm, but said ' she had expected a repetition of the attempts on her life so long as the law remained unaltered by which they could be dealt with only as acts of high treason.' In the *Life of the Prince Consort* we read: ' Sir Robert Peel hurried up from Cambridge, on hearing what had occurred, to consult with the Prince as to the steps to be taken. During this interview her Majesty entered the room, when the Minister, in public so cold and self-controlled, in reality so full of genuine feeling, out of his very manliness, was unable to control his emotion, and burst into tears.'

Although a hare-brained love of notoriety had quite as much to do with these attempts as any desire to kill, it had now become absolutely necessary to pass some law to meet such alarming offences against the person of the Sovereign. Accordingly, on the 12th of July the Premier introduced a Bill into Parliament making attempts on the Queen's life punishable as high misdemeanours by transportation for seven years, or imprisonment, with or without hard labour, for a period not exceeding three years. Further, the culprit was to be publicly or privately whipped as often and in such manner and form as the court should direct, not exceeding thrice. This measure became law on the 16th. Bean was brought to trial on the 25th of August following, at the Central Criminal Court. The pistol having missed fire, the capital charge was abandoned, and the hunchback was tried for misdemeanour. He was convicted upon this charge, and Lord Abinger sentenced him to eighteen months' imprisonment in Newgate.

To the anxiety caused by these dastardly attempts upon the life of the Sovereign succeeded a sad incident which caused deep grief to the Queen and her husband. On the 13th of July intelligence was received in London to the effect that the Duke of Orleans, while riding in his carriage, was suddenly thrown from it and killed on the spot. Her Majesty was much affected on receiving this deplorable news, and wrote an autograph letter of condolence to the Royal Family of France. This illustrious house and our own were connected by many ties, three members of the Coburg family—the near relatives of Queen Victoria and Prince Albert—having married three members of the French Royal Family. Her Majesty thus gave utterance to her own grief for the Queen Louise and for the young widow—a highly-cultured but physically weak German princess: ' My poor dearest Louise, how my heart bleeds for her! I know how she loved poor Chartres (the earlier title of the Duc d'Orleans), and deservedly, for he was so noble and good. All our anxiety now is to hear how poor dear frail Hélène (the Duchesse d'Orleans) has borne this too dreadful loss. She loved him so, and he was so devoted to her.'

But the time was not all sorrowful. Amongst the lighter and happier episodes of the summer of 1842 were the two visits of Mendelssohn, the celebrated composer, to the Queen and Prince Albert at Buckingham Palace. A most interesting and graphic account of the second visit was given by Mendelssohn himself, in a letter to his mother, and this account we reproduce :—

' I must tell you all the details of my last visit to Buckingham Palace. It is, as G. says, the one really pleasant and thoroughly comfortable English house where one feels *à son aise*. Of course, I do know a few others; but yet on the whole I agree with him. Joking apart, Prince Albert had asked me to go to him on Saturday at two o'clock, so that I might try his organ before I left England. I found him alone, and as we were walking away the Queen came in, also alone, in a simple morning dress. She said she was obliged to leave for Claremont in an hour; and then, suddenly interrupting herself, exclaimed: " But, goodness ! what a confusion ! " for the wind had littered the whole room, and even the pedals of the organ (which, by the way, made a very pretty feature in the room), with leaves of music from a large portfolio that lay open. As she spoke she knelt down and began picking up the music. Prince Albert helped, and I too was not idle. Then Prince Albert proceeded to explain the stops to me, and she said that she would meanwhile put things straight.

' I begged that the Prince would first play me something, so that, as I said, I might boast about it in Germany; and he played a chorale by heart, with the pedals, so charmingly and clearly and correctly, that it would have done credit to any professional; and the Queen, having finished her work, came and sat by him, and listened and looked pleased. Then it was my turn, and I began my chorus from *St. Paul*, " How lovely are the messengers." Before I got to the end of the first verse, they both joined in the chorus; and all the time Prince Albert managed the stops for me so cleverly—first a flute, at the *forte*

the great organ, at the D major part of the whole;
then he made a lovely *diminuendo* with the stops, and
so on to the end of the piece, and all by heart, that
I was really quite enchanted. Then the young
Prince of Gotha came in, and there was more
chatting; and the Queen asked if I had written any
new songs, and said she was very fond of singing my
published ones. " You should sing one to him," said
Prince Albert; and after a little begging she said she
would try the *Frühlingslied* in B flat—" if it is still
here," she added, " for all my music is packed up for
Claremont." Prince Albert went to look for it, but
came back saying it was already packed. " But one
might perhaps unpack it," said I. " We must send
for Lady ——," she said. (I did not catch the
name.) So the bell was rung, and the servants were
sent after it, but without success; and at last the
Queen went herself, and while she was gone Prince
Albert said to me: " She begs you will accept this
present as a remembrance," and gave me a little case
with a beautiful ring, on which is engraved—" V. R.
1842."

'Then the Queen came back and said: " Lady
—— is gone, and has taken all my things with her.
It really is most annoying." (You can't think how
that amused me.) I then begged that I might not
be made to suffer for the accident, and hoped she
would sing another song. After some consultation
with her husband, he said, " She will sing you something of Glück's."

'Meanwhile, the Princess of Gotha had come in;
and we five proceeded through various corridors and
rooms to the Queen's sitting-room, where there was a

gigantic rocking-horse standing near the sofa, and two big bird-cages, and pictures on the walls, and bound books on the table—music on the piano. The Duchess of Kent came in too ; and while they were all talking I rummaged about amongst the music, and soon discovered my first set of songs. So, of course, I begged her rather to sing one of those than the Glück, to which she very kindly consented ; and which did she choose ?—" *Schöner und Schöner schmückt sich !* "—sang it quite charmingly, in strict time and tune, and with very good execution. Only in the line " *Der Prosa Lasten und Müh,*" where it goes down to D, and comes up again chromatically, she sang D sharp each time ; and as I gave her the note both times, the last time she sang D, and there it ought to have been D sharp. But with the exception of this little mistake, it was really charming, and the last long G I have never heard better or purer or more natural from any amateur. Then I was obliged to confess that Fanny had written the song (which I found very hard, but pride must have a fall), and begged her to sing one of my own also. If I would give her plenty of help, she would gladly try, she said ; and then she sang the *Pilgerspruch, " Lass dich nurr,"* really quite faultlessly, and with charming feeling and expression.

' I thought to myself, one must not pay too many compliments on such an occasion ; so I merely thanked her a great many times, upon which she said : " Oh, if only I had not been so frightened ; generally I have such long breath." Then I praised her heartily, and with the best conscience in the world ; for just that part with the long G at the close she had done so well, taking the three following and connecting notes in the same breath, as one seldom hears it done ; and therefore it amused me doubly that she herself should have begun about it.

'After this Prince Albert sang the *Arndte-lied*, " *Es ist ein Schnitter ;* " and then he said I must play him something before I went, and gave me as themes the chorale which he had played on the organ and the song he had just sung. If everything had gone as usual, I ought to have improvised most dreadfully badly—for it is almost always like that with me when I want it to go well—and then I should have gone away vexed the whole morning. But—just as if I was to keep nothing but the pleasantest, most charming recollection of it—I never improvised better. I was in the best mood for it, and played a long time, and enjoyed it myself ; so that between the two themes I brought in the songs that the Queen had sung, naturally enough ; and it all went off so easily that I would gladly not have stopped ; and they followed me with so much intelligence and attention that I felt more at ease than I ever did in improvising to an audience. She said several times she hoped I would soon come to England again and pay them a visit ; and then I took leave. And down below I saw the beautiful carriages waiting, with their scarlet outriders ; and in a quarter of an hour the flag was lowered, and the *Court Circular* announced : " Her Majesty left the palace at twenty minutes past three." And I went off in the rain to the Klingemanns, and had the double pleasure of pouring out all my news to them and to Cécile.

'I must add that I begged the Queen to allow me

to dedicate my A minor Symphony to her, as that had really been the inducement to my journey, and because the English name on the Scotch piece would look doubly well.   Also I forgot to tell you how, just as she was going to begin to sing, she said, " But the parrot must go out first, or he will screech louder than I shall sing."   Upon which Prince Albert rang the bell ; and the Prince of Gotha said he would carry it out ; and I said, " Allow me," and carried the great cage out, to the astonishment of the servants.'

I have given this lengthy extract, because nothing can better illustrate or show forth the inner domestic life of the Queen and her husband.   Such glimpses as these are deeply interesting, as everything must be which tends to reveal the personal and human aspects of a monarch's nature.   We like to see and to feel that they are moved by the same emotions and aspirations as ourselves.   It is not mere curiosity which prompts this, but a feeling of kinship between the highest and the lowest of the sons and daughters of humanity.

Her Majesty's first visit to Scotland—the land for which she afterwards came to entertain such affection—was paid in the year 1842.   On the 29th of August the Queen and Prince Albert, accompanied by the Duchess of Norfolk and the Earl of Morton, as lady and lord in waiting, and other members of the household, embarked at Woolwich in the *Royal George* yacht, commanded by Lord Adolphus Fitzclarence.   When her Majesty arrived off Tilbury Fort—a place associated with the name of her illustrious predecessor, Queen Elizabeth—she was received with a royal salute from the guns of the fortress, and the troops in the garrison were drawn out and presented arms. The scene on the Gravesend shore, where considerable numbers of spectators had assembled, was very animated. The royal squadron was received with loud cheers as it passed, the Gravesend steamers hoisted their flags, and the different bands played 'God Save the Queen,' until the royal yacht was out of sight. It appears from the *Annual Register* that during the progress of the squadron to the North every tower and beacon along the coast vied in demonstrations of loyalty. The Mayor of Ipswich, with a party, came forth in a steamer to offer his obeisance; but the authorities of Sunderland, in the exuberance of their loyal feelings, were a day too early. Off Berwick, the *Modern Athens* of Dundee was the first Scotch vessel to welcome the Sovereign. She was shortly followed by other steamers, and all fired a royal salute in welcome. The Queen came on deck, and acknowledged the enthusiastic greetings of her Scottish subjects, who were delighted to see her wearing a Scotch shawl of Paisley make. The royal fleet entered the Firth of Forth about midnight on the 31st, and anchored for the night on the north side of the island of Inchkeith.

At nine on the morning of September 1st the Queen landed at Granton Pier, and proceeded direct to Dalkeith Palace, the splendid seat of the Duke of Buccleuch. The civic authorities of Edinburgh, who did not anticipate so early an arrival, were not prepared for her Majesty's reception. At night the city was brilliantly illuminated. As the royal visit to the Scottish capital was one of national importance, Edinburgh presented a spectacle such as had never

before been witnessed. An immense concourse of
people gathered together from all parts of the country,
journeying by steamer, rail, and stage-coach, while
some trudged on foot from the remotest districts of
the North.

The Queen, who had suffered severely from sea-
sickness during the latter part of her voyage, had
entirely recovered her health by the morning of the
2nd, and took a drive in the direction of Dalhousie
and Melville castles. Prince Albert, with the Duke of
Buccleuch, ascended Arthur's Seat.

Her Majesty yielded to the desire for a State procession through Edinburgh, which accordingly took
place on the 3rd. Having taken the city, as it were,
by surprise on her first entry, this new arrangement
was made to meet the wishes of the people, and to
compensate the civic authorities for their disappointment of the 1st, when they were unable to give
the Queen that right royal reception they had prepared
for her. The State procession was of a most successful
and gratifying character, and was described with great
circumstantiality of detail in all the Scotch and
English papers.

The Queen set out from Dalkeith Palace about half-
past ten o'clock A.M. Around her carriage were the
Royal Company of Archers. Her Majesty wore a
tartan plaid of the Royal Stuart pattern. As the
Queen entered the precincts of the royal grounds a
salute was fired from the Castle. Amidst the loud
cheers of the people the procession moved up the
Canongate and the High Street to the Cross, where
the city barrier was erected. Here the magistracy
were assembled to present the keys of the city to the

Sovereign, and the crowd was excessive. There were also drawn up at this spot the members of the Celtic Society, in the full costume of their respective clans. They saluted the Queen with their claymores in true Highland fashion, and her Majesty made a gracious acknowledgment. The society then formed in the rear of the royal *cortége*, and escorted her Majesty to the Castle. The procession halted in front of the Royal Exchange, about fifty yards from the barrier, where the Lord Provost advanced, and after delivering a brief address, presented the keys of the city to her Majesty.

The Queen, after receiving the keys, replied, with much dignity mingled with kindness of manner : ' I return the keys of the city with perfect confidence into the safe keeping of the Lord Provost, magistrates, and council.'

The procession then resumed its course up the High Street and Lawnmarket. On entering the esplanade of the Castle her Majesty was received by the Commander of the Forces, Sir Niel Douglas. Escorted by the Governor and the Fort Major, on either side, and holding the arm of her husband, her Majesty—followed by Sir Robert Peel, the Earl of Aberdeen, the Earl of Liverpool, the Duke and Duchess of Buccleuch, the Duchess of Norfolk, the Duke and Duchess of Argyll, and others—walked up the shelving slopes and through the narrow passages which lead to the upper part of the famous fortress, and proceeded to view all that it contained of novelty and interest. She seemed gratified and surprised at the sight of the celebrated gun, ' Mons Meg,' whose fortunes she appeared perfectly well acquainted with.

After viewing the magnificent scene over the Firth of Forth from the Mortar Battery, the Queen proceeded to the Half-moon Battery, and thence to the Old Barrack Square. The Crown Jewel Office was next visited, where are deposited the regalia of Scotland, which, after being lost for a long period, were recovered in 1818, chiefly through the instrumentality of Sir Walter Scott. Her Majesty was much interested in the insignia. Queen Mary's rooms were now visited, and here the Queen was accompanied by Prince Albert only. The chamber in which King James was born her Majesty regarded with special interest.

Everything of historical interest having been viewed, the Queen returned to the Castle gate, where she again entered her carriage. Amidst the loud cheering of the multitude she drove down the Castle Hill. In Bank Street there was a dense mass of spectators, and a serious accident occurred owing to the sudden rush of the crowd upon the extensive temporary gallery which had been erected at the foot of the Mound, within the railing at the northernmost angle of the East Princes Street Gardens. Shortly after the royal procession had passed the wooden structure gave way with a loud crash, and fifty persons were injured, two of them fatally. In Princes Street and Queensferry Street the crowd was enormous: thousands who could find no situation from whence a sight of the Sovereign could be obtained quickly traversed the road through which her Majesty was to pass until they were fortunate enough to meet with a coign of vantage.

Sir Thomas Dick Lauder has preserved some of the humorous incidents of the Queen's entry into Edin-

burgh in his memorial of the Sovereign's first visit to
Scotland. He states that on Castle Hill an elderly
woman succeeded by a *coup de main et de force* in
making her way past the guards; and having most
unceremoniously passed through the party in attendance on her Majesty, she exclaimed in a convulsive
state of excitement : ' Oh, will ye no let me see the
Queen ? ' The military pushed her back, but she was ·
not to be so easily beaten. She again squeezed forward until she stood within a yard of the royal
carriage. ' Hech, sirs ! ' she exclaimed, clasping her
hands, ' is that the Queen—is that the Queen ?
Weel, what have I no seen this day ? Eh ! but she's
a bonnie leddie ! ' The poor woman had not only
seen the Queen, but she was gratified by the Queen's
recognition of herself. Another anecdote is told in
illustration of the Queen's quickness of observation
and condescension on all such public occasions. A
gentleman who lived near Edinburgh said to his
servant on the evening of the Queen's first visit to the
city, ' Well, John, did you see the Queen ? ' ' Troth
did I that, sir.' ' Well, what did you think of her,
John ? ' ' Troth, sir, I was terrible feared afore she
came forrit—my heart was amaist in my mouth ; but
whan she did come forrit, od, I wasna feared at a' ;
I jist looked at her, an' she lookit at me, an' she
bowed her heid to me, an' I bowed my heid to her.
Od, she's a raal fine leddie, wi' fient a bit o' pride
aboot her at a'.'

On leaving Edinburgh, the royal party proceeded to
Dalmeny Park, where the Earl of Rosebery—the predecessor of the young statesman who now bears that
title—had provided a sumptuous luncheon. It had

O

been arranged that after the *déjeuner* the Queen should walk in the grounds which command a view of the Forth, the islands which stud it, and the heights beyond; but the rain fell heavily. A great multitude of persons had assembled on the lawn, however, undeterred by the weather; and in order not to disappoint them, her Majesty went to the library, whose windows opened upon the lawn, and advancing to the open window remained there for some time amidst the most enthusiastic demonstrations of loyalty. In the afternoon the Queen and Prince Albert left Dalmeny Park for Dalkeith, passing through Leith, which was *en fête*, and where her Majesty stopped to receive a civic address.

While the Queen had been viewing Edinburgh Castle, the foundation-stone of the Victoria Hall, and the buildings erected for the accommodation of the General Assembly, was laid by Lord Frederick Fitzclarence, Acting Grand Master Mason of Scotland, accompanied by the Earl of Buchan, Acting Depute, with the members of the Grand Lodge, and about 300 brethren of other lodges.

Sunday, the 4th of September, being the first Lord's Day which the Queen had spent in Scotland, her Majesty at noon attended divine service in a chapel in Dalkeith Palace, fitted up expressly for the use of the Royal Family and suite. The Rev. E. B. (afterwards Dean) Ramsay, of St. John's Episcopal Church, Edinburgh, officiated. A little ecclesiastical war followed upon this circumstance in the newspapers. The Presbyterians were greatly dissatisfied because her Majesty did not attend the Church of Scotland, and it was some time before their angry feelings were allayed. The arrangements for the Queen were made without any ' malice aforethought,' however ; and the Ministers ·in attendance upon her—Sir Robert Peel and the Earls of Aberdeen and Liverpool—did attend divine service in the parish church.

On the 5th her Majesty held a *levée* in Dalkeith Palace, which was attended by an extraordinary concourse of the nobility and gentry of Scotland. Holyrood House could not be used on the occasion, because of a contagious fever lately prevalent in the vicinity. The Queen received a number of deputations, including one from the Church of Scotland, and in replying to the address of the latter she said : ' I acknowledge with gratitude the inestimable advantages which have been derived from the ministrations of the Church of Scotland. They have contributed in an eminent degree to form the character of a loyal and religious people.' Addresses were also presented from the Universities of Edinburgh, Glasgow, St. Andrews, and Aberdeen, and from the Lord Provost and magistrates of Edinburgh.

The remainder of the Queen's Scotch visit was thoroughly enjoyed by the Sovereign and her husband. On the 6th they left Dalkeith and went to Queensferry, where they embarked in a royal steamer. Landing at North Ferry, in Fifeshire, they proceeded to Dupplin Castle, where they dined with the Earl of Kinnoull. The Lord Provost and town council of Perth attended to present an address, and subsequently her Majesty drove into Perth, where a handsome triumphal arch of Grecian architecture had been erected in honour of her visit. The Queen dined

and slept at Scone Palace, the seat of the Earl of
Mansfield. Next morning, at the solicitation of the
authorities of Perth, the Queen and Prince enrolled
their names in the Guildry Books, in imitation of the
precedents therein contained of King James VI. and
King Charles I. The following were the inscriptions :—

Dieu et Mon Droit.
VICTORIA R.
Scone Palace,
September 7th, 1842.

Treu und Fest.
ALBERT.
Scone Palace,
September 7th, 1842.

Taymouth Castle, the seat of the Marquis of Breadalbane, was next visited, and her Majesty's stay here
was rendered full of interest. She was received at
Dunkeld by a gallant array of Lord Glenlyon's clans-
men, 1000 in number ; and alighting from her
carriage she walked round the Green, witnessing the
performance of the Highland reel and other national
dances. On the approach to Taymouth Castle a
striking display was made of fine, tall Highlanders in
their national costume ; and in passing through the
park her Majesty accosted the Marquis with the
remark : ' Keeper, what a quantity of fine High-
landmen you have got ! ' A magnificent display of
fireworks greeted the Queen's arrival ; and the evening was passed in the exhibition of Highland
dancing on a platform formed under the windows of
the Castle.

Prince Albert was entertained on the 8th to a deer-stalking expedition, in which 150 men were engaged. The Prince was the only person who fired, and he killed nineteen roe-deer, besides several brace of grouse and other game. The Queen occupied herself in walking through the gardens of the Castle. She also visited the dairy, and, to the surprise and delight of the woman in charge, had some milk and a piece of bread. The amusements were continued on the 9th; and in the evening a ball was given, which her Majesty opened with the Duke of Buccleuch and the Prince with the Duchess.

On the 10th, previously to leaving Taymouth Castle, the Queen planted a fir and an oak tree in the grounds as a memorial of her visit. The royal party then embarked on Loch Tay, and were rowed up to Auchmore, a distance of sixteen miles. 'As the barges and boats proceeded slowly and majestically up the loch, they exhibited to the spectators a very beautiful sight. The surrounding scenery also was very grand; and its enjoyment, on the part of royalty, was enhanced by the singing of Gaelic songs by the boatmen, with which the Queen appeared to be highly pleased. Her Majesty landed at Auchmore; and after partaking of luncheon in the Marquis of Breadalbane's cottage, resumed the journey to Crieff, the drive to which—passing by Killin, Glen Ogle, Loch Earn, St. Fillans, and Comrie—was through very wild and romantic mountain scenery.' The party reached Drummond Castle at seven o'clock in the evening. Here the Queen was most cordially received by Lord and Lady Willoughby d'Eresby, whose guest she was.

A picturesque scene took place on the 12th, when a

hundred Highlanders in the Drummond tartan, some armed with Lochaber axes, others with swords and bucklers, paraded before her Majesty. An old man known as Comrie of Comrie, who claimed to be hereditary standard-bearer of the Perth family, displayed the very flag which was rescued by his great-uncle, after it had been taken by King George's troops at the battle of Culloden; and he also wore the same claymore which did service on that occasion. Early on the morning of the 13th the Queen and Prince Albert left Drummond Castle on their return south. On reaching the estate of Viscount Strathallan, her Majesty passed under a beautiful arch, over which was inscribed the words: 'Adieu! fair daughter of Strathearn'—an allusion to the title of the Queen's father as Duke of Kent and Strathearn.

At Stirling, an interesting incident occurred. The Provost, in receiving her Majesty, informed her that he had the honour to serve under the Duke of Kent for twenty-four years. The Queen was quite delighted, and replied: 'It gives me great satisfaction to meet, in the Provost of this town, one who has served under my revered father.' After visiting Stirling Castle, the royal party went on to Falkirk, and from thence pursued their journey towards Edinburgh, passing on the way the fine old ruin of Niddry Castle, the retreat of Mary Queen of Scots on her escape from Loch Leven. Her Majesty and the Prince Consort reached Dalkeith Palace at six o'clock, after a very fatiguing day.

It is mentioned as illustrating the accuracy with which the Queen's progress was carried out as regards time, that although no fewer than 656 horses were engaged in conveying her Majesty and suite to and from Taymouth Castle, with the exception of five minutes lost at Linlithgow, not the slightest delay occurred.

The freedom of the City of Edinburgh was conferred on the Prince Consort on the 14th, and Dr. Lee, Principal of the University of Edinburgh, also delivered to his Royal Highness the diploma of an honorary LL.D., conferred by the Senatus Academicus. The Queen and Prince subsequently drove to Roslin. The beautiful and perfect architecture of the chapel filled them, as it must fill every one, with astonishment and admiration. The royal party then drove round to Hawthornden and viewed the romantic scenery of the glen from the remains of the Castle. The Queen and the Prince remained for some time at the Poet's Seat, and next viewed with great interest the celebrated plane-tree under which the poet Drummond and Ben Jonson had met 250 years previously. The royal visitors went over the Castle and grounds, and then returned to Dalkeith Palace.

The Queen was so deeply impressed with the heartiness of her reception by all classes of her Northern subjects, that before leaving Scotland she caused the Earl of Aberdeen to write the following letter, in which she gave expression to her gratified feelings: 'The Queen cannot leave Scotland without a feeling of regret that her visit on the present occasion could not be further prolonged. Her Majesty fully expected to witness the loyalty and attachment of her Scottish subjects; but the devotion and enthusiasm evinced in every quarter, and by all ranks, have produced an impression on the mind of her Majesty which can never be effaced.'

Her Majesty quitted Scotland on the morning of the 15th of September, after a stay of exactly a fortnight in the Northern portion of her dominions. At Granton Pier she embarked on board the steamer *Trident*, belonging to the General Steam Navigation Company, with the flag of Sir Edward Bruce, Vice-Admiral of the White, flying at the fore. The steamer had a safe passage, and at 10 A.M. on the 17th the royal party landed at Woolwich amid the cheers of the assembled multitude and the thunder of cannon.

The Duke of Wellington received the Queen, the Prince, and the royal children on a visit at Walmer Castle, near Deal, on the 10th of November ensuing. The veteran soldier welcomed her Majesty at the gate of the Castle, and she ascended the grand staircase leaning upon his arm. The Queen was in excellent health and spirits, and soon after her arrival, it being a moonlight night, she walked out upon the ramparts, and enjoyed the fine view which presented itself from that elevation. For two or three weeks the royal visitors remained at Walmer, taking daily walks or drives in the neighbourhood. On one occasion the Queen and Prince took a very rough walk completely unattended except by their favourite dogs, and they went as far as the village of Kingsdown, calling on the way at the cottage of an old fisherman, and chatting for a short time with his daughter. On the night of the 22nd there was a fearful gale; and four Deal boatmen, in attempting to board a foreign ship in the Downs, in a distressed and hazardous state, were unfortunately drowned. Her Majesty, on being apprised of the circumstances, caused to be forwarded to the Mayor of Deal a cheque for £20, to be divided between the poor families which had been thus suddenly bereaved.

During her stay at Walmer, the Queen received the important and gratifying intelligence of the reconquest of Afghanistan by British troops, as well as the news of the conclusion of peace with China. On the 3rd of December, the Royal Family took leave of the Duke of Wellington and returned to Windsor, travelling the whole distance by road in closed carriages and four.

When Parliament assembled on the 1st of February 1843, the Queen was unable, for the first time since her accession, to open it in person. But not long after this we find that she manifested her anxiety for the highest interests of the people by returning a gracious answer to an address forwarded to her at the instance of the philanthropic Lord Ashley (the Earl of Shaftesbury of honoured memory), praying the Sovereign seriously to consider the best means of diffusing the blessings of a moral and religious education among the working classes.

The Duke of Sussex, uncle of the Queen, died on the 21st of April, at Kensington Palace, after lingering for many days in a serious condition. Prince Albert, on behalf of her Majesty, paid a visit of condolence to the sorrowing relatives. On the 3rd of May the body of the Duke lay in State, admission being given to all persons who were dressed in 'decent mourning.' There was an immense crowd at Kensington, for the deceased had been highly esteemed by all classes, and it was computed that 25,000 visitors passed through the chamber of death. The

Duke was interred at Kensal Green on the 4th with much ceremony, and the reports state that Prince Albert seemed to be more affected than any other person at the funeral.

Another daughter was born to her Majesty at Buckingham Palace on the 25th of April. The Prince Consort was present; but, with the exception of the Earl of Liverpool, Lord Steward of the House-hold, all the official personages arrived too late. They came just in time to see the first bulletin, and then left again, the Queen and infant being reported as pro-gressing most favourably. The infant Princess was christened on the 2nd of June, and received the names of Alice Maud Mary. The sponsors were the King of Hanover, Prince Ernest, the Princess Sophia Matilda, and Princess Feodore. The child grew up to be an especial favourite with the English people, who sym-pathized deeply with her in the many sorrows which marked her married life.

The Princess Augusta Caroline, eldest daughter of the Duke of Cambridge, was married on the 28th of June to the Hereditary Grand Duke of Mecklenburg-Strelitz. The wedding was solemnized with great splendour in the new Chapel Royal at Buckingham Palace, in the presence of the Queen and Prince Albert, and other royal relatives and guests, and the most distinguished personages in the kingdom. Amongst the guests of the Queen and Prince Albert were the King and Queen of the Belgians, and the Duchess of Kent. The following amusing passage in Dr. Raikes's *Journal* will show that jealousy of the Prince Consort had not yet died out in at least one very high quarter,—'This morning, at breakfast, the Duke of

Wellington said to me : " Did you hear what happened at the wedding ? " meaning that of the Princess Augusta of Cambridge.   Replying in the negative, he continued : " When we proceeded to the signatures, the King of Hanover was very anxious to sign before Prince Albert ; and when the Queen approached the table he placed himself by her side, watching his opportunity.   She knew very well what he was about, and just as the Archbishop was giving her the pen, she suddenly dodged round the table, placed herself next to the Prince, then quickly took the pen from the Archbishop, signed, and gave it to Prince Albert, who also signed next, before it could be prevented." The Queen was further anxious to give precedence at Court to King Leopold, and consulted me about it, and how it should be arranged.   I told her Majesty that I supposed it should be settled as we did at the Congress of Vienna.   " How was that ? " said she ; " by the first arrival ? "   " No, madam," said I, " alphabetically ; and then, you know, B comes before H."   This pleased her very much, and it was done.' The Queen sent a message to Parliament respecting the grant of an annuity of £3000 to the Princess Augusta.   The grant was stoutly opposed by Joseph Hume, but he was defeated by 223 votes to 57.

The first public result of the labours of the Royal Commission on the Fine Arts, of which Prince Albert was President, was witnessed in June 1843.   On the 29th of that month the Queen and the Prince Consort, accompanied by the King and Queen of the Belgians, visited an exhibition of cartoons in Westminster Hall.   They were prize cartoons for the decoration of the new Houses of Parliament.   Designs were afterwards carried out in frescoes, but unfortunately the process has not proved so durable as was expected at the time by the artists and experts concerned. Some time before the decoration of the Houses of Parliament, Prince Albert had also given orders for a series of fresco paintings from Milton's *Comus*, in eight lunettes, to decorate a pavilion in the grounds of Buckingham Palace. Amongst the distinguished artists employed were Maclise, Leslie, Landseer, Dyce, Ewins, and Stanfield. The Queen and Prince took great interest in the work, and made frequent visits to the pavilion to see how the artists were progressing. Ewins, in writing of this time, has observed that in many things the Queen and her Consort were a pattern to their age. 'They have breakfasted, heard morning prayers with the household in the private chapel, and are out some distance from the Palace, talking to us in the summer-house, before half-past nine o'clock, sometimes earlier. After the public duties of the day, and before dinner, they come out again, evidently delighted to get away from the bustle of the world to enjoy each other's society in the solitude of the garden. Here, too, the royal children are brought out by the nurses, and the whole arrangement seems like real domestic pleasure.'

The ordinary life at the Palace, as Lady Bloomfield has shown, was delightful in its simplicity, both as regards its occupations and its enjoyments. As maid-of-honour to the Queen at the time of which we are writing, the Hon. Georgiana Liddell (who afterwards became the wife of Lord Bloomfield, the diplomatist) was thrown constantly into the society of her Majesty, and the Queen seems to have had an especial affection for her. The following extracts from Lady Bloom-field's *Reminiscences of Court and Diplomatic Life* will be read with interest :—

'*Windsor Castle, Aug.* 12*th,* 1843.—I had a de-lightful ride with the Queen yesterday, who most kindly lent me her habit, hat, collar, and cuffs. Con-sidering the great difference in our figures, the habit fitted me wonderfully. . . . . We rode all about the park for two hours and a quarter, and I never enjoyed anything more. I do hope the Queen will continue to ride, because as neither Lady Dunmore nor Matilda Paget ever do, I should probably always have to accompany her Majesty. No one dined here last night, so we talked a great deal to the Queen, and afterwards played at *vingt-et-un,* and I won eight-pence, which was much for me, as I generally come off second-best in the round games. The Queen told us a funny anecdote of the little Princess Royal. Whilst they were driving the other day the Queen called her, as she often does, "Missy." The Princess took no notice the first time, but the next she looked up very indignantly, and said to her mother, "I'm not Missy, I'm the Princess Royal." She speaks French fluently, and she was reading the other day when Lady Lyttelton went up to her; so she motioned her away with her hand, and said, "*N'approchez pas moi, moi ne veut pas vous.*"

'The Duchess of Kent very kindly sent me an immense heap of music yesterday, vocal and instru-mental. I delight in looking over new music. We took a long drive, and the more I see of this lovely park the more I admire it; the scene varies so much, that almost every day I become acquainted with fresh beauties. The Queen went with the little Princess and the Duchess of Buccleuch in one of the small pony carriages, and before we started there was a little delay, so I witnessed a most interesting scene between the Duke of Wellington and the Princess. She looked at him very hard, and he bent down in the most gallant manner and kissed her tiny hand, and told her to remember him, as well she may. The Duke is looking very well, and rode part of the way with us, but he refrained from accompanying us all the time we drove, for the Queen drives so fast, it is very hard work riding by her carriage.

' *August 26th.*—We drove with the Queen and the little Princess yesterday. The latter chattered the whole time, and was very amusing. Prince Albert rode away to look at a house he is having built, and the carriage stood still till he returned. The Queen was talking to us, and not taking any notice of the Princess, who suddenly exclaimed, "There's a cat under the trees"—fertile imagination on her part, as there was nothing of the kind; but having succeeded in attracting attention, she quietly said, "Cat come out to look at the Queen, I suppose." Then she took a fancy to some heather at the side of the road, and asked Lady Dunmore to get her some. Lady Dunmore observed she could not do that, as we were driving too fast; so the Princess answered, "No, *you* can't, but *those girls* might get out and get me some " —meaning Miss Paget and me.'

The Queen's attachment to Miss Liddell was shown by the following letter, which her Majesty addressed to her maid-of-honour on learning of her engagement:—'Osborne, July 29, 1845.—My dearest Georgiana,—I received this morning your kind letter announcing your marriage with Mr. Bloomfield, which has surprised us most agreeably. I do not think you guilty of any inconsistency, and we only hope you will be *as* happy through a long life as *we are;* I *cannot* wish you *more* than this. I highly approve your choice, having a high opinion of Mr. Bloomfield; and I shall be much pleased to have, as the wife of my representative at St. Petersburg, a person who has been about me, whom I am so partial to, and who I am sure will perform the duties of her position extremely well. I pity you much for the painful separation from Mr. Bloomfield to which you will be subjected. Once more, repeating our sincere wishes for your happiness, and with our kind regards to your parents, who we hope are better, believe me, always yours affectionately, VICTORIA R.'

At the close of August 1843, her Majesty and the Prince went on a yachting expedition round the Isle of Wight, subsequently proceeding to Dartmouth, Plymouth, and Falmouth. At the last-named place, the Queen was rowed round the harbour in a barge, and Lady Bloomfield, who accompanied her Majesty, states that the crowd was awful. Vessels and boats of every description, large and small, filled to the utmost; and the moment they caught sight of the royal barge, the people seemed to lose their heads completely, left the helms to take care of themselves, and rushed to the side of the vessel nearest the barge, so that it was really alarming, and the Queen expressed great anxiety for her loyal subjects. Lord Adolphus Fitzclarence ordered the men to pull away as hard as they could when he saw an opening, so the royal barge outdistanced the pleasure boats and got

back safe to the yacht.   Here the Queen received the
Mayor, who, being a Quaker, asked permission to
remain with his hat on.

The royal party left Falmouth on board the *Victoria
and Albert*, and sailed for Cherbourg, in order that her
Majesty might pay her expected visit to King Louis
Philippe. In Lady Bloomfield's *Reminiscences* occurs
this entertaining passage : ' I remained on deck a long
time with her Majesty, and she taught me to plait
paper for bonnets, which was a favourite occupation of
the Queen's. Lady Canning and I had settled ourselves
in a very sheltered place, protected by the paddle-box,
and remarking what a comfortable spot we had chosen ;
her Majesty sent for her camp-stool and settled herself
beside us, plaiting away most composedly, when suddenly we observed a commotion amongst the sailors,
little knots of men talking together in a mysterious
manner ; first one officer came up to them, then
another, looking puzzled, and at last Lord Adolphus
Fitzclarence was called. The Queen, much puzzled,
asked what was the matter, and inquired whether we
were going to have a mutiny on board ? Lord Adolphus
laughed, but remarked that he really did not know
what *would* happen unless her Majesty would be
graciously pleased to remove her seat. "Move my
seat," said the Queen, "why should I ? What possible
harm can I be doing here ?" "Well, ma'am," said
Lord Adolphus, "the fact is, your Majesty is un-
wittingly closing up the door of the place where the
grog tubs are kept, and so the men cannot have their
grog !" "Oh, very well," said the Queen, "I will move
on one condition, viz., that you bring me a glass of
grog." This was accordingly done, and after tasting it,

the Queen said, "I am afraid I can only make the same remark I did once before, that I think it would be very good if it were stronger!" This of course delighted the men, and the little incident caused much amusement on board.'

The royal yacht passed Cherbourg and Dieppe without calling at either place, and at half-past five on the afternoon of September 2 came in sight of Eu. As soon as she was seen, King Louis Philippe, accompanied by the Duc d'Aumale and the Duc de Montpensier, Lord Cowley, and several of the suite, put off in the royal barge, and immediately came on board the yacht. The King embraced the Queen on both cheeks, and then kissed her Majesty's hand, and welcomed her most heartily to the shores of France. It was the first time an English Sovereign had visited France since the Field of the Cloth of Gold. At first the King seemed quite overcome; but he soon recovered himself, and spoke in excellent English. On the Queen leaving her yacht, the Royal Standard of England was lowered, and the Standards of England and France were hoisted on the King's barge.

Under a large canopy close to the shore were Queen Marie Amélie, the Queen of the Belgians, Madame Adélaide, the King's old sister, the Prince and Princess de Joinville, the Duchesse d'Orléans, the Prince and Princess Augustus of Saxe Coburg, and many others. As the royal barge approached they came close to the landing stage, falling close in line behind the Queen of the French. The King took the Queen of England by the hand and assisted her up the steps. As the two Queens advanced to meet each other, the most enthusiastic cheering broke forth from the spectators,

P

and the cannon boomed. Louis Philippe presented her Majesty to the Queen of the French, who took her by both hands and saluted her several times on both cheeks, with evident warmth of manner. The Queen of the Belgians, and other ladies of the Royal Family, then came forward, and also saluted her with great cordiality and affection. Prince Albert was presented to all the ladies in the same way. There were meanwhile continuous shouts of ' Vive la Reine Victoria ! ' ' Vive la Reine d'Angleterre ! ' and the two Queens were visibly moved by their emotion.

The various illustrious personages moved off in quite a mediæval procession for the Château d'Eu. The Castle is especially interesting as having been the scene of many historical events. William the Conqueror was married here, and it was long the residence of the Duc de Guise. The Queen's rooms were elegantly furnished with beautiful Beauvais tapestry, parquet floors, painted ceilings, and the pictures which were saved by the fidelity of servants during the French Revolution. In the evening there was a grand entertainment in the banqueting-room, when all the royalties were in high spirits. Queen Victoria had the Prince de Joinville on her right hand, and carried on a most animated conversation with him during the whole time of dinner; laughing and talking with much enjoyment and freedom. The Duchess of Orléans, being in widow's weeds, did not join the party at dinner, this being French etiquette ; but Queen Victoria visited her after dinner, and saw ' the young people,' to whom she paid such gratifying attentions that she speedily became a great favourite with all of them.

Sunday the 3rd was a quiet day, and as her Britannic Majesty had not a chaplain with her, she had prayers read in a private apartment by one of the persons in her suite. The members of the French Royal Family forbore from the gay amusements usual in France in compliment to the feelings of the English party.

A grand *fête champêtre* was the great event of the 4th. It was given by the King to his illustrious visitors, on the Mont d'Orléans, an elevated spot in the midst of the forest of Eu. A very pleasing and picturesque appearance was presented by the groups of gaily dressed persons who had assembled, and who mingled with the soldiers, gendarmes, and peasants. There was a splendid luncheon, the King of the French sitting at the centre of the table, with Queen Victoria on his right. A very interesting gathering of statesmen was to be seen further down the table, where M. Guizot was seated between Lord Aberdeen and Lord Liverpool. After luncheon the King gave his arm to Queen Victoria, and walked round the platform before the tent, being followed by Prince Albert with the Queen of the French. This presentation by the King of his youthful guest to the crowd led to a burst of cheers, which were again and again renewed till the departure of the whole party, and until they were out of sight on their way back to Eu.

In the evening there was a large dinner-party at the château, the guests numbering more than seventy; and after dinner there was a beautiful instrumental concert conducted by Auber. Lady Bloomfield states that the King had sent for the Corps de l'Opéra, in order to have an opera; but, unfortunately, they only brought two pieces—one ridiculed the English, and the other was said to be so improper that the Queen objected to it; so that the visitors had to content themselves with the musical performance, which was very good and well executed.

Prince Albert attended a review of the troops given in his honour on the morning of the 5th. In the afternoon the royal party visited the collegiate church of the Virgin and St. Lawrence of Dublin, which adjoins the château. 'We afterwards descended to the crypt,' writes Lady Bloomfield, 'where there are the ancient monuments of the Comtes d'Eu; they had recently been repaired, and are curious. The place was lighted with candles, and was exceedingly picturesque. The poor Duchesse d'Orléans went down with us, but was so overcome she was obliged to leave us; and when we returned into the body of the church, we found her and the Queen of the Belgians prostrate before one of the altars, and the Duchess was weeping bitterly. She had never appeared in public since the Duke's death till the Queen's arrival, and when she was seen for the first time, and was received with acclamations of "Vive la Duchesse d'Orléans!" she was completely overcome. She seemed a most amiable, charming person, and her two little boys were very pretty children. After seeing the church, we drove in *chars-à-bancs* to Tréport, where an immense multitude had collected, as it was rumoured that the Queen intended going on board the yacht. The sea was, however, too rough; so we returned to Eu, and walked round the gardens, and home through the pleasure-grounds. I was shown two beech-trees, which existed in the time of the Guises, and it is said the League was signed under their boughs.'

There was another forest *fête* on the following day, and on the 7th the Queen and Prince took leave of the King, expressing their warmest thanks for his great hospitality. The royal party embarked on board their yacht the *Victoria and Albert*, and sailed for England, being accompanied by a squadron of French yachts under the command of Prince de Joinville. Arriving off Brighton, the royal barge was lowered, and was rowed towards the eastern side of the pier by ten of the Queen's crew. The approach of her Majesty to the shore was the signal for loud cheering by thousands on the beach and on the cliffs. The bathing-women and the fishermen ran far out into the water, waving their hats and testifying the utmost joy. Her Majesty stood up again and again, and bowed and kissed her hand. The scene was very picturesque and heart-stirring, and this warm welcome from her own people made a deep impression upon the Sovereign.

A few days after her return, the Queen again left her native shores for Ostend, on a visit to the King and Queen of the Belgians. On landing at Ostend, her Majesty and Prince Albert were received by the King and Queen, and drove off to the royal palace at Laeken. On the 15th of September, the royal party went from Ostend to Bruges, and spent the day in visiting this quaint and venerable seat of the merchant princes of the Middle Ages, and which had further been the abode of the Counts of Flanders and the regal residence of the Dukes of Burgundy. Never had the old city presented a more brilliant or animated appearance than on the present occasion, when the royal visitors made their progress through its streets. As Queen Victoria and the Prince passed through the Grand Place, which they did several times during the day, the bells in the great tower or belfry above the Cloth Hall pealed forth 'Rule, Britannia,' 'God save the Queen,' and other English airs. Ghent, that other ancient and venerable city, was visited on the following day, and the Queen was deeply interested by the University, the convent of Belgian nuns, and the Cathedral of St. Bavon. At the last-named place she inspected the celebrated font in which the Emperor Charles V. was christened. On a triumphal arch in one of the principal streets of Ghent were inscriptions pointing out the fact that the city had been visited by Philippa of Hainault, Queen of England in 1343, and after the lapse of exactly five centuries by another Queen of England.

On the 19th the royal party left the palace at Laeken, and travelled by special train to Antwerp. They visited the cathedral, and also witnessed the antique pageant of the Giant, before the palace in the Place de Mer—described as 'the most perfect vestige of the ancient pageants now in existence in any city in Europe.' Next day the Queen and Prince embarked for England and landed at Woolwich on the morning of Thursday, September 21.

In October came a very interesting visit to Cambridge. The Queen and Prince Albert arrived at the lodge of Trinity College on the afternoon of the 25th, when they were received in State by the Chancellor of the University (the Duke of Northumberland) and a large number of Masters of Arts in residence.

Addresses were presented by Lord Lyndhurst, the high steward of the University, and Mr. Whewell, the Vice-Chancellor, and the heads of the University were presented to her Majesty. In the evening the Queen held a *levée*, and she remained for the night at Trinity College. Next morning she and the Prince proceeded to the Senate House, where the degree of LL.D. was conferred upon his Royal Highness with the usual ceremonies. After he had been duly admitted to the degree by the Vice-Chancellor, the Prince was invested with the doctor's scarlet robe, and took the velvet cap in his hand. A loud burst of cheering, accompanied with the waving of caps, went through the hall as his Royal Highness, thus equipped, walked back to his seat beside her Majesty. Amidst the cheering some cries were heard of ' Doctor Albert.'

The royal pair afterwards visited the various colleges, the University library, &c., and in the afternoon proceeded to Wimpole, the seat of the Earl of Hardwicke, about ten miles south-west of Cambridge. Although a select party was invited to meet the illustrious visitors, the visit was a strictly private one, in accordance with the Queen's wish. Her Majesty breakfasted at the early hour of eight next morning, and then enjoyed herself in the grounds. In the evening a splendid ball was given, to which the leading county families were invited. Colonel Ramsay, who was on escort duty with the Queen, has recorded some amusing incidents of this ball. One of these incidents was as follows :—' During the dancing several circles were formed. There was one reserved exclusively for her Majesty and Prince Albert, who waltzed together. In an adjoining circle, very much

crowded, an officer, who was dancing with a very
pretty girl, now the wife of a peer, burst out of it with
his partner, and said, "Let us go to some other circle."
Not observing the Queen, he said: "Halloa! there is
no one here;" and dashed in, waltzing in a somewhat
eccentric manner, with his elbows stuck out.   He just
escaped coming against her Majesty, who was seated.
We all rushed forward to stop them dancing, when
the Queen said, "Let them stay—they are very
amusing."   When they finished, they found themselves
directly opposite her Majesty, whose eyes were firmly
fixed upon them.   Their consternation was very great,
and they fled precipitately amid general laughter.'

The Queen paid other visits to several of her distinguished subjects towards the close of the year.
The Premier, Sir Robert Peel, had the honour of
receiving her at Drayton Manor, on the 28th of
November, when the visit was a complete success.
At the banquet given by Sir Robert, we read of the
Queen looking very nice in a pink silk gown with
three flounces.   After dinner she completely unbent,
and heartily enjoyed a game at patience with the
ladies.   Prince Albert went into Birmingham on the
29th, and visited the chief manufactories, as well as
the Town Hall, the Free Grammar School, the Proof
House, &c.   On the 30th he and the Queen visited
Lichfield, and went over the Cathedral.

From Drayton Manor her Majesty and the Prince
proceeded to Chatsworth, on a visit to the Duke of
Devonshire.   The Hon. Matilda Paget, who was in
waiting on the Queen, wrote concerning this visit, under
date Chatsworth, the 1st of December:—'The grandeur of this place far surpasses anything I could have

imagined. At half-past one the Queen and Prince went over the State rooms with the Duke, then after luncheon we drove out, and at half-past six we all went to see the conservatory lighted up. The ball last night was very pretty, in a grand banqueting-hall with a rococo ceiling. Mrs. Arkwright was there, and was taken up and presented to the Queen, who talked to her for some time. This evening there have been lovely fireworks, the cascades and fountains all lighted up with red and green lights, which had a fairy-like effect. I was so amused at the Duke of Devonshire coming up to me in the middle of it all, when every one was so amazed and excited, and saying, in an insinuating voice, "Do you like my little fireworks?" I went into dinner with Lord Beauvale, and his wife is charming. The Queen is well, and danced the country dance with Lord Leveson with much vigour, and her Majesty waltzed with the Prince. The royal magnificence of everything here is overpowering. No other place can come up to it. On Sunday there were prayers at eleven, and then we went to the kitchen garden. In the evening we walked through the statue gallery and conservatory, and there was some delightful music performed by the Duke's own band—some of Rossini's *Stabat Mater*, the *Creation*, &c. . . . . The Queen left Chatsworth at nine, and the Duke of Devonshire, who accompanied her Majesty as far as Derby, was in the highest spirits, and delighted at the way everything had gone off. At Chesterfield I helped the Queen to get up on a chair, that her Majesty might look out of a very high window. She took such very tight hold of my hand to prevent herself falling, that one said her Majesty is evidently not used to getting on chairs. The crowds at Derby and Nottingham were perfectly astonishing, especially at the latter place, which was more like Edinburgh than anything else, and we arrived here [Belvoir Castle, Dec. 4] at half-past one.' Belvoir, the Duke of Rutland's seat, was next visited, and from Belvoir her Majesty and the Prince returned to Windsor Castle, which was reached on the 7th.

The indoor and outdoor life of the Royal Family at Windsor have been happily described by Lady Bloomfield, and from her *Reminiscences* I select the following interesting extracts:—

' *Windsor Castle, Dec.* 15, 1843.—I went to the Queen's room yesterday, and saw her before we began to sing. She was so thoroughly kind and gracious. The music went off very well. Costa [Sir Michael] accompanied, and I was pleased by the Queen's telling me, when I asked her whether I had not better practise the things a little more, that "that was not necessary, as I knew them perfectly." She also said, " If it was *convenient* to me I was to go down to her room any evening to try the Masses." Just as if anything she desired could be *inconvenient !* . . . .

' We had a pleasant interview with the royal children in Lady Lyttelton's room yesterday, and *almost* a romp with the little Princess Royal and the Prince of Wales. They had got a round ivory counter, which I spun for them, and they went into such fits of laughter it did my heart good to hear them. The Princess Royal is wonderfully quick and clever. She is always in the Queen's room when we play or sing, and she seems especially fond of music, and stands listening most attentively, without moving.

'*Dec.* 18.—We walked with the Queen and Prince yesterday to the Home Farm, saw the turkeys crammed, looked at the pigs, and then went to see the new aviary, where there is a beautiful collection of pigeons, fowls, &c., of rare kinds. The pigeons are so tame they will perch upon Prince Albert's hat and the Queen's shoulders. It was funny seeing the royal pair amusing themselves with farming!

'*Dec.* 19.—My waiting is nearly over, and though I shall be delighted to get home, I always regret leaving my dear kind mistress, particularly when I have been a good deal with her Majesty, as I have been this waiting. We sang again last night, and after Costa went away, I sorted a quantity of music for the Queen; and then Prince Albert said he had composed a German ballad, which he thought would suit my voice, and he wished me to sing it. So his Royal Highness accompanied me, and I sang it at sight, which rather alarmed me; but I got through it, and it is very pretty. The Duchess of Kent has promised to have it copied for me. The Prince of Wales stayed some time in the room while we were practising. He was very attentive, and both he and the Princess Royal seem to have a decided taste for music. We sang some of my beloved Masses (Mozart's), and you cannot think how beautiful they are with all the parts filled up. Costa had composed a very pretty Miserere, which we also sang.'

The Queen had some strange visitors at Windsor near the close of the year—to wit, eight Indians of the Chippewa tribe. There were five chiefs, two women, a little girl, and a half-breed. They were under the charge of Mr. Catlin, the interpreter, and her Majesty received them in the Waterloo Gallery.

One of the chiefs made a speech, in the course of which he said that he was much pleased that the Great Spirit had permitted them to cross the large lake (the Atlantic) in safety, in order that they might see their great mother (the Queen), whom they had much wished to behold. They found everything in England to be far greater than they expected; they were especially pleased with the wigwam (Windsor Castle), which was very grand. But they should return to their own country quite happy and contented—'they thanked the Great Spirit they had enough to eat—they were satisfied.' Prince Albert shook hands with the chiefs, all of whom had fought for British interests. We are told that they looked exceedingly grave, and were dressed with large bunches of feathers on their heads, having on large skins, while their faces were dreadfully tattooed. The women had long black hair, and a dress which came down to their feet. They had quantities of coloured beads hung about them, and one had a small looking-glass. The chiefs danced two war-dances, which very much astonished and interested the Queen.

An accident occurred to her Majesty on the 5th of January, 1844, but happily it was not attended with serious results. The Queen, attended by the Marchioness of Douro, left Windsor in an open pony-phaeton and pair, driven by a postillion, in order to be present at the meeting of Prince Albert's harriers at the Manor House at Horton. The driver took too short a turn in entering the road near the Five Bells, and the near wheel of the carriage, from the rottenness of the side of the road—occasioned by a rapid thaw—sank into the ditch. The carriage was thrown against the hedge; the horse upon which the postilion was riding sinking in from the same cause. Her Majesty and the Marchioness of Douro were rescued from their perilous position by Colonel Arbuthnot, who was in attendance on horseback. The Queen accepted the offer of a pony-carriage belonging to Mr. Holderness, of Horton, and was driven back to Windsor, while a messenger was despatched for the Prince Consort. Some labourers who assisted in getting the carriage out of the ditch were liberally rewarded by command of the Queen.

The first public statue of her Majesty which had been erected in any part of her dominions was unveiled at Edinburgh on the 24th of January, in this year. It was a colossal statue by Mr. (afterwards Sir John) Steell, and it was placed in position on the colonnade of the Royal Institution, fronting Prince's Street. From the high elevation of the pedestal, the gigantic figure, which was nearly four times life size, assumed to the spectators almost natural proportions, and harmonized with the massive building on which it was placed. The whole composition was modelled on the severest principles of Grecian art, and it still remains a classic conception of much grandeur. Her Majesty is represented seated on a throne, with the diadem on her brow, while her right hand grasps the sceptre, and her left leans on the orb, emblematic of her extended sway.

The last days of January were saddened for the Queen and her Consort by the death of Prince Albert's father, the Duke of Saxe-Coburg-Gotha, at the age of sixty years. The Prince had been looking forward to a reunion in Germany, and now the Queen was called upon to write as follows to Baron Stockmar :—'Oh, if you could be here now with us! My darling stands so alone, and his grief is so great and touching. He says (forgive my bad writing, but my tears blind me) *I* am now *all* to him. Oh, if I can be, I shall be only too happy; but I am so disturbed and affected myself, I fear I can be but of little use.' The Prince, however, found deep solace in her affection, observing to an intimate friend that she felt and shared his grief, and was the treasure on which his whole affection rested. Prince Albert went over to Germany at Easter, and as he was now absent from the Queen for the first time since their marriage, both felt the separation poignantly. The letters written to his wife during his absence breathe the most affectionate solicitude. 'My own darling,' began the first of these letters, written at Dover, 'I have been here about an hour, and regret the lost time which I might have spent with you. Poor child, you will, while I write, be getting ready for luncheon, and you will find a place vacant where I sat yesterday; in your heart, however, I hope my place will not be vacant. I, at least, have you on board with me in spirit. I reiterate my entreaty, "Bear up," and do not give way to low spirits, but try to occupy yourself as much as possible; you are even now half a day nearer to seeing me again; by the time you get this letter you will be a whole one; thirteen more and I am again within your arms.'

On the 1st of February the Queen opened Parliament in person. The Irish Repeal agitation was at this time causing much concern, and State trials were proceeding in Dublin. Daniel and John O'Connell and six other prisoners were charged with conspiracy in endeavouring to obtain a repeal of the union between Great Britain and Ireland. Her Majesty, in receiving an address on the 2nd of February from the Corporation of Dublin, said : 'I receive with satisfaction the assurance that sentiments of loyalty and attachment to my person continue to be cherished by you. The legal proceedings to which you refer are now in progress before a competent tribunal, and I am unwilling to interrupt the administration of justice according to law.' O'Connell and his fellow-agitators were convicted, and sentenced to various terms of imprisonment; but an appeal being made to the House of Lords, the judgment was reversed. The Repeal agitation, however, did not flourish after the trial.

A curious but important domestic reform was inaugurated in the royal household at Windsor early this year. At the suggestion of her Majesty, all the unused bread of the various departments, which amounted to an enormous quantity in the course of the year, and which had hitherto been disposed of in an unsatisfactory manner, was directed to be given in future to the inmates of the several almshouses within the burgh of Windsor. A visitor at the Castle has referred to the enormous preparation and expense which were going forward every day, and to the strange sight which the royal kitchen almost daily presented. 'The fire was more like Nebuchadnezzar's "burning fiery furnace" than anything else I can think of; and though there is now no company at Windsor, there were at least fifteen or twenty large joints of meat roasting. Charles Murray told me that last year they fed at dinner 113,000 people. It sounds perfectly incredible; but every day a correct list is kept of the number of mouths fed; and this does not include the ball suppers, &c. &c., but merely dinners.'

A distinguished visitor arrived at Windsor in March, in the person of General Tom Thumb. He was under the charge of his guardian, the enterprising Barnum, and the General afforded much entertainment to her Majesty, Prince Albert, the Duchess of Kent, and the members of the royal household, by his extraordinary intellectual display. It was stated that his smart replies to the various questions put to him by the Queen caused great astonishment. Mr. Barnum subsequently wrote that 'surprise and pleasure were depicted on the countenances of the royal circle at beholding this remarkable specimen of humanity so much smaller than they had evidently expected to find him.' The General advanced with a firm step, and as he came within hailing distance, made a very graceful bow, and exclaimed: 'Good evening, ladies and gentlemen!' A burst of laughter followed this salutation.

The Queen then took him by the hand, led him about the gallery, and asked him many questions, the answers to which kept the party in an uninterrupted state of merriment. The General familiarly informed the Queen that her picture gallery was 'first rate,' and told her he should like to see the Prince of Wales. The Queen replied that the Prince had retired to rest, but that he should see him on some future occasion. The General gave them his songs, dances, and recitations; and after a conversation with Prince Albert

and all present, which lasted for more than an hour,
he was permitted to depart. As he retired, the
General was startled by the barking of the Queen's
favourite poodle, and he at once began an attack
upon that animal with his little cane. A funny fight
ensued, greatly to the merriment of the royal party.
A lord-in-waiting expressed a hope that the General
had sustained no damage in the encounter, adding
playfully that in case of injury to so renowned a personage, he should fear a declaration of war by the
United States.

In April General Tom Thumb paid a second and a
third visit to Buckingham Palace by command of the
Queen. The second visit was especially interesting
and amusing, and it has thus been described by
Mr. Barnum in his volume entitled *Struggles and
Triumphs* :—

'We were received in what is called the "Yellow
Drawing-room," a magnificent apartment, surpassing
in splendour and gorgeousness anything of the kind I
had ever seen. It is on the north side of the gallery,
and is entered from that apartment. It was hung
with drapery of rich yellow satin damask, the couches,
sofas, and chairs being covered with the same material.
The vases, urns, and ornaments were all of modern
patterns and the most exquisite workmanship. The
room was panelled in gold, and the heavy cornices
beautifully carved and gilt. The tables, pianos, &c.,
were mounted with gold inlaid with pearl of various
hues, and of the most elegant designs.

'We were ushered into this gorgeous drawing-room
before the Queen and royal circle had left the dining-
room; and as they approached the General bowed

Q

respectfully, and remarked to her Majesty that "he had seen her before;" adding: "I think this is a prettier room than the picture gallery; that chandelier is very fine."

'The Queen took him by the hand, and said she hoped he was very well.

'"Yes, madam," he replied; "I am first-rate."

'"General," continued the Queen, "this is the Prince of Wales."

'"How are you, Prince?" said the General, shaking him by the hand; and then, standing beside the Prince, he remarked: "The Prince is taller than I am; but I feel as big as anybody;" upon which he strutted up and down the room as proud as a peacock, amidst shouts of laughter from all present.

'The Queen then introduced the Princess Royal, and the General immediately led her to his elegant little sofa, which we took with us, and with much politeness sat himself down beside her. Then, rising from his seat, he went through his various performances, and the Queen handed him an elegant and costly *souvenir*, which had been expressly made for him by her order, for which he told her "he was very much obliged, and would keep it as long as he lived." The Queen of the Belgians (daughter of King Louis Philippe) was present on this occasion.'

On the third visit, King Leopold was present, and he put a multitude of questions to Tom Thumb. The General was dressed in a full Court suit. Queen Victoria desired him to sing a song, and asked him what song he preferred to sing. 'Yankee Doodle,' was the prompt reply. This answer was as unexpected by Mr. Barnum as it was by the royal party.

When the merriment which it occasioned had sub-sided, the Queen good-humouredly remarked: 'That is a very pretty song, General; sing it, if you please.' The General complied, and shortly afterwards took leave of his delighted and distinguished audience. The *souvenir* which her Majesty gave to Tom Thumb was very superb, being of mother-of-pearl set with rubies, and bearing a crown and the royal initials, 'V. R.' After each visit also a handsome sum was presented to Mr. Barnum.

The great Court event of the year was the visit of the Emperor of Russia—the hard, cold, cruel, hand-some, and imposing Nicholas. He was just in the prime of life, and struck every one by the grandeur of his bearing, though he must have thrown the officials of the royal household into a flutter, seeing that he slept upon straw, and always took with him a leathern case, which, at every stage of his journey, was filled with fresh straw from the stables. This strange potentate won upon the woman's heart of the Queen by his unstinted praise of her husband. 'No-where,' he said, 'will you find a handsomer young man; he has such an air of nobility and goodness.' There must really have been little in common, how-ever, between the Russian Bear and the gentle-natured Prince Albert.

The Emperor came in the Russian war-ship *Cyclops*, and landed at Woolwich on the 1st of June. He drove straight to the Russian Embassy. The King of Saxony also arrived on the same day at Buckingham Palace on a visit to her Majesty. On the 2nd, Prince Albert went to call upon the Emperor at the Russian Embassy, and the two illustrious personages

Q 2

met on the grand staircase. Their greeting was of the most affectionate and cordial kind. The Czar threw his arms round the neck of the Prince, and embraced him fervently, Prince Albert returning the salute. Very scant notice had been given of the Emperor's visit, but her Majesty expressed a strong hope that he would take up his abode at Buckingham Palace, and this he did after some days spent at Windsor. The Emperor paid visits to the various members of the Royal Family, and also to the Duke of Wellington, evincing the deepest interest in the veteran soldier.

On the 4th, the Emperor, the King of Saxony, and Prince Albert witnessed the races at Ascot, and on the following day there was a grand military review in the Great Park at Windsor. The greatest enthusiasm was manifested for the Iron Duke, who really attracted more attention than the Czar; but Wellington took off his hat, and waving it in the air, said to the people very earnestly : 'No, no ! not me—the Emperor ! the Emperor !' The people then warmly cheered the Czar. During the inspection of troops, the Emperor was most keenly interested in the 17th Lancers and 47th Foot. He surveyed them minutely, saying that he wished to see the regiments which had fought and gained our battles in India. On the approach of the Life Guards, the Duke of Wellington put himself at the head of his regiment, and advanced with it before her Majesty ; the spectacle calling forth an exhibition of unusual enthusiasm. In spite of the immense number of spectators present, not a single accident occurred during the day.

On the evening of this day, and for several succeeding days, there were splendid festivities at Windsor and at Buckingham Palace, and on the 8th of June the Duke of Devonshire gave a grand *fête* to the Emperor and the King of Saxony at his Grace's surburban villa at Chiswick. The Queen, Prince Albert, the Czar, and the King subsequently attended the opera at Her Majesty's Theatre, which was crowded in every part. On the 10th, the Emperor Nicholas left London on his return to Russia. During his stay in England, the Emperor's private gifts had been on the most lavish and princely scale, no one being forgotten; while as regards his public benefactions, he gave 1000 guineas to the Society for the Relief of Foreigners in Distress; £500 to the Nelson Testimonial Fund; £500 to the Wellington Testimonial Fund; a piece of plate, of the value of £500, to be annually run for at Ascot races; 200 guineas to the poor of St. George's parish; 100 guineas towards the formation of a Hospital for Distressed Germans in London, &c.

The Queen gave birth to a son on the 6th of August at Windsor Castle. The event was scarcely expected so soon, and only three hours before, her Majesty had signed the Commission for giving the royal assent to various Bills. The Queen's happy delivery was announced in the *Times* in precisely forty minutes after it had taken place at Windsor Castle; and as this was the first occasion on which the electric telegraph had been so used, the rapid publication of the news was considered very surprising. The young Prince was christened on the 6th of September in the names of Alfred Ernest Albert, being afterwards created Duke of Edinburgh. One of the sponsors

at the christening was the Prince Royal of Prussia
(now Emperor of Germany), who was then on a visit
to her Majesty.

As Byron and other poets and writers have
celebrated the virtues of the dog, it will not appear
trivial here to note the death of Prince Albert's
favourite greyhound, Eos. She had been the Prince's
companion since he was fourteen years of age, and
now after eleven years of affectionate and faithful
friendship, she was found dead without any previous
symptoms of illness. The remains were buried on the
top of the bank above the slopes of Windsor, and the
spot is marked by a bronze model of the hound.

The Queen had intended visiting Ireland in the
summer of 1844, but the unsettled condition of the
country rendered this unadvisable, and a second visit
to Scotland took the place of the projected Irish tour.
Her Majesty and the Prince left Windsor on the 9th
of September, taking the little Princess Royal with
them, the three other children being sent during their
parents' absence to the sea-side. The Queen and
Prince and 'little Vicky' embarked at Woolwich for
the North. Blair Castle had been placed at the
Queen's disposal by Lord Glenlyon, afterwards Duke of
Athole, for a brief sojourn. The royal party arrived
in the Tay early on the morning of the 11th, and
landed at Dundee. There was a great reception by
the loyal Scotch, which was repeated at Coupar-
Angus, and Dunkeld. Proceeding by way of Pit-
lochrie and through the beautiful Pass of Killiecrankie,
Blair Athole was reached at three in the afternoon.
Her Majesty was received at the Castle by the Master
and Lady Glenlyon.

This stay in the North was most delightful and refreshing to the royal travellers. Her Majesty took constant walks and drives in the romantic scenery with which the district abounds, visiting Glen Tilt, the Falls of Garry, Tulloch Hill, the Falls of the Tummel, Killiecrankie, and the Falls of Bruar. She also ascended Ben-y-Gloe, witnessed the Highland dancing; the fascinating sports of deer-stalking and otter-hunting; watched the women reapers in the glens, and otherwise entered with interest into the life of the people in this charming region. She gave considerable satisfaction by avowing a *penchant* for Athole brose—a very pleasant composition, which consists of honey, whisky, and milk. Only two incidents of a disturbing nature arose during the whole of the visit. The first occurred in the Pass of Killiecrankie, when at the most critical part of the Pass, near a narrow bridge, the leader horses in the carriage immediately behind that which contained the royal pair, got restive, plunged tremendously, and were nearly running in contact with the Queen's carriage. The animals at last threw their legs over the traces, and got so entangled as to arrest their progress. The royal equerries rode forward to assure the Queen that nothing serious had occurred, when she said, ' This is a pretty job, certainly,' and inquired which of the horses had been at fault. The answer was—' It was Wasp.' 'I thought as much,' said her Majesty; ' it was like him.'

The other unpleasant incident was not a vehicular but an ecclesiastical one. Her Majesty having attended the parish church of Blair Athole, where the worship was that of the Church of Scotland, the

Episcopalians were terribly enraged, and emptied the vials of their wrath in the newspapers. The Queen had intimated that she had gone North for the purpose of enjoying a period of strict quietude and seclusion, and she was surely not to blame for worshipping on this one occasion as she felt inclined. Bigotry, however, long kept the visit to the Church of Scotland open as a cause of theological strife,

The Queen was able to leave behind her almost entirely the heavier cares of her position, and she devoted herself to the rural recreations which had such a charm both for herself and her husband. The chroniclers of the time, however, were assiduous in following her movements, and we catch by their means many interesting glimpses of her Majesty's doings. It was her habit to rise with the sun, and to take her morning walk in the grounds, accompanied by the Prince Consort and the Princess Royal. 'Vicky' was always mounted on her Shetland pony when she accompanied her royal parents in their morning walk; but Prince Albert would sometimes take her in his arms, and point out any object within view that might attract the wondering fancy of a child. The Queen's piper, Mackay, who attended her during the whole of her Majesty's sojourn at Blair Athole, had orders to play the pibroch under the Queen's window every morning at seven o'clock; and at the same early hour a bunch of fresh heather, with some of the icy cold water from the celebrated spring at Glen Tilt, were presented to the Queen.

The following characteristic anecdote was published in one of the local journals :—'One morning about seven o'clock, a lady plainly dressed left the Castle;

who, though observed by the Highland guard on duty, was allowed to pass unnoticed, until after she had proceeded for a considerable distance ; when some one having discovered that it was the Queen, a party of the Highlanders turned out as a royal body-guard. Her Majesty, however, signified her wish to dispense with their services, and they all returned to their stations. The Queen, in the meanwhile, moved onwards through the Castle grounds, perfectly alone, until she reached the lodge, the temporary residence of Lord and Lady Glenlyon ; where, upon calling with the intention, as was understood, of making some arrangements for a preconcerted excursion to the Falls of Bruar, she was informed that his lordship had not yet risen. The surprise of the domestic may be conceived when her Majesty announced who was to be intimated as having called upon his lordship.

'On her return, her Majesty having taken a different route, and finding herself bewildered by the various roads which intersect the grounds in every direction, applied to some reapers whom she met to direct her to the Castle by the nearest way. They, not being aware to whom they spoke, immediately did so, by directing her Majesty across one of the parks, and over a paling that lay before her—which she at once climbed over, and reached the Castle—a good deal amused, no doubt, with her morning's excursion.'

Journeys up the hills on Scotch ponies was a favourite recreation with the royal pair. The Queen on these occasions proved herself a bold and expert horsewoman, disdaining, according to the reports, the broad winding paths of the hills, and venturing upon

more direct roads which presented obstacles that
would have deterred many other persons, including
even natives of the district. On one occasion she
ascended the hill of Tulloch, reaching the very top.
The view from this point was exceedingly fine, embracing a whole range of lofty mountains, including
Ben-y-Chat, Ben Vrackie, and Ben-y-Gloe, and also
the Falls of the Bruar and the Pass of Killiecrankie.
'It was quite romantic,' wrote the Queen afterwards.
'Here we were with only this Highlander (Sandy
McAra) behind us, holding the ponies—for we got off
twice and walked about. Not a house, not a creature
near us, but the pretty Highland sheep, with their
horns and black faces, up at the top of Tulloch,
surrounded by beautiful mountains.' To use her
Majesty's own language, it was the most delightful
and the most romantic ride she ever had.

When the time came for journeying South again
the Queen and her Consort left Scotland with great
regret ; they had begun to appreciate the beauty and
grandeur of its scenery, and the charms of solitude
which this 'land of the mountain and the flood'
afforded so abundantly. But they had afterwards a
permanent reminder of their visit to Blair Athole, for
the ponies ridden by the Queen, Prince Albert, and
the Princess Royal—and to which they had become
much attached—were presented to their royal riders
by Lord Glenlyon.

Louis Philippe, King of the French, arrived at
Windsor Castle, on the 8th of October, on a visit to
her Majesty. It was an event of great national
interest and importance, for that distinguished yet
unfortunate Sovereign was the first and only French

monarch who had ever landed in the British islands
on a visit of peace and amity. The British nation
hailed him with the heartiest demonstrations of
welcome. Prince Albert went down to Portsmouth
to receive him. The King was awaiting his arrival,
and eagerly advancing, he embraced the Prince, and
saluted him in the continental fashion, on each cheek.
The Prince returned the monarch's greeting with
warmth, though restraining himself to the English
modes. As the King landed a volley of cheers
went up from the spectators, whereupon his Majesty
bowed repeatedly on all sides, laying his hand on his
heart.

When the King and Prince reached Windsor Castle
they found the Queen waiting for them in the grand
vestibule fronting George the Fourth's gate. The
Queen advanced to the threshold, and in the most
cordial manner extended her arms, whilst Louis
Philippe and the Prince descended from the carriage.
The King's 'embrace of the Queen was very parental
and nice.' He was much moved, and his hand rather
shook as he alighted; his hat being off, his grey hair
was seen quite plainly. The Queen wrote this account
of Louis Philippe's arrival in her *Journal* :—' The King
said, as he went up the grand staircase to his apartments, " Heavens, how beautiful! " . . . . I never
saw anybody more pleased or more amused in looking
at every picture, every bust. He knew every bust,
and knew everything about everybody here in the
most wonderful way. Such a memory ! such activity!
It is a pleasure to show him anything, as he is so
pleased and interested. He is enchanted with the
Castle, and repeated to me again and again (as did

also his people) how delighted he was to be here ; how he had feared that what he had so earnestly wished since I came to the throne would not take place, and "Heavens! what a pleasure it is to give you my arm!"' The King had seen many vicissitudes, and the Queen wrote concerning a conversation with him during a banquet on the 8th : ' He talked to me of the time when he was "in a school in the Grisons, a teacher merely," receiving twenty-pence a day, having to brush his own boots, and under the name of Chabot. What an eventful life his has been ! '

On the 9th the King was duly installed, and with great pomp, a Knight of the Order of the Garter. Her Majesty sat in a State chair in the throne-room, wearing the blue velvet mantle of the Order, and having upon her head a diamond tiara. Round the table before her sat ten Knights Companions of the highest rank. The Sovereign announced the election in French, and the new knight was introduced by Prince Albert and the Duke of Cambridge. He was invested by the Queen with the George, and received the accolade, ' Albert then placed the garter round the King's leg,' wrote the Queen ; ' I pulled it through while the admonition was being read, and the King said to me, " I wish to kiss this hand," which he did afterwards, and I embraced him.' ' The ceremony,' as Sir Theodore Martin has observed, ' must have been pregnant with suggestions to all present who remembered that the Order had been instituted by Edward III. after the battle of Cressy, and that its earliest knights were the Black Prince and his companions, whose prowess had been so fatal to France.'

During his stay addresses were presented to the King by the corporations of Windsor, London, and Dover. In acknowledging the first, his Majesty said that the union of France and England was of great importance to both nations, but not from any wish of aggrandizement. France had nothing to ask of England, and England had nothing to ask of France, but cordial union. The King left England on the 13th, by way of Dover, having been unable to proceed by way of Gosport to Tréport, as he intended on the preceding day, in consequence of the swell in the Channel.

The Queen and the Prince Consort, after the departure of their guest, went upon a short cruise, and visited the house and grounds of Osborne, then the property of Lady Isabella Blatchford, but which were to be sold. Her Majesty was favourably impressed by the place, and as it was not far from London, and yet had all the advantages of a country house, the royal couple ultimately purchased it. On the 21st of October, the anniversary of the Battle of Trafalgar, the Queen and the Prince visited Nelson's ship, the *Victory*, then lying off Portsmouth. Her Majesty went to the quarter-deck, where there is a brass-plate bearing the inscription : ' Here Nelson fell.' The Queen gazed upon the inscription in silence, shedding tears the while. She also inspected the poop of the *Victory* with its inscription, ' England expects every man to do his duty.' In the cabin the Queen viewed the exact spot where Nelson breathed his last. Here she remained in reflection for some time, almost overpowered by the recollections which the scene awakened. On leaving the vessel, she requested that there should be no firing ; but she could not prevent the three tremendous British cheers which the tars raised instead.

London saw a splendid show on the 28th of October, when the Queen opened the new Royal Exchange. The procession was magnificent, and very similar to the one at the Coronation. From Buckingham Palace to the Exchange every place, hole, or cranny which commanded the smallest view of the route was crammed to suffocation. The Lord Mayor and Aldermen met the Queen at Temple Bar at twelve and escorted her to her destination. On alighting at the Exchange, she walked round the colonnade, and through the inner court. She then went upstairs, and walked through the second banqueting-hall to show herself ; subsequently receiving an address in a small room prepared for the purpose. After the address, she created the Lord Mayor (Sir William Magnay) a baronet. A few hours before his lordship had been in the most pitiable distress, for in going to receive her Majesty he had put on an enormous pair of jack-boots to protect himself from the mud ; and as the Queen approached he was unable to get them off—or at least one of them. He had one on and one off just as the Sovereign was about to draw up at Temple Bar, and in an agony of fright he ordered the attendants, who were tugging at the immovable boot, to let it alone and to replace the other one, which they did. These boots he was compelled to wear until after the ceremony.

The new buildings now opened formed the third Exchange. Gresham's original Exchange was destroyed in the Great Fire of London, and its successor was burnt down in 1838, one of the bells pealing forth the tune, 'There's nae luck aboot the house,' during the conflagration. In opening the third building, the Queen announced it as her pleasure that it should be hereafter called 'The Royal Exchange.' A grand *déjeuner* followed the opening ceremony, and in the evening there were great festivities in the City.

At Windsor Castle, on the 30th of October, the Queen received Sir Robert and Lady Sale; and her Majesty heard from the lips of the heroic lady a narrative of the privations to which she and other captives had been exposed in Afghanistan. Lady Sale went through fearful hardships during the disastrous retreat from Cabul. She was severely wounded on the second day of the march, and for nine days she was compelled to wear a habit that was like a sheet of solid ice, for having been wet through it had afterwards frozen. She was in captivity ten months, with her daughter, Mrs. Sturt, and the latter was confined of a child during the time in a tiny room without light or air. The baby lived, however, notwithstanding that its mother and Lady Sale were frequently twenty-four hours without food. Akhbar Khan treated them cruelly while pretending to be their friend. He said he would sooner part with all his prisoners than Lady Sale, for ' she was the only hold he had upon her devil of a husband ! '

On the 12th of November, the Queen and Prince Albert proceeded to Burghley House, near Stamford, on a visit to the Marquis and Marchioness of Exeter. Her Majesty was present at the christening of her host's infant daughter, to whom was given the name of Victoria Cecil. The Queen kissed her little namesake after the ceremony, and Prince Albert, who

stood godfather, presented her with a gold cup, bearing
the inscription, 'To Lady Victoria Cecil, from her godfather Albert.'   There were many things at Burghley
to remind the Queen of the visit paid to that seat by
her great predecessor, Elizabeth. Her Majesty returned
to London on the 15th, and a fortnight later occurred
the death of the Princess Sophia Matilda.   She was
the daughter of the Duke of Gloucester, George III.'s
brother, and sister of the succeeding Duke, who
married his cousin, Princess Mary.   The Princess was
buried on the 10th of December in St. George's
Chapel, Windsor.

In the ensuing January the Queen and Prince
Albert went on a visit to the Duke and Duchess of
Buckingham at Stowe.   It is not very pleasant to
read the details of a *battue* which took place in
honour of his Royal Highness, and at which the
Prince, the Duke, Sir Robert Peel, and others were
present.   Beaters to the number of fifty beat up the
game, and when they had successfully performed their
task, 'a regular running fire instantly commenced
upon the devoted hares.   The ground immediately in
front of the shooters became strewn with dead and
dying; within a semicircle of about sixty yards from
his Royal Highness, the havoc was evidently greatest.
The gun was no sooner to his shoulder than the
animal was dead.   In other cases wounded hares
vainly endeavoured to limp away, but every provision
had been made to avoid the infliction of prolonged
torture.   Keepers were in readiness to follow up and
kill such as were maimed.'   Pheasants were also
beaten up, and the total amount of game shot by the
party consisted of 200 hares, 100 pheasants, and one

snipe. Prince Albert shot 144 hares, 29 pheasants, and the only snipe killed. We are not surprised to learn that this and similar incidents gave much strength to the movement against the game laws. The Duke of Buckingham's *battue* was the reverse of manly sport, and the Prince would have done well had he resisted the entertainment provided in his honour. It could have afforded him no pleasure comparable with that which attends upon true sport.

A few days later the Queen and Prince Albert went on a visit to the Duke of Wellington at Strathfield-saye. The visit was made as private as possible, and the Duke's efforts to secure this were of a somewhat amusing character. To a newspaper representative, who applied for the facilities usually accorded on such occasions, the Duke wrote: ' Field Marshal the Duke of Wellington presents his compliments to Mr. ——, and begs to say that he does not see what his house at Strathfieldsaye has to do with the public press.' The Duke also caused a notice to be conspicuously posted in his grounds, desiring those who wished to see the house to drive up to the hall-door and ring the bell; but they were particularly requested not to walk on the flag-stones or look in at the windows. There was some company in the house, and the Duke's daily method of procedure has been thus described :—' The Duke takes the Queen in to dinner, sits by her Majesty, and after dinner gets up and says: " With your Majesty's permission, I give the health of her Majesty," and then the same to the Prince. They then adjourn to the library, and the Duke sits on the sofa by the Queen (almost as a father would sit by a daughter) for the rest of the

R

evening, until eleven o'clock; the Prince and the
gentlemen being scattered about in the library or the
billiard-room, which opens into it. In a large conservatory beyond, the band of the Duke's Grenadier
regiment plays through the evening.' Lawn-tennis
and shooting were the sports at Strathfieldsaye provided for the Prince, but instead of having a *battue*
the veteran Duke trudged through the hard fields
with his royal guest in quest of real sport. At all
the places which she visited the Queen planted trees
of some kind; the oak, however, being generallly
selected.

After the opening of Parliament in February 1845,
the Queen and the Prince Consort went down to
Brighton to make a short stay at the Pavilion. From
thence they visited Arundel Castle and Buxted Park.
During her stay at Brighton the Queen was exposed
to great annoyance in consequence of the rude behaviour of the crowd, who lay in wait to follow her in
her walk from the Pavilion to the pier. She was
very glad when the time came for taking possession
of Osborne, which she and the Prince did on the
29th of March following. The park and grounds
attached to this marine residence comprised upwards
of 300 acres, chiefly sloping to the east, and well
stocked with noble timber. The views from Osborne
are very extensive, commanding Portsmouth, Spithead, &c. A new mansion was subsequently built
for the Queen in lieu of the old house.

Her Majesty held a Court at Buckingham Palace
on May 21, to receive an address from the Lord
Mayor and Corporation of Dublin, inviting her to
visit Ireland. The very rumour that the Queen in-

tended to visit Ireland had filled every heart with gladness. In the course of her reply her Majesty said: 'Whenever I may be enabled to receive in Ireland the promised welcome, I shall rely with confidence on the loyalty and affection of my faithful subjects.'

On the 6th of June, at Buckingham Palace, the Queen gave a grand costume ball illustrating the period of George II. The precise period selected was the ten years from 1740 to 1750. The company numbered about 1,200, and amongst those present were the Duke and Duchess of Nemours and the Prince of Leiningen, then on a visit to her Majesty. Noblemen, ambassadors, statesmen, senators, and judges attended the ball. Ladies were most perplexed to fulfil all the points of the costume of the period, and it was *de rigueur* that they should thus appear. 'However, it was discovered that the powder made the complexion show more brilliant, and if the hoop disguised the figure, the stomacher displayed it; while both hoop and stomacher displayed the glowing jewellery, the rich and elegant lace, the splendid brocades, magnificent velvets, and gorgeous trimmings, that were the pride of the evening.' The men appeared in coats of velvet—crimson, black, or blue—adorned with gold or silver; and powdered wigs were universal. Many wore the dresses of their old ancestors copied from family portraits. The beauty of the ball was the Marchioness of Douro, daughter-in-law of the Duke of Wellington.

Her Majesty, as the Lady of the Feast, wore a magnificent dress of the period, rich with point lace, diamonds, &c., the chief part of which was from the

hoards of Queen Charlotte.   Prince Albert wore a
suit of crimson velvet and gold, the coat-lining and
waistcoat of white satin, with the insignia of the
Garter.   The Queen and the Prince Consort opened
the ball with a polonaise, followed by their most distinguished guests.   Then came a minuet in the throne-
room, headed by the Queen and Prince George of
Cambridge, with the Duchess of Nemours and Prince
Albert, and six other couples.   Various other dances
followed, and at midnight supper was served in the
great dining-room.   The ball closed with the old
country dance of ' Sir Roger de Coverley,' the Lady
of the Feast dancing with her husband.

The Queen and Prince Albert, accompanied by the
Lords of the Admiralty, inspected the Experimental
Squadron at Spithead on the 21st of June.   It was
a splendid spectacle to see the noble vessels as they
got under way.   The war-ships off Spithead at this
time had a total of 926 guns, 26,208 tons ; being
6,412 tons more than the fleet amounted to with
which England won the battle of the Nile.   After
the evolutions, the Queen passed through the squadron
on her return to Cowes, much gratified by the display
she had witnessed.

Her Majesty prorogued Parliament on the 9th of
August, and on the evening of the same day set out
with the Prince Consort on her first visit to Germany.
Such a tour must have had special interest for her,
seeing that Germany was not only her husband's
country, but that of her mother also.   The royal
party left Woolwich in the *Fairy*, the Queen's new
. yacht.   Lord Aberdeen, Lord Liverpool, Lady Gains-
borough, Lady Canning, and Sir James Clark were on

board.   For the first time in her many excursions by·
sea and land, the Queen had unfavourable weather.
Her Majesty and Prince Albert disembarked at
Antwerp, and went on to Malines, where they were
met by the King and Queen of the Belgians, who
escorted them through their dominions to Verviers
and Aix-la-Chapelle, where the King of Prussia was
in readiness to receive them.   Then came in succession Cologne, Bonn, and the royal palace of Bruhl.
At Bonn the Queen was quite pleased to meet with
some of her husband's old professors.   Of the Prince's
'former little house,' her Majesty writes: 'It was
such a pleasure for me to be able to see this house.
We went all over it, and it is just as it was—in no
way altered.   We went into the little bower in the
garden, from which you have a beautiful view of the
Kreuzberg—a convent situated on the top of a hill.
The *Siebengeberge* (Seven Mountains) you also see, but
the view of them is a good deal built up.'

One can imagine the delight with which the Prince
would point out to his wife the various places dear to
his youth, as well as the many other romantic spots in
which this part of Germany abounds.   Then also
there were the people of the 'fatherland' to interest
them both.   The King of Prussia behaved admirably,
and soon made the Queen feel perfectly at home in
her new surroundings.   In proposing the Queen's
health at a grand banquet in the palace of Bruhl his
Majesty said: 'There is a word of inexpressible
sweetness to British as well as to German hearts.
Thirty years ago it echoed on the heights of Waterloo
from British and German tongues, after days of hot
and desperate fighting, to mark the glorious triumph

of our brotherhood in arms.   This day, after a peace of thirty years' duration—the fruit of those arduous days—it resounds in the lands of Germany, on the banks of our noble Rhine.   That word is Victoria!   Gentlemen, empty your glasses to the bottom.   The toast is, " Her Majesty, the Queen of Great Britain and Ireland.   Long live Queen Victoria and her illustrious Consort ! " '

Baron Bunsen observed, with regard to the effect of this happy speech, that ' the Queen bowed at the first word, but much lower at the second.   Her eyes brightened through tears, and as the King was taking his seat again she rose and bent towards him and kissed his cheek, then took her seat again with a beaming countenance.'

On the 12th the royal visitors witnessed the inauguration of Beethoven's statue at Bonn, and in the evening there was a splendid spectacle on the river: Cologne was illuminated, and the Rhine was made one vast *feu-de-joie.*   'The royal party embarked in a steamer at St. Tremond, and glided down the river ; as they passed the banks blazed with fireworks and musketry ; at their approach the bridge glared with redoubled light, and, opening, let the vessel pass to Cologne, whose cathedral burst forth, a building of light, every detail of the architecture being made out in delicately coloured lamps—pinkish, with an under-glow of orange.   Traversing in carriages the illuminated and vociferous city, the King and his companions returned by the railroad to Bruhl.'   Another visit was paid to Cologne on the 13th, and when the Queen returned to Bruhl she was welcomed by the King and Queen of the Belgians, who had just arrived. In the evening a grand concert was given, at which Meyerbeer conducted in person, and a cantata which he had composed in honour of her Majesty was sung. Jenny Lind, Viardot, and Liszt were among the performers.

Next day the Queen and Prince Albert, with their host, steamed up the Rhine in the King's yacht, the *König.* Her Majesty seems at first to have been disappointed with the river; but as the vessel moved majestically along, breasting the current of the exulting and bounding stream, the Siebengebirge, with ' the castled crag of Drachenfels,' and the ' wild rocks shaped as they had turrets been,' crowning the grey summits of the Stronberg, and Wolherburg, and Hemmerich, burst upon the view; and her Majesty expressed her admiration and delight at the glorious spectacle in glowing terms.' This admiration was renewed when Coblentz came in view, with noble Ehrenbreitstein on the left. In the midst of all this picturesque scenery the smoke from the firing of twenty thousand troops, all eager to welcome the Queen, ' brought home to the imagination the din and lurid splendours of a battle.'

The august party made its halt for the day at the palace of Stolzenfels, whither Humboldt and Prince Metternich had come; but next day the King and Queen of Prussia took leave of their royal visitors, as the latter again set forth on their travels. On the 16th they reached Mayence; next day, being Sunday, was spent quietly : but on the Monday they pushed forward to Wurtzburg, and on the 19th entered Coburg, where they were received with every demonstration of delight. Here they found Duke Erestn

(the Prince Consort's brother) and King Leopold and
Queen Louise. There was a picturesque reception—
triumphal arches, &c., and young girls dressed in
white, who presented bouquets and verses. 'I cannot
say how much I felt moved on entering this dear old
place,' wrote the Queen, 'and with difficulty I restrained my emotion. The beautifully ornamented
town, all bright with wreaths and flowers, the numbers
of good affectionate people, the many recollections
connected with the place—all was so affecting.' The
Duchess of Kent had already arrived at Coburg on a
visit to her nephew, and she and the Duchess and
Dowager-Duchess of Coburg, Prince Albert's sister-in-
law and stepmother, welcomed the young royal couple.
The Queen said it was an affecting but exquisite
moment, and one which she should never forget.

The Queen and the Prince took up their residence
at the palace of Rosenau, which with kind thoughtful-
ness had been set apart for them by the Duke, and
they occupied the very room in which the Prince
Consort was born. Her Majesty thus wrote afterwards of the time and the place : 'How happy, how
joyful we were, on awaking, to find ourselves here, at
the dear Rosenau, my Albert's birthplace, the place
he most loves. He was so happy to be here with me.
It is like a beautiful dream.' Five or six days of
pleasure now followed, husband and wife going
about together everywhere. A visit was paid to the
fortress overhanging the town, which has Luther's
room in it, with his chair and part of his bed.
Kalenburg, another of the Duke's seats, was likewise
visited. On the 22nd the royal party were present
at a festival entitled the 'Feast of St. Gregorius,' a

species of carnival, in which the citizens and country people, their wives and children, disguised in fancy dresses, indulge in unrestrained gaiety. The Queen entered into the spirit of the festival, and astonished the children by conversing with them in their own language. 'Tired of dancing and processions, and freed from all awe by the ease of their illustrious visitors, the children took to romps, "thread-my-needle," and other pastimes, and finally were well pelted by the royal circle with *bons-bons*, flowers, and cakes.' Concerts and various sights filled up other days; and on the 25th, which was Prince Albert's birthday, there was another festival, which ended with a fancy ball. Her Majesty wrote concerning this day, which was the first the Prince had spent at Rosenau since he was fifteen: 'To celebrate this dear day in my beloved husband's country and birthplace is more than I ever hoped for, and I am so thankful for it! I wished him joy so warmly when the singers sang as they did the other morning!'

The family group broke up from Rosenau on the 27th, when the travellers left 'with heavy hearts.' They proceeded to Reinhardtsbrunn, a beautiful castellated hunting-seat of the Duke of Coburg. From thence they were to go on the following day to Gotha, on a visit to the Prince's grandmother, who was then seventy-four years of age. But the old lady astonished her grandchildren by travelling eight miles before breakfast in order to anticipate their visit. The Queen thus speaks of the meeting: 'I hastened to her, and found Albert and Ernest with her. She is a charming old lady, and though very small, remarkably nice-looking, erect and active, but unfortunately very deaf. She was so happy to see us, and kissed me over and over again. Albert, who is the dearest being to her in the world, she was enraptured to see again, and kissed so kindly. It did one's heart good to see her joy.' In the afternoon the royal travellers proceeded to Gotha, where they found many things to remind them touchingly of the late Duke, whose body had not yet been moved to its vault at Coburg. Next day there was a pic-nic in the Thüringerwald forest, with a deer-drive or battue. Stags were driven into an enclosure and shot, the ladies of the party looking on from a pavilion. Speaking of this sport, her Majesty has said in her Journal that 'none of the gentlemen like this butchery.'

The following day, which was Sunday, was spent quietly at Gotha. Then the last day came, 'with its inevitable sadness. "I can't—won't think of it," wrote the Queen, referring to her approaching departure. She drove and walked, and, with her brother-in-law and his Duchess, was ferried over to the "Island of Graves," the burial-place of the old Dukes of Gotha when the Duchy was distinct from that of Coburg. An ancient gardener pointed out to the visitors that only one more flower-covered grave was wanted to make the number complete. When the Duchess of Gotha should be laid to rest, with her late husband and his fathers, then the House of Gotha, in its separate existence, would have passed away. One more drive through the hay-fields and the noble fir-trees to the vast Thüringerwald, and "with many a longing, lingering look at the pine-clad mountains," the Queen and the Prince turned back to attend a ball given in their honour by the townspeople in the theatre.'

Next day, the 3rd of September, was a day of sorrowful farewells, and then the royal travellers turned their faces homewards. They stopped on the way at Eisenach, and visited the fortress of Wartburg, which has Luther for its hero, and St. Elizabeth, of Kingsley's *Saint's Tragedy*, for its heroine. The Queen and Prince Albert came afterwards to Fulda, then to Frankfort, and then to Biberich, on the Rhine; from whence they steamed to Bingen, where they went on board their own yacht *The Fairy*. As they were now going homeward, home was of course first in their thoughts, notwithstanding the beauty of the scenes which had given them such pleasure on first beholding them. At Antwerp, the travellers re-embarked in the royal yacht *Victoria and Albert*, but instead of sailing direct for English waters, they made for Tréport, to pay a flying visit to Louis Philippe, in response to the King's urgent entreaty. Off Tréport an unexpected contingency presented itself. It was low water when the yacht arrived, and as the shore shelves greatly here, there was water over a great extent of sands too shallow for a boat to swim. A happy thought on the part of the King of the French got the party out of their difficulties; 'and a reigning Queen, a King, a Prince Consort, a Prince of the Blood, a Duke of the Empire, and the Prime Minister of France, made a triumphal debarkation at a royal palace in a bathing-machine!' One day only, besides that of her arrival, could the Queen stay at Château d'Eu, but into that short time the King crowded as much entertainment as he possibly could, while he also took the oppor-

tunity of emphatically declaring his policy in regard
to the Spanish marriages. 'He would never consent,'
he said, 'to Montpensier's marriage to the Infanta of
Spain until her sister the Queen was married and had
children.'

There was a very affectionate parting between the
old and the young monarch, after which the Queen's
yacht stood for England. On the 10th her Majesty
and the Prince reached their home at Osborne, where
a joyous welcome awaited them as they ' drove up
straight to the house after landing ; for there, looking like roses, so well and so fat, stood the four
children.' The Queen has left it on record that this
visit to Germany was one of the most exquisite periods
of enjoyment in her whole life.

The ensuing winter of 1845-6 was a disastrous
one in some respects in our domestic history. In
England the railway mania had hurried many into
. ruin, while in Ireland there was fearful destitution
through the failure of the potato crop. The settlement of the great corn-law question was seen to be
imperative towards the close of 1845, and Sir Robert
Peel resigned office in order that Lord John Russell
and the Whigs might come in and grapple with this
long-vexed question. Lord John was unable to form
a Ministry, however, and on the 5th of December
Sir Robert Peel returned to power. He courageously
resolved to abolish the corn-laws, and although by
doing so he incurred great odium with his party, the
country generally acknowledged with gratitude his
great and disinterested services. The obnoxious corn
laws were swept away, and Peel's action was more
than justified by subsequent events.

During the thick of the political conflict the Queen gave birth, at Buckingham Palace, on the 25th of May, to her third daughter, Princess Helena, afterwards Princess Christian.

In the closing days of June the Government was defeated on its Irish Coercion Bill, a measure to check assassination in Ireland, and on the 6th of July the Prime Minister resigned office. The Queen felt the parting with Peel and Lord Aberdeen most keenly. Writing to King Leopold on the 7th she said: 'Yesterday was a very hard day for me. I had to part from Sir Robert Peel and Lord Aberdeen, who are irreparable losses to us and to the country. They were both so much overcome that it quite upset me. We have in them two devoted friends: we felt so safe with them. Never during the five years that they were with me did they ever recommend a person or a thing that was not for my or the country's best; and never for the party's advantage *only*. . . . . I cannot tell you how sad I am to lose Aberdeen; you cannot think what a delightful companion he was. The breaking-up of all this intercourse during our journeys is deplorable.' But the Queen had still one person on whose counsel she could rely, and one far dearer to her than her Ministers. 'Albert's use to me, and I may say to the country, by his firmness and sagacity in these moments of trial, is beyond all belief.'

The infant Princess was christened at Buckingham Palace on the 25th of July in the names of 'Helena Augusta Victoria.' The sponsors were the Duchess of Orleans, represented by the Duchess of Kent; the Hereditary Grand Duke of Mecklenburg-Strelitz; and the Duchess of Cambridge—the two latter being present at the ceremony.

A few days after this Prince Albert went to Liverpool, and formally opened the Albert Dock there; and on the following day his Royal Highness laid the foundation-stone of the Sailors' Home.   While the Prince was away the Queen wrote to Baron Stockmar : 'I feel very lonely without my dear master, and though I know other people are often separated, I feel that I could never get accustomed to it. . . . . Without him everything loses its interest.   It will always cause a terrible pang for me to be separated from him even for two days, and I pray God not to let me survive him.   I glory in his being seen and loved.'

Her Majesty and the Court, accompanied by the King and Queen of the Belgians, removed from Buckingham Palace to Osborne on the 7th of August. After a stay of five days here, the royal visitors returned to Belgium.   Baron Stockmar, who was over at Osborne at the time, was greatly impressed by the ripening powers of the Queen.   He thus expressed himself on this matter : 'The Queen improves greatly, and she makes daily advances in discernment and experience.   The candour, the tone of truth, the firmness, the considerateness with which she judges men and things, are truly delightful; and the ingenuous self-knowledge with which she speaks of herself is simply charming.'

On the 18th of August, her Majesty, the Prince Consort, and several members of the Royal Family, embarked on board the *Victoria and Albert* for a sail down the Channel.   They visited Weymouth, Babbicombe, and Mount Edgcumbe, and went up the

Tamar to visit the curious old house of Cothele. Sailing from Plymouth Sound, the royal party next visited Guernsey. They landed at St. Pierre, and drove through the principal parts of the island. Some days later, the Queen, the Prince, and their children again left Osborne in the royal yacht, and proceeded across the Channel to Jersey. In the course of this trip the Prince of Wales first appeared in his sailor's dress, and his appearance in nautical attire was hailed with rapturous delight by the officers and sailors on board the yacht. Her Majesty and Prince Albert were greatly charmed with the scenery of Jersey, which they thoroughly explored. From Jersey the royal party sailed to Falmouth, and on the 5th of September left that place and sailed along the coast of Cornwall as far as Land's End. In the *Fairy* they next went round the beautiful St. Michael's Mount. On Sunday, the 6th, her Majesty and the Prince having returned to the royal yacht from inspecting the old castle of St. Michael, the brief sea service was read by Lord Spencer. In the afternoon the whole party sailed from Mount's Bay, and the Queen and her family were rowed in the barge to see the curious caves in the Serpentine Rocks. Falmouth and Penryn were the next places visited, and subsequently the royal party went on board the *Fairy* and steamed up the rivers Truro and Tregony. On the 8th the Queen and Prince Albert landed at Fowey, and drove to the old castle of Restormel and the mine of that name, both belonging to the Duchy of Cornwall. At the mine the royal pair got into one of the trucks, and were dragged in by miners. In honour of the occasion the mine was lighted by candles, which

the miners carried in their hands. The royal party
then drove through the little town of Lostwithiel.
Returning from thence to the place of embarkation,
they set sail for the Isle of Wight, and arrived at
Osborne on the 10th. A few days later the Queen
and Prince took possession of that portion of their
new marine residence intended for their occupation.
We read pleasant accounts of the house-warming.
The Queen's health was drunk, and then that of her
husband. After it the Prince said, somewhat seriously,
'We have a psalm in Germany for such occasions,'
and then he began to quote the hymn in question,
which was Luther's. It was a paraphrase of the
121st Psalm, and Sir Theodore Martin gives this
translation of the quaint verse quoted by the
Prince:

'God bless our going out, nor less
 Our coming in, and make them sure;
God bless our daily bread, and bless
 Whate'er we do—whate'er endure;
In death unto His peace awake us,
And heirs of His salvation make us.'

We have already made some allusion to the Franco-
Spanish marriages, and something more is necessary
to be said here. Louis Philippe agreed in September
to that double alliance against which he had more
than once solemnly pledged himself to the Queen;
and the marriage of the Duc de Montpensier with the
Infanta Luisa was announced simultaneously with the
marriage of her sister, the Queen of Spain, to her
cousin the Duc de Cadiz. The King of the French no
doubt thought that he had outwitted Great Britain

and Europe by this policy, but he was destined to witness disastrous results from it. However, the marriages were arranged, and Queen Amélie was deputed to announce the fact to the Queen of England. Her Majesty sent a very dignified reply to the letter of the Queen of the French : ' You will perhaps remember,' she wrote from Osborne, on the 10th September, ' what passed at Eu between the King and myself. You are aware of the importance which I have always attached to the maintenance of our cordial understanding, and the zeal with which I have laboured towards this end. You have no doubt been informed that we refused to arrange the marriage between the Queen of Spain and our cousin Leopold (which the two queens had eagerly desired) solely with the object of not departing from the course which would be more agreeable to the King, although we could not regard the course as the best. You will therefore easily understand that the sudden announcement of this double marriage could not fail to cause us surprise and very keen regret.' The ' two queens' referred to by her Majesty were the young Queen of Spain and her mother the Queen Dowager Christina. The course which Queen Victoria did not regard as the best, but which she nevertheless respected, was the recognised one of confining the Queen of Spain's selection of a husband to a Bourbon Prince, a descendant of Philip V.

Her Majesty and Prince Albert visited the Queen Dowager at Cashiobury on the 19th of September and spent a few days with her in strict privacy. They then proceeded to Hatfield House, the seat of the Marquis of Salisbury, being met on the road by the

S

Marquis, the Duke of Wellington, and other noblemen and gentlemen, who formed an equestrian escort. Amongst the guests invited to receive the Queen were Lord John Russell, Lord Melbourne—who seems now to have quite fallen out of the Queen's life—and Lord and Lady Beauvale. At Hatfield the Queen was much interested in examining the famous Cecil papers. She found also much pleasure in outdoor recreation, visiting the vineyard, and the celebrated oak under which Queen Elizabeth was found sitting when she received the news of her accession. On the 1st of December, the Queen and the Prince Consort visited the Duke of Norfolk at Arundel Castle. Besides being the Premier of the nobility and hereditary Earl Marshal, his Grace now filled the political office of Master of the Horse. Elaborate preparations were made to receive the royal guests, while in the evening the Keep was brilliantly illuminated, and the whole town became one blaze of light. A sumptuous dinner was given to every poor person in Arundel. On the following day the Queen and Prince Albert each planted a young oak tree in the Small Park. From Arundel the visitors returned to Osborne House to spend Christmas.

The year 1847 opened very gloomily. The commercial depression from which the country had been suffering had been further aggravated, while the ravages of the potato disease had reduced the people of Ireland to a terrible condition of starvation and disease. Consequently when her Majesty opened Parliament in person on the 19th of January, the Royal Speech was not a cheerful document. Fortunately, foreign affairs were in a satisfactory condition, and as regards the home difficulties, the Government of Lord John Russell took prompt measures for relieving the distress in Ireland. They also brought in a new Irish Poor Law measure, which was quickly passed, together with other remedial legislation.

But the season in London, always inexorable, was not without its gaieties. The theatre saw the re-appearance of Fanny Kemble, whilst at the Italian Opera a new prima donna appeared, concerning whom the Queen thus wrote : ' Her acting alone is worth going to see, and the *piano* way she has of singing, Lablache says, is unlike anything he ever heard. He is quite enchanted. There is a purity in her singing and acting which is quite indescribable.' The new operatic star which thus suddenly came upon the horizon was that popular favourite, Jenny Lind.

Lord Campbell records an amusing incident which occurred at Court in February of this year : ' I had an audience,' says his lordship, who was then Chancellor of the Duchy of Lancaster, ' that her Majesty might prick a sheriff for the county of Lancaster, which she did in proper style, with the bodkin I put into her hand. I then took her pleasure about some Duchy livings and withdrew, forgetting to make her sign the parchment roll. I obtained a second audience, and explained the mistake. While she was signing, Prince Albert said to me : " Pray, my lord, when did this ceremony of pricking begin ? " *Campbell*—" In ancient times, sir, when Sovereigns did not know how to write their names." *Queen* (as she returned me the roll with her signature) : " But we now show we have been to school." '

One day, in the following month, Lord Campbell

and his wife and daughter dined at Buckingham Palace, and his lordship thus vivaciously describes the event : ' On our arrival, a little before eight, we were shown into the picture gallery, where the company assembled.   Bowles, who acted as master of the ceremonies, arranged what gentleman should take what lady.   He said, " Dinner is ordered to be on the table at ten minutes past eight, but I bet you the Queen will not be here till twenty or twenty-five minutes after.   She always thinks she can dress in ten minutes, but she takes about double the time."   True enough, it was nearly twenty-five minutes past eight before she appeared.   She shook hands with the ladies, bowed to the gentlemen, and proceeded to the *salle à manger*.   I had to take in Lady Emily de Burgh, and was third on her Majesty's right, Prince Edward of Saxe-Weimar and my partner being between us.   The greatest delicacy we had was some very nice oat-cake. There was a Highland piper standing behind her Majesty's chair, but he did not play as at State dinners.   We had likewise some Edinburgh ale.   The Queen and the ladies withdrawing, Prince Albert came over to her side of the table, and we remained behind about a quarter of an hour, but we rose within the hour from the time of our sitting down to dinner. . . . . On returning to the gallery we had tea and coffee.   The Queen came up and talked to me.   She does the honours of the palace with infinite grace and sweetness, and, considering what she is both in public and domestic life, I do not think she is sufficiently loved and respected.   Prince Albert took me to task for my impatience to get into the new House of Lords, but I think I pacified him, complimenting his taste. A dance followed. The Queen chiefly delighted in a romping sort of country dance, called the *Tempête*. She withdrew a little before twelve.'

Prince Albert was elected Chancellor of the University of Cambridge on the 28th of February, receiving 953 votes as against 837 given to his opponent the Earl of Powis. The installation of the Prince took place on the 6th of July, amid circumstances of great pomp and splendour, her Majesty being present at the investiture. The ceremony was performed in the hall of Trinity College. The journals report that the Queen, being seated on a chair of State on the dais, the new Chancellor (in his gorgeous robes of office), supported by the Duke of Wellington (Chancellor of the sister University of Oxford), the Bishop of Oxford, the Vice-Chancellor of Cambridge, and heads of houses approached, when the Chancellor read an address to her Majesty, congratulatory on her arrival. The Queen made a gracious reply, and the Prince retired with the usual profound obeisances—a proceeding which caused her Majesty some amusement.

A convocation was then held in the Senate House, the Royal Chancellor presiding, and the Queen attending as a visitor. There was great enthusiasm among the young gownsmen. Three German princes and other distinguished personages received honorary degrees. A grand dinner was given by the Vice-Chancellor, and in the evening there was a concert in the Senate House. The royal visitors occupied during their stay at Cambridge the Master's Lodge at Trinity College. Describing the incidents in Trinity Hall, Bishop Wilberforce wrote : 'The Cambridge scene was

very interesting.   There was such a burst of loyalty,
and it told so on the Queen and Prince.   E. would
not then have thought that he looked cold.   It was
quite clear that they both felt it as something new he
had earned, and not she given, a true English honour ;
and he looked so pleased and she so triumphant.
There were also some such pretty interludes when he presented the address, and she beamed upon him, and once
half smiled, and then covered the smile with a gentle
dignity, and then she said in her clear musical voice,
'The choice which the University has made of its
Chancellor *has my most entire approbation.*'   The
Queen herself observed in her diary :   ' I cannot say how
it agitated and embarrassed me to have to receive this
address and hear it read by my beloved Albert, who
walked in at the head of the University, and who
looked dear and beautiful in his robes, which were
carried by Colonel Phipps and Colonel Seymour.
Albert went through it all admirably, almost absurd,
however, as it was for us.   He gave me the address,
and read the answer, and a few kissed hands, and then
Albert retired with the University.'

The installation ode, written by the Poet Laureate,
William Wordsworth, was performed, next day, Tuesday, in the presence of the Prince Chancellor, with
great ceremony.   Her Majesty was again present as
a visitor, and there was an immense crowd to hear the
performance.   The ode contained many happy allu-
sions to the Queen and her consort.   The proceedings
were followed by a flower show and a magnificent
dinner at Trinity.   After dinner the royal guests
strolled forth to enjoy a private walk in the university
grounds.   The Queen has sketched this interesting

scene :—' Albert in his dress-coat, with a mackintosh over it, I in my evening dress and diadem, and with a veil over my head, and the Princes in their uniforms, and the ladies in their dresses and shawls and veils. We walked through the small garden, and could not at first find our way, after which we discovered the right road, and walked along the beautiful avenues of lime-trees in the grounds of St. John's College, along the water and over the bridges. All was so pretty and picturesque—in particular the one covered bridge of St. John's College, which is like the Bridge of Sighs at Venice. We stopped to listen to the distant hum of the town ; and nothing seemed wanting but some singing, which everywhere but here in this country we should have heard. A lattice opened, and we could fancy a lady appearing and listening to a serenade.' This scene might well have inspired some painter or poet.

On the Wednesday her Majesty held a levée in Henry VIII.'s drawing-room at Trinity Lodge, when the masters, professors, and doctors, with their ladies, were presented. The Prince Chancellor also held a levée, and received the Mayor and Corporation. Afterwards the Queen and Prince went to a public breakfast in the grounds of Trinity College, and this breakfast was no ordinary one, for it was attended by some thousands of the principal ladies and gentry of the eastern counties. In the afternoon the royal visitors returned to London, having, by their general bearing and condescension, riveted the chains of royalty upon her Majesty's Cambridge subjects.

The Queen resolved upon spending the early autumn of 1847 in Scotland. This was partly due to the

pleasure derived from her previous visit, and the beneficial effect it had upon her health, and also to the
strong desire of the Prince Consort to enjoy the really
fine sport of chasing the red-deer in their native
forests. Accordingly, on the 11th of August, her
Majesty and Prince Albert, with the Prince of Wales,
the Princess Royal, and the Prince of Leiningen left
Osborne in the *Victoria and Albert* yacht, with the
Fairy as tender. They made first for the Scilly
Islands, spending a night there, as the Queen suffered
from sea-sickness. This had disappeared next day,
and under more favourable weather the royal yacht
sailed through the Menai Straits—views of Snowdon
and of Carnarvon Castle being obtained—and past
the Isle of Man. The yachts, which were accompanied
by a fleet of war-vessels, then steered for the mouth of
the Clyde. The *Fairy* took her Majesty up the Clyde
as far as Dumbarton. The river was alive with ships
and boats of all descriptions; it seemed as if all
Glasgow had been suddenly seized with an aquatic fit.
The royal party minutely inspected the ancient and
celebrated Castle of Dumbarton. In returning, her
Majesty steamed past Greenock, and leaving Roseneath
on the right, passed on to Loch Long, a splendid lake
surrounded by grand hills, and reminding the visitors
of Switzerland. At Rothesay they went on board the
Victoria and Albert. The little Prince of Wales was
loudly cheered as Duke of Rothesay. The old castle
here was a relic of great interest.

On the 18th the royal party went through the
Kyles of Bute, that noble water-pass through verdure-
clad mountains. The Queen was much impressed by
the beautiful scene, which has moved every traveller

of whatever degree. The yachts next proceeded up
Loch Fyne, famous for its herrings as well as its
scenery. A pause had been made at Tarbert to
enable the travellers to view the expansive and magnificent panorama. 'The approach to Inveraray,' writes
the Queen in her *Journal*, 'is splendid; the loch is
very wide; straight before you a fine range of mountains splendidly lit up—green, pink, and lilac; to
the left the little town of Inveraray; and above it,
surrounded by pine woods, stands the Castle of Inveraray.'

The Queen and Prince had a true Highland reception. The Duke and Duchess of Argyll, the Duchess
of Sutherland, Lord Stafford, Lady Caroline Leveson-
Gower, and others, were waiting at the landing-place,
which was all ornamented with heather. There was
also the Celtic Society, with Campbell of Islay. The
royal visitors went by a beautiful winding drive to the
castle. Outside the house ' stood the Marquis of Lorne,
just two years old—a dear, white, fat, fair little fellow,
with reddish hair, but very delicate features, like both
his father and mother : he is such a merry, independent
little child. He had a black velvet dress and jacket,
with a " sporran," scarf, and Highland bonnet.' The
Queen little imagined that the child she thus saw was
to become the husband of one of her daughters, just as
she had little foreseen a similar event when she had
seen the little Prince Louis of Hesse on her German
tour.

From Inveraray the party proceeded to Ardrishaig,
at the head of the Crinan Canal. Passing through
the canal—which is a work of time, on account of its
eleven locks—they reached Crinan, where they spent

the night. Next morning they went through the
Sound of Jura and past the island of Kerrera to Oban,
which is the centre of some of the finest scenery in
Scotland. From thence they steered for Staffa, and
anchored close before the island. The Queen and all
her party were rowed in a barge towards the celebrated cave. Her Majesty thus speaks of the island
and the cave : ' The appearance it (the island) presents
is most extraordinary ; and when we turned the corner
to go into the renowned Fingal's Cave, the effect was
splendid—like a great entrance into a vaulted hall : it
looked almost awful as we entered, and the barge
heaved up and down in the swell of the sea. It is
very high, but not longer than 227 feet, and narrower
than I expected, being only 40 feet wide. The sea is
immensely deep in the cave. The rocks under water
were all colours—pink, blue, and green—which had a
most beautiful and varied effect. It was the first
time the British standard, with a Queen of Great
Britain and her husband and children, had ever entered
Fingal's Cave, and the men gave three cheers, which
sounded very impressive there.'

From Staffa the royal party went to Iona, where
the Queen and her ladies sketched the ruins of the
cathedral, while the Prince Consort and the Prince of
Leiningen inspected the sepultures of the ancient
kings and heroes of Scotland. Tobermory, in Mull,
was the next place visited, and from thence, on the
20th, the flotilla proceeded down the Sound of Mull
to Loch Eil, and anchored off Fort William. Prince
Albert landed here, and went to see Glencoe, celebrated
for its wild and rugged scenery, and the terrible
massacre of the Macdonalds in William III.'s time.

On Saturday, the 21st, Her Majesty and party quitted the squadron at Fort William, and proceeded by land to Ardverikie, on Loch Laggan, the place she had selected for her autumnal residence. 'I am quite sorry we shall have to leave our yacht,' she wrote, 'in which we have been so comfortably housed, and that this delightful voyage and tour among the western lochs and isles is at an end—they are so beautiful, and so full of poetry and romance, traditions and historical associations.'

Ardverikie, the estate upon which Her Majesty's temporary residence was situate, is said to have been used as a hunting park by King Fergus of Scotland. The present lodge was erected by the Marquis of Abercorn in 1840 ; it was now rented by Lord George Bentinck, who lent it to the Queen : it has since been destroyed by fire. It was a very plain and unpretentious building, and the greatest point of interest about it was that on the bare walls of two of the principal apartments Landseer had drawn masterly sketches of his inimitable productions, 'The Challenge,' and 'The Stag at Bay.' There was also, in a long corridor, a splendid collection of stags' heads, many of them with thirteen and fourteen points. In front of the house lay Loch Laggan, stretching away on either side, and having a total length of eight miles.

In this country abode the Queen enjoyed herself in riding, sketching, fishing, &c. Prince Albert followed exhilarating sport of various kinds with gun and rod, and made pedestrian excursions through the wild scenery adjacent; while the royal children found great delight in outdoor pastimes and in riding ponies. For four weeks this life of enjoyment and

of perfect retirement lasted. 'The Queen was greatly
delighted with the Highlands,' wrote Lord Campbell,
' in spite of the bad weather, and was accustomed to sally
forth for a walk in the midst of a heavy rain, putting
a great hood over her bonnet, and showing nothing of
her features but her eyes. The Prince's invariable
return to luncheon about two o'clock, in spite of
grouse-shooting and deer-stalking, is explained by his
voluntary desire to please the Queen, and by the intense hunger which assails him at this hour, when he
likes, in German fashion, to make his dinner.'

The royal party left Ardverikie on the 17th of September, and embarking on board the yacht, sailed for
the south, paying a visit to the Isle of Man, where the
Prince landed. Ultimately her Majesty and the
Prince, with their children, disembarked at the new
port of Fleetwood, and performed the rest of the
journey home by rail.

They reached Buckingham Palace on the evening of
the 21st. Upon this period of calm and peaceful
repose in the Highlands was shortly to supervene one
of profound care and anxiety

CHAPTER VI.

LAST YEARS OF WEDDED LIFE.

THE year 1848 was one of great upheaval amongst the States of Europe. France was the first to feel the force of the revolutionary movement. The policy of Louis Philippe, and especially his intrigues with a view to Bourbon aggrandisement, had long rendered the King very unpopular. The public discontent now found vent in revolution, and the dynasty was swept away, and a republic proclaimed.

The proud monarch and his family fled from Paris, and became fugitives and wanderers. The King succeeded in escaping to England, and landed at Newhaven in the name of 'John Smith.' Before his arrival the Queen had written to King Leopold: 'About the King and Queen (Louis Philippe and Queen Amélie) we still know nothing. We do everything we can for the poor family, who are indeed sorely to be pitied ; but you will naturally understand that we cannot make common cause with them, and cannot take a hostile position to the new state of things in France. We leave them alone ; but if a government which has the approbation of the country be formed, we shall feel it necessary to recognise it, in order to pin them down to maintain peace and the existing treaties, which is of the greatest importance. It will not be pleasant to do this, but the public good and the peace of Europe go before one's personal feelings.'

After Louis Philippe arrived at Claremont, he paid
a private visit to the Queen, by whom he was received
in the most affectionate and hospitable manner : and
this was her attitude towards the whole of the
members of the Orleans family. 'You know my love
for the family,' wrote her Majesty to Baron Stockmar ;
' you know how I longed to get on terms with them
again, and you said, "Time alone will, but certainly,
bring it about."   Little did I dream that this would
be the way we should meet again and see each other,
all in the most friendly way.   That the Duchess de
Montpensier, about whom we have been quarrelling
for the last year and a half, should be here as a fugi-
tive, and dressed in the clothes I sent her, and should
come to thank *me for my kindness*, is a reverse of fortune which no novelist would devise, and upon which
one could moralize for ever.' Some regret must surely
have passed through the mind of Louis Philippe himself, that he had not striven to govern, like the Sovereign of England, upon strict constitutional principles.

The effects of the revolutionary spirit were felt in
other countries—Italy, Spain, Prussia, and Austria ;
but in Belgium the attempts to incite the people
against the monarchy proved abortive, and the throne
of her Majesty's uncle remained secure.   This, however, was not the case with her brother and brother-
in-law, the Princes of Leiningen and Hohenlohe, who
were compelled to abdicate their seignorial rights.

In the midst of the general solicitude for the peace
of England during this time of convulsion the Queen
was delivered of her fourth daughter, the Princess
Louise.   The royal infant was christened at Buckingham Palace on the 13th of May following, receiving the

names of Louise Caroline Alberta, the first being the
name of the child's grandmother on the father's side,
and the last being the feminine form of her father's
name. The sponsors were the Duke Augustus of
Mecklenberg-Schwerin,the Duchess of Saxe-Meiningen,
and the Grand Duchess of Mecklenburg-Strelitz, but all
were represented by proxies. Prince Albert composed,
for the occasion, the music to the following chorale :—

> 'In life's gay morn, ere sprightly youth
>   By vice and folly is enslaved,
> Oh! may thy Maker's glorious name
>   Be on this infant mind engraved.
> So shall no shades of sorrow cloud
>   The sunshine of thy early days,
> But happiness, in endless round,
>   Shall still encompass all thy ways.'

Life and death are ever close together. Only a
few days after the birth of the Princess Louise, comes
the record of the death of Princess Sophia, the
youngest surviving daughter and twelfth child of
George III. and Queen Charlotte. She fell, as a shock
of corn fully ripe, at the age of seventy-one.

Not long after the birth of her daughter, the Queen
—whose thoughts were even then directed to her
people—wrote to King Leopold : 'I heard all that
passed, and my only thoughts and talk were political.
But I never was calmer, or quieter, or less nervous.
Great events make one calm; it is only trifles that
irritate my nerves.' Chartist disturbances were expected at this time, and there was considerable
discontent over the income-tax and the increased
grants for the army and navy. On the 13th of March
a Chartist meeting was held on Kennington Common,

but it did not prove itself so formidable as had been anticipated.· Great preparations were made, however, in view of possible outbreaks, and disturbances occurred in the north of England, and also in London. But the military and other authorities acted with promptitude, and the leaders of the movement having been arrested, the agitation subsided. The excitement in London, nevertheless, was at one time so great that nearly ₤00,000 special constables were sworn in, amongst them being Prince Louis Napoleon (afterwards Emperor of the French) and the Earl of Derby. When the danger was all over the Queen wrote to King Leopold : ' The Chartist meeting and procession have turned out a complete failure. The loyalty of the people at large has been very striking, and their indignation at their peace being interfered with by such wanton and worthless men, immense.' Irish agitation gave a good deal of trouble at this time, and eventually the three most prominent leaders, Mitchell, Meagher, and Smith O'Brien, were brought to trial for sedition. No conviction was obtained in the cases of Meagher and O'Brien, but Mitchell was found guilty and transported for fourteen years.

By way of showing the immense labour which devolved upon the Queen and Prince Albert, as well as the Foreign Secretary, during this year of trial and anxiety, it is stated that ' no less than twenty-eight thousand despatches were received by or sent out from the Foreign Office.'

The Queen prorogued Parliament in person on the 5th of September, and on the afternoon of the same day her Majesty and the Prince Consort, accompanied by the Prince of Wales, the Princess Royal, and

Prince Alfred, embarked in the royal yacht at Woolwich for Scotland. Their destination on this occasion was Balmoral Castle, which, on the recommendation of Sir James Clark, Prince Albert had leased from the Earl of Aberdeen. The royal squadron entered Aberdeen Harbour on the 7th, and on the following day her Majesty proceeded, amidst the most loyal demonstrations, to Balmoral. The place seems to have created a favourable impression upon the royal visitors from the first. ' It is a pretty little castle, in the old Scottish style,' remarked the Queen, in her *Journal*. ' There is a picturesque tower and garden in the front, with a high wooded hill : at the back there is a wood down to the Dee, and the hills rise all around.'

Sport and riding were the order of the day, and on the 16th the Queen ascended Loch-na-Garr on a pony led by Mr. Farquharson's head-keeper, Macdonald. Prince Albert endeavoured to stalk a deer, but in vain, and then he would occasionally make a detour after ptarmigan. When her Majesty had nearly reached the top of the mountain, the mist drifted in thick clouds, so as to hide everything not within a hundred yards or so. The ascent was determinedly finished, however ; but when the visitors descended, the wind blew a hurricane, and they were almost blinded with the mist. Another day was devoted to a ' drive ' in the picturesque wood of Balloch Buie, where Prince Albert shot a magnificent stag. The sport was successful, and every one was delighted, Macdonald and the keepers in particular ; the former saying that ' it was her Majesty's coming out that had brought the good luck.' The Queen was supposed to have ' a lucky foot,' of which the Highlanders think a great deal.

T

During her Majesty's stay in Scotland important events were transpiring abroad. England was comparatively quiet, though the sudden death of the Conservative leader, Lord George Bentinck, caused great sensation. In France, Prince Louis Napoleon had been elected by no fewer than five departments to the new French Chamber, while news came from Frankfort of a terrible riot in which two members of the German States Union were assassinated.

The royal party at Balmoral attended a 'gathering of the clans' at Invercauld, and were much interested in the wild and manly sports of the Highlanders. On the 28th, the Court left Balmoral for the South. Only a stay of a day was made in London, however, and then the Queen and her family proceeded to Osborne. In returning from their marine residence on the 9th of October, the royal party witnessed a sad accident in the Channel. The Queen's yacht passed the frigate *Grampus*, which had just returned from her station in the Pacific. The day was misty and stormy, but five women, relatives of the men on board the *Grampus*, had gone out in a small boat to meet them, being rowed by two watermen. A sudden squall swamped the boat, without the knowledge of any one on board the two vessels. The men on board a Custom-house boat, however, perceived a man clinging to the capsized boat, and immediately came up to render assistance. Prince Albert was the first person on board the *Fairy* to realize what had occurred. The Queen was quite overcome. The royal yacht was stopped, and one of its boats lowered, which picked up three women, two of whom were unfortunately dead. The storm was very violent, and Lord Adolphus Fitzclarence, the commander of the Queen's yacht, having decided that nothing further could be done, held on his course, affirming that it would be very unsafe to delay. The Queen and Prince Albert were strongly in favour of staying, and her Majesty felt the sad incident very much, for she wrote afterwards : 'It was a dreadful moment; too horrid to describe. It is a consolation to think we were of some use, and also that, even if the yacht had remained, they could not have done more. Still, we all keep feeling we might, though I think we could not. It is a terrible thing, and haunts me continually.'

In the ensuing month of November, Lord Melbourne, the Queen's first Minister—and a man to whom she had become much attached, in consequence of his almost paternal devotion to her in her early youth— passed away, having been for some time in seclusion. Her Majesty wrote concerning him: 'Truly and sincerely do I deplore the loss of one who was a most disinterested friend of mine, and most sincerely attached to me. He was, indeed, for the first two years and a half of my reign almost the only friend I had, except Stockmar and Lehzen, and I used to see him constantly —daily. I thought much and talked much of him all day.' The Queen also wrote in her *Journal* a day or two subsequently : 'I received a pretty and touching letter from Lady Palmerston, saying that my last letter to poor Lord Melbourne had been a great comfort and relief to him, and that during the last melancholy years of his life we had often been the chief means of cheering him up. This is a great satisfaction to me to hear.'

Parliament was opened by the Queen in person, on

T 2

the 2nd of February, and, in addition to its reference
to the continued Irish distress at home, the Royal Speech
lamented that a formidable rebellion had broken out in
the Punjab. The war proceeded with disastrous consequences, and although the fiercely contested battle of
Chillianwallah left the British masters of the field,
the Sikhs inflicted terrible losses upon our troops. Sir
Charles Napier was sent out, but before he arrived in
India Lord Gough had encountered the combined
forces of the enemy at Goojerat, and had totally
defeated them. The rebellion was suppressed, and
the Punjab was annexed to the British possessions in
India.

On the 19th of May another dastardly attack was
made upon her Majesty. After holding a Drawing
Room at Buckingham Palace, she went out in an open
carriage, with three of her children, to take a drive
round the Parks. Shortly before six o'clock the royal
carriage had arrived about midway down Constitution
Hill on its return, when a man who stood within the
railings of the Green Park discharged a pistol in the
direction of the Queen. He was immediately seized
by the bystanders, and would probably have been the
victim of lynch law, had not a park-keeper and a
constable interfered and arrested him. The carriage
stopped for a moment, but her Majesty, with great
coolness and decision, stood up, and motioned the
driver to go forward. The prisoner was brought up
and identified as one William Hamilton, of Adare, in
the county Limerick. He was a bricklayer's labourer,
who for five years past had led a roving life in
France and England. His last place of abode was in
Pimlico, in the house of a fellow-Irishman, whose

wife had lent him an old rusty pistol, ostensibly to make 'a sight in the air among the trees.' He was afterwards found in the Green Park under the circumstances narrated. Hamilton was put on his trial at the Central Criminal Court, when witnesses proved the presenting of the pistol at the carriage, and its explosion. The prisoner was sentenced to seven years' transportation.

The Queen's long-expected visit to Ireland was paid in August 1849. Her Majesty and Prince Albert, with their four children, embarked at Cowes on the 1st, in the royal yacht, and steered to the westward, convoyed by a squadron of four steamers. They arrived at the Cove of Cork at 10 P.M. on the following day, and came to anchor amidst the booming of artillery and the blaze of a universal illumination on sea and land. Next morning the most deafening cheers hailed her Majesty's first landing on Irish ground. The Queen received a number of addresses, and communicated her royal pleasure that the town of Cove should, in commemoration of its being the spot chosen for her landing, henceforth bear the name of Queenstown. The royal party re-embarked, and proceeded to Cork amid the enthusiastic shouts of thousands of Irish Celts. A royal progress was made through the city, the Queen being much struck by the noisy but good-natured crowd, and by the beauty of the women. The royal squadron next sailed to Waterford, and from there went on to Dublin. As the vessels came into Kingstown Harbour, and the Queen appeared on deck, there was a burst of cheering, renewed again and again, from some 40,000 spectators.

Early on the following day, Lord Clarendon, the Lord Lieutenant, and Lady Clarendon, with Prince George of Cambridge, the Archbishop of Dublin, and various officers of State, went on board to be in attendance on her Majesty. A deputation from the county of Dublin, headed by the Earl of Charlemont, presented an address. At ten o'clock the Queen and Prince Albert prepared to land, with their children. As the Queen's foot touched the shore, the royal standard swept aloft, the populace shouted, and the booming of the heavy guns veritably shook the earth. An eye-witness thus describes her Majesty's passage from the boat to the railway: 'It was a sight never to be forgotten, a sound to be recollected for ever. Ladies threw aside the old formula of waving a white pocket-handkerchief, and cheered for their lives, while the men waved whatever came first to hand—hat, stick, wand, or coat (for the day was very hot)—and rent the air with shouts of joy, which never decreased in energy till their beloved Sovereign was far out of sight. The Queen, turning from side to side, bowed repeatedly. Prince Albert shared in and acknowledged the plaudits of the people, while the royal children were objects of universal attention and admiration. Her Majesty seemed to feel deeply the warmth of her reception. She paused at the end of the platform for a moment, and again making her acknowledgments, was hailed with one universal and tremendous cheer as she entered the terminus. The royal party then went by rail to the capital.

The royal carriages were in waiting at the terminus, and her Majesty now made her progress through Dublin, having first received the keys of the city from

the Lord Mayor, and graciously returned them to him.
There was a triumphal arch of great size and beauty
at the entrance to the city, but it was the human
element all along the route which most deeply interested the Queen. 'It was a wonderful and stirring
scene,' she wrote; 'such masses of human beings, so
enthusiastic, so excited, yet such perfect order maintained. Then the number of troops, the different
bands stationed at certain distances, the waving of
hats and handkerchiefs, the bursts of welcome that
rent the air, all made it a never-to-be-forgotten scene
when we reflected how lately the country had been
under martial law.' Dublin, with its magnificent
Sackville Street, was greatly admired by the royal
visitors. In the midst of all the shouting and excitement, at the last triumphal arch, a tame dove, with
an olive-branch round its neck, was let down into the
Queen's lap—an incident which deserves recording to
the honour of some poetic Celt.

On the following day, the 7th, the Queen drove
into Dublin, and with the Prince Consort, who had
followed her on horseback, viewed the various public
buildings and institutions, including the Bank, the old
Parliament House, and Trinity College. In the afternoon, her Majesty visited Kilmainham Hospital, and
also went to College Green. Next day there was a
full Court and *levée* at the Castle, when congratulatory
addresses from the most important bodies in Ireland
were presented. On the 9th there was a grand
review in the Phœnix Park, and the day following
the Queen and Prince Albert, with Lord and Lady
Clarendon, went on a quiet visit to Carton, the seat of
the Duke of Leinster, 'Ireland's only duke.' Her

Majesty was much interested and amused by the Irish dancing and other things that she witnessed.

The royal party re-embarked at Queenstown the next day. 'As the yacht approached the extremity of the pier near the lighthouse, where the people were most thickly congregated, and who were cheering enthusiastically, the Queen suddenly left the two ladies-in-waiting, with whom she was conversing, ran with agility along the deck, and climbed the paddle-box to join Prince Albert, who did not notice her till she was nearly at his side. Reaching him, and taking his arm, she waved her right hand to the people on the piers.' She also ordered the royal standard to be lowered in courtesy to the cheering thousands on shore. Lord Clarendon said 'there was not an individual in Dublin who did not take as a personal compliment to himself the Queen's having gone upon the paddle-box and ordered the royal standard to be lowered three times.'

A very rough passage was experienced before the royal yacht anchored at three in the morning in Carrickfergus Road, about seven miles below Belfast. As there was not sufficient draught of water here for the *Victoria and Albert*, the illustrious party transferred themselves to the *Fairy*, in which vessel they glided up the Lough to Belfast. Here they were welcomed by Lord Londonderry and his family, Lord Donegal, and the Mayor of Belfast. Deputations of Presbyterians, and from the linen trade, &c., were received. The Queen knighted the mayor, as she had done his brother-mayor of Cork. The royal party landed and went to view the principal sights of the city. Her Majesty was greatly delighted with her reception by the Irish

people of all classes, and before leaving the country
she resolved upon creating her eldest son 'Earl of
Dublin,' a title which had been borne by her honoured
father.

The Queen intended to go on to Scotland from Belfast, but at the time of her proposed departure the
wind blew a hurricane, which continued throughout
the night, and the whole of the next day, Sunday.
Taking advantage of a momentary lull, however, the
royal squadron was enabled to make the voyage in the
afternoon of the last-named day.   After a very tempestuous passage, the royal yacht cast anchor in Loch
Ryan, on the western coast of Argyllshire ; Prince
Albert made a short detour from this point by Loch
Lomond, and rejoined her Majesty at Loch Goil,
whence they proceeded to Glasgow, where the honour
of knighthood was conferred upon the Lord Provost.
The Queen and the royal party inspected the fine
cathedral of Glasgow, and then departed by rail for
Stirling and Perth.

From the latter place the journey to Balmoral was
made entirely by the royal carriages, which bore
the distinguished visitors through some of the finest
of Highland scenery.   Balmoral was reached on the
15th.   The Queen remained in her Highland home
for about six weeks, enjoying, with her husband and
children, real privacy.   There were fewer servants and
attendants upon them than at any other time.   On one
occasion her Majesty accompanied the Prince Consort
on a distant excursion, and twice slept at a solitary hut
on an island on Loch Muich—the lake of darkness or
gloom. The Queen was impressed by the stern sublimity
of the scenery.   At her Majesty's Highland abode there

was trout-fishing, &c., by day, and whist with a
dummy in the evening, together with a walk round
the diminutive garden, ' where the silence and solitude,
only interrupted by the waving of the fir-trees, were
very striking.'

Greville was summoned to Balmoral in September,
to attend a Council called to order a prayer for relief
from the cholera, which was then committing its
ravages in London and elsewhere.   This picturesque
account of the Queen and Prince Albert at their
Scotch home appears in Greville's *Journal :* ' They live
there without any State whatever ; they live not merely
like private gentlefolks, but like very small gentlefolks—small house, small rooms, small establishment.
There are no soldiers, and the whole guard of the
Sovereign and the whole Royal Family is a single
policeman, who walks about the grounds to keep off
impertinent intruders or improper characters.   Their
attendants consisted of Lady Douro and Miss Dawson,
lady and maid-of-honour ; George Anson and Gordon ;
Birch, the Prince of Wales's tutor, and Miss Hildyard,
the governess of the children.   They live with the
greatest simplicity and ease.   The Prince shoots
every morning, returns to luncheon, and then they
walk and drive.   The Queen is running in and out
of the house all day long, and often goes about alone,
walks into the cottages, and sits down and chats with
the old women.

' I never before was in society with the Prince, or
had any conversation with him.   On Thursday morning John Russell and I were sitting together after
breakfast, when he came in and sat down with us,
and we conversed for about three-quarters of an hour.

I was greatly struck with him.   I saw at once (what
I had always heard) that he is very intelligent and
highly cultivated, and, moreover, that he has a
thoughtful mind, and thinks of subjects worth thinking about.   He seemed very much at his ease, very
gay, pleasant, and without the least stiffness or air of
dignity.   After luncheon we went to the Highland
gathering at Braemar—the Queen, the Prince, four
children, and two ladies in one pony carriage; John
Russell, Miss Hildyard, Mr. Birch and I in another;
Angus and Gordon on the box ; one groom, no more.
The gathering was at the old Castle of Braemar, and
a pretty sight enough.   We returned as we came,
and then everybody strolled about till dinner.   We
were only nine people, and it was all very easy and
really agreeable, the Queen in very good humour
and talkative; the Prince still more so, and talking
very well; no form, and everybody seemed at their
ease.'

The royal party left Balmoral on the 27th of
September, and travelled by way of Edinburgh and
Berwick, calling upon Earl Grey at Howick.   At
Reading they branched off for Gosport, and crossed
over from the latter place to Osborne.   A few days
after reaching their marine residence, the Queen and
Prince Albert were much moved on learning of the
death of Mr. Anson, the Prince's private secretary
and keeper of the Queen's privy purse.   These offices
were afterwards respectively filled by Colonel Phipps
and General Grey.

The new London Coal Exchange was opened on the
30th of October, and the Queen had intended to
perform the ceremony in person, but a slight attack

of chicken-pox prevented her.   Prince Albert took her place, and was accompanied by the Prince of Wales and the Princess Royal, who made their first appearance in public on this occasion.   The illustrious party went down the Thames in the royal barge, and there was a grand water pageant such as had not been seen for almost a century.   When the barge emerged from London Bridge there was a perfect forest of masts in the Upper Pool.   The landing-place was the Custom House Quay, from whence the royal party proceeded through a covered corridor to the principal entrance to the Coal Exchange.   After the opening ceremony there was of course the usual *déjeuner*, and the little Prince and Princess were much astonished at the enthusiasm with which the toast of their healths was received.   Prince Albert was much gratified with the whole proceedings, and said to his children as they re-embarked in the *Fairy*, 'Remember that you are indebted to the Lord Mayor for one of the happiest days of your lives.'

The Dowager Queen Adelaide died on the 2nd of December, at her country seat of Bentley Priory, at the age of fifty-seven years.   Towards the close of November, Queen Victoria had paid her last visit to her, afterwards writing to King Leopold : 'There was death written in that dear face.   It was such a picture of misery, of complete prostration, and yet she talked of everything.   I could hardly command my feelings when I came in, and when I kissed twice that poor dear thin hand.   I love her so dearly ; she has ever been so maternal in her affection to me.   She will find peace and a reward for her many sufferings.'   In accordance with the Queen Dowager's wishes, there

was no embalming, lying-in-state, or torchlight procession, and she was buried at Windsor without any
pomp or state.

Her Majesty's third son and seventh child was born
on the 1st of May 1850, and as this was the birthday
of the Duke of Wellington, it was determined to give
him the same name, Arthur. Writing to Baron
Stockmar, the Queen said : 'It is a singular thing
that this so much wished-for boy should be born on
the old Duke's eighty-first birthday. May that, and
his beloved father's name, bring the poor little infant
happiness and good fortune.' The child was christened
'Arthur William Patrick Albert.' The second name
was given after Prince William of Prussia (now the
Emperor of Germany), Patrick was in remembrance of
the Queen's visit to Ireland, and Albert was chosen
after the Prince Consort.

Only a few weeks after the birth of her child, a
most cowardly attack was made upon the Queen by
one Lieutenant Pate, a man of good family. As her
Majesty was leaving Cambridge House, where she had
called to inquire after the Duke of Cambridge, who
was seriously ill, Pate darted forward, and struck a
blow with a cane at her Majesty's face. The force of
the blow was broken by the bonnet, but a severe
bruise was inflicted on the Queen's forehead. The
perpetrator of this shameful outrage was a dandy, and
a conspicuous frequenter of the Parks. No motive
was ever assigned for the attack. At Pate's trial, the
usual plea of insanity was put forward, but the jury
declined to recognize it, and the prisoner was sentenced
to seven years' transportation.

Preparations were at this time being made for the

Great Exhibition, and Prince Albert was much chagrined at the opposition manifested in the press and in the House of Commons at the choice of Hyde Park as the site for the Exhibition. Immediately upon this came the melancholy news of the death of Sir Robert Peel, who met with an accident, which terminated fatally, while riding up Constitution Hill on the 29th of June. In all matters relating to the Exhibition the deceased statesman warmly supported the Prince, and after his death the latter wrote to Baron Stockmar: 'We are in deep grief; add to which, I cannot conceal from you that we are on the point of having to abandon the Exhibition altogether. We have announced our intention to do so, if on the day the vast building ought to be begun the site is taken from us.' To the Duchess of Kent the Prince wrote: 'Death has snatched from us Peel, the best of men, our truest friend, the strongest bulwark of the throne, the greatest statesman of his time!' Very different was the position Peel latterly occupied at Court compared with that he held at the time of the 'Bedchamber Plot,' which was the only misunderstanding her Majesty ever had with any of her Ministers.

The arbitrary action of Lord Palmerston as Foreign Minister at this juncture caused her Majesty and the Prince great concern. It was complained of him that in interviews he would apparently agree with the Sovereign's views, but would go away and write despatches in a completely opposite sense. Some of his own colleagues, Lord Lansdowne particularly, disapproved of Palmerston's proceedings; 'yet by their weak connivance he was allowed to set at defiance the

Sovereign, the Government, and public opinion, while the Queen could get neither redress nor support from Lord John Russell, and was forced to submit to such degradation.' Minutes submitted to the Queen in one form were changed by Palmerston into other forms; and Austria declined to send any ambassador to England, because he could not transact business with her Secretary of State. At length, matters reached such a pitch, that the Queen wrote a strong memorandum, which was submitted to Lord John Russell, and by him shown to Lord Palmerston, insisting upon the Foreign Secretary's rigid adherence to his duties, and indicating what she regarded as the exact nature of those duties.

The Queen and the Prince experienced considerable relief when the House of Commons decided that Hyde Park should be the site of the projected Great Exhibition. *Punch* had made fun of Prince Albert in connection with this subject, but he took its jokes very good-humouredly.

In July 1850, the popular Duke of Cambridge died. He was the youngest of the sons of George III. who attained manhood. Prince George, the present Duke, succeeded, and Parliament voted him £12,000 per annum in lieu of the £27,000 which his father enjoyed as the son of a previous Sovereign. Not long after the Duke of Cambridge's death, news arrived of the decease of Louis Philippe, ex-King of the French, in his seventy-seventh year. He had not long survived his reverse of kingly fortune.

Her Majesty and her family visited the North again in the autumn, calling on the way at Castle Howard, the seat of the Earl of Carlisle. From thence she proceeded to the Tyne, where she opened a splendid railway bridge, and she subsequently opened a second one over the Tweed. At Edinburgh, the Queen stayed for one night at Holyrood Palace, where she and the Prince, and their children, were deeply interested in the memorials and reminiscences of Mary, the hapless Queen of Scots. From Arthur's Seat, the royal party viewed the fair city of Edinburgh. On the second day of the visit Prince Albert laid the foundation-stone of the Scotch National Gallery, and made his first speech before an Edinburgh audience, acquitting himself very creditably. Later in the day, the Scott Monument, the High Street, the Canongate, Donaldson's Hospital, and the Queen's Park were visited. A brilliant circle assembled at Holyrood in the evening, including the Queen and the Prince, the Buccleuchs, the Roxburghes, the Mortons, the Belhavens, &c. It was in remembrance of this evening that some years later Lord Belhaven bequeathed to her Majesty a cabinet which had been brought by Queen Mary from France, and given by her to the Regent Mar, from whom it passed into the family of Lord Belhaven. It contained a lock of Queen Mary's hair, and a purse worked by her.

Next day the royal party travelled to Balmoral. The celebrated Braemar gathering was attended this year by the Queen and the whole of her family as well as by the Duchess of Kent. Another amusement was that of witnessing the spearing of salmon in the Dee. A singular and somewhat laughable incident occurred, which was thus described in one of Prince Albert's letters: 'Our people in the Highlands are altogether primitive, true-hearted and without guile,

Yesterday the Forbeses of Strath Don passed through here. When they came to the Dee, our people (of Strath Dee) offered to carry them across the river, and did so, whereupon they drank to the health of Victoria in whisky (*schnapps*), but as there was no cup to be had, their chief, Captain Forbes, pulled off his shoe, and he and his fifty men drank out of it.' The Forbeses marched through the grounds of Balmoral, 'piping' and cheering.

The stay at Balmoral was very pleasant, but it was not without causes of anxiety. The visit of General Haynau, the Austrian woman-whipper, caused great indignation in London, and in connection with a disturbance at Barclay's Brewery during Haynau's visit, Lord Palmerston wrote a despatch which had to be recalled.

The Queen of the Belgians was seriously ill during the stay of her Majesty in the Highlands, and immediately after the return of the Court to Osborne she died, leaving the Queen's uncle Leopold bitterly to lament her loss.

Great sensation was caused in the following winter by the issue of a Papal Bull redistributing the Roman Catholic bishoprics in England, and placing a Cardinal Archbishop at their head. The Pope's policy was strongly resented by the Prime Minister, Lord John Russell, who introduced the Ecclesiastical Titles Bill. The Universities of Oxford and Cambridge presented formal protests to the Queen, which her Majesty acknowledged. Like many of the more sober judges of the ·question, the Queen felt that the Pope could do no harm; he might do what he pleased, but he could never make England Catholic ; and this sensible

U

view prevailed throughout the country as the momentary excitement passed away.

Lady Lyttelton, who had been governess to the royal children for eight years, retired from that post in January 1851. She was the daughter of the second Earl Spencer, and married at twenty-six the third Lord Lyttelton. At the time of her retirement from the Queen's service she was fifty-four, and she desired to spend the remainder of her life in rest and repose. Writing of her farewell, Lady Lyttelton said: 'I was sent for to my last audience in the Queen's own room, and I quite broke down and could hardly speak or hear. I remember the Prince's face, pale as ashes, and .a few words of praise and thanks from them both, but it is all misty; and I had to stop on the private staircase and have my cry out before I could go up again.' Her ladyship was succeeded by Lady Caroline Barrington—sister of Earl Grey—who remained in the Queen's household until her death in 1875.

The greatest domestic event of 1851, and indeed of many years, was the opening of the Great Exhibition in Hyde Park. This precursor of so many international festivals was held in the palace of glass designed by Sir Joseph Paxton, who was knighted for his services. Prince Albert chose the motto of the exhibition—'The earth is the Lord's and the fulness thereof; the world, and they that dwell therein;' and from all quarters of the universe came goods and treasure to the great central storehouse, which peacefully represented the progress of the human race in art, science, industry, and commerce. Never had such a triumph been witnessed in all that concerns the internal welfare and advancement of States and Empires.

The inaugural ceremony took place on the 1st of May, and it is almost superfluous to say that it was a most imposing sight. The Queen and Prince Albert and all the royal children, as well as the Duchess of Kent and the young Count Gleichen, were present. The Park presented a wonderful spectacle, and the scene in the streets recalled that of the Coronation Day. The Queen wrote a graphic account of the ceremony in her diary, and as it takes us below the surface, and exhibits the inner emotions of her Majesty, as well as the main features of the ceremonial on this great day, I shall make extracts from her account in preference to those given in the daily journals. The following are the chief passages in the Sovereign's description :—

' At half-past eleven the whole procession in State carriages was in motion. The Green Park and Hyde Park were one densely crowded mass of human beings, in the highest good-humour and most enthusiastic. I never saw Hyde Park look as it did, as far as the eye could reach. A little rain fell just as we started, but before we came near the Crystal Palace, the sun shone and gleamed upon the gigantic edifice, upon which the flags of all the nations were floating. We drove up Rotten Row, and got out at the entrance on that side.

' The glimpse of the transept through the iron gates, the waving palms, flowers, statues, myriads of people filling the galleries and seats around, with the flourish of trumpets as we entered, gave us a sensation which I can never forget, and I felt much moved.

U 2

We went for a moment to a little side room where we left our shawls, and where we found mama and Mary (now Princess of Teck), and outside which were standing the other Princes. In a few seconds we proceeded, Albert leading me, having Vicky at his hand, and Bertie holding mine. The sight as we came to the middle where the steps and chair (which I did *not* sit on) were placed, with the beautiful crystal fountain just in front of it, was magical, so vast, so glorious, so touching. One felt—as so many did whom I have since spoken to—filled with devotion more so than by any service I have ever heard. The tremendous cheers, the joy expressed in every face, the immensity of the building, the mixture of palms, flowers, trees, statues, fountains—the organ (with 200 instruments and 600 voices, which sounded like nothing), and my beloved husband, the author of this "Peace Festival," which united the industry of all nations of the earth—all this was moving indeed, and it was and is a day to live for ever. God bless my dearest Albert! God bless my dearest country, which has shown itself so great to-day! One felt so grateful to the great God who seemed to pervade all and to bless all! The only event it in the slightest degree reminded me of was the Coronation, but this day's festival was a thousand times superior. In fact, it is unique, and can bear no comparison, from its peculiarity, beauty, and combination of such different and striking objects. I mean the slight resemblance only as to its solemnity; the enthusiasm and cheering too were much more touching, for in a church naturally all is silent.

'Albert left my side after "God save the Queen"

had been sung, and at the head of the Commissioners
—a curious assemblage of political and distinguished
men—read me the report, which is a long one, and
to which I read a short answer.   After this the
Archbishop of Canterbury offered up a short and
appropriate prayer, followed by the "Hallelujah
Chorus," during which a Chinese mandarin came forward and made his obeisance.*   This concluded, the
procession began.   It was beautifully arranged, and
of great length—the prescribed order being exactly
adhered to.   The nave was full, which had not been
intended; but still there was no difficulty, and the
whole long walk from one end to the other was made
in the midst of continued and deafening cheers and
waving of handkerchiefs.   Every one's face was
bright and smiling, many with tears in their eyes.
Many Frenchmen called out, "*Vive la Reine!*"   One
could of course see nothing but what was here in the
nave, and nothing in the courts.   The organs were
but little heard, but the military band at one end had
a very fine effect as we passed along.   They played
the march from *Athalie.*   The beautiful Amazon in
bronze, by Kiss, looked very magnificent.   The old
Duke and Lord Anglesey walked arm-in-arm, which
was a touching sight.   I saw many acquaintances
amongst those present.

   'We returned to our own place, and Albert told
Lord Breadalbane to declare that the Exhibition was
opened, which he did in a loud voice: "Her Majesty
commands me to declare this Exhibition open," which

---

* This incident was not provided for in the official programme.
It was purely spontaneous on the part of the mandarin, who
was apparently overcome by the solemnity of the scene.

was followed by a flourish of trumpets and immense cheering. All the Commissioners, the Executive Committee, &c., who worked so hard, and to whom such immense praise is due, seemed truly happy, and no one more so than Paxton, who may be justly proud; he rose from being a common gardener's boy. Everybody was astonished and delighted; Sir George Grey (Home Secretary) in tears.

'The return was equally satisfactory; the crowd most enthusiastic, the order perfect. We reached the Palace at twenty minutes past one, and went out on the balcony and were loudly cheered. The Prince and Princess (of Prussia) quite delighted and impressed. That we felt happy—thankful—I need not say; proud of all that had passed, of my darling husband's success, and of the behaviour of my good people. I was more impressed than I can say by the scene. It was one that can never be effaced from my memory, and never will be from that of any one who witnessed it. Albert's name is immortalized, and the wicked and absurd reports of dangers of every kind which a set of people—viz., the *soi-disant* fashionables and the most violent Protectionists spread—are silenced. It is therefore doubly satisfactory that all should have gone off so well, and without the slightest accident or mishap. . . . . Albert's emphatic words last year, when he said that the feeling would be "*that of deep thankfulness to the Almighty for the blessings which He has bestowed upon us here below,*" have been this day realized. . . . .

'I must not omit to mention an interesting episode of this day—viz., the visit of the good old Duke on this his eighty-second birthday to his little godson, our dear little boy. He came to us both at five, and gave him a golden cup and some toys, which he had himself chosen, and Arthur gave him a nosegay.

'We dined *en famille*, and then went to the Covent Garden Opera, where we saw the two finest acts of the *Huguenots* given as beautifully as last year. I was rather tired ; but we were both so happy, so full of thankfulness ! God is indeed our kind and merciful Father !'

Lord John Russell congratulated the Queen upon the triumphant success of the day's proceedings. All the arrangements had been most perfectly carried out. In addition to 25,000 people within the building, it was calculated that nearly 700,000 people were assembled on the route between it and Buckingham Palace ; yet the Home Secretary was able to report to her Majesty next day that there had not been one accident or one police case due to this assemblage. Such a circumstance was probably unexampled in the history of great popular celebrations. Well might the Queen assert that this Exhibition of 1851 would contribute to give imperishable fame to Prince Albert, while the day of its opening, the 1st of May, would ever remain 'the proudest and happiest of her happy life !'

The Queen and the Prince Consort entered into other enjoyments at this time. They heard Rachel in the *Andromaque*, were present when Macready took leave of the stage, and attended a performance at Devonshire House on behalf of the newly formed Guild of Literature and Art, when Charles Dickens, Douglas Jerrold, John Forster, and others, appeared in *Not so Bad as We Seem*. The Prince was also very prominent in charitable and scientific enterprises, and manifested a deep interest in the British Association.

A grand fancy ball was given by the Queen at Buckingham Palace on the 13th of June. All the characters and costumes were drawn from the Restoration period. Her Majesty and the Prince were superbly dressed. Four national quadrilles—English, Scotch, French, and Spanish—were danced; and subsequently there was a 'Rose' quadrille. In opening the general ball, which followed, the Queen danced the *Polonaise* with Prince Albert, the Duke of Cambridge, and Prince Edward of Saxe Weimar. Prince Albert next danced with the Duchess of Norfolk, the premier peeress, and after supper the Queen danced with the Prince of Leiningen. Lady Ashburton appeared as Madame de Sévigné, and the Countess of Tankerville as the Duchesse de Grammont, whom she personated in right of her mother-in-law, Corisande de Grammont, granddaughter of Marie Antoinette's friend, Gabrielle de Polignac. Mr. Bancroft Davies, Secretary of the United States Legation, appeared as William Penn; and there were many other assumptions of distinguished characters. Miss Burdett Coutts and Lady Londonderry surprised every one by their dazzling display of jewels. The Duke of Wellington was in the scarlet and gold uniform of the period; Lord Galway was in a plain cuirass and gorget; while Mr. Gladstone—*mirabile dictu*—appeared as a judge of the High Court of Admiralty in Charles's reign, 'in a velvet coat turned up with blue satin, ruffles and collar of old point, black breeches and stockings, and shoes with spreading bows.'

The City also gave a grand ball at the Guildhall on

the 9th of July, to celebrate the opening of the
Exhibition.   The Queen and Prince Albert, and large
numbers of the aristocracy, were present.   The great
hall in which the ball took place was splendidly fitted
up.   There was a striking array of banners em-
blazoned with the arms of the nations and cities represented at the Palace in Hyde Park, while the compartments beneath the balconies were filled with
pictorial representations of the finest and most striking
contributions in the Exhibition.   After the dancing,
supper was served in the crypt, which was made to
represent an old baronial hall.   On leaving, her
Majesty thanked Lord Mayor Musgrove for his hospitality, and announced her intention of creating him
a baronet.   Prince Albert told Baron Stockmar that
this City ball passed off most brilliantly, and that a
million of people remained till three in the morning
in the streets, and cheered her Majesty on her return
with great enthusiasm.

On the 27th of August the Queen, Prince Albert,
and several of the royal children, left London for
Balmoral, travelling for the first time by the Great
Northern Railway.   A halt was made at Peterborough,
where her Majesty had a kindly interview with the
venerable Bishop, Dr. Davys, who had been the tutor
of her childhood.   Boston, Lincoln, and Doncaster
were next visited, the royal party stopping for a night
at the last-named town, selecting the Angel Inn for
their resting-place.   Going on next day to Edinburgh,
her Majesty and the Prince drove through the city, and
remained for the night in the State apartments of
Holyrood Palace.   The honour of knighthood was
conferred on the Lord Provost of Edinburgh.

Balmoral was reached on the evening of the 29th.
The castle and domain had now become royal property.
The estate extended to upwards of seven miles in length
and four in breadth. The stay this year was not marked
by any special incidents, though several features of
interest attended the return journey. Leaving her
Highland residence on the 7th of October, the Queen
journeyed with her family to the South. Between
Forfar and Glasgow the axle of a carriage truck
became ignited, and the carriage had to be disengaged;
while between Glasgow and Edinburgh one of the
feeder-pipes from the tender to the engine burst with
a loud explosion. No evil results occurred from these
misadventures. At Lancaster the royal party alighted
to view John of Gaunt's ancient castle. The Queen
and the Prince then proceeded to Croxteth Park, the
seat of the Earl of Sefton. From thence, on the
following day, a royal progress was made through
Liverpool, in accordance with previous arrangements.
Great preparations had been made for her Majesty's
reception, but the weather was disastrously unfavourable. The rain poured down in torrents, and all
objects were concealed in a deep mist. The Queen
and the Prince, nevertheless, courageously went
through the whole of the programme; and the streets
were crowded with persons whose loyalty defied the
elements. The royal party visited the Docks, and
sailed round the mouth of the Mersey. They then
visited the Town Hall and St. George's Hall. At the
Town Hall addresses were presented, and her Majesty
knighted the Mayor, Mr. John Bent. From Liverpool the royal party went by barges on the Bridge-
water Canal to Worsley Hall, the seat of the Earl of

Ellesmere. Next day was a grand gala day at Manchester. There was a royal progress through the town, the Queen being received everywhere with the utmost enthusiasm; and in Peel Park nearly 80,000 children, belonging to all religious denominations, were arranged in fourteen tiers of galleries. It was· during this royal visit that Sir John Potter received his knighthood. Her Majesty returned to Worsley Hall, and next day the royal travellers journeyed to Watford, where they took carriages to Windsor.

The Queen paid a farewell visit to the Exhibition on the 14th of October, and shortly afterwards it was dismantled. During the five and a half months it had remained open, the visitors had been 6,200,000, and the total receipts £500,000.

Several events of moment occurred before the close of the year. In November the King of Hanover died. He was the fifth and last surviving son of George III. and Queen Charlotte, and as Duke of Cumberland he had been anything but popular. Louis Kossuth came over to England in the autumn of 1851, and created intense interest and excitement. But the most startling incident of all this year occurred on the 2nd of December, that fatal day which witnessed the *coup d'état* of Louis Napoleon. By the aid of the army, the ambitious Bonaparte ruthlessly violated the rights of the people, laying the foundation of his power in bloodshed and despotism. A good deal of ill-feeling resulted between England and France, but all fears of French aggression ultimately died out. Lord Palmerston was compelled to resign in consequence of his too-ready acceptance of the *coup d'état* and his acquiescence in the measures of

Louis Napoleon; but he had his revenge early in the following year, when he was mainly instrumental in overthrowing the Liberal Government on its Militia Bill.

The year 1852 was one of appalling disasters. Early in January the splendid mail steam-ship *Amazon* was destroyed by fire as she was entering the Bay of Biscay. Out of a total of 161 persons on board no fewer than 140 perished. Amongst those who met a terrible fate on this occasion was that admirable writer, Mr. Eliot Warburton. Another fearful catastrophe occurred in April, when her Majesty's steam troop-ship *Birkenhead* went down near the Cape of Good Hope. Heart-rending accounts were published of the disaster from survivors. Out of 630 persons on board, chiefly military passengers and their wives and children, only 194 were saved. A third catastrophe, which occurred at home, was the bursting of the Bilberry reservoir, near Holmfirth, on the borders of Yorkshire and Lancashire. An immense destruction of life and property ensued. Nearly one hundred persons perished; and, as an example of the wreck and ruin involved, it may be stated that one family who the night before were worth £10,000, were reduced to ask for clothes to cover them. More than 7,000 persons were instantly rendered destitute, and the total damage was estimated at £600,000. Her Majesty was greatly moved on learning of these dire calamities.

When the London season commenced this year, an interesting correspondence took place between the King of the Belgians and the Queen. The former was afraid lest the wear and tear of London life should have an injurious effect upon her Majesty.

The Queen's reply set her uncle's mind at rest:
' The London season for us consists of two State balls
and two concerts. We are hardly ever later than
twelve o'clock at night, and our only dissipation is
going three or four times a week to the play or
opera, which is a great amusement and relaxation to
us both. As for going out as people do here every
night to balls and parties, and to breakfasts and teas
all day long besides, I am sure no one would stand it
worse than I should; so you see, dearest uncle, that
in fact the London season is nothing to us.'

While her Majesty was staying at Osborne in the
summer, she received news of the death of Count
Mensdorff, who had married the sister of the Duchess
of Kent, and was consequently uncle by marriage both
to the Queen and Prince Albert. Princess Hohenlohe
came over on a visit at this time; she was in great
distress and anguish, having just lost her eldest
daughter from consumption.

In July the Queen and Prince Albert made a
marine excursion along the Devonshire coast, and in
the ensuing month they went over to Brussels on
a brief visit to King Leopold. Shortly after their
return, her Majesty received intimation that a large
legacy had been bequeathed to her absolutely by an
eccentric barrister of Lincoln's Inn, named John
Camden Nield. The testator had inherited a large
fortune from his father, which he had greatly increased by his penurious habits. Mr. Nield's personalty
was sworn under £250,000.

The Court proceeded to Balmoral in August, and
on the 16th of the following month, while on an
excursion to the Glassalt Shiel, the Queen received

intelligence of the death of the greatest of her subjects. The illustrious Wellington, 'the great Duke,' had passed away at Walmer, after a few hours' illness, and with no suffering, at the patriarchal age of eighty-three. Keenly did her Majesty feel this great loss, for the Duke had in a measure held towards her the triple capacity of father, hero, and friend. In the plenitude of her grief, and with an exaggeration of language which will be understood in consequence, she spoke of him as 'England's, or rather Britain's, pride, her glory, her hero, the greatest man she had ever produced.'

Thousands of British hearts, however, echoed the Queen's sentiment when she wrote that 'one cannot think of this country without "the Duke," our immortal hero!' Full justice was done by the Queen in the following passage to the great soldier's character: 'In him centred almost every earthly honour a subject could possess. His position was the highest a subject ever had—above party—looked up to by all—revered by the whole nation—the friend of the Sovereign—and how simply he carried these honours! With what singleness of purpose, what straightforwardness, what courage, were all the motives of his actions guided.

'The Crown never possessed—and I fear never *will*—so devoted, loyal, and faithful a subject, so staunch a supporter! To *us* (who, alas! have lost now so many of our valued and experienced friends) his loss is *irreparable*, for his readiness to aid and advise, if it could be of use to us, to overcome any and every difficulty, was unequalled. To Albert he showed the greatest kindness and the utmost confidence. His experience and knowledge of the past were so great too ; he was a link which connected us with bygone times, with the last century. Not an eye will be dry in the whole country.'

While the pessimism of grief pervaded this tribute, it indicated very clearly the characteristics of the man whom all Britain mourned as with one heart. The body of the Duke was brought up to London, and conveyed to Chelsea Hospital, where it lay in State for four days, and was viewed privately on the first day by the Queen and Prince Albert and their children.   On the 18th the great Duke was laid to rest in St. Paul's Cathedral, the funeral being such as had never before been celebrated for any Englishman. At the close of the funeral rites in the Cathedral, the body was lowered into the vault amid the solemn strains of the 'Dead March.' A sense of depression, of personal loss, then came over the vast assembly. Prince Albert, it is stated, was deeply moved, and the aged Marquis of Anglesey, the octogenarian companion in arms of the deceased, by an irresistible impulse stepped forward, placed his hand on the sinking coffin that contained the remains of his chief in many battles, and burst into tears. Verily, a prince and a great man had fallen in Israel !

In December 1852 the Derby-Disraeli Government fell upon its Budget, which was attacked with great force by Mr. Gladstone.   Lord Aberdeen became Prime Minister, and his Ministry included many of the leading Whigs and Peelites, Mr. Gladstone being Chancellor of the Exchequer for the first time.

Across the Channel, the French Empire had just been declared, and Louis Napoleon had made his public entry into Paris as Emperor.

On the 19th of March 1853 a disastrous fire broke out in Windsor Castle, which at one time placed that magnificent structure and the whole, of its contents in jeopardy. Fortunately, the flames were subdued and the injury was confined to the ceilings of the dining-room in the Prince of Wales's Tower, and two floors of bedrooms immediately over it, which were practically destroyed. The fire was supposed to have originated from the heating of the flues. The Court was at Windsor at the time, and the Queen, in writing upon the fire to the King of the Belgians, said : ' Though I was not alarmed it was a serious affair, and an acquaintance with what a fire is and with its necessary accompaniments, does not pass from one's mind without leaving a deep impression. For some time it was very obstinate, and no one could tell whether it would spread or not. Thank God, no lives were lost.' The principal treasures in the State rooms were removed in safety on the announcement of the outbreak.

The eighth child of her Majesty, and her fourth son, was born at Buckingham Palace on the 7th of April. He was named Leopold George Duncan Albert, the first name being after King Leopold, the second after the King of Hanover, and the fourth after Prince Albert. The third name was a compliment to Scotland. With regard to the name of Leopold, the Queen said to her uncle, ' Stockmar will have told you that Leopold is to be the name of our fourth young gentleman. It is a mark of love and affection which

I hope you will not disapprove. It is a name which is the dearest to me after Albert, one which recalls the almost only happy days of my sad childhood.' When the young Prince arrived at manhood it was arranged to retain this popular name of Leopold by styling his Royal Highness ' Prince Leopold, Duke of Albany.'

On the 21st of June there was a splendid military spectacle at Chobham, when a sham fight and a series of military manœuvres were carried out before the Queen and Prince Albert, the King and Queen of Hanover, and the Duke and Duchess of Coburg, then on a visit to the English Court. Queen Victoria excited great admiration as she rode down the lines, dressed in a half-military riding-habit, and mounted on a splendid ebony steed.

That royalty is subject to the ordinary ills of humanity was proved early in July, when various members of the Queen's family were attacked with measles. The Prince of Wales was the first sufferer, but he was quickly convalescent; Prince Albert suffered more virulently; the Princess Royal and the Princess Alice took the infection mildly, and the Queen also suffered from a very mild attack of the disorder. All happily recovered without any serious consequences; but the disease was subsequently conveyed by the Queen's visitors to the Courts of Hanover and Belgium.

Her Majesty held a grand naval review at Spithead on the 11th of August, and there were present with her as spectators the Prince of Prussia, the Crown Prince and Princess of Würtemburg, and three Russian archduchesses. The sight was splendid, as the noblest

x

vessels in the British fleet passed majestically along, and afterwards engaged in mimic warfare.

On the 29th of August, the Queen and Prince Albert, with the Prince of Wales and Prince Alfred, crossed over from Holyhead to Dublin, to visit the Exhibition of Art and Industry which had been opened in the Irish capital. It was an offshoot of the Hyde Park Exhibition. On landing, the royal party were received by the Lord Lieutenant, the Archbishop of Dublin, the Duke of Leinster, and numerous other peers and dignitaries. The same enthusiasm was shown by the crowds of spectators as on the occasion of the previous visit. Her Majesty took a walk in the Phœnix Park in the afternoon, and a drive in the evening, when Dublin was brilliantly illuminated. Next day, the Queen and the Prince, and their two children, were received in State at the Exhibition; an address was presented to her Majesty, thanking her for her support of the Exhibition, and her contributions; and in her reply the Queen eulogized the manner in which the enterprise had ·been carried out, 'with no pecuniary aid but that derived from the patriotic munificence of one of her Irish subjects.' This subject was Mr. Dargan, who had erected the Exhibition building at his own expense, and who now came forward and kissed hands amid the loud applause of the assembly.

The royal visitors remained in Dublin for a week, evincing great interest in the various Irish manufactures and industries. On the afternoon of one day the Queen and Prince Albert drove out to Mount Annville, the residence of Mr. Dargan. Her Majesty would have made its owner a baronet, but he was anxious that this should not be done.

On the 3rd of September the royal party left
Kingstown in the *Victoria and Albert*, and crossed
over to Holyhead.   Here they transferred themselves
to the *Fairy*, and cruised along the beautiful shores of
Carnarvon Bay.   Returning to Holyhead, they proceeded thence by rail to Scotland, reaching Balmoral
on the afternoon of the 6th.   The only event of
interest during the Queen's stay at her Highland
home this year was the laying the foundation-stone
of the new house at Balmoral.   This was done, with
all due ceremony, on the 28th of September.   The
Rev. Mr. Anderson, parish minister of Crathie, prayed
for a blessing on the work, and then her Majesty
affixed her signature to a parchment recording the
day upon which the foundation-stone was laid.

The Court returned to Windsor Castle earlier than
usual, in consequence of the critical state of affairs in the
East of Europe.   In reply to the movement of Russian
troops across the Danube the Turks declared war, and the
French and English Governments notified to the Czar
that if any further warlike steps were taken against
Turkey, the Allied fleets would enter the Black Sea,
and take up the cause of the Porte.   Meanwhile,
there were dissensions in the English Cabinet, and
when Lord Palmerston, who represented the strong
British war feeling, withdrew from the Government,
great popular excitement ensued.   There was loud
talk about Court prejudice and intrigue, and it was
openly said that Prince Albert was acting as a hostile
influence 'behind the Throne' against Lord Palmerston and the wishes of the people.   The feeling was
now as strong against the Prince as it had been in his
favour a few years before.   Tories and Liberals were

X 2

alike embittered against him. Writing to Baron
Stockmar, the Prince said : ' One word more about the
credulity of the public. You will scarcely credit that
my being committed to the Tower was believed all
over the country—nay, even "that the Queen had
been arrested." People surrounded the Tower in
thousands to see us brought to it. . . . . It was anything but pleasant to me that so many people could
look upon me "as a rogue and traitor," and I shall
not be at ease until I see the debate in Parliament
well over.; for it is not enough that these rumours
should be dispelled for the time—they must be knocked
on the head, and the disease radically cured. Then,
what has occurred may be of the greatest service for
the future.' The Queen wrote to Lord Aberdeen : ' In
attacking the Prince, who is one and the same with
the Queen herself, the Throne is assailed, and she
must say she little expected that any portion of her
subjects would thus requite the unceasing labours of
the Prince.' In January 1854, when Parliament met,
the calumnies against the Prince were completely
refuted by Lord Aberdeen in the House of Lords, and
Lord John Russell in the House of Commons. Lord
Campbell, Lord Derby, and Mr. Walpole, all high constitutional authorities, vindicated the right of the
Prince to support the Sovereign by his advice in all
matters of State.

Her Majesty heartily rejoiced when the clouds
lifted, and a letter she wrote to Baron Stockmar, on
the anniversary of her marriage, showed the strength
of her womanly feelings. ' This blessed day,' she
observed, ' is full of joyful, tender emotions. Fourteen happy and blessed years have passed, and I con-

fidently trust many more will, and find us in old age
as we are now—happy and devotedly united.   Trials
we must have ; but what are they if we are together ? '
A family masque was performed on this occasion, in
which all the royal children took part.   At one point
in the proceedings the Princess Helena appeared as
Britannia, and pronounced a blessing on the Queen
and Prince, in the name of all the Seasons, which had
been represented respectively by the Princess Alice,
the Princess Royal, Prince Alfred, and the Prince of
Wales.

Not long after this peaceful scene, war was declared
against Russia, and on a cold March morning a painfully interesting incident was witnessed in front of
Buckingham Palace, when the Fusiliers marched past,
cheering the Queen heartily.   Her Majesty was much
touched over the farewell to her gallant troops, now
setting out for the East.   There were many sorrowing
friends to bid good-bye to the soldiers.   High and low
felt the grief of parting, and amongst the former was
the Duchess of Cambridge, who bade farewell to her
son, now the Commander-in-Chief.   Some days later
the Queen went to Spithead, to view the magnificent
fleet under Sir Charles Napier, before it sailed for the
Baltic.

Her Majesty's birthday was this year spent at
Osborne, and to commemorate the occasion, the royal
children were presented with the Swiss cottage in the
grounds, for their own youthful use and behoof.   Undeterred by wars and rumours of wars, the young
Princes and Princesses enjoyed themselves exceedingly.
Each had a flower and vegetable garden, greenhouses,
hothouses and forcing-frames, nurseries, tool-houses,

and even a carpenter's shop. All worked at gardening
con amore. On this juvenile property there was also a
building, the ground-floor of which was fitted up as a
kitchen, with pantries, closets, dairy, and larder; and
the young Princesses might sometimes be seen arrayed
à la cuisinière, floured to the elbows, and deep in the
mysteries of pastry-making, or cooking the vegetables
from their own gardens, preserving, pickling, baking,
&c. The Queen resolved to give all her children a useful
training. She further taught them to love and appreciate Nature by keeping up for their benefit a museum
of natural history, furnished with curiosities collected
by the royal party in their rambles and researches.
The children were taught the structure of animals,
plants, and birds.

A thoroughly friendly alliance having been established between England and France, Prince Albert
went over to Paris in September, on a special visit
of some days to the Emperor Napoleon. Shortly
after his return the Court proceeded to Balmoral,
where the news reached it of the victory of the Alma.
During this visit to Scotland the Queen listened for
the first time to one who was afterwards honoured by
her warm friendship, the Rev. Norman Macleod. His
sermon greatly impressed her, while she was still more
deeply moved by his sympathetic prayer for 'the
dying, the wounded, the widow, and the orphan.'
Returning from Balmoral by Edinburgh, the royal
party visited Gateshead, where there had been a
terrible conflagration, and Great Grimsby, with its
splendid docks.

All the interest of the country now centred in the
war news, the Queen sharing the feeling of anxiety
in all its intensity. In October came the ever-

memorable charge of the Light Brigade at Balaclava, and on the 5th of November the brilliant but costly victory of Inkermann. Then ensued a disastrous period of mismanagement in the Crimea. Her Majesty thus wrote to Lord Raglan: 'The sad privations of the army, the bad weather, and the constant sickness, are causes of the deepest concern and anxiety to the Queen and Prince. The braver her noble troops are, the more patiently and heroically they bear all their trials and sufferings, the more miserable we feel at their long continuance. The Queen trusts that Lord Raglan will be *very strict* in seeing that no unnecessary privations are incurred by any negligence of those whose duty it is to watch over their wants.' But the serious blundering and mismanagement continued, and the only light in the gloom was the noble-hearted service rendered by Florence Nightingale and the ladies who went out with her to the East as nurses.

Her Majesty felt so keenly the hardships endured by the troops and the prolonged siege of Sebastopol, that when Lord Cardigan returned to England and visited her at Windsor, one of the royal children said to him: 'You must hurry back to Sebastopol and take it, else it will kill mama!' A motion for a Sebastopol inquiry was brought forward in the House of Commons by Mr. Roebuck, and this led to the dissolution of the Ministry. Lord Palmerston formed a new Government, and prosecuted the war with vigour. On the 2nd of March Europe was startled by the news of the death of the Emperor Nicholas, an event due as much to the failure of his plans in the Crimea as to the chilling influences of the 'Generals, January and February.'

The Queen and the Prince visited the wounded soldiers at Chatham on the 3rd of March. During the same month a sale of water-colour drawings took place in London for the benefit of the widows and orphans of officers killed in the Crimea, and a clever and spirited drawing by the Princess Royal, then a girl of fifteen, was sold (amongst other pictures) for a large sum. In April the Emperor and Empress of the French arrived at Windsor Castle on a visit to the Queen. By a curious coincidence the Emperor's bedroom was the same which had been occupied on previous occasions by the late Emperor Nicholas and Louis Philippe. Her Majesty has thus recorded the reception of her Imperial guests: 'I cannot say what indescribable emotions filled me, how much all seemed like a wonderful dream. These great meetings of Sovereigns, surrounded by very exciting accompaniments, are always very agitating. I advanced and embraced the Emperor, who received two salutes on either cheek from me, having first kissed my hand. I next embraced the very gentle, graceful, and evidently very nervous Empress. We presented the Princes (the Duke of Cambridge and the Prince of Leiningen) and our children (Vicky, with very alarmed eyes, making very low curtsies); the Emperor embraced Bertie; and then we went upstairs, Albert leading the Empress, who in the most engaging manner refused to go first, but at length with graceful reluctance did so, the Emperor leading me, expressing his great gratification at being here and seeing me, and admiring Windsor.' The 'two salutes on either cheek' which her Majesty alludes to, gave great offence to the French Republicans, and to English sympa-

thizers with the Republic, who spoke of Louis Napoleon
as 'a villain,' and 'a traitor.'

The Queen was delighted with the Empress, finding
her 'full of courage and spirit, yet so gentle, with
such innocence and *enjouement*, that the *ensemble* is
most charming. With all her great liveliness, she
has the prettiest and most modest manner.' Addresses
were received, and reviews of troops were held in
honour of the Emperor. There was also a grand ball
in the Waterloo Room, when the Queen danced a
quadrille with her Imperial visitor. She writes that
the Emperor danced with great dignity and spirit,
and adds: 'To think that I, the granddaughter of
George III., should dance with the Emperor Napoleon,
nephew of England's greatest enemy, now my nearest
and most intimate ally, in the Waterloo Room, and
this ally only six years ago living in this country in
exile, poor and unthought of.' Success gilds many
careers which in themselves are neither noble nor
exalted.

There was a Council of War on the day after the
Emperor's arrival, and subsequently he was invested
with the Order of the Garter. Bishop Wilberforce,
who was present at the Chapter, describes Louis
Napoleon as 'rather mean-looking, small, and with a
tendency to *embonpoint;* a remarkable way, as it were,
of swimming up a room, with uncertain gait; a small
grey eye, looking cunning, but with an aspect of softness about it too. The Empress, a peculiar face from
the arched eyebrows, blonde complexion; an air of
sadness about her, but a person whose countenance at
once interests you.'

A splendid banquet was given to the Emperor and

Empress in the Guildhall, and the guests also went in State with the Queen and Prince to the Italian Opera. The carriages had to make their way through what was literally a sea of human beings. The audience in the Opera-house was immense, and the cheering most enthusiastic when her Majesty led the Emperor to the front of the royal box, being followed by Prince Albert with the Empress. Next day the Queen and Prince accompanied their Imperial guests to the Crystal Palace at Sydenham. All went off well, though her Majesty was anxious about the Emperor's reception by the people. 'I felt, as I leant on the Emperor's arm,' she wrote afterwards, 'that I was possibly a protection for him. All thoughts of nervousness for myself were lost. I thought only of him, and so it is, as Albert says, when one forgets oneself, one loses this great and foolish nervousness.'

A second Council relating to the Crimean War was held at Windsor on the 20th of April. The Queen was present, and took such a profound interest in public affairs, that she said it was one of the most interesting scenes she was ever present at, and one which she would not have missed for the world. The Emperor and Empress left on the 21st, and the Prince Consort escorted them to Dover. A memorandum written by the Queen showed that she anticipated much, in a political sense, from the Imperial visit.

A touching scene was witnessed on the 21st of May, in front of the Horse Guards, when her Majesty distributed medals to some of the heroes of the war in the East. Many of these gallant soldiers had been sadly injured and mutilated in their country's cause,

and some were so weak that they could scarcely stand
to receive the medals.   Tears of gratification stood in
their eyes, that they should receive these honourable
distinctions from the Queen's own hands.   Some of
the officers were wheeled past her Majesty in Bath-
chairs, and one of these was young Sir Thomas
Troubridge, who had had both feet carried off in
battle, but who insisted on commanding his battery to
the end, only desiring his limbs to be raised in order
to stop the loss of blood.   The Queen leaned over Sir
Thomas's chair and handed him his medal, telling him
that she appointed him one of her *aides-de-camp;*
whereupon he replied, 'I am amply repaid for everything.'

Four of the royal children—Prince Arthur and
Prince Leopold, and the Princesses Louise and Alice—
were attacked with scarlet fever in the summer.   The
disease was not very virulent, however, and fortunately
did not spread.

On the 18th of August her Majesty, accompanied
by Prince Albert, the Prince of Wales, and the Princess
Royal, went over to France on a visit to the Emperor
and Empress.   Never since the infant Henry VI. was
crowned at Paris in 1422, had an English Sovereign
been seen in the beautiful French capital.   The Queen's
visit was therefore a remarkable event, and it was
doubly significant as marking the close of the ' natural
enmity' which for centuries had exasperated two
hostile nations.   The royal party landed at Boulogne,
where they were received by the Emperor, who saluted
the Queen, kissing her hand and both cheeks.   It was
late when the visitors made their progress through
Paris, but her Majesty saw enough of the capital to be

struck by its beauty and magnificence. The Palace of St. Cloud was placed at the disposal of the Queen and Prince Albert.

The following day being Sunday her Majesty kept it as in England. On Monday, the Palais des Beaux Arts, a portion of the Great Exposition d'Industrie, was visited. Lunch was had at the Elysée, and then Nôtre Dame, the Hôtel de Ville, the Place de la Bastille, and other memorable places, were visited. The Queen and the members of her family quite won the hearts of the French people by their frank and winning manners. Tuesday was devoted to Versailles, with a State visit to the Opera in the evening. The Emperor was completely drawn out of his usual impassiveness by the conversation of the Queen, and the interest she manifested in everything. The Municipality of Paris gave a splendid ball in the Hôtel de Ville on the evening of Thursday—a ball which is said to have surpassed in brilliancy and magnificence all previous experience. Next day there was a review of 45,000 troops in the Champ de Mars, and a visit to the Hospital of the Invalides, to see the resting-place of the great Emperor Napoleon. The Palace of St. Germains was visited on Saturday, and at night there was a grand *fête* at the Palace of Versailles. The illuminations were magnificent, and when they closed with a representation of the towers and battlements of Windsor Castle, there was a loud burst of applause from the spectators, succeeded by the strains of 'God save the Queen' from the orchestras.

After two more days filled with delightful or imposing scenes, the royal visitors left Paris on the return journey, and proceeded to Boulogne, where—

accompanied by the Emperor—her Majesty reviewed the magnificent army encamped on the heights.   At nine on the following morning the English Court embarked for Osborne.

Through the Earl of Clarendon, her Minister in attendance, the Queen addressed the following official letter to Sir George Grey expressive of the great pleasure the visit to France had afforded her : 'The Queen is profoundly sensible of the kindness with which she has been received by the Emperor and Empress, and of those manifestations of respect and cordiality on the part of the French nation by which she has everywhere been greeted.   On personal and political grounds the visit to Paris has afforded the highest gratification to her Majesty.'

One or two incidents during this visit are especially worthy of mention.   In the course of a quiet drive which the Queen took with the Emperor, she explained her friendly attitude towards the Orleans family, which it had been said would displease the Emperor.   She told him that they were her friends and relations, and that she could not abandon them in their adversity, though politics were never touched upon between her and them.   The Emperor understood the situation and accepted the explanation.   Prince Albert's birthday was celebrated in the course of the visit, and the Emperor gave him a picture by Meissonier, and the Empress a mounted cup carved in ivory.   In her diary subsequently, the Queen wrote concerning her parting with the Empress at Paris : 'When all was ready, the Empress could not bring herself to face the ordeal, and the Emperor said to the Queen that if she would go to her room it would make her come.   When we went in, the Emperor called her: " Eugénie, here is the Queen ; " and she came and gave me a beautiful fan, and a rose and heliotrope from the garden, and Vicky a beautiful bracelet, set with rubies and diamonds, containing her hair.' At Boulogne, where the Emperor bade farewell to his guests, the Queen and the Emperor embraced, and the latter shook hands warmly with the Prince Consort, the Prince of Wales, and the Princess Royal. Once more, at the side of the vessel, her Majesty pressed her late host's hand, and embraced him, saying: 'Adieu, Sire.' When the Emperor saw her looking over the side of the ship towards his barge, he called out : ' Adieu, Madame, au revoir ;' to which the Queen replied : ' Je l'espère bien.'

Early in September the English Court proceeded to Balmoral. The new house, though not yet complete, was sufficiently advanced for occupation, and as the Queen entered the hall an old shoe was thrown after her for good luck. On the 10th, the Duchess of Kent, who was staying at Abergeldie, went over to Balmoral to dinner. Lord Granville, Minister in attendance upon her Majesty, received a telegram this day from General Simpson, stating that Sebastopol was in the hands of the Allies. ' God be praised for it ! ' wrote the Queen, who, like the rest, could scarcely realize the good though long-desired news. Guns were fired and bonfires lit, and there was a great scene of excitement in this distant corner of the Highlands.

This visit to Balmoral was also memorable for its happy domestic news. The Prince of Prussia had some time before made a proposal of marriage for the Princess Royal on behalf of his only son, Prince

Frederick William, then twenty-four years of age.
As the Princess was only fifteen, however, the Queen
and her husband resolved that the question should
not be forced, that time must be afforded so that the
Princess might have an opportunity of knowing more
of the Prince, and of seeing whether her affections
willingly tended in that direction.   Nevertheless, the
young wooer came over to Balmoral on a visit, and
all-potent Love settled the difficulty, as he has done
thousands of times both before and since.

Writing in her diary on the 29th of September,
her Majesty tells briefly the story of the Prince's
wooing : ' Our dear Victoria was this day engaged to
Prince Frederick William of Prussia, who had been
on a visit to us since the 14th.   He had already
spoken to us on the 20th of his wishes ; but we were
uncertain, on account of her extreme youth, whether
he should speak to her himself, or wait till he came
back again.   However, we felt it was better he should
do so ; and during our ride up Craig-na-Ban this
afternoon, he picked a piece of white heather (the
emblem of " good luck ") which he gave to her, and
this enabled him to make an allusion to his hopes and
wishes as they rode down Glen Girnoch, which led to
this happy conclusion.'

Shortly after the return of the Court from Balmoral, the King of Sardinia (our ally in the Crimean
War) came to England on a visit to her Majesty,
and was splendidly entertained at Windsor.   Several
addresses were presented to the King during his stay,
and he was invested with the Order of the Garter.

On the last day of January 1856, the Queen
opened Parliament in person under auspicious cir-

cumstances. Two months later the war in the East
was at an end, and peace was signed. London and
the provinces rejoiced greatly over the event. Though
our troops had suffered severely in the Crimea, British
pluck had once more triumphed, and, together with
her Allies, England had gained the victory over the
Russians. But the struggle had been a fierce and
deadly one, and peace was everywhere welcomed with
enthusiasm. Lord Palmerston, who had done much
to ensure the later successes of the British arms, was
created a Knight of the Garter.

The Queen and Prince Albert reviewed the troops
at Aldershot on the 18th of April, remaining in camp
over night in a pavilion prepared for their use. At
the first day's review her Majesty wore a field-marshal's
uniform with the Star and Order of the Garter, and
a dark blue riding-habit. She also visited the sick
and wounded soldiers in the Chatham hospitals, being
deeply moved by the sad cases of some of the men
whom she visited in the wards. One had received
four dreadful wounds in the Redan, losing both feet;
another had had thirteen pieces of his skull removed;
while a third had received thirty-one wounds in the
cavalry action at Balaclava. The Queen distributed
liberal donations amongst the sufferers. On the 23rd
of April she held a naval review at Spithead, which
was on an unprecedented scale, both as to the amount
of force engaged and the number of spectators
attracted. Addresses were moved to the Queen by
both Houses of Parliament' on the conclusion of the
war and the signing of peace, and in the upper House
Lord Ellesmere, the mover, gave utterance to the
national sentiment when he referred to the deep debt

of gratitude which the country owed to Florence
Nightingale.   The Lords and Commons went in procession to Buckingham Palace to present their
addresses to the Queen, and her Majesty subsequently
gave a State ball to celebrate the peace.   Some days
later she laid the foundation-stone of the military
hospital at Netley.

The Princess Royal was confirmed in the private
chapel, Windsor, on the 20th of March.   Two months
later, while her affianced bridegroom was on a visit to
England, an accident occurred to her Royal Highness
which might easily have proved fatal.   When engaged
in sealing a letter at a table, the Princess saw with
horror that the sleeve of her light muslin dress had
caught fire.   Fortunately, Princess Alice and her
sister's governess, Miss Hildyard, were in the room,
and they wrapped the hearthrug round the Princess
Royal, thus no doubt saving her life.   The Princess
showed great self-possession, though suffering much
pain.   Her arm was burnt from below the elbow to
the shoulder, but not so severely as to cause permanent disfiguration.   When the accident occurred,
she uttered no cry, but she said, 'Don't frighten
mama; send for papa first.'

The Queen had several royal visitors this summer.
First came King Leopold, always specially welcome,
with his younger son and his daughter, Princess
Charlotte, and subsequently the Prince and Princess
of Prussia, who, in the course of the next two years,
were to find a daughter in the Princess Royal.

Her Majesty paid another visit to Aldershot in July,
and reviewed the troops returned from the Crimea.
As the officers and four men of each of the regiments

Y

which had been under fire 'stepped out' of the ranks,
the Queen stood up in her carriage and thus addressed
them : ' Officers, non-commissioned officers, and soldiers,
I wish personally to convey through you to the regiments assembled here this day my hearty welcome on
their return to England in health and full efficiency.
Say to them that I have watched anxiously over the
difficulties and hardships which they have so nobly
borne, that I have mourned with deep sorrow for the
brave men who have fallen in their country's cause,
and that I have felt proud of that valour which, with
their gallant Allies, they have displayed on every field.
I thank God that your dangers are over, while the
glory of your deeds remains ; but I know that should
your services be again required, you will be animated
with the same devotion which in the Crimea has rendered you invincible.' A great cry of ' God save the
Queen ' rent the air when the mellifluous voice became
silent ; helmets, bearskins, and shakos were thrown
aloft, and the Dragoons rendered the scene still more
picturesque by waving their sabres.

The Guards were welcomed home on the next day
by her Majesty, and about this time a very sad and
touching incident occurred at Buckingham Palace.
Lord Hardinge, the Commander-in-Chief, was suddenly
struck down by paralysis while having an audience
with the Queen. His lordship resigned his appointment (in which he was succeeded by the Duke of
Cambridge), and died not long afterwards.

The Queen and her family reached Balmoral on the
30th of August this year. The new house was quite
finished, and the old one had been demolished. This
favourite residence of the Queen is not far from Bal-

later, where the railway now ends, Aberdeen having previously been the end of her Majesty's railway journey. Two roads run from Ballater, following the course of the river—one passing through Crathie and the other leading through the fir and birch woods of Abergeldie. From both roads are to be obtained glimpses of the three great mountain ranges, Cairngorm, Glengairn, and Lochnagar. Balmoral was originally Prince Albert's property, as Osborne was the Queen's. He purchased this Highland estate, and 'it was by a bequest in his will that it came, with all its memories, to his widow.' Three different monuments to the Prince, on as many elevations above the Castle, at once attract the eye. The highest, which is a conspicuous object from many points of view, is a gable-like cairn, where the tenantry and others assemble on the Prince's birthday to drink to his memory; the second is a figure of the Prince, attended by his greyhound, Eos; and the third is an obelisk erected by the tenantry and servants to their master.

Balmoral Castle is a reddish-granite structure in the baronial style. Over the principal entrance are the coats-of-arms, and two bas-reliefs which indicate the character of the building. One of these shows a hunting-lodge under the patronage of St. Hubert, supported by St. Andrew of Scotland and St. George of England, and the other represents groups of men engaged in Highland games. Inside, the house is full of relics of the chase, and of expeditions made in the district. The furniture is Scotch, with hangings and carpets representative of various royal tartan sets. The rooms are, of course, not so large as in the royal palaces proper; but they are commodious enough for the restricted circle which has always gathered there with her Majesty. The ball-room is a long and picturesque hall, one story in height, bearing numberless Highland devices on its walls. The yearly ball was an event which many looked forward to, in addition to the royal children, some of whom at least greatly distinguished themselves in Highland reels.

Crathie Church is a little white building standing upon a green and wooded eminence, and looking across the Dee to Balmoral. The gallery of the church, which is the principal seated part of the structure, contains the Queen's pew and that of the Prince of Wales. There are two stained windows in the building, the gifts of her Majesty in memory of her sister, the Princess Hohenlohe, and of Dr. Norman Macleod. The finest orators in the Church of Scotland have preached in this little building, and amongst their auditors have been celebrated British statesmen and men of letters. Near to the Castle are the Queen's cottages, whose occupants are admirably looked after, and who possess many reminders of a concrete character of her Majesty and her family. Then there is the one shop in the place, and probably the only shop in her dominions in which the Queen has herself indulged in the favourite feminine occupation of 'shopping.' Amongst other northern places whose names have long been familiar to the Queen's subjects is Abergeldie, first associated with the Duchess of Kent, and more recently with the Prince and Princess of Wales. The house is of white stone, with a single-turreted tower. The spot which her Majesty most favours in the vicinity of Balmoral is the romantic district which includes Alt-na-Giuthasach and the

Glassalt Shiel.   The Queen's modest dwelling on the
Glassalt stands near the head of a loch two miles long,
and is built quite close to the waters of the lake.

There is little wonder, especially considering its
associations with the Prince Consort, that the Queen
came to love Balmoral dearly.   It was one of the
happiest of royal homes, and it has become endeared
to her Majesty by her annual residences there for
upwards of thirty years.   It was the birthplace of
many hopes, as it was the home of unclouded happiness for an all too brief period; and its memories are
now the most ineffaceable from the Queen's affections,
as she looks back through a long vista to the time
when she first visited it with the beloved partner of
her life.

In November 1856, while the Court was at Windsor, the Queen received intimation of the death of her
brother, the Prince of Leiningen, from apoplexy.   He
was in his fifty-third year, and left behind him two sons,
the elder of whom, Prince Ernest, entered the English
navy.   Her Majesty felt the Prince's death very
keenly.   Writing to King Leopold, she said: ' Oh !
dearest uncle, this blow is a heavy one, my grief very
bitter.   I loved my dearest, only brother, most tenderly. . . . . We three were particularly fond of each
other, and never felt or fancied that we were not real
geschwister [children of the same parents].   We knew
but one parent, *our* mother, so became very closely
united, and so I grew up ; the distance which difference of age placed between us entirely vanished.'

A pleasing international incident occurred in
December, when the Queen accepted from the
American people the gift of the *Resolute,* one of the

English ships which went to the North Seas in search of Sir John Franklin. It had been abandoned in the ice, but had been discovered by an American vessel and conveyed across the Atlantic refitted.

The Queen's fifth daughter, and last and ninth child, was born at Buckingham Palace, on the 14th of April 1857. The infant Princess received the names of Beatrice Mary Victoria Feodore. A few days after her birth there was another death in the Royal Family, the Duchess of Gloucester—the last of the children of George III.—passing away in her eighty-third year. The Queen thus wrote of her to her uncle : ' Her age, and her being a link with bygone times and generations, as well as her great kindness, amiability, and unselfishness, rendered her more and more dear and precious to us all, and we all looked upon her as a sort of grandmother.'

The approaching marriage of the Princess Royal having been announced to Parliament, the House of Commons, in a spirit of liberality which was gratifying to her Majesty, voted an annuity of £8,000 to the Princess, and a dowry of £40,000.

Amongst the visitors to Osborne in the summer were the Archduke Constantine, Admiral-in-Chief of the Russian Navy, and the young Archduke Maximilian of Austria—the destined husband of the Queen's cousin, Princess Charlotte of Belgium. Don Pedro of Portugal—whose marriage with the Princess Stephanie of Hohenzollern Prince Albert had been desired to negotiate—also came over to England ; and Prince Frederick William too spent some time in wooing at Osborne.

Prince Albert opened the Fine Art Exhibition at

Manchester in May ; and on the 25th of the following
month the Queen formally conferred upon him, by
letters patent, the title of ' Prince Consort.' It was
deemed advisable to take this step in order to ensure the
due recognition of the Prince's rank at foreign Courts.

An interesting spectacle was witnessed in Hyde
Park on the 26th of June, when her Majesty made
the first distribution of that much-coveted distinction,
the Victoria Cross, or Cross of Valour. There was a
vast concourse of spectators, who cheered lustily as
the Queen rode up to the place appointed for the
ceremony. The ' mighty men of valour' were called
up one by one (to the number of sixty-two), and the
Queen, with that singular air of majesty and grace
which sits upon her so naturally on all occasions of
State, pinned the cross upon each man's breast with
her own hands. The Prince Consort saluted the
recipient with a courteous gesture, and he retired a
proud and happy man. As each brave man withdrew
from the Queen's side, the spectators saluted him with
clapping of hands and loud cheers. The Victoria
Cross is in the form of a Maltese cross, formed from
the cannon captured at Sebastopol. The riband is
blue for the Navy and red for the Army. The royal
crown is in the centre of the cross, surmounted by
the lion. On the clasp are two branches of laurel,
and from it the cross hangs, supported by the initial
' V.' The decoration carries with it a pension of
£10 per annum.

The Queen and the Prince Consort, with their four
elder children and Prince Frederick William of
Prussia, paid a visit to Manchester in July. The
royal party received addresses, visited the Exhibition,

and made a progress through the streets to Peel Park,
where a statue of her Majesty had just been erected.
Towards the close of the month Prince Albert went
over to Brussels to attend the marriage of the Princess Charlotte and the Archduke Maximilian. Who
could foresee the terrible close of this happy and
apparently auspicious union ? While the Prince was
away, the Queen wrote to King Leopold: ' You cannot think how much this costs me [her husband's
absence], nor how completely forlorn I am and feel
when he is away, or how I count the hours till he
returns. All the numerous children are as nothing to
me when he is away. It seems as if the whole life of
the house and the home were gone.'

There was a happy visit to Balmoral in September;
and this extract from the Queen's *Journal* shows the
deep interest which the Sovereign took in the humblest of her subjects and neighbours: ' Albert went
out with Alfred for the day, and I walked out with
the two girls and Lady Churchill, stopped at the
shop, and made some purchases for poor people and
others; drove a little way, got out and walked up the
hill to Balnacroft, Mrs. P. Farquharson's, and she
walked round with us to some of the cottages to show
me where the poor people lived, and to tell them who
I was. Before we went into any we met an old
woman, who, Mrs. Farquharson said, was very poor,
eighty-eight years old, and mother to the former dis-
tiller. I gave her a warm petticoat, and the tears
rolled down her old cheeks, and she shook my hands,
and prayed God to bless me: it was very touching. I
went into a small cabin of old Kitty Kear's, who is
eighty-six years old—quite erect, and who welcomed

us with a great air of dignity. She sat down and
spun. I gave her, also, a warm petticoat; she said,
" May the Lord ever attend ye and yours, here and
hereafter; and may the Lord be a guide to ye, and
keep ye from all harm." . . . .

'We drove back, and got out again to visit old
Mrs. Grant [Grant's mother], who is so tidy and clean,
and to whom I gave a dress and handkerchief, and she
said, " You're too kind to me, you're over kind to me,
ye give me more every year, and I get older every
year." After talking some time with her, she said, " I
am happy to see ye looking so nice." She had tears
in her eyes, and speaking of Vicky's going (marriage),
said " I am very sorry, and I think she is sorry herself;" and having said she feared she would not see
her (the Princess) again, said : " I am very sorry I
said that, but I meant no harm; I always say just
what I think, not what is fut " (fit). Dear old lady ;
she is such a pleasant person. Really the affection of
these good people, who are so hearty and so happy to
see you taking interest in everything, is very touching
and gratifying.'

The stay at Balmoral this season was overshadowed
by the terrible news of the mutiny in India, and the
massacre at Cawnpore. The intelligence of the
dramatic relief of Lucknow alleviated the gloom a
little, but the Queen was sorely distressed at the
severity of the measures adopted to avenge the native
cruelties. The mutiny was happily suppressed, and in
the succeeding year Parliament rendered a great
service to India herself by placing that vast de-
pendency under the immediate control and government of the Queen.

On the 25th of January 1858, the Princess Royal was married to Prince Frederick William of Prussia, now the Crown Prince of Germany. For days before, the ceremony had been the common topic of conversation in society. The Princess was very popular, and the many splendid gifts she received were some slight evidence of this popularity. Several interesting and touching incidents are recorded in connection with the marriage. Before the service on the Sunday preceding, the Princess Royal gave the Queen a brooch with the Princess's hair, clasping her mother in her arms as she did so, and telling her that she hoped to prove worthy to be her child. Her Majesty felt the approaching parting with her daughter very deeply. She has recorded her feelings on the morning of the wedding, when she felt more nervous even than her child, for she was now solicitous for another, and had not 'that blessed feeling, elevating and supporting, of giving herself up for life to him whom she loved and worshipped—then and ever.' This thought had sustained her on her own wedding-day. Just previous to setting out for the ceremony, a daguerreotype was taken of the family group, father, mother, and daughter, but the Queen trembled so that her own likeness came out very indistinctly.

The marriage was celebrated in the Chapel Royal of St. James's, and all the members of the Royal Family were present, besides many other illustrious and noble guests. Her Majesty wore a train of lilac velvet, with petticoat of lilac and silver moire antique, and a flounce of Honiton lace; corsage ornamented with diamonds, the Koh-i-noor as a brooch; headdress, a magnificent diadem of diamonds and pearls.

The Prince Consort and King Leopold were in field-marshal's uniforms; the Prince of Wales and the other Princes in Highland costumes; and the Princesses Alice, Helena, and Louise—who went hand-in-hand behind their mother in the procession—wore white lace over pink satin, with daisies and blue cornflowers in their hair. The bridegroom, who looked very soldierly and stately, was in the blue uniform of a Prussian General. When he appeared in the chapel he bowed low to the Queen and to his mother. The bride came into the chapel walking between her father and King Leopold, the latter being both her godfather and grand-uncle. She wore a white dress of moire and Honiton lace, with wreaths of orange and myrtle blossoms. Her train was borne by eight bridesmaids, the unmarried daughters of dukes, marquises, and earls, and the very flower of English beauty and nobility. Their names were as follows:—Lady Susan Pelham Clinton, Lady Emma Stanley, Lady Susan Murray, Lady Victoria Noel, Lady Cecilia Gordon Lennox, Lady Catherine Hamilton, Lady Constance Villiers, and Lady Cecilia Molyneux. The bridesmaids were in white tulle, with wreaths and bouquets of pink roses and white heather.

The *Annual Register* states that as the Princess advanced to the altar she paused, and made a deep reverence to her mother, the paleness of her face flushing to a deep crimson the while. A similar observance was made to the Prince of Prussia. The bridegroom then came forward, and, dropping on one knee, took her hand and pressed it with an expression of fervent love and admiration. The marriage cere-many was performed by his Grace of Canterbury, assisted by the Bishops of London, Oxford, and Chester, and the Dean of Windsor. At its conclusion, the 'Hallelujah Chorus' was sung. As soon as the ring had been placed on the Princess's finger, the cannon were fired, and telegrams despatched to Berlin.

The congratulations to the bride were given amid a scene of strangely conflicting but very human emotions. The Princess gave way to her pent-up feelings, and threw herself upon her mother's bosom, her whole form heaving with agitation. The Queen, whose feelings also now became uncontrollable, warmly embraced her daughter again and again. Prince Frederick William next claimed his privilege with a gentle firm embrace, and then the bride's father enfolded her in his arms. The bridegroom kissed first the hand and then the cheek of his father and mother, saluted the Prince Consort and King Leopold in German fashion, and was embraced by the Queen. The Princess was about to kiss her father-in-law's hand, but he drew her towards him, and kissed her cheek. The familiar strains of Mendelssohn's 'Wedding March' were heard as the bride and bridegroom went forth from the chapel hand-in-hand.

Buckingham Palace, to which the royal procession returned, was in a state of friendly siege, being environed by a dense crowd. In response to repeated bursts of cheering, her Majesty appeared on the balcony with the royal children, and then retiring, led back the bride by the hand, and presented her to her loyal subjects. Prince Frederick William also stood forward, and placing himself by the side of his wife, the happy couple stood together hand-in-hand, and received the vociferous greetings of the multitude.

The bride and bridegroom subsequently left for Windsor, where they were to spend the honeymoon.

The day was observed as a general holiday throughout the United Kingdom, and in the evening London was brilliantly illuminated. Only two days after the marriage the Court removed to Windsor, and her Majesty created her royal son-in-law a Knight of the Order of the Garter. On the 29th, the Court and the newly married couple returned to Buckingham Palace. In the evening a State visit was paid to Her Majesty's Theatre, when *The Rivals* and *The Spitalfields' Weaver* were performed. Addresses of congratulation poured in upon the bride and bridegroom on the following day.

The 31st was a Sunday, and apprehensive of the coming separation, the Queen wrote : ' God will carry us through, as He did on the 25th, and we have the comfort of seeing the dear young people so perfectly happy.' The Princess, however, was much distressed at the thought of parting, and said to her mother : ' I think it will kill me to take leave of dear papa.' The separation came on the 2nd of February, and there was not a dry eye in the Palace. Wrote her Majesty : ' I clasped her in my arms, and blessed her, and knew not what to say.' And again : ' I kissed good Fritz, and pressed his hand again and again. He was unable to speak, and the tears were in his eyes.' The Prince Consort and the Prince of Wales, and Prince Alfred, accompanied the Prince and Princess Frederick William to Gravesend. The last farewell of the tender father to his daughter on this snowy winter's day was very affecting. The Queen keenly felt the separation for long after, but both she and her husband began to find solace in the loving assiduities of the Princess Alice.

The year 1858 was a busy one for the Sovereign. In the month following her daughter's marriage the Palmerston Government went out of office on the Conspiracy Bill, and Lord Derby became Premier, though he had only a short lease of power. In May the Prince Consort went over to Germany for a brief visit, and in June he accompanied the Queen to Stone-leigh Abbey, the seat of Lord Leigh. Her Majesty visited Birmingham, and also opened the People's Museum and Park at Aston. The royal party stayed for a night at Aston Hall, and the Queen had for her boudoir the room in which Charles I. slept when his army was on its way from Shrewsbury to relieve Banbury Castle. Warwick Castle was visited next day, in the evening of which the Court returned to London.

Early in August, her Majesty and the Prince Consort, with the Prince of Wales, visited the Emperor of the French on the occasion of the inauguration of Cherbourg. The Queen received 'such a salute from the ships and fortress itself as seemed to shake earth and sky.' The Emperor and Empress visited the Queen and Prince on board the royal yacht, and after they had gone, her Majesty went below and occupied herself in reading, nearly finishing 'that most interesting book *Jane Eyre*.' Next day the royal party landed and drove through the town. In the evening there was a State dinner on board the French ship *Bretagne*. As the relations between England and France were not quite so cordial as they had been, her Majesty was a little nervous as to the possible character of the speeches, but in proposing the 'Health of his Illustrious Visitors,' the Emperor declared his adherence to the French alliance with England.   Next day the Queen and Prince returned to Osborne in time to dine with their other children.   After dinner they danced a merry country dance with them on the terrace.

A few days later her Majesty and the Prince Consort crossed over to Antwerp in the royal yacht, and proceeded to pay a visit to their daughter in her German home.   During a halt at Düsseldorf, Prince Albert received a telegram announcing the death of his faithful valet, Cart, who had accompanied him to England, and had been in his service since the Prince was a child of eight.   It was a severe blow both to the Prince and his wife.   'All day long the tears would rush into my eyes,' wrote her Majesty ; 'he was the only link my loved one had about him which connected him with his childhood, the only one with whom he could talk over old times.'

But the happy meeting with her child modified this grief.   Next day, on the arrival of the royal party at the Wildpark Station, near Magdeburg, they found the Princess waiting for them on the platform with a nosegay in her hand.   She stepped into the carriage, and the Queen says : 'Long and warm was the embrace as she clasped me in her arms ; so much to say and to tell, and to ask, yet so unaltered ; looking well, quite the old Vicky still.   It was a happy moment, for which I thank God ! '   Her Majesty stayed at the Palace of Babelsburg during her visit, which extended over fourteen days.   Flying visits were paid to Berlin, Potsdam, and Charlottenburg.   When the time came for parting, it was more keenly felt by the Queen than had

been the original separation almost, for, as her Majesty
wrote : ' All would be comparatively easy were it not
for the one thought, that I cannot be with her at that
very critical moment when every other mother goes to
her child.'

On the 6th of September, the Queen interrupted
her journey to Scotland by staying at Leeds to open the
new Town Hall, a building second only to St. George's
Hall, Liverpool, in size and beauty. She had a
memorable reception from all ranks and classes of the
people. After the opening ceremony, her Majesty
knighted the Mayor, Mr. Fairbairn, who is described
in her *Journal* as a ' perfect picture of a fine old man,'
and as looking in his crimson velvet robes and chain
of office ' the personification of a Venetian doge.'

The first grandchild of the Queen was born at
Berlin on the 27th of January 1859. The infant
Prince's mother was then only nineteen years of age,
and his grandmother only forty. At his christening
the child had forty-two godfathers and godmothers.
In April came the confirmation of the Princess Alice,
respecting whom the Queen wrote : ' She is very good,
gentle, sensible, and amiable, and a real comfort to
me.' At this time the Prince of Wales was travelling
in Italy, and Prince Alfred was on board his ship in
the Levant. In the midst of war rumours the great
Volunteer movement was established in England. The
new Parliament was opened in June, and in the
course of the same month Lord Derby resigned the
Premiership, and was succeeded by Lord Palmerston.

The Queen and the Prince Consort made a yachting
excursion to the Channel Islands in August, and then
proceeded to Balmoral. As the meeting of the British

Association was held at Aberdeen in September, Prince Albert presided over the conference, and afterwards entertained two hundred members of the Association at a Highland gathering at Balmoral. During her stay in the North this year, the Queen made successful ascents of three famous Highland mountains—Morven, Lochnagar, and Ben Macdhui, the last being the loftiest mountain in Scotland, and upwards of 4000 feet high. Before returning to the South, the Queen opened the great Glasgow waterworks, which have their fountain-head at Loch Katrine, and which cost the city of St. Mungo altogether nearly £1,500,000. From Balmoral the Court returned to Osborne, where a very happy and 'a merry Christmas' was spent this year.

Parliament was opened by the Queen in person on the 24th of January, and she was accompanied for the first time by the Princesses Alice and Helena. Her Majesty was not so occupied in State matters as to forget art and literature. In the Academy Exhibition this year was Phillips's picture of the 'Marriage of the Princess Royal,' the Queen's property, and now hung in the great corridor at Windsor Castle. The Queen and Prince were great admirers of Tennyson's new work, the *Idylls of the King*, also of 'George Eliot's' *Adam Bede*, and at Osborne there hangs, as a pendant to a scene from the *Faery Queene*, a representation of the young squire watching Hetty in the dairy. Another royal link with literature was the appointment of Sir Arthur Helps as Clerk of the Privy Council, in June.

Her Majesty received the officers of Volunteer rifle corps at a special *levée* at St. James's Palace on the

z

7th of March, and on the 23rd of June following she held a great Volunteer review in Hyde Park. The Queen drove to the ground in an open carriage, accompanied by the King of the Belgians, the Princess Alice, and Prince Arthur. The Prince Consort and the Prince of Wales were on horseback. The scene presented was one worthy of note in a nation's history, for the 20,000 citizen soldiers reviewed were a practical embodiment of the patriotic spirit which animated the whole of the country. Her Majesty also attended the first meeting of the National Rifle Association at Wimbledon in July. She instituted a handsome annual prize of £200, and fired the first shot at the meeting, the rifle being so arranged that when she touched the trigger the shot struck the bull's-eye, and caused three points to be scored for the fair shooter.

Many domestic events occurred during the year. The Prince of Wales went out to Canada, and had a most successful progress through the Dominion, with a visit to the American President at Washington. It was arranged that Prince Alfred should also visit a distant English colony, and land at the Cape of Good Hope. It was hoped that these visits would strengthen still further the friendly bonds existing between England and her dependencies. In July, a daughter was born to the Prince and Princess Frederick William, at Potsdam, and the infant Princess received the baptismal names of Victoria Elizabeth Augusta Charlotte.

On the way to Balmoral in August the Court halted at Edinburgh, where the Queen held a Volunteer review in the Queen's Park. From every point of view the review was successful, and the whole scene was animated and picturesque in the highest degree. Out of

a total of 30,000 Scotchmen who had enrolled themselves as Volunteers, and many of whom dwelt in
regions beyond the railway, upwards of 18,000
appeared in battle array before her Majesty. The
spectators, who numbered hundreds of thousands,
occupied the vast natural slopes of Arthur's Seat, from
the summit down to the great expanse of hill-ground
shelving down in front of Salisbury Crag. 'The view
presented to all these spectators was in the highest
degree romantic. In the grassy hollow below was the
long line of the Volunteers, massed in battalions,
their ranks flanked by the quaint towers of Holyrood,
while still further to the west rose, pile above pile, the
antique buildings of the ancient capital, terminated by
the fortress-rock. Behind rose the Calton Hill, and
far beyond that the blue Frith, and the distant hills.'
The Queen came upon the ground accompanied by her
venerable mother, the Duchess of Kent, the Princes
Arthur and Leopold, and the Princesses Alice, Helena,
and Louise. The Prince Consort was on horseback,
surrounded by a group of the Scottish nobility and
lords-lieutenant. At the close of the march past, the
whole force reformed in line, and, advancing, presented
arms and saluted. Her Majesty having acknowledged
the salute, 'the men burst into enthusiastic cheers,
which, being taken up by the multitudes assembled on the
hills in front, a sound arose, the like of which the high
places of "Auld Reekie" had never before re-echoed.'

Shortly after the Queen's arrival at Balmoral, news
came of the death of the Duchess of Kent's only
surviving sister, the widow of the Grand Duke Constantine of Russia. Her Majesty and the Prince
Consort, with the Princesses Alice and Helena,

ascended Ben Macdhui during their stay, and, as the
weather was most favourable, a splendid view was
obtained. A still longer expedition followed, which
necessitated a stay for a night of the whole royal
party at a village inn. As they travelled incognito,
a certain amount of piquancy was added to the
adventure.

After their return South, the Queen and the Prince
Consort, with the Princess Alice, paid a visit to the
ancestral States of the Saxe-Coburg Gothas. They
embarked in the *Victoria and Albert* at Gravesend, on
the 22nd of September, and reached Antwerp the
following evening. Next day the King of the Belgians arrived, and escorted the travellers through his
dominions. The Prince Regent of Prussia met them
at Aix-la-Chapelle, and accompanied them for some
distance, and they were welcomed at Frankfort by the
Princess of Prussia and the Grand Duke and Duchess
of Baden. The Queen and the Prince reached Coburg
on the 25th, where they were received by the Duke
and Duchess, and also the Prince and Princess Frederick William. One sorrowful incident had occurred,
which threw a gloom over the visitors: this was the
death of the Dowager Duchess of Coburg, the mother
of the Prince Consort. The Grand Duchess and the
Princess Royal consequently appeared in the deepest
German mourning, with long black veils. The Queen
writes that as she met her daughter there was ' a
tender embrace, and then we walked up the staircase.
I could hardly speak, I felt so moved, and quite
trembled.'

The holiday passed in a quiet fashion, but it was
nearly marred by what might have proved a terrible

and even fatal accident to the Prince Consort. His
Royal Highness was driving alone in an open carriage
when the horses took fright, and ran away at full
gallop towards a spot where a bar was put up to
guard a level railway-crossing, and in front of which
a waggon was already waiting. Foreseeing that a
crash was inevitable, the Prince jumped out and
escaped with several bruises and cuts, while the driver
was thrown out and seriously injured. The Queen
was informed of the accident and of her husband's
escape before more alarming reports could reach her;
and in gratitude for the Prince's preservation, she
founded a charity to provide for young men and
young women, of good character, suitable provision on
their marriage and settlement in life.

The royal travellers left Coburg on the 10th of
October, and proceeded by Mayence and Coblentz to
Brussels. In consequence of a very severe cold with
sore throat, her Majesty remained as the guest of her
uncle for three days. She had never been so seriously
unwell since her childhood. Happily she made a good
and quick recovery. During her enforced inactivity,
we learn that Lady Churchill read to her *The Mill on
the Floss*. The royal visitors left Brussels on the 16th,
and reached Windsor on the following day.

Prince Louis of Hesse-Darmstadt came over to
England in December, and his betrothal to the
Princess Alice came about during this visit. Her
Majesty in giving an account in her *Journal* of 'how
it all happened,' wrote: 'After dinner, whilst talking
to the gentlemen, I perceived Alice and Louis conversing before the fireplace more earnestly than
usual, and when I passed to go to the other room

both came up to me, and Alice in much agitation said
he had proposed to her, and he begged for my blessing.   I could only squeeze his hand, and say
"Certainly," and that we would see him in our room
later.   We got through the evening work as well as
we could.   Alice came to our room . . . . agitated but
quiet. . . . .   Albert sent for Louis to his room, went
first to him, and then called Alice and me in. . . . .
Louis has a warm, noble heart.   We embraced our dear
Alice and praised her much to him.   He pressed and
kissed my hand, and I embraced him.   After talking
a little we parted; a most touching, and to me
most sacred, moment.'

In the closing days of this year the Prince Consort
suffered from one of those painful gastric attacks
which had unfortunately now become somewhat frequent with him.

Early in 1861 Prince Frederick William became
Crown Prince of Prussia by the death of his uncle.
At home, there were two events at this time of interest
to the royal circle.   The Prince of Wales matriculated
at Cambridge, and the Queen and Prince celebrated
the twenty-first anniversary of their wedding-day.
Writing to King Leopold, her Majesty observed : ' Very
few can say with me that their husband, at the end
of twenty-one years, is not only full of the friendship,
kindness and affection which a truly happy marriage
brings with it, but of the same tender love as in the
very first days of our marriage.'

But a heavy trial was impending over the royal
house, though not that supreme sorrow which was also
to be experienced before the close of this disastrous
year.   The Duchess of Kent, now in her seventy-sixth

year, was showing alarming symptoms of breaking
health.   She had just lost her faithful and attached
secretary, Sir George Couper, and to this loss succeeded physical suffering for the Duchess herself,
as she had been called upon to undergo a surgical
operation for a complaint affecting her right arm.
On the 15th of March, while ' resting quite happily
in her armchair,' the Duchess was seized with a
shivering fit, from which serious consequences were
apprehended.   The Queen, the Prince, and Princess
Alice left Buckingham Palace immediately on receiving
the information, and reached Frogmore in two hours,
which seemed to her Majesty like an age.

The Prince Consort first went up to see the
Duchess, and when he returned with tears in his eyes,
the Queen knew what to expect.   She went up the
staircase with a trembling heart, and entered her
mother's room.   ' Here,' she afterwards wrote, ' on a
sofa, supported by cushions, the room much darkened,
sat, leaning back, my beloved mama, breathing
rather heavily—in her silk dressing-gown, with her
cap on, looking quite herself.'   One of the attendants
whispered that the illustrious patient's end would be
easy, whereupon the Queen writes in her diary : ' Oh,
what agony, what despair was this !   Seeing that our
presence did not disturb her, I knelt before her, kissed
her dear hand, and placed it next my cheek ; but,
though she opened her eyes, she did not I think know
me.   She brushed my hand off, and the dreadful
reality was before me, that for the first time she did
not know the child she had ever received with such
tender smiles !   I went out to sob. . . . . I asked the
doctors if there was no hope.   They said they feared

none whatever, for consciousness had left her. . . . . It was suffusion of water on the chest which had come on.'

The Queen remained through the night by the side of the unconscious sufferer. In the morning her husband took her away for a short time, but she soon returned to her vigils. Holding the Duchess's hand, she sat down on a footstool and awaited the issue. 'I fell on my knees,' subsequently wrote her Majesty, 'holding the beloved hand, which was still warm and soft, though heavier, in both of mine. I felt the end was fast approaching, as Clark went out to call Albert and Alice, I only left gazing on that beloved face, and feeling as if my heart would break. . . . . It was a solemn, sacred, never-to-be-forgotten scene. Fainter and fainter grew the breathing; at last it ceased, but there was no change of countenance, nothing; the eyes closed as they had been for the last half-hour. . . . . The clock struck half-past nine at the very moment. Convulsed with sobs, I fell on the hand and covered it with kisses. Albert lifted me up and took me into the next room—himself entirely melted into tears, which is unusual for him—and clasped me in his arms. I asked if all was over; he said, "Yes." I went into the room again after a few minutes, and gave one look. My darling mother was sitting as she had done before, but was already white. O God! how awful, how mysterious! But what a blessed end! Her gentle spirit at rest, her sufferings over.' The Prince Consort bade his daughter Alice 'comfort mama,' and the Princess Royal came over from Germany with the same filial purpose.

Great respect was shown by the Houses of Parliament and the whole nation to the memory of the deceased. The Duchess bequeathed her property by will to the Queen, and appointed the Prince Consort sole executor. Her remains were interred in the vault beneath St. George's chapel, Windsor, on the 25th of March. The pall-bearers were six ladies, and the Prince Consort was chief mourner. Her Majesty and her daughters remained at home 'to pray together, and to dwell on the happiness and peace of her who was gone.' The allowances which the Duchess of Kent had made to her elder daughter, the Princess Hohenlohe, and to her two grandsons, Prince Victor Hohenlohe and Prince Edward of Leiningen, were continued by the Queen, who also pensioned her mother's servants. Frogmore, the house associated with the Duchess's last days, and in which the heir to the Prince of Wales was unexpectedly born some years later, has received many visits from her Majesty, who has loved to linger amidst its peaceful scenes, and to recall the joys of the past before death made its cruel inroads upon the royal circle.

There was mourning at Osborne after the death of the Duchess, but more joyous events soon supervened. On returning to Buckingham Palace in April, the Queen announced to the Privy Council the forthcoming marriage of the Princess Alice. Parliament voted a dowry of £30,000 and an annuity of £6,000 to the Princess. Prince Louis came over at Whitsuntide, and had the misfortune to suffer from measles, which he communicated to Prince Leopold, who suffered severely, and with permanent ill effects. Other visitors in the summer were King Leopold and the Crown Prince and Princess of Prussia, with their children. These were succeeded by the King of Sweden and his son, and the Archduke Maximilian and his wife. The Queen spent the birthday of the late Duchess of Kent at Frogmore.

In August her Majesty and the Prince paid another visit to Ireland. They were accompanied by Prince Alfred (who had just returned from the West Indies) and the Princesses Alice and Helena. The Prince of Wales was already in Ireland, serving in the Curragh Camp, and the royal party attended a field-day at the Curragh. This was followed by a visit to the Lakes of Killarney, which her Majesty greatly enjoyed, naming a point in the course of a row on one of the lakes. The Prince Consort was also much moved by the grandeur and beauty of the scenery, exclaiming again and again, 'This is perfectly sublime!' There was a stag-hunt at Killarney, and there were delightful visits to Kenmare House and Muckross Abbey.

On the 29th the royal visitors left Ireland and proceeded to Balmoral, which was reached on the 31st. Here the usual free and unconstrained life was led for some weeks, but in the midst of her deep happiness the Queen sometimes felt an undercurrent of sadness. Her reflection after an enjoyable excursion to Cairn Glaishie was, 'Alas! I fear our last great one. The Court left Balmoral on the 22nd of October, and slept that night at the Palace of Holyrood. Next day the Prince Consort performed two interesting public acts at Edinburgh—namely, the laying of the foundation-stone of the new General Post-office, and afterwards that of the Industrial Museum of Scotland. The royal party arrived at Windsor the next day.

Fortunate for humanity is it that a veil lies between

it and the future.   Little could any member of the
happy royal party which now journeyed southward
imagine that for one of its members, and that the
noble and self-sacrificing Prince Consort himself, the
last journey had been made to Balmoral, and that
the ceremonials at Edinburgh were the last public
acts which it was the will of Providence he should
perform.   Take the moment only given thee, O man,
and live it as it should be lived !

CHAPTER VII.

DEATH OF THE PRINCE CONSORT.

A PROFOUND and melancholy interest attaches to all the details published by Sir Theodore Martin concerning the illness and death of the Prince Consort. Death often strikes waywardly; it takes those who desire to live; and leaves those who are ready to die. But in the case of the Prince the great enemy found him ready; he was perfectly prepared for the end. It is stated that not long before his fatal illness he said to the Queen: 'I do not cling to life. You do; but I set no store by it. If I knew that those I love were well cared for, I should be quite ready to die to-morrow.' It has never been accurately ascertained how the fever under which he sank originated; but it is strongly surmised that the first predisposing cause was the Prince's visit to Sandhurst on the 22nd of November. He went to inspect the buildings for the new Staff College and Military Academy, and as the day was one of incessant rain, he suffered from exposure and fatigue. Next day came news of the distressing death of the young King of Portugal, and other members of his family, from malignant typhoid fever; and this intelligence weighed heavily upon the Prince's spirits.

On the 24th, which was Sunday, the Prince complained of being full of rheumatic pains, and he wrote

in his diary that he had scarcely closed his eyes
for the past fortnight. Next morning, although the
weather was cold and stormy, he travelled to Cambridge to visit the Prince of Wales. He still got
worse, and on the 28th became greatly disturbed
at the news of the American outrage on the British
flag by the seizure of the *Trent*. Civil war had broken
out in the United States, and the English steamer,
Trent, in coming from Havannah to England with the
English mails, had on board, among other passengers,
Messrs. Slidell and Mason, who had run the blockade
from Charlestown to Cuba, and were proceeding to
Europe as envoys sent by the Confederates to the
Courts of England and France. The *Trent* was met by
the *San Jacinto*, a Federal war-ship, and the commander of the latter, Captain Wilkes, boarded the
Trent, and demanded the surrender of Slidell and
Mason, and their companions. The envoys, to relieve
the English captain from his embarrassment, sur-
rendered themselves. There was great excitement in
England when the facts became known, and the
British Government took a high tone—too high a
tone, thought the Prince, whose last public act was the
writing of a draft to Lord Russell in correction of his
draft to the English ambassador at Washington.
This document, while sufficiently dignified, was of a
conciliatory character, and it was accepted by Ministers
and favourably received by the American Government.
The ominous cloud which had been gathering on the
horizon, now happily blew over. In response to the representations made, the American President ordered
the release of the gentlemen who had been seized.

Though very' ill, the Prince continued to go out,

and wrapped in a fur-lined coat on one occasion he witnessed a review of the Eton College Volunteers. On Sunday, December 1st, he walked out on the terrace, and attended service in the chapel, and notwithstanding his weakness he insisted upon 'going through all the kneeling.' Low-fever was next mentioned, and this greatly discomposed her Majesty, especially as she remembered the terrible mortality from this cause in the Portuguese royal family. But in speaking of his own illness, the Prince said that it was well it was not fever, 'as that, he felt sure, would be fatal to him.' Lord Palmerston, who was not one as a rule to take gloomy views, was so alarmed by what he heard at the Castle, that he suggested the calling in of another physician. Dr. Jenner and Sir James Clark, however, reassured the Queen with the hope that the fever which was feared might pass off.

There was now nothing left to do but to wait and hope for the best; but unfortunately the Prince lost strength daily, and there would sometimes be 'a strange wild look' upon his face. He would smile when his pet child, Princess Beatrice, was brought to him, but his most constant companion was the Princess Alice. The Prince had long resisted the entreaties of the medical men that he should undress and go to bed, and when at length he was prevailed upon to do this it was too late. Fever having unmistakably declared itself, knowledge of the unfavourable change could no longer be kept from the Queen, who was almost broken down by her grief. As she expressed it in her diary, she seemed to be constantly living 'in a dreadful dream.' The sufferer was moved on the 8th of December into a more commodious room, and as fate would have it, it was the very room in which both William IV. and George IV. had died. At the Prince's request a piano was brought into the room, and his daughter Alice played two hymns—one of them, 'A strong tower is our God.' During the playing his eyes were filled with tears.

The day was Sunday, and in a letter written by a member of the Queen's household shortly after the Prince Consort's death, the following touching passages described the events of the day: 'The last Sunday Prince Albert passed on earth was a very blessed one for the Princess Alice to look back upon. He was very ill, and very weak, and she spent the afternoon alone with him, while the others were in church. He begged to have his sofa drawn to the window, that he might see the sky and the clouds sailing past. He then asked her to play to him, and she went through several of his favourite hymns and chorales. After she had played some time she looked round and saw him lying back, his hands folded as if in prayer, and his eyes shut. He lay so long without moving that she thought he had fallen asleep. Presently, he looked up and smiled. She said: "Were you asleep, dear papa?" "Oh, no," he answered, "only I have such sweet thoughts." During his illness his hands were often folded in prayer; and when he did not speak, his serene face showed that the "happy thoughts" were with him to the end. . . . .

'The Princess Alice's fortitude has amazed us all. She saw from the first that both her father's and mother's firmness depended on her firmness, and she set herself to the duty. He loved to speak openly of his condition, and had many wishes to express. He loved to hear hymns and prayers. He could not speak to the Queen of himself, for she could not bear to listen, and shut her eyes to the danger. His daughter saw that she must act differently, and she never let her voice falter, or shed a single tear in his presence. She sat by him, listened to all he said, repeated hymns, and then when she could bear it no longer, would walk calmly to the door, and rush away to her room, returning with the same calm and pale face, without any appearance of the agitation she had gone through. Of the devotion and strength of mind shown by the Princess Alice all through these trying scenes it is impossible to speak too highly. Her Royal Highness has indeed felt that it was her place to be a comfort and support to her mother in this affliction, and to her dutiful care we may perhaps owe it that the Queen has borne her loss with exemplary resignation, and a composure which under so sudden and so terrible a bereavement could not have been anticipated.'

Returning to the last days of the Prince, the illness obtained such hold that Dr. Watson and Sir Henry Holland were called in. While the doctors regarded the case as grave, they by no means thought it hopeless. The great irritability and restlessness of the Prince, which were characteristic symptoms of the disease, gave way to delight when the Queen was by his side. The patient would tenderly caress her cheek, and whisper loving words in German, such as 'Dear little wife, good little wife.' By the 12th of December it became manifest that the fever and the shortness of breathing had increased. There was also a probability of congestion of the lungs, and on the 13th Dr. Jenner was compelled to make known to her Majesty that the illness was very serious. The Prince was wheeled into the next room, according to custom for the last few days, but he sat with his hands clasped, gazing abstractedly out of the window.

Princess Alice now summoned the Prince of Wales from Cambridge on her own responsibility. Next morning, however, Mr. Brown, of Windsor, the medical attendant of the Royal Family for twenty years, told the Queen that he thought the Prince much better, 'and that there was ground to hope the crisis was over.' As Mr. Brown knew the Prince's constitution well, this news was felt to be very reassuring. Unfortunately, the apparent improvement proved only to be that brief recovery which frequently comes before the end. As the Queen entered the sick-room on the morning of the 14th, she was more than ever struck by the unearthly beauty upon the patient's face. His eyes were dazzlingly bright, but they were fixed on vacancy, and did not notice her entrance. The medical men were now extremely anxious, and to the Queen's inquiry whether she might go out for a breath of air, responded, 'Yes, just close by, for a quarter of an hour.' Going out upon one of the terraces with the Princess Alice, they heard a band playing in the distance, whereupon the Queen burst into tears and returned to the Castle.

Although Sir James Clark said he had seen a recovery in worse cases, the Queen gave way to despair as she saw the dusky hue stealing over her husband's face. Some hours passed without further change. In the afternoon, after the Prince had been wheeled into the middle of the room, the Queen went up to him

A A

and saw with dismay that his life was fast ebbing away. The sufferer ejaculated in German his last loving words : ' Good little wife,' kissed her, and with a moaning sigh laid his head upon her shoulder. He dozed and wandered, speaking French sometimes. All his children who were in England came into the room, and one after the other took his hand, Prince Arthur kissing it as he did so, but the Prince made no sign of knowing them. He roused himself, and asked for his private secretary, but again slept. Three of the gentlemen of the household, who had been much about the Prince's person, came up to him and kissed his hand without attracting his attention. All of them were overcome; only she who sat in her place by his side was quiet and still. So long as enough air passed through the labouring lungs, the doctors would not relinquish the last grain of hope. Even when the Queen found the Prince bathed in the death-sweat, so near do life and death still run, that the attendant medical man ventured to say it might be an effort of nature to throw off the fever.

But the last hope was at length abandoned. Not long before the end came, the Queen bent over her husband and said in German: ' It is your little wife.' The dying man recognized the voice, and answered by bowing his head and kissing the Queen. The sands of life were now rapidly running out. The Queen retired into the next room to weep, but she was soon sent for again into the chamber of death. She knelt by her husband's side, holding his hand, their children also kneeling around; while the Queen's nephew, Prince Ernest Leiningen, the gentlemen of the Prince's suite, General Bruce, General Grey, Sir Charles Phipps, the

Dean of Windsor, and the Prince's favourite German valet Löhlein, reverently watched for the end. The Prince died at a quarter to eleven o'clock, thus passing, in his forty-third year, to 'where beyond these voices there is peace.'

The great bell of St. Paul's tolled at midnight, spreading the mournful news over the vast city. Early on the following day, which was Sunday, the sad intelligence was flashed by telegraph to all parts of the Empire. In the churches, the omission of the Prince Consort's name from the Litany told many for the first time of the calamity which had fallen upon the nation. There was not a house in the land that was not saddened by the news, while the hearts of all the people went out to the Queen, who was thus made 'a widow at forty-two.' There had seemed such a long period of married happiness still in store for her; and now all was over. The sorrow which continued to be expressed recalled in its intensity the national mourning for the Princess Charlotte. 'All diversities of social rank and feeling were united in one spontaneous manifestation of sympathy with the widowed Queen and the bereaved family; for the loss of the husband and father was instinctively felt to be as grievous to the most exalted rank as to the humblest. The highest family in the realm had lost, indeed, with scarce a warning or a presentiment of woe, the manly soul, the warm heart, the steady judgment, the fertile mind, the tender voice, and the firm hand, that for twenty-one years had led, and guided, and cheered them through the trials and dangers inseparable from theirs as from every position. Through a period of many trials he had been the dearest friend and

most devoted servant of his Sovereign ; while it was
known to her subjects that her Majesty fully valued
the blessing of the love and care of so good and so
wise a husband and companion.'

The news of her father's death was communicated
to the Princess Royal at Berlin ; and it was also
conveyed to Prince Leopold at Cannes under specially
painful and melancholy circumstances.   The young
Prince was in great grief over the death of his
governor, General Bowater, who had just expired in a
chamber next to that of his Royal Highness, when
a telegram came announcing the still more crushing
calamity of the Prince Consort's death.   The message
was directed to the dead general. When it was opened
it was found to contain the dreadful tidings : ' Prince
Albert is dead ! '   The anguish of Prince Leopold
knew no bounds, and he called out in his desolation :
' My mother ! I must go to my mother.'   The child's
sobs and tears were most touching, as he exclaimed
in his grief : ' My mother will bring him back again.
Oh ! I want my mother ! '

At Windsor there was great solicitude for the
Queen and the Princess Alice.   For three days they
suffered terribly, and her Majesty's weakness was
so great that her pulse could scarcely be felt.   The
Princess afterwards said that she wondered how her
mother and herself had lived through these first
bitter days.   The Queen ' spoke constantly about
God's knowing best, but showed herself broken-
hearted.'   At length the country was relieved on learning that exhausted nature had somewhat recovered
itself, and that the Queen had slept.

Her Majesty was again and again urged to leave Windsor before the funeral, but she wept bitterly, and said her subjects were never advised to leave their homes or the remains of those lost to them. It was only when the safety of her children was pleaded as a means of giving them immunity from the fever, that she was prevailed upon to leave Windsor and repair to Osborne. Attired in her deep widow's mourning, she set out in the strictest privacy, accompanied only by the Prince of Wales and the Princesses Alice and Helena.

But before going to her desolate home in the Isle of Wight, her Majesty visited Frogmore to choose a site for a mausoleum, where her husband and herself were yet to lie side by side. Leaning on the arm of the Princess Alice, she walked round the gardens, and selected the spot for the ultimate and final reception of the Prince's remains. Then she left for Osborne, in all her sorrow and loneliness.

The funeral took place at Windsor on the 23rd of December. The service was held in St. George's Chapel, where had assembled the company who had received commands to be present at the ceremony, including the Ministers of the Cabinet, the foreign ambassadors, the officers of the household, and representatives of the nobility and the higher clergy. The Knights of the Garter were in their stalls, and representatives were present of all the foreign States connected by blood or marriage with the late Prince. The chief mourner was the Prince of Wales, who was supported by his brother Arthur, a boy of eleven. There were also present the Duke of Saxe-Coburg, the

Prince's brother, the Crown Prince of Prussia, the sons
of the King of the Belgians, Prince Louis of Hesse,
Prince Edward of Saxe-Weimar, Count Gleichen, the
Duc de Nemours, and the Maharajah Dhuleep Singh.

When the coffin arrived, bouquets from Osborne
were placed upon it.   One bouquet of violets, with a
white camellia in the centre, was from the Queen.
At the head of the coffin stood the Prince of Wales,
with his brother and uncle, the Lord Chamberlain
being at the foot, and the other mourners grouped
around.   The service was taken by the Dean of
Windsor.   The grief of the young Princes for their
father, as well as that of the Duke of Saxe-Coburg
for his beloved brother, greatly moved the spectators.
The Prince of Wales, himself overcome, spoke a few
soothing words to his little brother, and for a short
time both seemed comforted.   As the body was committed to its resting-place in the vault, a guard of
honour of the Grenadier Guards, of which the Prince
Consort had been colonel, presented arms, and minute-
guns were fired at intervals by Horse Artillery in the
Long Walk.   The Thirty-ninth Psalm, Luther's Hymn,
and two chorales were sung during the funeral service
and while the coffin was uncovered and lowered in the
grave.

During the last moments the spectacle was very
touching.   The two Princes hid their faces and sobbed
bitterly, and almost every other person present was
overcome by his emotion.   It was a solemn period
when the coffin began slowly to sink into the vault;
the half-stifled sobs of the mourners were audible from
all parts of the choir.   The silence could almost be

felt as the coffin gradually descended and finally disappeared from view. The service being concluded,
Garter King-at-Arms advanced to the head of the
vault, and proclaimed the style and titles of the deceased Prince. When he came to the prayer for her
Majesty, for the first time during her reign the word
'happiness' was left out, and only the blessings of
'life and honour' were besought for her. As the
strains of the Dead March in *Saul* pealed forth, the
mourners advanced to take a last look into the deep
vault. The Prince of Wales approached first, and
stood for one brief moment with hands clasped, looking
down; then all his fortitude suddenly deserted him,
and bursting into a flood of tears, he hid his face, and
was led away by the Lord Chamberlain.   Prince Arthur
now seemed more composed than his elder brother; it
seemed as though his unrestrained grief had exhausted
itself in tears and sobs.   Heartfelt sorrow was depicted on the face of every mourner, as one by one
they slowly left the side of the vault.

Throughout the country there was long and genuine
mourning for the 'blameless Prince.'

This is not the place in which to attempt an exhaus-
tive estimate of the character of the Prince Consort.
But it has been well remarked that his influence for
good, alike in the affairs of State, over public morals,
and over the sentiments and conduct of private life—
his interest in the arts, in the sciences, and in those
manufactures into which art and science enter as vivi-
fying forces, were ever alive, ever present, and ever
most beneficially exerted.   He was wise and temperate
in his judgment of public events; and he influenced

the counsels of a great nation in its relations with
foreign States by a love of order united with an equal
love of freedom.   In private life he was deservedly
beloved.   While the Sovereign mourned the counsellor, the wife sorrowed for the tender and affectionate
husband; and the children who had profited so much
by his love and guidance, have since risen up to 'call
his memory blessed.'   No man could well exchange
worlds under happier conditions.

CHAPTER VIII.

EARLY DAYS OF WIDOWHOOD.

NOTWITHSTANDING the cheering sympathy of the Princess of Hohenlohe and the King of the Belgians—who came over to Osborne on a mission of consolation—the daily sense of her loss pressed heavily upon the Queen. 'There is no one near me to call me "Victoria" now!' she is said to have exclaimed on the morning after her bereavement, and this touching expression strongly illustrates her great loneliness. But she did not forget the sorrow of others in her own, and when, within a month of the death of the Prince Consort, the fearful disaster occurred at the Hartley Colliery, by which 204 lives were lost, her Majesty sent a message, to the effect that 'her tenderest sympathy is with the poor widows and mothers, and that her own misery only makes her feel the more for them.'

In February, the Queen took leave of the Prince of Wales, who went on a lengthened tour in the East, accompanied by Dean Stanley and General Bruce. Gradually the Sovereign began to evince a renewed interest in State affairs, and the Princess Alice was made the great medium of communication between her and her Ministers. On the 1st of May the International Exhibition was opened, amid much pomp and ceremony. In his Inauguration Ode, the Poet

Laureate thus happily recalled Prince Albert's deep interest in these peaceful triumphs of art and commerce—

> 'O, silent father of our kings to be,
> Mourned in this golden hour of jubilee,
> For this, for all, we weep our thanks to thee!'

About this time, when a dear friend expressed her surprise at finding the Queen more calm than after her mother's death, her Majesty said, 'I have had God's teaching, and learned to bear all He lays upon me.' The Queen spent her birthday at Balmoral, and summoned thither the Rev. Dr. Norman Macleod, whose ministrations she had found most helpful. He preached a sermon, in which he dwelt upon the duty of resignation, for he believed that the lesson was necessary to her Majesty, who appeared not sufficiently reconciled to her loss. The manly fulfilment of his duty was received in a truly noble spirit by the Queen, who not only wrote him a tender letter of thanks in recognition thereof, but summoned him to her room. 'She was alone,' the Doctor writes, in his account of the interview. 'She met me with an unutterably sad expression, which filled my eyes with tears, and at once began to speak about the Prince. She spoke of his excellences—his love, his cheerfulness; how he was everything to her. She said she never shut her eyes to trials, but liked to look them in the face; how she would never shrink from duty, but that all was at present done mechanically; that her highest ideas of purity and love were obtained from him, and that God could not be displeased with her love.'

The marriage of Princess Alice to Prince Louis of

Hesse—which had been delayed by the Prince Consort's death—took place at Osborne, on the 1st of July, the ceremony being of a private character. The Archbishop of York officiated, his Grace of Canterbury being indisposed. The Queen attended in deep mourning, and without a vestige of State. The Prince of Wales, and the Princes Alfred, Arthur, and Leopold were present, and the Princess's bridesmaids were her sisters—the Princesses Helena, Louise, and Beatrice, and the Princess Anna of Hesse. The bride, who was given away by her uncle, the Duke of Saxe-Coburg Gotha, wore a dress of Honiton lace, made after a design furnished by her deceased father. The Queen conferred on the bridegroom the rank of Royal Highness. The Princess Alice was already a great favourite with the English people, and her departure for the Continent shortly after the wedding was followed by many heartfelt wishes and blessings.

The Queen went to Balmoral with her children in August, and on the 21st there was an expedition to the top of Craig Lowrigan, where her Majesty and each of the elder Princes and Princesses laid a stone on the foundation of the Prince's cairn. The royal party also went to the summit of Craig Gowan on the late Prince's birthday. On the 1st of September her Majesty left England for Germany, accompanied by all her sons and daughters who were still at home. A passing visit was made to King Leopold at Laeken, and here the Queen had her first interview with her future daughter-in-law, the Princess Alexandra of Denmark. At the German hunting-seat of Reinhardtsbrunn, in Thuringia, her Majesty was joined by the Crown Prince and Princess of Prussia and their children, and by Prince Louis and Princess Alice, and Prince Alfred. Before leaving Germany the Queen visited the venerable Baron Stockmar at Coburg, and heard from his lips many reminiscences of the dead Prince. After her return to England, her Majesty welcomed her daughter Alice, with her husband, Prince Louis, on a visit, and subsequently the Princess Alexandra came over from Denmark on a brief visit.

The remains of the lamented Prince Consort were removed on the 18th of December from the vault beneath St. George's Chapel to the noble mausoleum prepared for them by the Queen and the royal children at Frogmore. This memorial edifice stands in Frogmore Park. It is cruciform in plan, with a cell in the crossing, and the arms directed towards the cardinal points. The cell is lighted by three semicircular windows in the clerestory. It is decorated externally with polished shafts of Aberdeen granite; the roof is of copper, octagonal in plan, with a square tower, surmounted by a gilt cross. The transepts are square in plan, lighted by a clerestory to correspond with the cell. The whole exterior of the mausoleum is faced with Aberdeen and Guernsey granite, and with different coloured building stones; the interior is also faced with variously-coloured marbles and stones, and is decorated with statues. Beneath the dome of the cell is placed the sarcophagus of the Prince, upon which rests a recumbent figure of the deceased by Baron Marochetti. The ceremonial observed on the removal of the Prince's body was strictly private. The coffin was placed in a hearse, and the Prince of Wales and his brothers and Prince Louis of Hesse followed as mourners. After a brief appropriate service, the coffin was placed in the sarcophagus. The Princes then arranged upon it the wreaths of flowers which their sisters had woven with their own hands 'to rest over the breast of the fondest and noblest of fathers.'

On one of the closing days of this year the Duchess of Sutherland presented to the Queen a sumptuously bound Bible, the gift of 'loyal English widows.' Her Majesty returned the following beautiful letter of thanks for this offering: 'My dearest Duchess,—I am deeply touched by the gift of a Bible "from many widows," and by the very kind and affectionate address which accompanied it. . . . . Pray express to all these kind sister-widows the deep and heartfelt gratitude of their widowed Queen, who can never feel grateful enough for the universal sympathy she has received, and continues to receive, from her loyal and devoted subjects. But what she values far more is their appreciation of her adored and perfect husband. To her, the only sort of consolation she experiences is in the constant sense of his unseen presence, and the blessed thought of the eternal union hereafter, which will make the bitter anguish of the present appear as naught. That our Heavenly Father may impart to "many widows" those sources of consolation and support, is their broken-hearted Queen's earnest prayer. . . . . Believe me, ever yours most affectionately, VICTORIA.'

London, and indeed the whole of England, was alive with pleasurable excitement on the 7th of March, when the Princess Alexandra, 'Sea-kings' daughter from over the sea,' arrived off Gravesend as the bride-elect of the heir to the British Crown. She was accompanied by her father, mother, brother, and sister, and was met by the Prince of Wales, who drove with her through the streets of London amid the cheers of an enthusiastic crowd. The royal party went by train to Slough, where they were received by the Princes of Prussia and Hesse, and Princes Leopold and Arthur. Eton was not reached till a little past six. There was heavy rain here, but it did not damp the ardour of the Eton boys, who gave nine hearty cheers for the Danish Princess. The royal party proceeded by carriages to Windsor. In one of the rooms of the Castle the Queen and the Princesses Louise and Beatrice were anxiously awaiting their arrival. Her Majesty gave her new daughter a warm motherly greeting.

The wedding took place in St. George's Chapel on the 10th of March. The Queen, attended by the Hon. Mrs. Bruce, was present in the royal closet, in widow's weeds, but she took no part in the brilliant ceremonial. All the members of the Royal Family attended, and the general company included many illustrious and distinguished personages. The Prince of Wales wore a full general's uniform, with the stars of the Garter and the Indian Order, and the ribbon and band of the Golden Fleece round his neck. Over his uniform was the mantle of the Garter. The bride, whose beauty touched all hearts, and who was in her nineteenth year, wore a dress of white satin and Honiton lace, with a silver moiré train. She also wore the necklace, earrings, and brooch of pearls and diamonds which were the gift of the bridegroom; a *rivière* of diamonds, given by the Corporation of London, and valued at £10,000; an opal and diamond bracelet, given by the Queen; a diamond bracelet, given by the ladies of Leeds ; and an opal and diamond bracelet, given by the ladies of Manchester. On reaching the *haut pas*, the bride made a deep and reverent curtsey to the Queen, and during the service her Majesty was much affected. A spectator indeed observed, as a characteristic feature of the marriage, that all the English Princesses wept behind their bouquets on beholding their brother waiting for his bride alone, and without the support of the beloved father who was gone. After the ceremony, the bride and bridegroom returned to the Castle, alighting at the grand entrance, where they were received by the Queen. The marriage was attested in the White Room, and then the wedding-breakfast was served in the dining-room to the royal guests, and in St. George's Hall to the diplomatic corps, &c. The Prince and Princess of Wales subsequently left Windsor for Osborne, to spend their honeymoon. London and all the large towns were brilliantly illuminated in the evening, and the rejoicings over this happy event were kept up for some days. The crowds were so dense in the City to witness the illuminations on the 10th that six persons were crushed or trodden to death, and this melancholy circumstance drew a very sympathetic letter from the Prince of Wales addressed to the Lord Mayor. Marlborough House was selected as the town residence of the bride and bridegroom, and Sandringham as their country house.

During the stay of the Princess Louis of Hesse at Windsor she gave birth to a Princess. The Queen watched over her daughter with affectionate solicitude at this interesting time.

On the 9th of May her Majesty paid a long visit to

the military hospital at Netley, the foundation-stone of which she had laid seven years before. On that occasion she had been accompanied by the Prince Consort, who took a great interest in the hospital, and afterwards visited it many times. This later visit by the Queen was strictly private. Before she went into the hospital, her Majesty went first to view the foundation-stone. She bore the visit firmly, though she was evidently moved by painful reminiscences. Subsequently she went through a great many of the wards. In one ward an old soldier from India lay nearly at the point of death. When the Queen had spoken to him, he said : "I thank God that He has allowed me to live long enough to see your Majesty with my own eyes.' The Queen and the Princess Alice were much touched by this speech, which evidently came from the heart. As her Majesty passed along, the corridors were thronged with Indian invalids, fine old soldiers, bearded and bronzed, some of whom were overcome with emotion at the kindly recognition of their Sovereign. The women's quarters were next visited, and altogether the Queen walked over several miles of ground. Wherever she went, her royal and womanly bearing deeply affected all who were honoured by her kindly notice and attention.

Her Majesty paid a visit to Belgium and Germany in August and September, being accompanied by the Princesses Helena and Beatrice and Princes Alfred and Leopold. The royal party crossed over from Greenhithe to Antwerp in the *Victoria and Albert*. The King of the Belgians received the Queen and her children at Scharbeck, and drove with them to Laeken. From thence the royal party travelled to the Castle of

Rosenau, near Coburg, where her Majesty made a considerable stay, and where she was joined by the Crown Prince and Princess of Prussia, and Prince and Princess Louis of Hesse. Though shattered in health, the Queen received visits from the King of Prussia and the Emperor of Austria. Leaving Rosenau on the 7th of September, the Queen spent a day with her daughter, the Princess Alice, and her family, at Kranichstein, near Darmstadt, and then returned to England.

The Court went to Balmoral in August. The Prince's cairn on Craig Lowrigan had been completed. It forms a fine sharp pyramid of granite, thirty-five feet high, and can be seen for miles from the valley. The cairn bears the following inscription :—' To the beloved memory of Albert, the great and good Prince Consort. Raised by his broken-hearted widow, Victoria R. August 21st, 1862. "He being made perfect in a short time fulfilled a long time ; for his soul pleased the Lord ; therefore hastened He to take him away from among the wicked.' (Wisdom of Solomon, iv. 13, 14.) This Scripture passage is said to have been chosen by the Princess Royal.

On the 15th of September the Queen went to Blair, to visit the Duke and Duchess of Athole. The Duke was suffering from an incurable illness, but he received her Majesty, and presented her with the white rose, which, according to tradition, is presented by the Lords of Athole on the occasion of the Sovereign's visit. The Queen went into the Duke's little room, which was full of rifles and other implements of sport, and sat with him for some time. When the time came for leaving, writes her Majesty in her *Journal*,

' the poor Duke insisted on going with me to the station, and he went in the carriage with the Duchess and me. At the station he got out, walked about, and gave directions. I embraced the dear Duchess, and gave the Duke my hand, saying, " Dear Duke, God bless you ! " He had asked permission that his men, the same who had gone with us through the glen on that happy day two years ago, might give me a cheer, and he led them on himself. Oh ! it was so dreadfully sad ! ' The Duke of Athole died in the following year from cancer.

An alarming accident happened to the Queen on the 7th of October, as she was returning with the Princesses Alice and Helena from an expedition to Altnagiuthasac. The usual coachman, Smith, was driving the royal party, but after proceeding about two miles in the darkness, though along a good road, the carriage turned over on its side, and all the occupants were precipitated to the ground. Her Majesty came down very hard, with her face upon the ground. Both horses were also down, and the scene was one of danger and anxiety. John Brown called out in despair, ' The Lord Almighty have mercy on us ! Who did ever see the like of this before ? I thought you were all killed.' The Princesses were entangled by their clothing, but were eventually released without injury. The traces of the carriage were cut, and the horses got up unhurt. The ladies then sat down in the carriage, covered with plaids. The Queen's face was a good deal bruised and swollen, and a little claret was all that could be got to bathe it with. After sitting for some half-hour in the dark, a servant who had gone on before with the ponies, feeling alarmed lest a disaster should have occurred, returned to the spot with the ponies. The Queen and her daughters then rode home. No one at Balmoral knew what had happened, but her Majesty told her sons-in-law, the Crown Prince of Prussia and Prince Louis of Hesse, who had long been awaiting the arrival of the party.

A few days afterwards the Queen went to Aberdeen to unveil the statue of the Prince Consort. She has left on record how terribly nervous she was, and that she longed not to have to go through the ordeal. Her Majesty was accompanied by the Crown Prince and Princess of Prussia, Prince and Princess Louis of Hesse, Princesses Helena and Louise, and Princes Arthur and Leopold. The day was very wet. There was a long, sad, and melancholy procession through the crowded streets of Aberdeen, where all were kindly, but all were silent. The Queen trembled during the ceremony, which was the first she had attended in public since her husband's death. An address was presented, and her Majesty knighted the Provost, a reply being afterwards forwarded to the address. The Prince's statue, by Marochetti, was considered to be very faithful and lifelike. After it had been unveiled, the Queen, who appeared much depressed, scanned it for some time narrowly.

On the 14th of December, the anniversary of the Prince's death, the Queen, accompanied by all the members of the Royal Family, proceeded at an early hour from Windsor Castle to the Royal Mausoleum at Frogmore, where a devotional service was held. This has since been observed as an annual custom, and all the members of the household, including the servants, are likewise permitted to pay their tribute of love and respect to the memory of the Prince. This wonderfully beautiful tomb, as the Princess Alice described it, with all its elaborate decorations, was erected at a cost of upwards of £200,000, which was entirely defrayed from her Majesty's privy purse.

A joyful but unexpected event occurred at Frogmore on the 8th of January 1864, when the Princess of Wales was prematurely confined of a son, Prince Albert Victor. There was no nurse in attendance, and no preparation had been made for the advent of 'the little stranger,' who had not been expected until March. The Queen was immediately apprised of the happy news of the birth of a direct heir to the Crown. The Prince was christened at Buckingham Palace on the first anniversary of his parents' marriage. The Princess of Wales made a speedy recovery, and congratulations poured in upon the Prince and Princess, and also upon the Queen, on the birth of the infant Prince.

Her Majesty's birthday was kept in May 1864 with all the old tokens of state and rejoicing, which had not been observed since 1861. There were the usual salutes from the Tower and the Park, and a grand review of the household troops on the parade behind the Horse Guards. In the following August, on her way to Balmoral, the Queen inaugurated a statue of the Prince Consort at Perth. She was accompanied on this occasion by several members of her family, and by the Duke and Duchess of Saxe-Coburg Gotha. In the following year,

Prince Alfred, on attaining his majority, was formally adopted by the Duke of Saxe-Coburg as his heir.

On the 1st of January 1865 the Queen once more manifested her solicitude for her subjects by causing a letter to be written to the directors of the leading railway companies, calling attention to the increasing number of accidents which had lately occurred on various lines of railroad. 'It is not for her own safety,' wrote Sir Charles Phipps, ' that the Queen has wished to provide in thus calling the attention of the company to the late disasters; her Majesty is aware that when she travels extraordinary precautions are taken; but it is on account of her family, and those travelling upon her service, and of the people generally, that she expresses the hope that the same security may be insured for all as is so carefully provided for herself. The Queen hopes it is unnecessary for her to recall to the recollection of the railway directors the heavy responsibility which they have assumed since they have succeeded in securing the monopoly of the means of travelling of almost the entire population of the country.' This letter received from the press and from the directors of the various railway companies the attention which its importance deserved.

Her Majesty visited the Consumption Hospital at Brompton on the 14th of March, going through the four galleries called respectively the 'Victoria,' the 'Albert,' the 'Foulis,' and the 'Jenny Lind.' She entered many of the wards, speaking to several of the bed-ridden patients, and bestowing kindly smiles and sympathizing looks upon all; and then she visited in turn the chapel, the vestry, the library, and the kitchens.

When England was startled by the sad news of the assassination of Abraham Lincoln, the Queen wrote with her own hand a touching letter of condolence to the widow of the late President. Addresses upon the untoward event were presented to the Crown by the two Houses of Parliament, and to these addresses her Majesty returned the following reply :—' I entirely participate in the sentiments you have expressed in your address to me on the subject of the assassination of the President of the United States, and I have given directions to my Minister at Washington to make known to the Government of that country the feelings which you entertain, in common with myself and my whole people, with regard to this deplorable event.'

On the 8th of August the Queen left England on a visit to Germany, accompanied by Prince Leopold and the Princesses Helena, Louise, and Beatrice. The illustrious party embarked at the Royal Arsenal pier on board the steam yacht *Alberta,* under the command of Prince Leiningen. Coburg was reached on the 11th, and the Queen at once proceeded to Rosenau. The birthday of the Prince Consort was celebrated by the inauguration of a costly monument to his memory at Coburg. It took the shape of a gilt bronze statue, ten feet high, which was unveiled in the public square of the town. On the conclusion of the ceremony, the Queen, accompanied by her children, walked across the square, and handed to the Duke of Saxe-Coburg a large bouquet of flowers, which he laid on the pedestal. All the children did the same, until the flowers rose to the feet of the statue. Princess Alice writes of the ' terrible sufferings ' of the first three years of the Queen's widowhood, but adds that after the long storm came rest, so that the daughter could tenderly remind the mother, without reopening the wound, of the happy silver wedding which might have been this year, when the royal parents would have been surrounded by so many grandchildren in fresh young households. The royal family returned from Germany on the 8th of September, visiting King Leopold at Ostend on the journey.

Her Majesty spent September and October in the Highlands. In addition to an expedition to Invermark she went to Dunkeld on a visit to the Duchess of Athole. This visit was strictly private, and the Queen found comfort in the companionship of the Duchess, who, like herself, had been bereaved of her husband. ' The life was even quieter than at Balmoral. Her Majesty breakfasted with the daughter who accompanied her, lunched and dined with the Princess, Duchess, and one or more ladies. There were long drives, rides, and rows on the lochs, sometimes in mist and rain, among beautiful scenery, like that which had been a solace in the days of deepest sorrow ; tea amongst the bracken or the heather, or in some wayside house ; friendly chats, peaceful readings.'

In October the popular Premier, Lord Palmerston, died, and the Queen keenly felt his loss, forgetting the intractability he had displayed some years before. But the year 1865 closed with a much greater personal loss than this: on the 9th of December her Majesty's uncle, King Leopold, passed away at the age of seventy-six. In the deceased King, Queen Victoria not only mourned a dear relative, but a faithful friend and counsellor—one whose sympathy and advice had been constant and unfailing ever since she ascended the throne.

CHAPTER IX.

THE earliest occasion on which her Majesty attended
any State ceremony after the death of the Prince
Consort was on the 6th of February 1866, when she
opened the first session of her seventh Parliament.
The event attracted much attention, and gave great
satisfaction. Enthusiastic crowds lined the whole
route of the procession to the Houses of Parliament.
In the House of Lords the scene was one of great
splendour, peers and peeresses being resplendent in
their robes and jewels. After prayers had been read
by the Bishop of Ely, at a signal from the Usher of
the Black Rod the whole assembly rose *en masse*—
peers, peeresses, bishops, judges, and the foreign
ambassadors—to receive the Prince and Princess of
Wales. The Princess was escorted to the place of
honour on the woolsack, immediately fronting the
throne. Shortly afterwards the whole assembly rose
again; the door to the right of the throne was flung
open, and the Queen entered, preceded by the State
officials. Her Majesty, who was attired in half-
mourning, walked with slow steps to the throne, stopping on the way to shake hands with the Princess of
Wales. The Queen wore a deep purple velvet robe
trimmed with white miniver, and a white lace cap
à la Marie Stuart; around her neck was a collar of

brilliants, and over her breast the blue riband of the
Order of the Garter.   During the proceedings and
the reading of the royal speech the Queen sat silent
and motionless, with her eyes fixed upon the ground.
She appeared wrapt in contemplation, and was doubtless moved by reminiscences of the time when she
stood, proud and happy, with her husband by her side,
and took an active part in this august ceremony.
When the Lord Chancellor had concluded the reading
of the speech, her Majesty rose from the throne,
stepped slowly down, kissed the Prince of Wales, who
sat almost at her feet, and shook hands with Prince
Christian.   Escorted by the heir to the Crown, and
followed by the Princess of Wales and the Duke of
Cambridge, the Queen retired by the door at which
she had entered, with the usual ceremonies in which
heralds and Garter kings-of-arms delight.

A new decoration, styled the Albert Medal, was
instituted by royal sign-manual in March.   It was
to be awarded to those who should, after the date of
the warrant, endanger their own lives in saving, or
endeavouring to save, the lives of others from ship-
wreck or other peril of the sea.

On the 13th of March, for the first time during
five years, the Queen visited the camp at Aldershot,
and reviewed the troops in garrison.   She was accompanied by Princess Helena and the Princess Hohenlohe.
The inspection was followed by a grand march past
of the regiments, and then the royal party drove
through the South Camp by way of the Prince Consort's library to the artillery and cavalry barracks,
and by the main road past the Memorial Church to
the Pavilion, where luncheon was served.   In the

afternoon there was a review of the cavalry, artillery, pontoon, and military trains. Not long afterwards her Majesty paid a second visit to Aldershot, the cause of this latter visit being the presentation of a new pair of colours to the gallant 89th Regiment, in lieu of the battered shreds which the corps had with great distinction borne in all parts of the world for the past thirty-three years.

The eminent American philanthropist, Mr. Peabody, having about this time added to his splendid gift for the improvement of the dwellings of the poor of London another munificent donation, the Queen signified her intention of presenting him with a miniature portrait of herself, specially painted. She would gladly have conferred upon him either a baronetcy or the Grand Cross of the Order of the Bath, but he felt himself debarred from accepting such distinctions. In thanking the Queen for the honour done him for his efforts in connection with the poor of London, Mr. Peabody wrote: 'Next to the approval of my own conscience, I shall always prize the assurance which your Majesty's letter conveys to me of the approbation of the Queen of England, whose whole life has attested that her exalted station has in no degree diminished her sympathy with the humblest of her subjects. The portrait which your Majesty is graciously pleased to bestow on me I shall value as the most precious heirloom that I can leave in the land of my birth, where, together with the letter which your Majesty has addressed to me, it will ever be regarded as an evidence of the kindly feeling of the Queen of the United Kingdom towards a citizen of the United States.'

Two marriages were celebrated in the royal circle in 1866. The first was that of the Princess Mary of Cambridge to Prince Teck, which took place at the village church of Kew on the 12th of June. The Queen was present, and looked remarkably well, but it was noticed that she was attired in mourning so deep that not even a speck of white relieved the sombreness. On the 5th of July her Majesty's third daughter, the Princess Helena, was married in St. George's Chapel, Windsor Castle, to Prince Christian of Schleswig-Holstein, the bride being in her twenty-first and the bridegroom in his thirty-sixth year. The Princess was accompanied to the altar by her mother and the Prince of Wales, and the Queen gave her daughter away.

The war in Germany this year saw the husbands of two of the Queen's daughters ranged on opposite sides. During the progress of the war in the immediate vicinity of Darmstadt the third daughter of our Princess Alice was born. The mother was deeply concerned for her husband in the field, but eventually he was restored to her in safety. Austria was utterly worsted in the conflict, and Prussia ultimately annexed Hanover, Hesse-Cassel, &c., as the spoils of victory.

In October the Queen evinced her interest in the sanitary concerns of the people by opening the fine new waterworks at Aberdeen. In 1806 the daily water supply of Aberdeen was only 60,000 gallons, but the new waterworks would furnish a supply of 6,000,000 gallons of pure water from the Dee. An address was presented to the Queen by the Commissioners, and her Majesty, speaking for the first time

in public since her great loss, said : ' I have felt that
at a time when the attention of the country has been
so anxiously directed to the state of the public health,
it was right that I should make an exertion to testify
my sense of the importance of a work so well calculated as this to promote the health and comfort of
your ancient city.'

The Queen again came forth from her seclusion
in February 1867, when she once more opened Parliament in person.   The Reform question was the all-
absorbing one occupying the public attention, and
before the session closed the Conservative Government
succeeded in carrying a measure which provided for a
large extension of the suffrage.

In the course of the year there appeared the interesting work entitled *The Early Years of H.R.H.
the Prince Consort*, compiled under the direction of
her Majesty by Lieut.-General the Hon. C. Grey.   In
this book the Queen pays an affectionate tribute to the
virtue and character of her deceased husband, and the
biography contains much material furnished directly
by the Sovereign herself.   ' No homage which the
Queen has paid to her husband's memory is more
expressive than the humility and simple confidence
with which she has in these pages trusted to the
world particulars relating to herself.   The candour
with which she has published the events that led to
their engagement, and their feelings and impressions,
is not more striking than the assiduous self-denial
which causes the interest always to centre in the
Prince.   The Queen is kept out of sight whenever her
presence is not required to illustrate his life.'   What
the book gives is ' not merely the privilege of over-

hearing the tale of love and grief, whispered by a mother to her children, but a great argument of history, a resolute attempt to make the nation understand the most illustrious character the Royal Family has possessed since the accession of the dynasty. To accomplish this high purpose, the Queen has not shrunk from the sacrifices which men seldom make, and monarchs never.'

On the 20th of May her Majesty in person laid the first stone of the Hall of Arts and Science at Kensington Gore. This important edifice, which is now known as the Royal Albert Hall, was to be available for the following objects:—Congresses, both national and international, for purposes of science and art; performances of music, distributions of prizes by public bodies, *conversazioni* for the promotion of science and art, agricultural, horticultural, and industrial exhibitions, and displays of pictures and sculpture. The ceremony at the laying of the foundation-stone was of an imposing character. The Queen was accompanied by the Princesses Louise and Beatrice, Prince Leopold and Prince Christian; and she was received by the Prince of Wales, the Duke of Edinburgh, the Lord Steward, and the Lord Chamberlain : her Majesty wore deep mourning, a plain widow's cap and a dark crape mantle. The Princesses wore dresses of green and white, and Prince Leopold a Highland dress. The Prince of Wales, bowing to his mother, handed her a beautiful bouquet. The Queen, as she took it, kissed both her elder sons, and went forward into the building, being received by the whole company with hearty cheers, waving of handkerchiefs, and clapping of hands. The Queen advanced to the edge of the raised dais, and curtsied three times, first to the right, next to the left, and then to those in front of her. The Prince of Wales read an address to the Queen, who replied, contrary to custom with her, in a scarcely audible tone of voice. She referred to the struggle with which she had nerved herself to take part in the day's ceremony, but said she had been sustained by the thought that she was assisting to promote the accomplishment of the Prince's great designs. To his memory, the Queen continued, 'the gratitude and affection of the country are now rearing a noble monument, which I trust may yet look down on such a centre of institutions for the promotion of art and science as it was his fond hope to establish here.'

In June the Queen of Prussia arrived at Windsor Castle on a visit to the Queen ; and in the following month the Sultan was also hospitably housed for a time at the Castle. His Majesty was made the centre of a round of gaieties and celebrations at the Crystal Palace and elsewhere ; but a grand naval review, at which he was present, off Spithead, was spoilt by tempestuous weather. The Sultan left England much impressed by his visit. On the day before his departure from Buckingham Palace the Queen received at Osborne another illustrious visitor in the person of the Empress of the French.

On the 20th of August the Queen left Windsor for Balmoral, paying a visit on the way to the Duke and Duchess of Roxburghe at Floors Castle. The procession from Kelso to the castle was quite a triumphal one, and at one point a beautiful scene was witnessed, when fifty young ladies and girls dressed in white, and wearing chaplets of ivy, strewed the road with exquisite bouquets of flowers. At night, beacon-fires were lit on the hill-tops over a wide extent of country, there being no fewer than thirteen bonfires on the Duke of Roxburghe's estate, so that the fires may be said to have ranged from the Eildons to the Cheviots. The Queen visited Melrose Abbey and Abbotsford on the 22nd, and Jedburgh on the succeeding day. At Abbotsford she inspected the memorials of Sir Walter Scott, and acceded to a request to write her name in the Great Wizard's journal; though she afterwards wrote in her own *Journal* that she felt it to be presumption on her part to do so. On the 24th she proceeded to Balmoral. During her stay in the North she paid a visit to Glenfiddich, the shooting-lodge of the Duke of Richmond. The luggage having failed to arrive on the same day as the travellers, the Queen and her ladies were compelled to dine in their riding-skirts, and her Majesty put on a black lace veil belonging to one of her attendants, which was arranged as a coiffure. On the 15th of October, the engagement day of the Queen and Prince Consort, a statue of the Prince was unveiled at Balmoral.

In February 1868 her Majesty received an address of loyalty and affection from the Irish residents in London, a demonstration evoked by the Fenian conspiracy and the Clerkenwell outrage. The address was signed by 22,603 persons.

An exciting debate took place in the House of Commons early in May, arising out of Mr. Disraeli's interview with the Queen after the defeat of the Government on Mr. Gladstone's Irish Church Resolutions. The Premier stated that he had recommended a dissolution of Parliament to her Majesty, but that he

had afterwards placed his resignation at her disposal
if she should be of opinion that it would conduce to a
more satisfactory settlement of the Irish Church
question.   Mr. Gladstone and other members strongly
censured the use that had been made of the Queen's
name, as well as the policy of the Premier, which
condemned the House of Commons by anticipation
if any of its votes should be displeasing to the Government.

Great indignation was caused in England by the
news that the Duke of Edinburgh, while accepting
the hospitality of the friends of the Sailors' Home at
Clontarf, near Port Jackson, New South Wales, had
been shot in the back by one O'Farrell.   The wound,
happily, was not fatal : the ball was extracted, and in
eight days the Duke was sufficiently recovered to go
on board his ship.

On the 13th of May the Queen laid the foundation-
stone of the new buildings for St. Thomas's Hospital,
and in her reply to the address presented to her she
referred to the founding of the Hospital by her royal
predecessor Edward VI., and to the interest which her
late husband always took in it.   She also alluded to
the fortunate preservation of her son, the Duke of
Edinburgh, from the hand of an assassin.   In Windsor Park, on the 20th of June, there was a review of
27,000 Volunteers by the Queen, the day being
observed as a holiday by most of the public offices
and large business establishments of London.

Her Majesty left England on a visit to Switzerland
on the 5th of August, travelling incognita as the
Countess of Kent : *en route* she stayed for a day at
the English Embassy, Paris, where she received the

c c

Empress Eugenie.   She proceeded next day by rail
to Lucerne.   During their sojourn at this place, the
Queen and her children—Prince Leopold and the
Princesses Louise and Beatrice—occupied a beautifully
situated residence called the Villa (Pension) Wallace.
It stands on a hill overlooking the town, with the
Righi on the left, and Mont Pilatus, distinguished by
its serrated ridge, upon the right, and the lake and
snowy St. Gothard range of Alps immediately in
front.   After enjoying for a month the delightful
scenery of Switzerland, her Majesty left Lucerne on
the 9th of September, reached Windsor Castle on the
11th, and proceeded to Balmoral on the 14th. During
her stay in her Scottish home she interested herself, as
usual, in all the doings of the humble occupants of the
cottages on the estate.   One of the typical visits she
was accustomed to pay to the cottagers has thus been
described by the Rev. Dr. Guthrie, who had himself
visited this particular cottar's home :—'Within these
walls the Queen had stood, with her kind hands
smoothing the thorns of a dying man's pillow.   There,
left alone with him at her own request, she had sat
by the bed of death—a Queen ministering to the comfort of a saint—preparing one of her humblest subjects
to meet the Sovereign of us all.   The scene, as our
fancy pictured it, seemed like the breaking of the day
when old prophecies shall be fulfilled : kings become
nursing fathers, and queens nursing mothers to the
Church.'   Whether at the Scotch communion service,
or at a deathbed or the graveside, the Queen testified
by her presence and sympathy to the oneness of
humanity.

Before the close of the year there appeared the

Queen's volume, *Leaves from the Journal of our Life in the Highlands, from* 1841 *to* 1861,' &c. &c. While the work laid no claim to the dignity of history or the gravity of literature, it had qualities of its own which ensured a ready acceptance amongst all readers. These records were not originally intended for publication, but, as her husband had passed away, the Queen decided to give them to the world, in order that it might learn how great was the loss which she and England had sustained by the death of so good and able a man as the Prince Consort.   Her Majesty sent a copy of this volume to Charles Dickens, as a gift from ' one of the humblest of writers to one of the greatest.'

The Queen visited the City of London on the 6th of November 1869, for the purpose of opening the new bridge over the Thames at Blackfriars, and the new viaduct over the Fleet Valley from Holborn Hill to Newgate Street.   The citizens of London gave a warm welcome to their Sovereign after her prolonged absence from their midst.   The journey from Paddington to Blackfriars Bridge—the Queen was accompanied by the Princesses Louise and Beatrice and Prince Leopold—was a continued ovation.   After the ceremony at the bridge her Majesty proceeded to the new Holborn Viaduct, where there was an immense assemblage of people, who greeted her with the liveliest acclamations.   Having declared the Viaduct open, the Queen drove by way of Holborn to Paddington.   The Lord Mayor gave a banquet at the Mansion House in the evening, when the Queen's reply to the address presented was read, expressive of the pleasure it had afforded her to visit the City, to open new works in which she recognized ' the spirit of enterprise and improvement which has ever characterized the citizens of London.'

Another very interesting ceremony was witnessed in May 1870, when the Queen, accompanied by the Prince and Princess of Wales, formally opened the new buildings erected for the University of London in Burlington Gardens. The address presented made reference to the fact that it was in the year of her Majesty's accession to the throne that the University began its labours ' for the encouragement of a regular and liberal course of education among all denominations of the subjects of the Crown; ' and it further offered dutiful thanks to the Queen for consenting to open a building granted by Parliament and fully satisfying all the requirements of the University. Lord Granville, as Chancellor of the University, read the address, to which her Majesty replied, and then said in firm and clear tones, ' I declare this building open.' Many distinguished visitors were present, who were all cordially received, but the warmest greetings were extended to Mr. Gladstone, Mr. Disraeli, and the Indian religious reformer, Baboo Keshub Chunder Sen.

The year 1870 was an eventful one upon the Continent. The war between France and Germany—in which the Queen's sons-in-law, the Crown Prince of Prussia and Prince Louis of Hesse were engaged—led to the re-making of the map of Europe so far as France and Germany were concerned ; and as one result of the deadly struggle the Emperor and Empress of the French were driven into exile. Under changed and melancholy conditions Queen Victoria visited the Empress Eugenie at Chislehurst towards the close of the year.

Her Majesty's stay at Balmoral in 1869 had been diversified by a most enjoyable visit of ten days to Invertrossachs, from which point the royal party explored some of the most beautiful lake scenery in Scotland.   The visit to Balmoral in the autumn of 1870 was marked by a happy incident of another description.   On the 3rd of October the Princess Louise became engaged to the Marquis of Lorne, eldest son of the Duke of Argyll.   The engagement took place during a walk from the Glassalt Shiel to the Dhu Loch.   The Queen writes in her Journal : ' We got home by seven.   Louise, who returned some time after we did, told me that Lorne had spoken of his devotion to her, and proposed to her, and that she had accepted him, knowing that I would approve. Though I was not unprepared for this result, I felt painfully the thought of losing her.   But I naturally gave my consent, and could only pray that she might be happy.'   Dr. Macleod, who had long known Lord Lorne, told the Queen that he had a very high opinion of him, and that ' he had fine, noble, elevated feelings.'

The year 1871 was a very anxious one for the Queen, as during its course another daughter left the parental roof on her marriage, while before it closed the life of the Prince of Wales was in imminent danger.

Her Majesty opened Parliament in person on the 9th of February.   The royal speech, however, was read by the Lord Chancellor, and as he proceeded the Queen sat with eyes cast down and perfectly still, a slight movement of her fan being all that was at any time perceptible.   The chief home topics of in-

terest were the approaching marriage of the Princess
Louise and the agitation for army reform, which ultimately ended in the abolition of purchase.

The marriage of the Princess Louise to the Marquis
of Lorne was solemnized at St. George's Chapel,
Windsor, on the 21st of March. The ceremony was
distinguished by much pomp. The Duke of Argyll
attracted special attention when he appeared in 'the
garb of old Gaul,' with kilt, philibeg, sporran, and
claymore complete. The bridegroom, who was supported by Earl Percy and Lord Ronald Gower, looked
pale and nervous. All the members of the Royal
Family were present. The bride was supported on
the right by the Queen, and on the other side by the
Prince of Wales and the Duke of Saxe-Coburg and
Gotha. The bridesmaids were dressed in white satin
decorated with red camellias, with long and drooping
leaves; and the bride wore a white satin robe, with a
tunic of Honiton lace of ingenious and graceful design.
In this tunic were bouquets composed of the rose, the
shamrock, and the thistle, linked together by a floral
chain, from which hung bouquets of various flowers.
The veil, which was of Honiton lace, was worked from
a sketch made by the Princess Louise herself. When
the Bishop of London put the usual question as to the
giving away of the bride, the Queen replied by a
gesture, and then the bishop joined the hands of the
young couple. At the close of the ceremony the
Queen lovingly embraced her daughter. The bride
and bridegroom left Windsor for Claremont, to spend
the honeymoon. For their London residence, rooms
were allotted to them in Kensington Palace.

Her Majesty opened the Royal Albert Hall on the

29th of March, in the presence of the members of the Royal Family, the chief officers of State, and a large and distinguished assembly, consisting of some 8,000 persons. On the entrance of the Queen the whole audience rose to receive her, and remained standing while the National Anthem was performed. At its conclusion the Prince of Wales read an address to her Majesty. The Queen handed to the Prince a written answer, and said in a clear voice : ' I wish to express my great admiration of this beautiful hall, and my earnest wishes for its complete success.' A prayer was offered by the Bishop of London, and then the Prince exclaimed : ' The Queen declares this hall to be now opened.' The announcement was followed by a burst of cheering, the National Anthem, and the discharge of the park guns. The opening was cele-brated by a concert, under the direction of Sir Michael Costa, who composed a cantata expressly for the occa-sion. The cost of the hall was estimated at £200,000, and—what is probably unique in the history of public buildings—this cost was not exceeded.

Early in April the Queen, accompanied by Prince Leopold, paid a visit to the Emperor Napoleon and the Empress Eugenie at Chislehurst. The Emperor was suffering greatly both in mind and body, but he was much touched by this manifestation of friendship.

On the 21st of June her Majesty opened the new St. Thomas's Hospital, and knighted the treasurer, Mr. Francis Hicks.

The Queen did not return from her usual visit to Balmoral until a late period this autumn, and when she reached Windsor, on the 25th of November, she was met by the disturbing news that a feverish attack

from which the Prince of Wales had for some time
been suffering had assumed a grave aspect. A bulletin,
issued by Drs. Jenner, Gull, Clayton, and Lowe, stated
that the Prince's illness was typhoid fever. Her
Majesty proceeded to Sandringham on the 29th. The
Princess Louis of Hesse and her children were staying
at Sandringham, and the Queen at once despatched the
Prince of Wales's three elder children and those of
the Princess Louis to Windsor. Princess Alice remained at Sandringham to share the vigils of the
Princess of Wales. The news of the Prince's illness
created profound sorrow and solicitude throughout the
United Kingdom. As the fever continued to run its
course for some days without any alarming symptoms,
her Majesty returned to Windsor ; but on the 8th of
December a very serious relapse occurred. The life
of his Royal Highness was in imminent danger, and
the Queen and all the members of the Royal Family
hurried to Sandringham. For some days the whole
nation was plunged in gloom, and the excitement
respecting the daily bulletins was intense. By the
Queen's desire, special prayers were used on and after
the 10th in all churches and chapels of the Establishment. Prayers also went up from the Jewish syna-
gogues and from Catholic and Dissenting churches.
The national anxiety and suspense were continued
until the night of Wednesday, the 14th—the anniversary of the Prince Consort's death—when there
was a slight amelioration of the worst symptoms, and
the invalid obtained long-needed and refreshing sleep.
From that day forward the Prince continued gradually
to recover. The Queen returned to Windsor on the
19th of December, and on the 26th she wrote the

following letter to her people : ' The Queen is very anxious to express her deep sense of the touching sympathy of the whole nation on the occasion of the alarming illness of her dear son, the Prince of Wales. The universal feeling shown by her people during those painful, terrible days, and the sympathy evinced by them with herself and her beloved daughter, the Princess of Wales, as well as the general joy at the improvement of the Prince of Wales's state, have made a deep and lasting impression on her heart, which can never be effaced.   It was indeed nothing new to her, for the Queen had met with the same sympathy when, just ten years ago, a similar illness removed from her side the mainstay of her life, the best, wisest, and kindest of husbands. The Queen wishes to express at the same time, on the part of the Princess of Wales, her feelings of heartfelt gratitude, for she has been as deeply touched as the Queen by the great and universal manifestation of loyalty and sympathy.   The Queen cannot conclude without expressing her hope that her faithful subjects will continue their prayers to God for the complete re-covery of her dear son to health and strength.'

The 27th of February 1872 was observed as a day of national thanksgiving for the Prince's recovery.   A more joyous and successful celebration was never witnessed in London.   The progress of her Majesty and the Prince and Princess of Wales and Princess Beatrice to St. Paul's was one con-tinuous ovation.   Amid the incessant cheering cries were heard of ' God save the Queen ! ' and ' God bless the Prince of Wales ! '   His Royal Highness in-sisted upon continually removing his hat in response to the congratulations. At Temple Bar the City sword was presented and returned, after which the Lord Mayor remounted his horse and rode before the Queen to St Paul's. The sight in the cathedral, where 13,000 persons were gathered, was very imposing. The Queen, who had the Prince of Wales on her right and the Princess of Wales on her left hand, took the Prince's arm, and walked up the nave to the pew specially prepared for the Royal party. The service began with the *Te Deum*, and then there was a special form of thanksgiving, which opened as follows : ' O Father of mercies, O God of all comfort, we thank Thee that Thou hast heard the prayers of this nation in the day of our trial; we praise and magnify Thy glorious name for that Thou hast raised Thy servant Albert Edward, Prince of Wales, from the bed of sickness.' The sermon was preached by the Archbishop of Canterbury, his text being taken from the Epistle to the Romans : ' Members one of another. When her Majesty left the Cathedral, the Lord Mayor and Aldermen led the procession to the bounds of the City. After reaching Buckingham Palace the Queen and the Prince of Wales appeared for a short time on the central balcony. In the evening London was brilliantly illuminated. Her Majesty on the following day issued a letter to the people, stating how deeply touched and gratified she had been by the immense enthusiasm and affection exhibited towards her son and herself on their progress through the capital.

Only two days after this happy event, the Queen was returning from a drive in the park, her carriage having just entered the courtyard when a lad suddenly rushed forward to the left-hand side of the carriage,

and held out a pistol in his right hand and a paper in
his left. He next rushed to the other side and held the
pistol and the paper at the full stretch of his arms
towards the Queen, who was then seated to his right,
appearing quite calm and unmoved. The lad was
speedily seized by her Majesty's personal attendant,
John Brown. The pistol proved to be unloaded. On
the offender's person a knife was found, and also a
petition, written on parchment, for the release of the
Fenian prisoners. He had managed to scale some iron
railings about ten feet high, and thus gained access to
the courtyard. He proved to be an Irish youth named
Arthur O'Connor, seventeen years of age, and a clerk
to an oil and colour firm in the Borough. Great
popular indignation was aroused in consequence of the
outrage, and coming so close after the thanksgiving
service, it accentuated the loyalty of the people towards
the Queen. O'Connor was subsequently brought to
trial, and sentenced to one year's imprisonment with
hard labour, and a whipping with a birch rod. The
Queen had for some time past contemplated instituting
a medal as a reward for long or faithful service
among her domestic servants, and she now inaugurated
the institution by conferring on John Brown, her
faithful attendant, a medal in gold, with an annuity of
£25, as a mark of her appreciation of his presence of
mind and of his devotion on the occasion of the
attack made upon her Majesty.

While the Queen was at Balmoral in the ensuing
June she received tidings of the death of her valued
friend and spiritual adviser, Dr. Norman Macleod. The
Queen and all her household were much affected by
the loss. The deceased had on many occasions cheered

and comforted the Sovereign in times of trouble. 'No one ever raised and strengthened one's faith more than Dr. Macleod,' wrote her Majesty.   'His own faith was so strong, his heart so large, that all, high and low, weak and strong, the erring and the good, could alike find sympathy, help, and consolation from him.   How I loved to talk to him, to ask his advice, to speak to him of my sorrows, my anxieties!   But, alas! how impossible I feel it to be to give any adequate idea of the character of this good and distinguished man.'

On the 1st of July, the Queen, accompanied by the Duke of Edinburgh, the Princesses Louise and Beatrice, and Prince Leopold, visited the national memorial erected in Hyde Park to the memory of the Prince Consort.   This magnificent and costly monument was then complete, save for the statue of the Prince, which was to be executed by Mr. Foley, and to form the central and principal figure. The structure, which is very elaborate in all its parts, reaches to a height of 180 feet, and terminates in a graceful cross.

Her Majesty visited Dunrobin in September, and laid the memorial stone of a monument to the memory of her dear friend the Duchess of Sutherland in the grounds of Dunrobin Castle.   The stone bore a brass plate, with a suitable inscription, closing thus: 'This foundation-stone was laid by Queen Victoria of England, in testimony of her love and friendship, 9th of September 1872.'

Before the month closed her Majesty received intelligence of the death of her beloved sister, the Dowager Princess of Hohenlohe Langenburg, who expired at Baden-Baden.   There was ever a warm attachment between the two illustrious ladies, and the

Princess was deeply mourned, not only by the Queen, but by a wide circle. The Duke of Edinburgh and Prince Arthur went over to Germany to the funeral, at which also were present the Emperor of Germany and the Prince and Princess Louis of Hesse.

A strange and chequered career came to a close in January 1873, when the Emperor Napoleon died after much physical suffering at Chislehurst. Messages of sympathy with the Empress Eugenie and the Prince Imperial were sent by the Queen and various European Sovereigns.

On the 2nd of April the Queen paid a visit to Victoria Park, and her appearance in the East End was welcomed with great enthusiasm by large crowds of her poorer subjects, who lined both sides of the thoroughfares. It seemed as though every court and alley of this densely populated portion of the metropolis had poured forth all its occupants of both sexes, who vied with each other in their demonstrations of loyalty.

A sad and fatal accident befell one of the Queen's grandsons, Prince Frederick William of Hesse, at Darmstadt, on the 28th of May. Shortly before eight o'clock in the morning, the nurses had as usual brought the royal children into Princess Alice's bedroom. 'On this occasion there were but three—viz., Prince Ernest, Prince Frederick William, and the baby, Princess Victoria. Out of the bedroom opened a bathroom, into which Prince Ernest ran. The Princess, knowing the window to be open, as was also the one in her bedroom, hastily got up and followed the child, leaving Prince Frederick William and the baby on the bed. During her short absence, Prince Frederick William let a toy with which he was playing fall out of the window, and while trying to recover it he fell a height of twenty feet to the ground. The Princess, hearing a noise, rushed back, but only in time to see the unhappy child in the air. Her shrieks soon brought assistance, but all efforts were useless, and the poor little fellow died about eleven o'clock. He had been weakly from his birth, but he was of a gay and lively disposition, and his death caused profound sorrow to his parents, with whom much sympathy was felt.' As an illustration of the rigidity of Court etiquette it may be mentioned that, while Court mourning was ordered in England for the little prince, there was none ordered in Darmstadt, as the deceased child was not twelve years old.

During their stay in Scotland, in September, the Queen and Princess Beatrice spent a week at Inverlochy, near Ben Nevis, Lord Abinger having placed his seat there at her Majesty's disposal. The Queen afterwards went through the Caledonian Canal, greatly enjoying its beautiful scenery. From Inverness the royal travellers went on to Balmoral.

On the 23rd of January 1874 the Duke of Edinburgh was married to the Grand Duchess Marie of Russia, the ceremony taking place in the Winter Palace at St. Petersburg. In the succeeding March the royal couple made a public entry into London. A heavy snowstorm somewhat marred the proceedings, but the Queen, with the Duchess and the Duke of Edinburgh and Princess Beatrice, drove through the streets of the metropolis in an open carriage. On arriving at Buckingham Palace the newly wedded couple met with an ovation from a large crowd of persons who had assembled in front of the palace.

In April her Majesty visited Gosport, and inspected the sailors and marines of the Royal Navy who had gallantly borne their part, with three regiments of the army, in the successful campaign against the Ashantees. At a later period she personally conferred the medals awarded for conspicuous gallantry during the Ashantee war upon nine seamen and marines. In connection with this war Sir Garnet Wolseley received the Order of St. Michael and St. George, and Lord Gifford that of the Victoria Cross.

On the occasion of the jubilee meeting of the Royal Society for the Prevention of Cruelty to Animals, held on the 22nd of June, the Queen, through Sir Thomas Biddulph, addressed a letter to the President, Lord Harrowby. Her Majesty desired to give expression to her warm interest in 'the success of the efforts which are being made at home and abroad for the purpose of diminishing the cruelties practised on dumb animals. The Queen hears and reads with horror of the sufferings which the brute creation often undergo from the thoughtlessness of the ignorant, and she fears also sometimes from experiments in the pursuit of science. For the removal of the former the Queen trusts much to the progress of education, and in regard to the pursuit of science she hopes that the entire advantage of those anæsthetic discoveries from which man has derived so much benefit himself in the alleviation of suffering may be fully extended to the lower animals.'

The interesting festival of Hallowe'en was celebrated on a great scale at Balmoral on the 4th of November. As soon as darkness set in, her Majesty and the Princess Beatrice, each bearing a large torch, drove out in

an open phæton. A procession, consisting of the
tenants and servants on the estates, followed, all
carrying huge lighted torches.   They walked through
the grounds and round the Castle, and the scene was
very weird and striking.   There was an immense
bonfire in front of the Castle, and when the flames
were at the highest a figure dressed as a hobgoblin
appeared on the scene, drawing a car surrounded by a
number of fairies carrying long spears, the car con-
·taining the effigy of a witch.   A circle having been
formed by the torch-bearers, the presiding elf tossed
the figure of the witch into the fire, where it was
speedily consumed.   Reels were then begun, which
were danced with great vigour to the stirring bagpipe
strains of Willie Ross, the Queen's piper.   The Queen
and Princess Beatrice, who remained as spectators of
the show, were highly entertained.

A pleasing international incident occurred on the
3rd of December, when her Majesty received at
Windsor an address of thanks from the French nation
for the services rendered by the English people to the
sick and wounded in the war of 1870–71.   The
address was contained in four large volumes, which
were beautiful as works of art; and by command of
the Queen these volumes were placed in the British
Museum, in order that the public might have an
opportunity of inspecting them.

There appeared this year the first volume of Sir
Theodore Martin's *Life of the Prince Consort*—a
work valuable for giving a complete picture of the
man ; and amongst other tributes to the Prince was
the erection of the statue to his memory at the termination of the Holborn Viaduct.   This statue was

presented to the Corporation by a wealthy gentleman of the City.

Many distinguished men who had been personally honoured by the Queen passed away in this and the following year. The mournful death-list included Bishop Wilberforce, Sir E. Landseer, Charles Kingsley, W. C. Macready, and her Majesty's literary adviser and clerk of the Council, Sir Arthur Helps.

It had been announced that the Queen would open Parliament in person in February 1875, but the alarming illness of her youngest son, Prince Leopold, prevented her from carrying out her design. The Prince had been seized with typhoid fever during the Christmas vacation at Osborne (though the disease had been contracted at Oxford University), and for a long time a fatal termination was feared to his illness. Happily, however, he eventually' recovered. As the Princess Alice said, he had already been given back three times to his family from the brink of the grave.

Her Majesty was an involuntary witness of a lamentable accident which occurred as she was crossing over from Osborne to Gosport in the royal yacht on the 18th of August. A yacht called the *Mistletoe*, belonging to Mr. Heywood, of Manchester, ran across the bows of the *Alberta*, and a collision took place. The *Mistletoe* turned over and sank, and the sister-in-law of the owner was drowned. The master, who had been struck by a spar, also died afterwards, but the rest of the crew were saved. The Queen was greatly distressed by the occurrence, and personally aided in restoring one of the sufferers to consciousness. Colonel Ponsonby some time afterwards addressed a letter to the Commodore of the Royal Victoria Yacht

Club, deprecating the constant practice of private yachts in approaching the royal yacht from motives of loyalty or curiosity. As the Solent is generally crowded with vessels in summer, this was a very dangerous custom, which might lead to lamentable results, and the Queen hoped it would be discontinued. This letter gave rise to much controversy; and as it appeared immediately after the verdict of the Gosport jury, which attributed the disaster partly to error on the part of the officers of the royal yacht, it was interpreted as an expression of the Queen's opinion that the master of the *Mistletoe* was to blame. Her Majesty hastened to remove this impression, and an explanation was published from Colonel Ponsonby to the effect that his letter was written three weeks before the verdict had been pronounced, and was not in any way intended to anticipate that verdict by laying the blame on either party.

The Queen paid a visit to the Duke and Duchess of Argyll at Inveraray in September, and from thence proceeded to Balmoral. At Crathie, on the 21st of October, her Majesty and Princess Beatrice attended the funeral of Mr. John Brown, father of the Queen's attendant. The weather was wet and bleak, but the Queen and her youngest daughter followed on foot from the house to the hearse, which, from the nature of the roads, could not be got near the door. After the hearse had moved off, her Majesty returned to the house, and stayed some time, endeavouring to comfort the widow. Most of the members of the Court attended the old man's funeral.

In October the Prince of Wales left England for his lengthened tour through her Majesty's Indian dominions. He met with a grand reception in Bombay, and his birthday was kept in India. The Prince visited the chief wonders of India, including the caves of Elephanta. There was an elephant hunt in Ceylon, and an illumination of the surf. Colombo, Bombay, Baroda, Calcutta, and Madras were all visited. The tour was in every respect a perfect success, and created a most favourable impression amongst the Queen's Indian subjects. In the following year the Royal Titles Bill was passed, and her Majesty was proclaimed Empress of India.

The Queen made many public appearances in 1876. Early in February she opened Parliament in person, and on the 25th of the same month attended a State concert given at the Albert Hall, when she was accompanied by the Princess of Wales, Princess Beatrice, and Prince Leopold, and received by the Duke of Edinburgh. Another of her Majesty's personal friends, Lady Augusta Stanley, passed away on the 1st of March, and the Queen erected a memorial cross to her memory in the grounds at Frogmore. On the 7th of March her Majesty opened a new wing of the London Hospital, which had been built by the Grocers' Company at a cost of £20,000. Altogether the sum of £90,000 was contributed by public subscription for the enlargement of the hospital. The statue of the Prince Consort in the Albert Memorial was unveiled on the 9th, without any ceremony. This splendid recognition of a Queen's affection and a nation's gratitude was now complete. Towards the close of March the Queen proceeded to Germany for a visit of some weeks—during which she visited her sister's grave—travelling under the name of the

Countess of Kent. On the homeward journey, on the 20th of April, her Majesty rested at Paris, and had an interview with Marshal Macmahon, the French President. On the 2nd of May she reviewed the troops at Aldershot; the march past took place in the midst of a violent hailstorm. On the 13th the Queen opened a loan collection of scientific instruments at South Kensington Museum; and on the 27th her birthday was kept in London with more than customary public rejoicings in honour of the Prince of Wales's return from India.

The Albert Memorial at Edinburgh was unveiled by the Queen with great ceremony on the 17th of August. The memorial, which is in Charlotte Square, consists of a colossal equestrian statue of the Prince Consort, in field-marshal's uniform and bare-headed, standing on a pedestal, at the four corners of which are groups of figures looking up to the central figure. The sculptor of the whole composition was Mr. John Steell, upon whom and Professor Oakeley, the composer of the chorale which was sung on the occasion, her Majesty conferred the honour of knighthood. The Queen took up her quarters at Holyrood Palace for two days, and in her diary she records the coincidence that the last public appearances of both her husband and her mother were made in Edinburgh. The ceremony of unveiling the statue passed off very successfully. The Queen was well seen by her subjects, for she insisted upon standing throughout the whole ceremony, although chairs of State had been prepared for her and Princess Beatrice and Prince Leopold. As the memorial was uncovered the band played the 'Coburg March,' which much touched her Majesty.

She walked round the statue, and expressed her complete satisfaction with the work.

On the 26th of September the Queen presented new colours to the 79th Regiment, 'Royal Scots,' at Ballater. The rain came down in torrents. After the piling of the drums, her Majesty handed the new colours to the two sub-lieutenants, who were kneeling, and addressed them in these words : ' In entrusting these colours to your charge, it gives me much pleasure to remind you that I have been associated with your regiment from my earliest infancy, as my dear father was your colonel. He was proud of his profession, and I was always told to consider myself a soldier's child. I rejoice in having a son who has devoted his life to the army, and who, I am confident, will ever prove worthy of the name of a British soldier. I now present these colours to you, convinced that you will always uphold the glory and reputation of my first Regiment of Foot—the Royal Scots.' The Queen was terribly nervous while speaking.

Her Majesty again opened Parliament in person on the 8th of February 1877. The year was comparatively uneventful at home, and in September the Queen visited Loch Maree, staying at the Loch Maree Hotel for a week, and greatly enjoying the magnificent scenery which Ross-shire affords. She made several sketching excursions, and has left a pleasant record of her whole sojourn in her Journal.

Lord Beaconsfield was honoured by a visit from her Majesty at Hughenden in December. The little town of High Wycombe was almost beside itself with enthusiasm as the Queen drove through. The Premier received his royal visitor at the door of Hughenden Manor. The Queen and Princess Beatrice lunched with Lord Beaconsfield, and remained about two hours. Before leaving the Queen planted a tree on the lawn in front of the house, to serve as a memorial of her visit, and Princess Beatrice planted another tree close by.

The Queen's grandchild, Princess Charlotte of Prussia, was married at Berlin, in February 1878, to the hereditary Prince of Saxe Meiningen; and her cousin, Princess Elizabeth of Prussia, was married at the same time to the hereditary Grand Duke of Oldenburg. Early in the summer the Queen's cousin, the blind ex-King of Hanover, died at Paris in exile; his body was brought to England and interred in the vaults of St. George's Chapel, Windsor.

On the 29th of April the Queen held an investiture of the Imperial Order of the Crown of India at Windsor Castle. The following ladies were introduced separately to her Majesty, and personally invested with the badge of the Order : The Marchioness of Salisbury, the Marchioness of Ripon, the Countess Dowager of Elgin, the Countess of Mayo, Lady Hobart, Lady Jane Emma Baring, Baroness Napier of Ettrick, Baroness Lawrence, Lady Northcote, Lady Temple, Lady Denison, and Mrs. Gathorne Hardy.

Amid a heavy storm of rain her Majesty reviewed a portion of the fleet at Spithead. In consequence of the confined space, the crowds of shipping and small boats, the violent squalls of wind, and the occasional blinding showers, certain projected evolutions were abandoned.

At the close of the month the Queen, with the

Princess Beatrice and Prince Leopold, proceeded to Scotland, paying a visit on the way to the Duke and Duchess of Roxburghe at Broxmouth. While here she received news of Madame Van de Weyer's death, and her Majesty wrote in her diary : ' Another link with the past gone, with my beloved one, with dearest uncle Leopold, and with Belgium ! ' Not long afterwards the Queen's faithful friend and servant, Sir Thomas Biddulph, died at Abergeldie Mains. Her Majesty visited him, and found him able to converse. ' He said, " I am very bad." I stood looking at him, and took his hand, and he said : " You are very kind to me ; " and I answered, pressing his hand, " You have always been very kind to me." ' The Queen further records that ' under a somewhat undemonstrative exterior, Sir Thomas was the kindest and most tender-hearted of men.'

Her Majesty was much shocked on learning of the dreadful catastrophe which occurred on the Thames off Woolwich on the 3rd of September, when the *Princess Alice* steamboat, in returning from a pleasure trip, was run down by the *Bywell Castle*. By this terrible disaster some six hundred persons lost their lives.

The Marquis of Lorne, who had been appointed Governor-General of Canada, sailed for the Dominion in November, accompanied by the Princess Louise. The heartiest good wishes followed them in their new sphere.

A severe gap was made in the Royal Family in December by the death of the lamented Princess Alice. Some time before, diphtheria had broken out in the Darmstadt household, and every member of it was attacked in succession. Princess Marie, who was only four years old, died on the 16th of November. The Princess caught the infection as the result of her devoted attention to others, and from having on one occasion rested her head, from sheer sorrow, on the Duke's pillow, without having taken the necessary precautions. She made all her preparations in the event of death. Once she was heard to murmur in her sleep, ' Four weeks—Marie—my father.' On the morning of her death, having just taken some refreshment, she said, ' Now I will again sleep quietly for a longer time.' These were her last words, as she slept the sleep which knows no earthly waking, passing away on the 14th of December, the seventeenth anniversary of her father's death. Few princesses have been more warmly beloved than the Princess Alice. The remains of the Princess were interred in the mausoleum at Rosenhöhe, on May 18, the Prince of Wales, Prince Leopold, and Prince Christian being amongst the mourners. A beautiful recumbent figure in white marble of the Princess, in which she is represented as clasping her infant daughter to her breast, has been placed near the tomb, as a token of the loving remembrance of her brothers and sisters. The Queen issued a letter to her subjects expressing her heartfelt thanks for the universal and most touching sympathy called forth by the death of her beloved daughter.

During the month of January 1879 Edward Byrne Madden was tried at the Central Criminal Court for sending threatening letters to the Queen. Being found of unsound mind, he was ordered to be detained during her Majesty's pleasure. Madden was of Irish parents, but was born at Bruges. He developed a mania for threatening Sovereigns, and before the charge against him in England, had already been confined in Austrian, Belgian, French, and American asylums for threatening the lives of the Emperor Francis Joseph, King Leopold, Napoleon III., and President Johnson.

In March the Duke of Connaught was married to the Princess Louise of Prussia, at St. George's, Windsor. Some days later the Queen left England with the Princess Beatrice for Lago Maggiore, where they remained for four weeks. News reached them of the death of Prince Waldemar, one of the sons of the Crown Prince and Princess of Germany, from fever. Her Majesty returned to England on the 24th of April, travelling by way of Milan, Turin, Paris, and Cherbourg.

On the 12th of May the Queen's first great-grandchild, the daughter of the Princess of Saxe Meiningen, was born. A fortnight later her Majesty proceeded to Balmoral, and, accompanied by the Princess Beatrice, she inspected the cross of Aberdeen granite which an affectionate mother had reared to a beloved daughter. The cross bears this inscription : ' To the dear memory of Alice, Grand Duchess of Hesse, Princess of Great Britain and Ireland. Born April 25, 1843. Died December 14, 1878. This is erected by her sorrowing mother, Queen Victoria. " Her name shall live, though now she is no more." '

Her Majesty was at Balmoral when she received the mournful news of the death of the Prince Imperial, who was slain in the Zulu war. The Queen could not at first credit the news, but it was confirmed by a telegram from Lady Frere, despatched from the Government House, Cape Town. Her Majesty feared for the effect of the terrible news upon the Empress Eugenie, and thus wrote in her Journal: ' To think of that dear young man, the apple of his mother's eye, born and nurtured in the purple, dying thus, is too fearful, too awful; and inexplicable and dreadful that the others should not have turned round and fought for him. It is too horrible!'

The Queen opened Parliament in person on the 5th of February 1880, and on the ensuing 25th of March left England for Baden Baden and Darmstadt. She was present at the confirmation of her grandchildren, the Princesses Victoria and Elizabeth, daughters of the Duke and the late Duchess of Hesse; and she also visited the grave of their mother at Rosenhöhe. Her Majesty in the following September welcomed the Duke of Connaught and his bride at Balmoral, where a cairn had been erected in their honour.

The last month of this year and the early months of 1881 were signalized by three great losses in English literature and politics. George Eliot died in December 1880, Carlyle in February 1881, and the Earl of Beaconsfield in the following April. The Conservative leader was buried at Hughenden, and the Queen and Princess Beatrice visited the funeral vault while it was still open, and placed flowers upon the coffin. At a later period a monument was erected in Hughenden Church to Lord Beaconsfield ' by his grateful and affectionate sovereign and friend, Victoria R.I. Kings love him that speaketh right (Prov. xvi. 13).'

Prince Leopold was created Duke of Albany in

June 1881, and took his seat in the House of Lords.

On the 19th of September, President Garfield died after a long and painful struggle, the victim of an assassin. When it was known that he had succumbed to his wounds, the utmost sympathy was manifested throughout Europe, and the English Court went into mourning, a custom hitherto only observed in regard to the death of crowned heads. The President was buried on the 24th. One of the largest and most exquisite of the floral decorations on the bier bore a card with the inscription: ' Queen Victoria to the memory of the late President Garfield : an expression of her sorrow and her sympathy with Mrs. Garfield and the American nation.'

Not many months afterwards another attempt was made on the Queen's own life. On the 2nd of March 1882, her Majesty, accompanied by Princess Beatrice, was entering her carriage at Windsor station, on returning from London, when she was fired at by a man named Roger Maclean, who was at once arrested. Fortunately, neither the Queen nor any one else was injured. It was discovered that the antecedents of Maclean were perfectly respectable, but that he had fallen into want. He was committed for trial on a charge of high treason, but being found not guilty on the plea of insanity, was sentenced to be confined during her Majesty's pleasure. In both Houses of Parliament addresses were unanimously adopted, expressing horror and indignation at the attempt made on the Queen's life, and congratulations on her escape.

Her Majesty left England on the 14th of March

accompanied by Princess Beatrice, on a visit to Mentone, travelling by way of Portsmouth, Cherbourg, and Paris. The royal travellers returned to Windsor on the 14th of April, having had a very rough passage from Cherbourg to Portsmouth.

A fortnight later the marriage of the Duke of Albany to Princess Helen of Waldeck was celebrated in St. George's Chapel, Windsor, in the presence of the Queen and the Royal Family. The young couple had Claremont assigned to them as their residence, and the usual parliamentary provision was made.

An interesting ceremony took place at Epping on the 6th of May. The Queen and Princess Beatrice went in State from Windsor to the forest, where they were received by the Lord Mayor and Sheriffs, the Duke of Connaught as Ranger of the Forest, &c. An address was presented by the Corporation of London, after which her Majesty declared the forest dedicated to the use and enjoyment of the public for all time. Upon her return to Windsor the Queen received the melancholy news of the assassination of Lord Frederick Cavendish and Mr. Burke in Phœnix Park, Dublin. Towards the end of May, Albert Young, a railway clerk at Doncaster, was sentenced at the Old Bailey to ten years' penal servitude for sending a letter to Sir Henry Ponsonby threatening to murder the Queen.

On the 17th of August her Majesty presented new colours to the 2nd battalion Berkshire Regiment (the 66th) at Parkhurst, Isle of Wight. This gallant regiment lost its old colours in the engagement with Ayoub Khan, at Maiwand, on July 14, 1880, when 370 of its officers and men were killed, including its commanding officer, Colonel Galbraith.   Two of the companies wore the Afghan cross, struck in memory of the march from Cabul to Candahar.

When the Egyptian war broke out the Duke of Connaught was amongst the officers who accompanied Sir Garnet Wolseley into Egypt.   The progress of the campaign was watched with much solicitude by the Queen and the Duchess of Connaught, who were at Balmoral during the thick of the engagements.   News at last arrived of the great British victory at Tel-el-Kebir.   'How anxious we felt, I need not say,' wrote the Queen in her Journal, 'but we tried not to give way.   I prayed earnestly for my darling child, and longed for to-morrow to arrive.   Read Korner's beautiful *Gebet vor der Schlacht, Vater ich rufe Dich* ("Prayer before the Battle: Father, I call on Thee").   My beloved husband used to sing it often.' A telegram arrived at Balmoral: 'A great victory; Duke safe and well;' and this was succeeded by a fuller one containing the words, 'the Duke of Connaught is well and behaved admirably, leading his brigade to the attack.'   This message diffused great joy and thankfulness over the royal circle.   The Duke and Duchess of· Albany arrived at Balmoral in the midst of the rejoicings, and were warmly welcomed after their bridal tour.   The healths of the bride and bridegroom having been drunk with Highland honours, the Queen requested her son to propose a toast 'to the victorious army in Egypt,' coupled with the name of the Duke of Connaught.   The toast was received with pride and enthusiasm.

On the 18th of November the Queen reviewed in St. James's Park about 8,000 troops of all arms who had recently returned from service in Egypt. After parading before her Majesty, the troops marched by way of Birdcage Walk, Grosvenor Place, Piccadilly, and Pall Mall, where they were enthusiastically received by large crowds. Three days later the Queen distributed Egyptian war medals to the generals and representatives of various branches of the service at Windsor; and she also delivered a brief address to those present. On the 24th she held an investiture of orders conferred for distinguished service in Egypt.

The new Law Courts in the Strand, which had been erected after the designs of Mr. G. E. Street, R.A., were formally opened by the Queen on the 4th of December. There was an imposing ceremonial, her Majesty being received in the hall by the judges and representatives of the Bar. The Prime Minister and a great number of other distinguished persons were present. Lord Chancellor Selborne was advanced to the rank of an earl on this occasion, and the honour of knighthood was conferred upon the treasurers of the various Inns of Court.

The year 1883 was an uneventful one in the life of the Queen as regards public appearances; but in March her subjects learnt with regret that she had sustained a somewhat severe accident. It appears that while her Majesty was at Windsor Castle she slipped upon some stairs, and, falling, sprained her knee. The accident was at first regarded as of slight consequence, but it became the source of much pain and inconvenience. A month later the *Court Circular* announced that the effects of the sprain were still so severe as to prevent her walking, or even standing for more than a few seconds. Eventually these ill effects passed away, but not until the expiration of a year from the time of the accident.

A great trial befell her Majesty in 1884 by the untoward death of her youngest son, the Duke of Albany. From his childhood upward the Prince had been of delicate health. Alike from inclination and necessity, he had always been given to studious pursuits. As he reached manhood he was not only proficient in music and painting, but developed strong literary tastes. He had an excellent and refined judgment, and had gathered copious stores of book learning. He lived a comparatively retired life, suffering much from a constitutional weakness in the joints, and from a dangerous tendency to hæmorrhage, which rendered the extremest care necessary. On several occasions his life was in danger from sudden and severe fits of indisposition. His intellectual gifts, combined with his ill-health, rendered him an object of pride as well as of solicitude to the other members of the Royal Family. Towards the close of his existence he seemed, by the interest he took in literature and science, and the graceful public speeches which he delivered, about to take the place once held by his honoured father. He had a happy marriage, and in 1883 a daughter was born to him, to whom was given the name of his beloved and revered sister, Alice.

The career of this much-esteemed Prince, however, was cut prematurely short. In March 1884 he went to Cannes to avoid the inclement east winds, leaving the Duchess behind him at Claremont. His stay in the south of France proved of considerable service in restoring his health; but on the 27th of March, as he was ascending a stair at the Cercle Nautique, he slipped and fell, injuring the knee which had been hurt on several occasions before. The accident did not at first seem serious, and the Duke wrote a reassuring letter to his wife from ·the Villa Nevada, whither he had been conveyed. A fit of apoplexy supervened during the following night, however, and at three o'clock on the morning of the 28th he expired in the arms of his equerry, Captain Perceval. When the fatal news reached Windsor it was gently broken to the Queen by Sir H. Ponsonby. Though almost overwhelmed with her own grief, her Majesty's thoughts turned at once to the young widow at Claremont.

The Prince of Wales went over to France to bear the remains of· his brother back to England. The Queen and the Princess Christian and Princess Beatrice met the body at the Windsor railway station. On reaching the Castle, it was conveyed to the chapel, where a short service was held in the presence of her Majesty and her children. The afflicted Duchess of Albany bent one last look upon the bier. The funeral took place on the 5th of April, the Prince of Wales being chief mourner. The father-in-law and the sister-in-law of the deceased Prince were also present. The Queen entered St. George's Chapel leaning on the arm of the Princess of Wales, and followed by the Princess Christian, the Princesses Louise and Beatrice, and Princess Frederica of Hanover. The Duchess of Albany and the Duchess of Edinburgh were too ill to attend the funeral. The Dean of Windsor conducted the service, and when he came to the words, ' earth to earth, ashes to ashes, dust to dust,' Lord Brooke, the intimate friend of the deceased, cast a handful of earth upon the coffin.   With deep and evident emotion the spectators mournfully gazed upon the flower-laden coffin as it was slowly lowered into the vault and disappeared from view.

Addresses of condolence to the Queen and the widowed Duchess were passed by both Houses of Parliament, and these addresses reflected the high sense of the Prince's mental powers and moral worth left upon those who were brought into contact with him.   Earl Granville in the Lords, and Mr. Gladstone in the Commons, eloquently dwelt on the many claims which the memory of the Prince had upon the affectionate regard and admiration of his country-men.   So universal and spontaneous was the national regret for the lamented Duke, that the Queen published a letter thanking her people for their sympathy with herself and her daughter-in-law in their affliction.

After some months of comparative seclusion, the Queen and Princess Beatrice left England on the 31st of March for Aix-le-Bains.   From thence they proceeded on the 22nd of April to Darmstadt, travelling by way of Geneva, Berne, and Bâle.   At Darmstadt her Majesty assisted at the confirmation of her grand-daughter, Princess Irene of Hesse, which took place in the Chapel Royal.

The Queen returned to Windsor on the 2nd of May.   During this year she thanked the New South Wales and other colonies for their prompt offers of co-operation in the event of the extension of the war in Egypt ; presented medals to a party of non-commissioned officers and men from the Soudan ; and

E E

visited the sick and wounded soldiers from the Soudan at Netley Hospital.

On the 23rd of July 1885 the marriage of Princess Beatrice with Prince Henry of Battenberg was celebrated at Whippingham Church, Isle of Wight, in the presence of the Queen, the Royal Family, and a distinguished party of English nobility and others; but no representatives of the German reigning dynasties attended. Provision was made by Parliament for the Prince and Princess, and a Naturalization Bill on behalf of the former carried through both Houses. With this wedding the Queen saw the last of her children united in the bonds of matrimony. It may be stated here that the sons and daughters of the Queen have already become parents of thirty-four princes and princesses, twenty-nine of whom are living, and twenty of them resident in England.

Her Majesty has erected many monuments at Windsor to those whom she holds in loving remembrance. One of the chief attractions of the Albert (formerly the Wolsey) Chapel—beautifully restored by the Queen—is a pure white marble figure of the Prince, represented as a knight in armour, with the epitaph on the pedestal, ' I have fought the good fight, I have finished my course.' In St. George's Chapel are five monuments. The first is an alabaster sarcophagus to her father; the second, a white marble statue to King Leopold, whom the Queen has described as her second father; the third monument is to her Majesty's aunt, the Duchess of Gloucester; the fourth to the late King of Hanover; and the fifth to the son of King Theodore of Abyssinia. The young Prince died in England, and his monument bears the

epitaph : 'I was a stranger, and ye took me in.'
Theed's admirable group of the Queen and her husband stands at the entrance to the corridor which runs
round two sides of the quadrangle of the Castle. The
corridor contains many pictures and mementoes of
events and persons relating to the Queen's life and
reign. At Frogmore is Marochetti's recumbent figure
of the Prince, and space has been left for a similar
statue of her Majesty. There are also memorials of
Princess Alice and of the Queen's dead grandchildren
in the mausoleum. In an upper chamber belonging
to a separate vault is a statue of the Duchess of Kent
by Theed. At Osborne are many groups, statues, and
busts of the Queen's children and other relatives,
which serve to remind her Majesty—if she needed
such reminders—of the happy years in the past.

The Queen once more opened Parliament in person
in January 1886. She was received with deafening
shouts of welcome by the crowds assembled along
the route from Buckingham Palace to Westminster.
There was a brilliant scene in the House of Peers,
where the Prince of Wales and other members of the
Royal Family, and a gorgeously apparelled throng of
peers and peeresses, had already assembled before her
Majesty's arrival. As the Queen entered the House
the Prince of Wales stepped down from his State chair
and raised his mother's hand to his lips, her Majesty
moving to him with a graceful gesture. The Queen
then took her place on the throne. She was dressed
in black velvet trimmed with ermine, and wore the
Koh-i-noor as a brooch, a small coronet, the Order of
the Garter, and the family Orders. The representatives of the people having arrived from the Lower

House, the Queen handed the manuscript of the Royal Speech to the Lord Chancellor, who proceeded to read it in clear and firm tones. Her Majesty then left the House and returned to Buckingham Palace amid enthusiastic greetings from the people, similar to those which had marked her progress to Westminster.

The year was destined to be fruitful in political surprises. The Conservative Ministry were defeated on the labourers' allotment question during the debates on the Address, and resigned office. Mr. Gladstone became Prime Minister, and introduced his Home Rule measure. Being defeated in this, he appealed to the country. The elections were unfavourable to him, and he resigned; Lord Salisbury once more returning to the helm of State with a Conservative Government.

On the 24th of March the Queen laid the foundation-stone of the new Medical Examination Hall of the Royal Colleges of Physicians and Surgeons, on the Victoria Embankment. Her Majesty was accompanied by Princess Christian and Prince and Princess Henry of Battenberg, and appeared to be in very good health. She was evidently much gratified at the many marks of respect and loyalty paid to her by the people. The ceremony took place in a spacious pavilion, holding about 1,000 persons. The Prince of Wales, Princess Louise, Prince Christian, the Duke of Cambridge, and the Marquis of Lorne awaited the arrival of Her Majesty, whose advent was heralded by the strains of the National Anthem. The proceedings began with a prayer offered by the Archbishop of Canterbury, followed by a hymn sung by the Savoy choristers to the Prince Consort's tune

'Gotha.' The President of the Royal College of Surgeons then read an address. The Queen in her reply said : 'The erection of this hall is mainly due to the efforts you have made, in conjunction with the President of the Royal College of Physicians (Sir W. Jenner), with whom I have been long personally acquainted, and whose eminent abilities and far-seeing knowledge have justly placed him in the foremost rank of those who have benefited mankind.' A number of lengthy documents relating to the origin of the hall, and to the two corporations, were then presented to the Queen, and these were mercifully taken as read. The stone, which bore the following inscription, and in which were placed the usual mementoes, was then lowered to its bed :—'Victoria, Queen of Great Britain and Ireland, Empress of India, laid with her own hand this stone—24th March 1886.' The Prince of Wales, who has a ripe experience in laying foundation-stones, admirably assisted his mother in well and truly laying the stone of the new hall. The Archbishop pronounced the benediction, and after a stay of a few minutes her Majesty left the pavilion.

On the afternoon of the same day, while the Queen was taking a drive along Constitution Hill, a man ran out from the footway, and approaching close to the carriage, threw a letter into the vehicle. The package was immediately thrown out again, and as the man was stooping down to pick it up, he was surrounded by a number of spectators and the police, and arrested. The Queen continued her drive, though she had been somewhat startled by the incident. The offender was taken to King Street police station. He gave his name as Thomas Brown, and was apparently about thirty-five years of age. The paper which he threw was a petition, setting forth that the writer had been in the army, but had been discharged and sent to a lunatic asylum. Having been released from there, he again enlisted, suppressing all knowledge of his previous discharge and its cause. On the facts being discovered he was tried by court-martial and dismissed the service without a pension. He now pleaded that a pension should be granted to him, as he had served her Majesty for twenty-three years. After his second dismissal he had again been for some time in a lunatic asylum. As the doctors were not prepared to certify to his insanity, out of consideration for his general good character, Brown was released from custody.

The Colonial and Indian Exhibition—the most successful and extensive of a series of admirable exhibitions at South Kensington—was opened by the Queen on the 4th of May. The Prince of Wales was the actual promoter, the executive President, and practically the director of this Exhibition, which reflected the highest credit upon the energy and exertions of his Royal Highness. The opening ceremony was very imposing, both from the dense crowds in the vicinity of the Exhibition and the brilliant gathering within the building. Her Majesty was received with the most fervent greetings. As she entered the hall the fact was announced by a flourish of trumpets. She was received by the Prince of Wales, and joined by the Princess of Wales, the Duchess of Edinburgh, the Duchess of Connaught, and other ladies of the Royal Family. The Prince of Wales and the Duke of Connaught each kissed her

hand, and were in return kissed on the cheek by
their royal mother.   A procession was formed, which
proceeded through the main portions of the building
to the Royal Albert Hall, where the opening ceremony
was to take place.   Here the scene was brilliant in
the extreme.   The Queen was conducted by the
Prince of Wales to the royal daïs, where she took
her seat on the throne.   The National Anthem was
then sung, the first verse in English and the second
in Sanskrit.   At its conclusion hearty cheers were
given for her Majesty.   An ode followed, written for
the occasion, at the special desire of the Prince of
Wales, by the Poet-Laureate, and set to music by Sir
A. Sullivan.   It was sung by Madame Albani and
the choir, and it was observed that after each verse
the Queen smiled her thanks to the singer and clapped
her hands.   The Prince of Wales next read an address
setting forth the nature of and the reasons for the
Exhibition.

Her Majesty made the following reply :—' I receive
with the greatest satisfaction the address which you
have presented to me on the opening of this Exhibition.   I have observed with a warm and increasing
interest the progress of your proceedings in the
execution of the duties intrusted to you by the
Royal Commission, and it affords me sincere gratification to witness the successful results of your judicious
and unremitting exertions in the magnificent exhibition which has been gathered together here to-day.
I am deeply moved by your reference to the circumstances in which the ceremony of 1851 took place,
and I heartily concur in the belief you have expressed
that the Prince Consort, my beloved husband (had he

been spared), would have witnessed with intense
interest the development of his ideas, and would, I
may add, have seen with pleasure our son taking the
lead in the movement of which he was the originator.
I cordially concur with you in the prayer that this
undertaking may be the means of imparting a stimulus
to the commercial interests and intercourse of all
parts of my dominions, by encouraging the arts of
peace and industry, and by strengthening the bonds
of union which now exists in every portion of my
empire.'

At the conclusion of the speech the Prince of
Wales kissed the Queen's hand, but she, drawing him
towards her, kissed him on the cheek.   The Lord
Chamberlain, at the command of her Majesty, then
declared the Exhibition open, the announcement being
marked by a flourish of trumpets and the firing of a
royal salute in Hyde Park.   A prayer was offered
up by the Archbishop of Canterbury; the Hallelujah
Chorus was performed by the choir; and Madame
Albani sang with thrilling effect, 'Home, Sweet Home.'
The Queen then bowed to the company, and amid loud
and prolonged cheers descended from the daïs, and,
traversing the whole breadth of the building, mounted
the steps to the royal entrance.   As she took her
departure, followed by the Royal Family, she expressed
to Sir P. Cunliffe Owen her great satisfaction with the
Exhibition.

Only a few days after this ceremony the Queen
visited Liverpool, where she opened an International
Exhibition of Navigation, Commerce, and Industry.
Her Majesty was accompanied by the Duke of Connaught and the Prince and Princess Henry of Batten-

berg. During her visit the Queen stayed at Newsham
House. The Exhibition was opened on the 11th of
May, the Queen being the centre of a brilliant throng
upon a specially erected throne, while the vast body
of spectators numbered some thirty thousand persons.
As soon as her Majesty had taken her place the
orchestra performed an overture by Mr. F. H. Cowen,
with which had been incorporated by royal permission a chorale composed by the late Prince Consort.
An address was then read by the Mayor, and presented to the Queen in a casket. Her Majesty, in
clear tones, read a reply expressive of her gratification
in witnessing so successful an exhibition. A prayer,
offered by the Archbishop of York, and a performance
from Mendelssohn's 'Hymn of Praise,' followed. The
National Anthem having next been sung, the Mayor
presented to her Majesty a golden key, which she
turned in a model lock, and at her command Lord
Granville declared the Exhibition open. The doors of
the building flew open, and the fact being signalled
to the North Fort, the guns were fired. Her Majesty
knighted the Mayor, who rose Sir David Radcliffe
amid loud cheers. The royal party then left the
Exhibition and returned to Newsham House. Liverpool
was brilliantly illuminated in the evening, and the
Mayor gave a grand banquet at the Town Hall.

On the 12th there was a royal progress through the
streets of Liverpool. The thoroughfares were lavishly
decorated by private citizens as well as by the municipal
body. The Town Hall and St. George's Hall were
especially gay in appearance, and in front of the latter
place a grand stand had been erected, which accommodated five thousand persons. There was a grand

procession of trade and friendly societies, embracing
16,000 persons, with vehicles, bands, and banners.
Although unfortunately the weather was very wet, the
programme was carried out in its entirety. The Queen
and the royal party left Newsham House at three
o'clock, and as the cavalcade drove through the streets
it was everywhere loudly cheered. The route lay past
the Exhibition and through Sefton Park. At the
plateau in front of St. George's Hall her Majesty
halted to receive an address from the Corporation of
Liverpool. Presentations were then made to the
Queen, after which the royal *cortége* drove off to the
Prince's Pier-head. Here the distinguished party embarked on board the ferry steamer *Claughton*, and
steamed town the river on the Lancashire side,
returning up the stream near the Cheshire shore. The
Claughton went as far as the Sloyne, and steamed
round the *Great Eastern*, which was then lying there.
Her Majesty also had an opportunity of seeing the
training and reformatory ships moored in the Mersey,
and the boys of those vessels gave her a warm reception. The return journey through the streets
of Liverpool was made in somewhat better weather.
The Queen did not reach Newsham House until seven
o'clock, when she was much fatigued, after four hours
of driving and sailing.

Her Majesty left Liverpool on the 13th amid
warm popular demonstrations. Before entering the
train at the Exhibition station she expressed to the
Earl of Sefton her deep gratitude for the cordiality
with which she had been received in Liverpool. She
then turned to the Mayor and told him how much
pleasure she had derived from the reception she had

met with from all classes. The royal train steamed out of Liverpool at ten o'clock A.M., and reached Windsor at 3.15. Through Sir Henry Ponsonby the Queen gave £100 to the poor of Liverpool, and to Lady Radcliffe she presented a costly diamond bracelet, expressing at the same time her gratification at all that had been done for the comfort of herself and her children. The *Court Circular* afterwards stated that her Majesty was fatigued by all her exertions during the three days of her visit, but that she was greatly gratified and touched by the warm and kind reception which she and the Duke of Connaught and Prince and Princess Henry of Battenberg met with from all classes of her subjects at Liverpool.

On the 30th of June the Queen opened the Royal Holloway College for Women at Mount Lee, Egham. The college owed its being to the munificence of the late Mr. Thomas Holloway. It was erected and endowed at a cost of a quarter of a million sterling, and it offers every luxury and comfort for young ladies who may be fortunate enough to pursue the various branches of higher education within its walls. The list of visitors on the opening day included a large number of persons distinguished in all ranks of life. The Queen, with Princess Beatrice, the Duke of Connaught, Prince Henry of Battenberg, and Princess Louis of Battenberg, and suite, drove from Windsor Castle by way of Frogmore and Runnymede to Egham. At the entrance of the college her Majesty was met by Mr. G. Martin Holloway, who conducted her to the chapel, where the ceremony was appointed to take place. The choir sang an ode written by Mr. Martin Holloway, and set to music by Sir George Elvey, after

which the Archbishop of Canterbury offered up a
prayer. The royal party then visited the picture
gallery, where the contractor, Mr. Thompson, presented
to her Majesty a gold key to typify the nature of the
function which she had consented to perform in
opening the college. The key was most elaborate and
costly in its design · and construction, consisting of
gold work, with a laurel wreath of diamonds. After
passing through the other portions of the college, the
Queen at length reached the daïs erected in the upper
quadrangle, from which she was formally to open the
college. When she had taken her seat upon the chair
of State which had been provided, an address was presented to her Majesty by Mr. Martin Holloway, setting
forth the designs and intentions of the founder of the
college. The Queen returned the following reply :—
'I thank you for the loyal address which you have
presented to me on behalf of the governors and
trustees of this college. In opening this spacious and
noble building it gives me pleasure to acknowledge the
generous spirit which has been manifested in the com-
pletion by voluntary effort of a work promising so
much public usefulness. I gladly give the assurance
of my goodwill to the administration to whom the
college is about to be entrusted, and I earnestly hope
that their efforts to promote the objects for which
it has been founded and planned by your relative may
be rewarded by a career of abiding success.' The
Earl of Kimberley, who was standing on the Queen's
left, then stepped forward and said : 'I am commanded by her Majesty to declare this college open.'
This announcement was the signal for a flourish of
trumpets, after which the benediction was pronounced

by the Archbishop of Canterbury, and the proceedings terminated. The Queen and the royal party left the building amid loud and continuous expressions of loyalty.

With this latest of the public ceremonials in which her Majesty has engaged the present chapter may fitly conclude. We are now passing through the fiftieth year of the Queen's reign, but by the Sovereign's desire the Royal Jubilee will not be formally celebrated until the year has run its course. In all quarters of the world that celebration has already excited the utmost interest in advance, and every member of the Anglo-Saxon race is looking forward with affectionate and loyal solicitude to the time when, amidst universal rejoicing, we shall be able to say that it is an accomplished fact.

CHAPTER X.

CHARACTERISTICS.—CONCLUSION.

IN approaching the end of this biographical sketch of her Majesty there are still some aspects of the Sovereign's life and character which demand attention. It will have been seen that, in compiling the foregoing narrative, I have mainly kept in view the Queen herself, and that if I had attempted to trace in detail the social, domestic, foreign, and political movements of her reign, this work would have vastly increased in magnitude. The history of these movements can be read elsewhere ; my object has been to trace the career of our beloved Monarch from her birth down to the jubilee year of her reign—presenting her as child, maiden, wife, mother, and Queen. I am conscious of many imperfections in the work, but I trust the reader will forgive these in the interest which he must feel in the life of one under whose benignant rule it is his happiness to live.

Amongst the attractive features of the Queen's character has been her consistent admiration for men of genius. She is really cosmopolitan in this respect. The actress Rachel, Jenny Lind, and others received valuable mementoes from her; and as far back as 1839 she invited Daniel Webster to stay at Buckingham Palace. The great contemporary poets and novelists of England and America have exercised considerable fascination over her—Tennyson, Longfellow, Dickens, and George Eliot; and in an interview she had with Carlyle she quite charmed the philosopher of Chelsea by her considerate and unaffected demeanour. An amusing story is related of Campbell the poet. At her Majesty's coronation he wrote to the Earl Marshal, saying : ' There is a place in the Abbey called " The Poets' Corner," which suggests the possibility of there being room in it for living poets also.' This gained him a ticket of admission, and he was so delighted with the young Queen's bearing that he thus gave expression to his admiration : ' On returning home I resolved, out of pure esteem and veneration, to send her a copy of all my works.   Accordingly, I had them bound up, and went personally with them to Sir Henry Wheatley, who, when he understood my errand, told me that her Majesty made it a rule to decline presents of this kind, as it placed her under obligations which were not pleasant to her.   " Say to her Majesty, Sir Henry," I replied, " that there is nothing which the Queen can touch with her sceptre in any of her dominions which I covet ; and I therefore entreat you to present them with my devotion as a subject."   But the next day they were returned.   I hesitated to open the parcel, but on doing so I found, to my inexpressible joy, a note enclosed, desiring my autograph on them.   Having complied with this wish, I again transmitted the books to her Majesty, and in the course of a day or two received in return this elegant portrait engraving, with her Majesty's autograph, as you see, below.'

Evidences of the Queen's sympathetic nature will have been apparent all through this biography.   One of the latest examples of it is found in her letters on the death of Principal Tulloch, made public by Mrs. Oliphant. Writing to the Rev. W. W. Tulloch from Osborne, under date Feb. 13, 1886, her Majesty said: 'I am stunned by this dreadful news: your dear, excellent, distinguished father also taken away from us, and from dear Scotland, whose Church he so nobly defended. I have again lost a dear and honoured friend, and my heart sinks within me when I think I shall not again on earth look on that noble presence, that kindly face, and listen to those words of wisdom and Christian large-heartedness which used to do me so much good. But I should not speak of myself when you, his children, and your dear mother, and our beloved Scotland lose so much. Still I may be, I hope, forgiven if I do appear egotistical, for I have lost so many, and when I feel so *alone*. Your dear father was so kind, so wise, and it was such a pleasure to see him at dear Balmoral! *No more! Never again!* These dreadful words, I so often have had to repeat, make my heart turn sick. God's will be done! Your dear father is at rest, and his bright spirit free! We must not grieve for him. When I saw you at Balmoral you seemed anxious about him, and I heard the other day he could not write. Pray convey the expression of my deepest sympathy to your dear mother, whose health I know is not strong, and to all your family. I mourn with you. Princess Beatrice is deeply grieved, and wishes me to express her true sympathy with you all. I shall be most anxious for details of this terrible event.—Ever yours truly and sorrowingly,

'VICTORIA R. & I.'

Addressing Mrs. Tulloch some days later, and in anticipation of the funeral, her Majesty wrote: 'You must allow one who respected, admired, and loved your dear distinguished husband to write to you, though personally unacquainted with you, and to *try* to say what I feel. My heart bleeds for you—the dear worthy companion of that noble, excellent man, so highly gifted and large-hearted, and so brave! whose life is crushed by the greatest loss which can befall a woman. To me the loss of such a friend, whom I so greatly respected and trusted, is *very great ;* and I cannot bear to think I shall not again see him, and admire that handsome, kindly face and noble presence, and listen to his wise words, which breathed such a lofty Christian spirit. I am most anxious to visit you, and trust that you will allow me to do so quite quietly and privately, as one who knew your dear husband so well, and has gone through much sorrow, and knows what you feel and what you suffer. Pray express my true sympathy to all your children, who have lost such a father. My thoughts will be especially with you to-morrow, and I pray that God may be with you to help and sustain you.'

The same sympathetic feeling extended to persons in the humbler ranks of life. Some years ago, the wives of two Cornish miners, who were anxious to join their husbands in Nova Scotia—but were unable to provide that portion of money necessary to secure an emigration grant from the Cornwall Central Relief Committee—wrote to her Majesty and acquainted her with their poverty and their great desire. The Queen caused inquiries to be instituted, and these being satisfactory, she very kindly commanded the necessary

F F

sum of £10 to be sent to the humble occupants through the rector of Illogan.

The love of the Queen for domestic life has had a great deal to do in binding her children together in the bonds of fraternal affection. They are a happy and united family, and this comes chiefly from the example set them by their parents. It has been said that to know the real character of such a Sovereign as Victoria we must look away from the glittering palace life of London and Windsor to the secluded dales and mountain nooks of the Scotch Highlands; to the little village church of Crathie; to her numerous unostentatious charities; to her ardent attachment to home, her constant longing after domestic tranquillity, her motherly love for her offspring; a dislike of display, and a positive aversion to the pomp and pageantry of public life. While admiring greatness in all walks of life, she has ever put goodness before it.

In the course of last year a statement got abroad to the effect that her Majesty had lately invested £1,000,000 in the purchase of ground-rents in the city of London. Sir Henry Ponsonby thus gave a categorical denial to the report, in a letter to Major Ross, M.P.: 'The Queen has bought nothing and possesses nothing in the city of London; she has invested no money in ground-rents, and she does not possess a million to invest.'

The humblest tributes to the Queen have sometimes been the most striking. For example, there was that paid to her by the Welsh nurse of Prince Arthur, the wife of a mason at Rhyl, when she wound up her description of Court life with the expression that ' the

Queen was a good woman, quite fit to have been a poor man's wife as well as a Queen.' This homely nurse made the further remark, that the royal children were 'kept very plain indeed—it was quite poor living —only a bit of roast meat and perhaps a plain pudding.'

It would be easy to recall many tender illustrative examples of the Queen's solicitude for others, but one or two must suffice. The governess of the royal children was for several years the orphan daughter of a Scottish clergyman. During the first year of her residence at Windsor her mother died. Before her death the governess had been anxious to resign her charge, in order to go and nurse her. The Queen would not hear of her sacrificing her post altogether, but said to her in tones of gentle sympathy, "Go at once to your mother, child; stay with her as long as she needs you, and then come back to us. I will keep your place for you. Prince Albert and I will hear the children's lessons; so in any event let your mind be at rest in regard to your pupils.' The governess went and returned. On the anniversary of her mother's death she was quite broken down with grief. The Queen went to her and said, 'I meant to have given orders that you should have this day entirely to yourself. Take it as a sad and sacred holiday—I will hear the lessons of the children.' Then she added: 'To show you that I have not forgotten this mournful anniversary, I bring you this gift,' clasping on her arm a mourning bracelet with a locket for her mother's hair, marked with the date of that mother's death.

The Queen never forgets any person towards whom

she has been drawn, and when she was away on State
business at Edinburgh she turned aside to visit the
grave of a young Italian dressing-maid in Rose-
bank Cemetery, over which she had erected a chaste
and simple monument. The deceased maid seems to
have won in a remarkable degree the affection of her
royal mistress. When her Majesty left Balmoral for
the South some seasons ago, she promised to bring
the daughter of a cottar a toy in the following year.
Important State affairs intervened, and the Queen
went over to France on a visit to the Emperor. The
promise was forgotten on one side, that of the Highland girl; but not so on the other, for on arriving at
Balmoral next season the Queen presented the
humble lassie with the promised toy, remarking : ' See,
I have not forgotten you.'

The incumbent of Osborne has furnished a most
interesting picture of a cottage interior, showing the
Queen as a Scripture-reader. The incumbent had
occasion to visit an aged parishioner, and on arriving
at the house he found, sitting by the bedside, a lady
in deep mourning, reading the Word of God. He
was about to retire, when the lady remarked : ' Pray
remain. I should not wish the invalid to lose the
comfort which a clergyman might afford.' The lady
retired, and the clergyman found lying on the bed a
book, with texts of Scripture adapted to the sick; and
he found that out of the book portions of Scripture
had been read by the lady in black. This lady
visitor was the Queen of England.

Her Majesty has outlived all her early friends and
faithful servants. All who officiated at her coronation
have passed into the land of shadows; and of the

distinguished statesmen then living only one, Mr. Gladstone, remains.   Amongst personal friends the Queen has been called upon to mourn the loss of the good Duchess of Sutherland and Lady Augusta Stanley.   Then, too, Archbishop Tait, Dr. Macleod, Dean Stanley, and Principal Tulloch, have all gone. If she has tasted all the happiness of human life, she has tasted likewise all its bitterness, for Death has ever been busy laying his finger here and there upon her beloved friends, relatives, and associates.

The Royal Jubilee of 1887 will recall the memorable events of a memorable period in British history.   The Queen's reign is coincident with the most surprising progress at home and abroad.   It has been the age of railways, of trans-oceanic steaming, and of the telegraph; of free trade, parliamentary reform, and the abolition of the Corn Laws.   There has been no stagnation, not even for a brief period, in the arts and sciences.   While some peoples have risen and others have fallen during the last fifty years, the English race has continued to spread and multiply, and to exhibit evidences of its vitality in all quarters of the world.   With much of this progress, and the attachment of the nation to constitutional liberty, the name of the Queen is inextricably associated.   The historian of the future will adopt the language of our living poet, and say :

> ' Her Court was pure, her life serene ;
>   God gave her peace, her land reposed,
>   A thousand claims to reverence closed
> .   In her as mother, wife, and queen.'

The late Earl of Carlisle once happily observed that the glories of her Majesty's reign were ' the glories of peace, of industry, of commerce, and of genius; of justice made more accessible; of education made more universal; of virtue more honoured; of religion more beloved; of holding forth the earliest gospel light to the unawakened nations; the glories that arise from gratitude for benefits conferred; and the blessings of a loyal and chivalrous because a contented people.'

Through years of revolution abroad, of shock and change, of wars and popular tumults, we have seen the Sovereign of England conspicuously manifesting the influence and power of virtue, and bearing a name untouched by any suspicion and unblemished by any reproach. Notwithstanding the 'fierce light that beats upon a throne,' the character of the Sovereign has borne the test of that light, and has enshrined itself in the hearts of her people. It is considerations like these which have made her reign as noble as it has been illustrious; and they must invest her jubilee with a double interest and significance. As men compute life, her Majesty is not yet advanced in age—her years thus far number but sixty-seven; and I therefore close with an aspiration that will find an echo in the breast of every Englishman, be his political opinions or abstract theories of government what they may: for many years to come, whether at the festive board or at public celebrations, at home or abroad, on land or on sea, may Britons be able to raise the loyal and affectionate cry of "God save the Queen!"

PRINTED BY BALLANTYNE, HANSON AND CO.
LONDON AND EDINBURGH